From the Files of

Madison Finn

Read all the books about Madison Finn!

Don't miss the Super Editions

From the Files of
Madison Finn

BF4E*
*Best Friends Forever

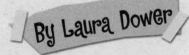
By Laura Dower

Books 4-6

HYPERION
New York

For Rich and the monkeys

Special thanks to Karl for teaching me
how to use a PC

Caught in the Web text copyright © 2001 by Laura Dower
Thanks for Nothing text copyright © 2001 by Laura Dower
Lost and Found text copyright © 2002 by Laura Dower

From the Files of Madison Finn is a trademark of Disney Enterprises, Inc.

All rights reserved. No part of this book may be reproduced or transmitted in any form or by any means, electronic or mechanical, including photocopying, recording, or by any information storage and retrieval system, without written permission from the publisher. For information address Hyperion Paperbacks for Children, 114 Fifth Avenue, New York, New York 10011-5690.

Printed in the United States of America

First compiled edition, 2006
3 5 7 9 10 8 6 4 2

The main body of text of this book is set in 13-point Frutiger Roman.

ISBN 1-4231-0287-8
Library of Congress Cataloging-in-Publication Data on file

Visit www.hyperionbooksforchildren.com

Caught in the Web

Chapter 1

"So even though this guy was dead, his heart was still beating under the floor?" Hart Jones cried. "For real?"

"Well," Mr. Gibbons said. "Not exactly, Hart. But your imagination's working. That's good."

Madison Finn shifted in her chair. English class was giving her the creeps today.

Mr. Gibbons continued to pace in front of the class as he explained more meaning behind "The Tell-Tale Heart." He replayed a recording of the classic short story by Edgar Allan Poe.

. . . The beating grew louder, louder! I thought the heart must burst. . . .

This narrator's voice was weirder than weird.

. . . Until, at length, I found that noise was not
within my ears . . .

"So his mind was playing tricks on him," Hart said
aloud.

Mr. Gibbons clapped, excited. He liked it when his
students gave good answers.

Hart always said things in class that made teachers smile. He was smarter than smart. This was probably why Madison had been crushing on him since
seventh grade started. Plus, he was cute.

Way back in elementary school Hart had chased
her around the school yard, but Madison always
ignored him. Back then, Hart had been nothing
more than a big geek. But something had changed
over the years. His family moved away from their
neighborhood in Far Hills. They moved back again
when Hart was suddenly popular. Even Madison's
enemy, Ivy Daly, appeared to have both eyes on him.

Fiona Waters leaned over to Madison. The beads
on her braids clinked against the desk.

"Was Hart Jones just looking over *here*?" Fiona
asked. "I swear I saw him. I swear."

"No way," Madison said firmly, turning in her
chair. She shrugged off Fiona with a casual
"Whatever." For a friend who was usually pretty
spaced out, Fiona was paying an awful lot of attention to people Madison "liked" and "didn't like."

Hart had absolutely not glanced over in
Madison's direction.

Had he? Now Madison wasn't sure.

Madison's lips were Ziploc-sealed shut when it came to boys. Only her secret computer files and her secret online friend Bigwheels knew the whole truth about her feelings for Hart and everything else.

Across the classroom, Ivy's hand shot into the air. She looked like a boa constrictor ready to strike. She had her elbows up on her desk and her red hair was all fluffed out around her head.

"Mr. Gibbons?" Poison Ivy hissed. "Can't you just tell us why the man killed the other man again?"

A kid from the back row laughed out loud. "Duh, weren't you listening?"

"Duh, yourself." Ivy turned around and glared. "I was so listening!"

"Excuse me." Mr. Gibbons clapped again because he wanted everyone to be quiet. He handed a spiky-haired girl in the front row a stack of papers. "I think we've talked about 'The Tell-Tale Heart' for long enough, class. Now, take one of these sheets and pass the rest along. . . ."

Madison saw the word *Boo!* in giant black letters on the page. A cluster of black bats winged across the top. Underneath, Mr. Gibbons had printed random facts about the origins of the upcoming holiday.

Much to Madison's surprise, the Halloween described on this paper had very little to do with the holiday she'd understood all her life. Centuries ago in Europe, Halloween was named "Samhain." Mr. Gibbons pronounced it "soh-wen." Samhain started out as a Celtic holiday.

"Wait! Wait! Who are the Celtics again?" Ivy asked aloud.

"Just one of the best basketball teams *ever*," Fiona's brother, Chet Waters, snapped.

Mr. Gibbons laughed. "You're right, Chet. But the real Celtics, or Celts, mentioned here were people from ancient Ireland. At the time we're talking about, in the fifth century B.C., Samhain, or Halloween, was the day their summer ended. On your sheet there's more information—and I added a crossword on the other side. . . ."

Madison loved word games. She flipped the page over instantly. This crossword was shaped like a witch's hat.

"Pssst! Maddie?" Fiona asked, leaning over toward Madison's desk. "Can you sleep over on Saturday? I'm going to ask Aimee too. My mom said it was okay."

"Cool!" Madison smiled. She loved sleepovers.

Madison timed herself filling in all the crossword puzzle blanks. Three minutes later, she'd scribbled the answer to each clue, finishing up just before the class bell. It was a personal record.

Fiona grabbed Madison's arm as they walked out.

"My mother says she'll make minipizzas and Cherry Garcia sundaes in honor of your favorite ice cream flavor," Fiona bubbled. "At the sleepover I mean. And my dorky brother, Chet, won't be there, so we can rent any old movie we want. I am soooo excited!"

Madison stopped short in front of a display case as they walked down the hall together. "Look," she said, motioning to Fiona. She pointed to a bright orange sign inside the cabinet:

Something to Scream About!
Halloween Dance
Friday, October 27, from 6 to 9 P.M.

"Yeah! Aren't you excited?" Fiona asked when she read the sign. "Seventh-grade dance committee meeting's tomorrow. We have to do the decorating and food and stuff like that."

Madison acted happy, but deep down, the dance had her a little worried. School dances usually meant a girl needed to be able to do three things: get boys to like her, pick out a cooler-than-cool outfit, and dance. Madison wasn't sure she could do *any* of those things.

She considered the possibility that maybe her luck was changing, however. Seventh grade was a new start, Madison told herself, so maybe all the tricks of the past would now turn into *treats*?

Madison headed over to Mrs. Wing's classroom to

help download some documents onto the school Web site. She'd been helping with the site since school started, usually after school and during free periods.

Staying after school could be a very good thing. Especially today. Madison knew Mom would be home late because of a meeting. Aimee had dance troupe. Fiona had soccer. If she stayed after school, Madison could avoid being alone so much. She'd get to walk home with her friends, after all.

On the way home, Aimee started chattering about the Halloween dance, but Fiona wanted to talk about sleepover plans exclusively. Madison asked Aimee if she could bring her mother's Ouija board.

"What's a wee-jee?" Fiona looked confused.

"You know, Fiona," Madison said. "You sit around in the dark and move this little pointer on the game and ask the ghosts to come and play. Like ooooooh, I'm so scared!"

"You shouldn't mock ghosts, Maddie," Aimee said. "Seriously."

"Aimee!" Madison groaned.

"There *are* ghosts everywhere," Aimee said with a straight face, pointing to an old building they passed on the route home. "Everywhere. You saw *The Sixth Sense*."

"There are *no* ghosts in Far Hills." Fiona shuddered. "Would you quit saying spooky stuff?"

"Yeah, Aim. I've had the jeebies all day," Madison said, thinking back to the story from English class.

"See? That's because you do believe me!" Aimee smirked.

As the sunlight faded, all the houses seemed soaked in an eerie, orange glow. While clouds and night sky gathered overhead, light played tricks on the sidewalk.

"You never know when there are ghosts around. They could be at school or anywhere. That's all I'm saying," Aimee said, hustling ahead of her friends.

Madison and Fiona looked at each other and then rushed to catch up. All Aimee's ghost talk *had* changed their minds a little. Suddenly every bush along the side of a dreary road was hiding a monster, every shadow on a deserted street was a beast on the loose, and every noise was the sound of heavy, plodding footsteps. . . .

Madison was so relieved to finally reach her front porch. She pulled her house key out of her bag. Phineas T. Finn, Madison's pug, greeted her with a big, wet, doggie smooch when she walked in the door. She couldn't hear anything at first except the dog's heavy breathing and snorting in her ears.

. . . Until, at length, I found that noise was not within my ears. . . .

Her mind wandered back to "The Tell-Tale Heart" again. Ghost stories at school and on the way home were definitely *not* a good idea. Especially when she was home alone.

Madison called Mom's cell phone to check in. After getting the automatic voice mail system and not a real live Mom, she left a long message. Nerves made her ramble on a little bit longer than usual.

As she entered her bedroom, Madison flicked on the light and knelt down to look under the bed. But the only things Madison saw were a sock covered in dust, a notepad with Phin's chew marks, and one very dirty nickel.

Madison checked every closet and corner and crevice.

She even peeked behind the shower curtain in the hall bathroom.

What if there were ghosts in Far Hills?

Relieved when she found nothing resembling a ghost, Madison shook off her jeebies, slipped out of her sneakers, and sat down at her desk. She dialed her mom once again and got a busy signal this time. Mom was probably getting her messages. She'd be home soon, anyway.

Madison hadn't checked her laptop computer for e-mails yet today, so she powered it up. It was still sitting open on her bedroom desk exactly where she'd left it plugged in that morning. One click and the motor hummed again. After the home screen illuminated, Madison's e-mailbox flashed with a *ping*.

FROM	SUBJECT
✉ Bob1A1239	Invest NOW $$$

Who was Bob1A1239? His name looked like a real name, like a person from school. It annoyed Madison to think that someone was e-mailing her while pretending to be a regular guy. He wasn't real! She knew it must be an advertisement and immediately deleted the message. Dad always said to do that when she didn't know the sender.

FROM	SUBJECT
✉ Eggaway	Computer?
✉ Boop-Dee-Doop	Spooktacular SALE
✉ JeffFinn	FW: Ha Ha Halloween

Unlike Bob1A1239's message, the remaining notes in Madison's mailbox were from a more familiar crew.

Egg needed homework questions for Mrs. Wing's computer class.

Boop-Dee-Doop, an online clothes store for girls, was having a sale.

And Dad had sent along another one of his jokes. Madison always tried to guess the punch line.

What do you put on a Halloween sundae?

Whipped scream was the answer. She guessed it right away, but she still giggled. Dad's e-mails were like happy shots. It didn't even matter if she'd heard a joke before.

Madison opened a saved document and typed the sundae joke into her Dad file. It was joke number thirty-two so far this month. After that she went into her file marked "Social Studies." She'd created folders for every single subject with ongoing vocabulary lists. Tonight she had to study terms about archaeology. Her teacher, Ms. Belden, said she might be popping a pop quiz tomorrow.

Madison didn't want to take any chances.

By the time she memorized the definitions, it was already six o'clock. Her stomach was grumbling. Her e-mailbox *pinged* again.

```
FROM                   SUBJECT
Webmaster@bigfis   Are you CAUGHT IN THE
```

The new e-mail was an announcement from her favorite Web site, bigfishbowl.com. Text at the top flashed orange and white in honor of the season. The words looked like candy corns.

```
From: webmaster@bigfishbowl.com
To: Members Only
Subject: Are you CAUGHT IN THE WEB?
New Contest!
Date: Mon 16 Oct 11:50 AM
Are you caught in the WEB?
Well, get snagged NOW!

The big fins at bigfishbowl.com want
```

YOU to write us a mystery for
Halloween. We provide the story
starter and you provide the thrills!
This is a special contest for
bigfishbowl members ONLY.

Contest entries due Friday,
October 27.

To enter the contest: Every winner
MUST begin with the story starter
below. Write a story of no more
than five hundred words. The winner
will have their mystery posted on
our site and get a mystery game
valued up to $25.

IT WAS A DARK AND STORMY NIGHT.
THE HOUSE WAS DEAD QUIET, EXCEPT
FOR . . .

"Dinner!"
Madison jumped. The message disappeared from
the screen. Her pulse was racing so hard all of a sudden that she mouse-clicked the wrong icon on her
computer screen.

"Whoa! Mom scared me," Madison said to Phin.

"Madison!" the downstairs voice bellowed again.
"Sorry I'm late! Is Phinnie up there with you?"

"Yes!" Madison bellowed back.

"Rowrooooo!" Phinnie howled.

11

"Come downstairs!" Mom yelled again. "I got takeout, honey bear! Come and eat!"

Madison wasn't surprised about the menu. Mom had a habit of providing on-the-run dinners for the two of them. Madison usually categorized these meals as "Scary Dinners" in her computer files.

After inhaling the takeout Chinese vegetables and crunchy noodles, Madison started over-thinking.

She thought about the contest.

She thought about ghosts.

She thought about what she wanted for dessert.

"Penny for your thoughts," Mom said gently, reaching into a white, greasy bag. She produced a slice of cake in a pink plastic carton with frosting smudged on the side.

Had Mom eavesdropped on her mind? Madison contemplated the chocolate, double-butter-cream universe sitting on the table.

Mmmmmm.

She couldn't wait to take the first bite.

 Caught in the Web

Maybe if I could write scary stories, I'd win this new Caught in the Web contest on bigfishbowl. Can my writing possibly compare to Edgar Allan Poe's "The Tell-Tale Heart?"

I could write a "My Teacher Is Really a Vampire" story. I'd write it about my science teacher, Mr. Danehy, since he

really bites. But who would read
that?

Maybe I should just write about Ivy Daly
and Hart Jones dancing together at the
school dance. Now *that's* scarier than
scary.

Here's the truth: the only Halloween
story I'm gonna be able to write is "The
Tell-Tale *Hart*," without the *e* and without
me.

Rude Awakening: Life gets tricky around
Halloween.

Chapter 2

The Far Hills Halloween Dance Committee meeting was scheduled to begin at three o'clock on Tuesday, just after the last class bell rang. Madison was so excited about the meeting that she had a hard time focusing on her end-of-the-day social studies pop quiz.

She wasn't the only one. Aimee and Fiona were just as distracted. In fact, Fiona was doubly distracted because after the dance meeting she had soccer. It was the end of the season, and important games were coming up. She couldn't miss a single practice.

Fiona had considered skipping the dance committee altogether, but Madison convinced her to change her mind. The Halloween dance was *the* turning point at Far Hills. It meant that seventh graders could finally be a part of junior high. They were responsible for planning the important tasks like decorations, food, and music.

Aimee wasn't going to miss *any* of it. All four of her older brothers had gone to Far Hills Junior High.

Her oldest brother, Roger, told his sister the dance was an inauguration ceremony. "Like you're finally a member of junior high," Roger said. "Not just some visitor."

Her brother Dean, a high school senior, said the dance had been a great way to get noticed and to "meet babes."

Doug, the ninth grader who'd been to the dance only two years before, said the food was the best part. He hadn't actually *danced*, but he said the decorations "rocked."

Only Billy, Aimee's second-oldest brother, had voiced a negative opinion. He said the "dumb dance was so boring."

But he would say that. *Billy* was so boring.

Unfortunately, Aimee's brothers couldn't really help Madison figure out what she needed help with the most, like what outfit to wear or how to dance. More than anything, Madison wanted to dance with Hart.

Just as she thought about Hart, he walked into Señora Diaz's classroom. Madison nearly gasped out loud.

It was a sign. It was just like the night before

when she'd been thinking about eating dessert and Mom gave her chocolate cake.

"Hey, Finnster," Hart said, sliding into a seat in the front row. His hand grazed her shoulder accidentally as he walked by.

She felt her face get all red, so she tried to focus all of her energy onto a poster of Barcelona, Spain, that was hanging directly ahead of her on Señora Diaz's wall. It said Paradise. She stared at the words until they got fuzzy.

Fiona whispered from behind. "Hey, Maddie, did you see that Web contest on bigfishbowl?"

Madison turned around. "Uh-huh. I'm gonna do it," Madison mumbled. She was happier than happy to get her mind off Hart. "Are you?"

Fiona shook her head.

"What are we talking about?" Aimee asked from one row over. "Are we talking about the dance?"

"No, *we're* talking about an Internet contest," Fiona said. "On bigfishbowl."

Out of the corner of her eye, Madison tried to watch Hart *and* talk to her friends at the same time, but it wasn't working so well. Hart was turned halfway toward them, wearing a jewel-green shirt that made his eyes sparkle. She still had a ghost of a feeling where his hand had brushed her arm.

"Earth to Maddie," Fiona joked.

"Oh. Sorry." Madison snapped back to the conversation. "Bigfishbowl. Yeah, the Web site, Aimee, where you can go online and chat. You know."

"I know *that*, Maddie." Aimee chuckled. "But I'm pretty much clueless about online chatting." Madison didn't understand how Aimee's dad could have a cybercafé in his bookstore, while Aimee still hadn't gotten her own screen name.

"But you are the queen of chatting, Aimee," Madison teased. "Just not on the computer."

"Which is why you just have to sign up!" Fiona commanded. "Then the three of us can meet up on bigfishbowl and talk. You can get your own screen name. It'll be the best, Aimee."

Fiona explained how she and her brother, Chet, had twin screen names. She was Wetwinz with a *z*, and her brother Chet was Wetwins with an *s*. Aimee agreed that was pretty inventive.

The classroom began to slowly fill up. Madison counted sixteen volunteers. Even Egg and his good buddy Drew were there.

Señora Diaz charged in behind students. *"Hola, estudiantes!"* she proclaimed, a little out of breath. *"Cómo están? Tienen ganas de que llegue el baile?"*

Most kids didn't have a clue about what was said since they were in beginners' French, not Spanish. But Egg tried to help. "She wants to know if we're excited about the dance," he explained.

If anyone could translate Señora Diaz, Egg could. Señora Diaz was his real-life mother.

"Thank you for your help, Walter," Señora said sweetly, as if she were pinching his cheek. Egg muttered something under his breath. Madison knew he hated it when Señora called him by his real first name like that. Mothers who were teachers were way more embarrassing than plain old ordinary mothers.

"Señora Diaz." Aimee's hand was up in the air. "Are we supposed to wear costumes to this dance?"

A kid in a blue jacket sitting near the door asked, "Do we have to pay?"

"Is there going to be stuff to eat?"

"Will there be a live band?"

"Settle down, everyone." Señora inhaled deeply and scratched her head with her pen. "Let's go slowly. *Estámos preocupados, no?* Lots of ground to cover."

A couple of kids groaned. Egg leaned across a desk and whispered, "What are *you* going to the dance as, Maddie? A dork?"

"Quit it," Madison growled.

"Silencio!" Señora said as she handed a piece of paper to someone in the front row. "Please pass this sheet around and sign up your names and homeroom and phone number. This is our committee contact sheet."

They would be splitting up into task teams for whatever needed to get done. Seventh graders had all the grunt work of the dance. Eighth and ninth graders just had to show up.

"Are we doing a scary hallway?" Aimee asked. "My brothers said we always do—and that it's the best part of the whole dance."

"*El Vestíbulo! Sí!* Of course!" Señora Diaz said. *Vestíbulo* was the Spanish word for "hallway." In addition to decorating the main part of the gymnasium with streamers and signs, designated areas of the gym would be set aside with aisles of space just wide enough for kids to pass through in the dark. Curtains were drawn all around that space to form a labyrinth. No one could tell which direction was which once inside the curtains. Plus students volunteered to "stand and scare" as unwitting visitors passed through.

"You scream as kids go by," Señora said. "*Un grito!* Right, Walter?"

Egg shrank down into his chair.

All Drew could do was snort. He always laughed when Egg got embarrassed. He laughed whenever Egg did *anything.*

Madison was busy deciding what task team she wanted to help with most. She knew she didn't want to scream in the scary hallway. She didn't want to deal with food, either. That was too messy.

Decorating seemed like the best option. She got along well with crepe paper, balloons, and masking tape. Madison had an eye for color, especially the deep orange of construction paper pumpkins.

Thwack!

The door slammed open and the entire room got as silent as a tomb. Everyone turned.

Ivy walked in fifteen minutes late. She said, "Sorry," but she didn't look very sorry. She flipped her hair twice. "This is the Dance Committee, yeah?"

"Take a seat, dear," Señora Diaz said, motioning down toward the front.

"Ex-cuse me," Ivy said, stepping over someone's bag. She made a big scene, stepping on four kids just to get to the one empty chair down near Señora's desk. It was the chair next to Hart.

Madison glared at the space between their seats. She imagined a force field or fence between them. One touch, and *pzzzzzzt!*

"Look who's here—" Aimee whispered, gently nudging Madison. "Figures."

By the time she got settled, Ivy's late entry had caused so much commotion that the meeting was temporarily off track. Egg and Drew were cracking each other up. One kid in the back row even had a Gameboy out.

"Atención!" Señora Diaz yelled. "Jacob, put that computer game away now or I'll confiscate it. Look, I think we need to make a dance committee rule that any latecomers to meetings will be excused—permanently—unless I get some valid note or explanation. Is that clear?"

Madison wished Señora would "permanently excuse" Ivy right then and there.

"Ahem." Ivy cleared her throat and spoke up in a soft voice that sounded nothing like the obnoxious Ivy Madison knew. "I'm really, really, *really* sorry about being late, Señora."

"Oh?" Señora Diaz crossed her arms. "And your note?"

"I don't have a *note* exactly, but I was at the nurse . . . and next time of course I'll get one. I am sooooo sorry."

"What a liar!" Madison thought. She knew for a fact that Ivy had been nowhere near the nurse that day. She wasn't *sick*! She'd probably been in the girls' bathroom, putting on lip gloss. Ivy sounded so sticky sweet, but Madison knew about the poison that bubbled underneath.

As Señora got the meeting focused again, Fiona raised her hand to be excused for soccer. Señora sighed and reluctantly let her leave.

"Before you go, what task team do you want to be on?" Señora asked as Fiona gathered her things.

Fiona said, "Food," without missing a beat.

Señora asked who else wanted to be a food volunteer. Almost every boy in the room raised his hand. Madison thought at first that was because they all wanted to be around Fiona. But it wasn't. These boys were just plain hungry.

After Fiona left, Señora began signing up names for the dance and music task team list. Aimee's hand shot into the air right away to be the dance task team leader. After all, she was the best dancer in seventh grade. It made the most sense. Not even Rose, Ivy's dancing drone, challenged Aimee when it came to this.

Aimee leaned over to ask Drew if he'd help pull together all the music, too. Drew's father was mega-rich. The Maxwells had a recording studio right there on their own property. He could make the best Halloween mix ever.

"Who would like to help lead our decorating crew?" Señora Diaz asked next. Ivy's hand went up. So did Madison's.

"Well." Señora seemed pleased by their double enthusiasm. "What do you each have to say?"

Ivy started talking as if she'd already been put in charge. "I think, as class president, I know what the decorating for our dance should be. I would like to organize decorations. And I really think I can handle the scary hallway setup, too . . ."

"Fair enough," Señora Diaz said. "Señorita Finn? Would you like to add anything?"

"Well . . . just . . ." Madison cleared her throat. "I just wanna say that—" The words got stuck on the way out.

"Madison," Ivy interrupted in her hideous, sticky-sweet voice. Madison's stomach curdled. "I really think we both know who'd be better at taking care of the decorating, don't we?"

Madison didn't know what to say to that.

But Aimee did.

"Excuse me," Aimee interrupted. Her face was blotchy and Madison feared she might haul out and punch Ivy right there. She looked *that* mad. Aimee took things very personally when it came to Poison Ivy.

"We do know who'd be better, Ivy. But I think Madison would like to give *you* a chance, too."

Gotcha!

Madison covered her mouth, surprised—and grateful.

Drew snorted again.

Ivy acted stunned.

"Now, girls," Señora chimed in. "I don't think we need that kind of talk." She looked squarely at both girls, squinting and thinking for a moment. Madison sat still. Ivy flipped her hair.

Señora spoke up. "There's more than enough work to go around for two or more people. I think Madison and Ivy should *both* lead this task team."

"What?" Ivy and Madison said at the same time. "You mean—"

"*Sí!*" Señora Diaz said in Spanish emphatically. "You will lead the decorating task team *together*. That is my final decision."

In one fleeting moment, Señora Diaz had sealed Ivy and Madison's Halloween dance fates. Now Madison and Poison Ivy weren't only partnered in science class—they were matched up *after* school, too.

The decorators worked on the to-do list for the

scary hallway first. It started out okay—without any fights or disagreements. Madison hoped it would stay that way. She scribbled some notes. Everyone had great ideas, and the meeting lasted over an hour. When Madison got home, the notes on her laptop became an official file on her laptop.

 Halloween Dance: To Do

- Get vibrating rubber hands with fake blood (Ivy)
- Plastic ax from props in basement
- Brain gelatin mold (home ec?)
- Eyeballs suspended from the ceiling (if possible)
- Sheets (everyone bring one set plus curtains)
- Sound effects music (esp. screaming—Mrs. Montefiore in the music dept.)
- Monster makeup (green, white clown makeup, black nail polish from Rose S.)
- Dry ice machine (Principal Bernard to help get)
- Bats, rats, and spiders (Madison)

Madison decided she'd be the best person to make spiders, roaches, and moths out of black and brown construction paper. Her love of animals and all things creepy-crawly made her perfect for the job.

Ivy decided that she wanted to put up all the balloons. Probably because the boys were already talking about playing with the helium machine. Madison wondered if that was Ivy's key motivation: blow up balloons, meet boys. Then again, everyone loved the idea of inhaling helium and talking like a squeaky Munchkin. Ivy always did things that were popular.

Suddenly Madison's e-mail box blinked. It even had a red exclamation mark next to it.

Importance: high!
From: Bigwheels
To: MadFinn
Subject: Happy Columbus Day?
Date: Tues 17 Oct 5:20 PM
I know I'm like 2 wks late, but did
I say happy Columbus Day? Or is
that holiday just a bad joke? My
old camp friend said Columbus didn't
really discover America. Is that
true? I figured you'd know.

Mom & Dad are officially back
together. Did I tell you that
already? Dad bought her flowers
yesterday, so I am feeling happy.
They were roses. Mom keeps humming,
though, and it's getting on my
nerves.

How is that guy you have a crush
on? What is his name again? Write
back or else, okay?

Yours till the peanut butters,

Bigwheels

P.S. Do you have a Halloween dance
at your school? I have to make
cupcakes for mine. I bet you're
making posters for the dance on
your computer, you're so good at
that artistic stuff.

P.P.S. What are you dressing up as
for Halloween?

**Madison clicked REPLY immediately. Sometimes
the way she and Bigwheels thought and talked
about the same things was *scary*. Her keypal hadn't
guessed that Madison would be on the decoration
committee, but anything else she talked about was
so true.**

From: MadFinn
To: Bigwheels
Subject: Re: Happy Columbus Day?
Date: Tues 17 Oct 6:10 PM
Hi!!!!! Thanks for writing back &
for your advice.

To answer all your comments and
questions in order (sort of):

1. Happy Columbus Day to you, too.
2. There are some people who think
   Columbus wasn't the only guy.
   That's true. My mom almost produced
   a documentary on that subject. (Did
   I tell you that she makes movies?
   Mostly nature stuff, but sometimes
   profiles on famous people, too,
   like Christopher Columbus.)
3. I am so happy about your parents.
   WOW!
4. My crush is doing okay (see my
   question below).
5. We DO have a Halloween dance. I
   can't believe you asked me that
   question! We just met about
   it today. I was put on the
   decorating committee, BUT
   there's just one problem (see my
   question).

Now my questions for you.

1. How can I get my enemy (you
   know) away from the guy I like?
   She's after him, I know it!
2. How can I be on a dance
   committee when my enemy is in

charge? She's everywhere I go.
Help!!!

Okay, that's all for now. Bye!
WRITE BACK.

Yours till the scare crows,

MadFinn

P.S. Do you make up scary stories
or just poems? Just curious.
Bigfishbowl is having a special
Halloween writing contest. Are you
entering?

She clicked SEND and watched the e-mail disappear. Madison was thinking about how great it would be if Bigwheels wrote something for the contest, too.

But then Madison thought some more.

What would it be like to compete against a keypal at that contest? Competition got in the way of everything. Competing with Ivy for the decorations committee and for Hart was enough for one day.

Let the Halloween games begin.

Chapter 3

As soon as Madison arrived home from school the next day, she yanked her nubby brown sweater from the closet and down over her head. Her hair got static-electrified when she did that. She had an entire halo of split ends.

It was extra chilly in the house. Fall was beginning to make moves toward winter.

Madison wanted to power up her laptop and open her new file called "Caught in the Web." She had spent a half hour trying to write a story for the Halloween Web contest on her favorite site during free time in Mrs. Wing's class.

Unfortunately, she had zero ideas.

She also had zero time. Her dad and his new girlfriend, Stephanie, Madison, and Aimee were going on a late afternoon trip to Peterson's Farm. The four of them were going to get pumpkins and cider, a Finn tradition begun by Dad and his family years ago.

Madison had invited Fiona to come along, too, but Fiona had an important soccer practice (again).

Peterson's Farm was a half hour outside of Far Hills in a town called West Lake. There wasn't actually much of a lake there anymore, but when Dad was little, his parents brought him there every summer to swim and every winter to ice skate. Within a mile of the place, Dad usually got nostalgic.

"Do I look fat in this sweater, Mom?" Madison asked, walking back into the kitchen. She'd chosen brown corduroys to color-coordinate her bottom with the top.

"You look nice and warm," Mom said, ignoring the fat part of the question. "Now, don't forget to get me some of that corn relish at the farm, okay? And wear your Timberlands, not those sneakers. It's muddy out."

"It should be *you* going with us, Mom," Madison said, picking at cookies that had been left on the kitchen counter. "It's just not the same anymore . . ."

"Maddie," Mom said. She stopped what she was doing, leaned over, and gently rubbed a finger behind Madison's ear. "Look, Maddie, I know it's hard. I know this is the first real fall since your father and I split up—"

Madison rolled her eyes, so Mom grabbed her gently by the shoulders.

"Madison, later on this week you and I will do something that's fun just for us. Like making pies— or raking all the leaves in the backyard."

"Raking? That's your idea of fun?" Madison moaned. "Are you kidding?"

"Of course I'm only kidding!" Mom looked right into Madison's eyes again. It felt like she was staring right through her skin, bones, and everything.

Madison didn't feel like talking all of a sudden. She just hugged Mom.

"Honey bear," Mom continued to speak. "You'll love going up to West Lake. I know it. And you like Dad's girlfriend . . . what's her name?"

"Stephanie," Madison said. Mom sometimes forgot little details like names.

"Yes, *Stephanie*," Mom repeated slowly. "Well, you said you like her. What's the problem?"

"She's just not you," Madison said.

Mom squeezed her daughter around the middle. "Do me a favor and try to have a good time, Maddie. Try."

Tap tap.

Aimee was outside the kitchen door, face pressed so her lips went splat like a big guppy mouth kissing the glass. She'd changed her outfit since school, too.

Tap tap tap tap.

"I'm coming!" Madison said, opening the sliding doors.

"Hiya!" Aimee blurted, dancing inside. "Hey, Mrs. Finn!"

When she said "Finn," Phin, the dog, came running to say hello.

"Well, Aimee," Mom said. "Don't you look as pretty as always!"

Aimee grinned and struck one of her dancer poses. "Thank you."

"And that's a nice sweater," Madison said, rolling her eyes and half laughing. "Is it new?"

Aimee was wearing a black ski sweater with a big purple stripe.

"Oh my God, *this*? Not even. And it makes me look so *huge*," Aimee quipped. "You're not supposed to wear stripes across. Totally unflattering. But I thought it would be warm, so I wore it. It's wicked cold out today."

"You've got a lot of energy this afternoon," Mom declared.

"My brother Roger made me herbal tea when I got home from school," Aimee said. "You know how he always makes these drinks with ginger and ginseng. It's good for you."

Madison had never eaten or drunk anything with ginseng in it. It sounded too mysterious. She glanced at her own outfit and compared it to what Aimee had on. Aimee always seemed to dress the part of cool while Madison usually felt uncool in comparison.

Honk honk.

Aimee peeked out the window. "It's your dad, Maddie! Bye, Mrs. Finn!"

"That was good timing, huh?" Madison said, looking at Mom. It seemed hard to believe Dad was in the driveway on time. Mom said that in fifteen years of marriage, Jeff Finn had *never* been on time.

Dad stuck his head out the window to wave to Mom, who was standing on the porch. Mom waved limply and walked back inside.

Approaching the car, Madison saw Stephanie seated in the front seat. Stephanie had been riding up front since she'd begun dating Dad. Madison had a sinking feeling she would *never* ride shotgun in Dad's car again.

Madison and Aimee jumped in the back.

"How was school today, girls?" Dad asked, pumping the gas pedal. He started driving and asking so many questions that Madison was sure he must have had six cups of coffee. Dad was like a little kid when he got excited.

"So we have the entire afternoon planned out," Dad explained. "First the pumpkin patch—then cider—hmmm—what time is it, Stephanie?"

Stephanie turned to the girls in the backseat and winked as she said to Dad, "Slow down, will ya, Speed Racer? It's almost four o'clock."

The two friends chuckled. The farm closed up shop after six. They had plenty of time to get there and find the right pumpkins.

"Your dad got a new digital camera that we're going to try out," Stephanie said. "Did he tell you, Maddie?"

Dad spied Madison in the rearview mirror and smiled. "You up for a photo session, girls?"

"Yeah, I guess. I'm sure Aimee is," Madison teased.

"Hey!" Aimee laughed. "Well, I don't mind having my picture taken, if that's what you're asking, Mr. Finn." She gave Madison's shoulder a gentle nudge.

"That's good!" he said.

"How come you guys aren't at work or something?" Aimee asked.

Stephanie laughed. "Aren't days off a wonderful thing? We had a business meeting this morning. Saved the afternoon for you two."

"We'll beat the Saturday rush at the farm," Dad said. "You girls finished your homework like we agreed, right?"

Madison and Aimee nodded from the backseat.

Outside the car, tree branches shook their dead yellow, red, and orange leaves off in the wind. Madison pressed her nose up to the window on the passenger side and watched as her warm breath fogged up the cool glass. She traced a smiley face with her index finger. Aimee leaned over and used her fingers to draw squiggles in the same spot.

Soon they were driving through the farm gates.

34

After they parked, Dad led them to the horse cart transporting guests into the pumpkin patches.

Madison, Aimee, and Stephanie posed for a photo op in front of "Megasquash," a display of enormous zucchinis. Aimee stuck a piece of hay in her mouth and twirled around, working overtime to be the center of attention. Madison laughed hysterically while Dad clicked away.

The greatest thing about Dad's digital camera was that he could eliminate or retake bad pictures right away. Madison already guessed which picture she'd be downloading as a screen saver for her laptop. She and Aimee had hammed it up with a scarecrow in overalls.

The air on the farm smelled more and more like everything fall was supposed to smell like: horses, smoke from a chimney, apples, more hay. Madison took a deep breath of cool air. It was getting duskier outside.

"Look at this one, Maddie! It has boobs!" Aimee screeched when they jumped off the cart into the pumpkin patch. She held up a giant orange pumpkin with two funny-looking bumps on the side.

Madison laughed and ran over to join Aimee. They sorted through plump ones, round ones, flat ones, and even green ones. Stephanie found a teeny patch that had been picked over already by some crows. Dad found a pumpkin so big that it barely fit in the wagon they were using.

At five o'clock, Madison and Aimee ordered cups of cider at one of the farm stands and sat out on a picnic bench, even though it was a little too chilly to sit in one place for very long.

"How did you meet Mr. Finn?" Aimee asked, blowing on the cider before taking her first sip. She was so good at asking the right questions. Madison envied Aimee's ability to say whatever was on her mind.

Stephanie said that she was a computer sales rep. and met Madison's dad at a technology conference a few months back. In her head, Madison tried to do the math just to make sure that Dad had started dating Stephanie *after* the big D.

They had.

"Steph—" Dad started to groan. "Do you girls really wanna hear this?"

"Of course we do, Mr. Finn!" Aimee blurted. "Every detail. Like, what were you wearing when you met?"

"I think I had on a gray sweater." Stephanie chuckled. "And plaid pants."

"Plaid? Ohhh!" Aimee bristled like plaid was bad. She continued with her questions. "Have you ever been married before?"

Madison couldn't believe Aimee would ask something so personal.

Stephanie smiled. "Well, not exactly."

"What does 'not exactly' mean?" Madison asked.

"Well, here's the thing. I was engaged," Stephanie said. "Once. I was engaged, but I didn't go through with it. Couldn't go through with it."

"And am I glad for that," Dad said, wrapping his arm around Stephanie's back and leaning in to kiss her head.

Dad looked up just in time to see the expression on Madison's face. It was a "why did you just do that?" look. It had taken Madison her whole life to get used to Dad kissing Mom. Now she had to get used to Dad kissing someone else?

Eeeeeuuuw.

Madison remembered to grab a jar of Mom's favorite relish as they left the farm. She triple-checked the label to make sure it was the correct kind: extra spicy, Peterson's specialty.

Dad paid for all the pumpkins, including the one with boobs, and the relish, and then the foursome headed back to his Far Hills loft. He was preparing a "Finn Feast," or so he said. Stephanie promised she'd toast pumpkin seeds.

While Madison's dad and Stephanie cooked dinner, Madison logged on to Dad's newfangled computer with its slick chrome edges. Aimee just watched at first. Then she sat down and grabbed the mouse.

"Let's go to that fish site you were talking about yesterday," Aimee said. "With Fiona. You know the one."

"You mean bigfishbowl.com?" Madison asked.

Aimee nodded. "I wanna get a screen name. Can we do it now? Tonight?"

Madison smiled. After all this time, she was so happy to hear that Aimee wanted to log on for real. It meant the three friends could gab on the computer in three-way conversations. Finally. They signed on under Madison's screen name to start. Madison punched in her secret password.

The home page was a giant advertisement for the Caught in the Web Halloween story contest, with flashing spiders and cobwebs and witches floating past on on-screen broomsticks. If you moved the cursor over one of the fish inside the bowl, you saw its skeleton.

All at once, a shaded green box popped up. The cursor blinked quickly.

ENTER SCREEN NAME

"I don't know what my name should be, Maddie. Whaddya think? Twinkle toes?" Aimee joked. "Bertha big butt? Ha! You're good at nicknames. You gave Egg his nickname, didn't you?"

Madison laughed out loud. "Yeah, right." She had.

They punched in a perfect screen name for Aimee's personality.

BALLETGIRL

The screen flashed like a strobe light.

NAME TAKEN. SELECT ANOTHER. MAY WE RECOMMEND BALLETGIRL12?

"That's lame. What's the twelve for?" Aimee

asked, disappointed. "Are there really eleven other ballerinas on this Web site? I don't get this."

"Wait!" Madison exclaimed, punching in a different name without any numbers. She typed "BALLETGRL"—without the *l* for a change.

That worked.

At long last, Aimee was an official online member of the bigfishbowl community. She announced her name and her password out loud as she punched it in, like she was ordering something at the deli.

"BALLETGRL! POINTE!"

Aimee had a hard time keeping secrets. Even her own.

After dinner, the duo signed online again to test Aimee's new membership privileges in chat rooms and beyond. When Madison noticed that Wetwinz was online, she helped Aimee send her first Insta-Message ever.

They asked Fiona about soccer practice that day, and Fiona wrote back in an instant:

I can't believe this is YOU! That is so wow. C u!

"What's that?" Aimee asked, pointing to the letters *C* and *U* at the end of the message. She didn't understand Web lingo yet.

"C U. It's 'See you.' Get it? It's like computer shorthand. You'll pick it up after a while."

Then Madison took her turn logging in. Dad poked his head into the room to say it was time to pack up for home. Madison ran to the bathroom, leaving Aimme to surf the site by herself.

Aimee was zoned out on bigfishbowl.com, clicking from screen to screen, searching for a chat room. She couldn't believe the made-up names she encountered: ChuckD4Ever, PrtyGrrl88, and Brbiedoll.

All of a sudden, there was an Insta-Message up on the screen.

"Hey!" Aimee cried out to Madison. "What's this?"

"Huh?" Madison asked, walking back in.

"Who is Bigwheels?" Aimee said, eyes locked on the screen.

 Aimee

My BFF finally got online! But here's
the problem—Bigwheels was online at the
exact same time!

Aimee was sitting there staring at the
Bigwheels Insta-Message on my dad's computer
screen. I just flipped. I hit DELETE and
told Aim it must be a wrong screen name,
like a wrong number on the phone. Then I
punched the RESET key and the computer went
black. Why didn't I just tell her?

Rude Awakening: The truth IS out there.
I'm just not ready to share it yet.

Thursday afternoon, Madison was *still* feeling
weirder than weird about avoiding Bigwheels

online. It was like the flu. She couldn't shake it. What was the big deal about telling Aimee that Bigwheels existed, anyway?

She looked away from the computer screen to see if the librarian or anyone else was loitering in the school media center. She was up here in the middle of a Thursday test block. Her teacher, Mr. Sweeney, had given her one of those "get out of math free" cards. Madison always tried to play her cards right, which usually meant finding a computer somewhere. She loved the chance to escape into her files, even if it was only for the briefest moment.

Once again she scanned the room to make sure no one was staring her way or spying.

Madison punched the side of her computer power tower with her fist to get it thumping and chugging, but that didn't help much. The media center machine was a real dinosaur. Hitting it only made the monitor buzz like some kind of angry, prehistoric insect.

From across the library where she was typing, Madison saw the flash of someone entering the library and did a double take. Most seventh-grade kids were at lunch, class, or study hall right now. The eighth- and ninth-grade classes were away on a day trip into the city.

Who was that?

It was hard not to be a little bit paranoid.

As soon as she saw funny hair sticking out all over the place, Madison felt better. She knew that head. It was Drew, standing by the biography section.

Madison waved and turned back to her files. But she heard something else. Breathing.

"Boo!"

Madison leaped out of her chair.

"You should watch what you write when people are around, Maddie." It was Egg. And he was breathing, right behind her—with lousy milk breath on top of everything else.

"Egg, you stink," Madison gasped. She meant it both ways.

"Yeah, but I gotcha!" Egg cackled like he'd just played the best trick ever. "When are you gonna get a clue? I GOTCHA!"

He was so good at scaring the wits out of her and everyone else whenever he got the chance.

From across the room, Drew smiled wide. Was he laughing? Madison frowned. No more Little Miss Nice Guy with any of these boys, Madison thought. Drew was probably just Egg's lookout.

She had been tricked.

"Whatcha doing?" Egg asked. "What *are* you writing?"

"None of your beeswax, Egg. You are so nosy!"

Madison hid the computer monitor screen with both palms pressed flat and quick-saved her document. She pulled her disk out of the computer and casually shoved it into her orange bag.

"Maddie, why are you always up here alone?" Egg asked. "You living up here or what?"

Drew walked over. "Er . . . Egg, the bell's about to ring."

"I'm going to get you guys back for this." Madison pursed her lips. "*Both* of you."

"Yeah right." Egg cackled again. "For your information, I'm not a little scaredy-cat. . . ."

"Egg, the bell's going to ring any minute." Drew tugged on Egg's sleeve.

"Yeah, yeah." Egg moaned.

Madison got up to walk away.

"Hey, wait up!" Egg called after her. "You didn't answer my question."

"You didn't *ask* a question," Madison grumbled. She kept right on walking, out of the library and into the main stairwell. Whatever it was that Egg had to say, Madison wasn't in the mood. She already felt bad enough with the whole lying-to-Aimee thing. She didn't need Egg trouble!

Madison made her way to science class. The room was chaos today, with kids talking and standing everywhere except their assigned seats. There was no teacher in sight. Madison slipped uncomfortably into her assigned seat next to Poison Ivy.

On the other side of Ivy, Hart sat perched on his lab stool, nose in his notebook. Madison tried to catch his eye, just to say hello, but she couldn't see him and he couldn't see her. Every time she leaned forward, Ivy leaned forward. Whenever she pushed backward, Ivy pushed back, too.

Hart was out of reach and out of sight.

The worst part about Hart being so close and yet so far was all the secondhand listening. Ivy and Hart were having one of those drippy, flirty conversations.

"Whassup?"

"Not much. Whassup with you?"

"Nothing."

"So . . . what's going on?"

"Nothing. What's going on with—"

Drip, drip, DRIP!

Madison screamed inside her own head. She couldn't understand why Hart was so nice to Ivy. Was he worked up over Ivy's red, flowing hair? Was he under some kind of weird spell? (It was Halloween, after all.)

Or worst of all—did he like her?

That would be a real nightmare.

Five minutes after class should have begun, their regular teacher Mr. Danehy, still hadn't arrived. A joker standing in the middle of the room said there was some kind of ten-minute rule they could follow if the teacher wasn't there soon. No teacher after ten minutes meant class was automatically canceled. Madison wished for that. It would be like getting a "get out of class free" card, only better. It meant escape from Poison Ivy.

Chet took the delay as another opportunity to stand up in front of the class and act like a clown. He liked to pretend he was the teacher, testing his bad imitation of Mr. Danehy's unidentifiable accent.

In the middle of all the fuss, the door to room 411 opened with a whoosh.

Chet froze. He thought he'd been caught red-handed in the act of impersonating a teacher.

But Mr. Danehy wasn't the one standing there. It was a substitute teacher from central casting. And he was taller than tall.

Everyone scurried into their seats and shut up.

The big guy who'd arrived on the scene was wearing an average-looking white shirt, loose green tie, and khaki pants. But he was anything but ordinary. He leaned against the doorway casually so his head almost hit the top of the frame. Madison figured he must be seven feet tall.

"Hello, seventh-grade science class," the big guy grunted as he entered, eyes scanning the room. Everyone in class nodded back like a bunch of robots. They weren't sure who this was, but they knew he wasn't someone to mess with. "I'm Mr. Stein," he said gruffly, writing it up on the board. "S-t-e-i-n."

He stepped back with a clop, kicking a wadded-up piece of paper on the floor. His hair was a jet-black helmet. The only thing missing was bolts in his neck.

"Did you say you were Mr. Stein?" Chet blurted. "As in Frank-en-stein?" He chuckled at his own joke.

Mr. Stein chuckled right back. "Not Frank. *Bob.*"

"Ha!" Chet burst out laughing. "That's funny!"

"Yeah, well," Mr. Stein continued. "I'm the funny science sub. What can I say? Now, let's get to work."

The rest of the class laughed out loud as Mr. Stein told a couple more jokes about werewolves. Then he asked everyone to pull out their textbooks. He wrote the formal assignment from Mr. Danehy on the board.

Read pages 101 to 151.

"I know that's a lot for thirty minutes, so do as much reading as is humanly possible," Mr. Stein urged, shuffling a few papers in front of him. "But no talking, okay?" He sat down at Mr. Danehy's desk with a thunk.

Chet leaned over to Hart and whispered, "Am I crazy, or is this guy a walking science experiment?"

Madison sighed audibly. "Shhh!" She opened her textbook to do the reading. There had been enough monstrous moments for one day.

A few minutes later, however, kids got restless. First they started to mumble. Despite Mr. Stein's instructions, whispering came over the room like a breeze. Madison was trying as hard as she could *not* to listen to any of it, but she couldn't help overhearing Ivy's whispers to Hart because they were just a foot away.

"Hart, are you asking anyone to the Halloween dance?" Ivy was using her soft, sweet voice.

"Nah," Hart answered. "I'm just gonna go with some friends."

Ivy leaned in closer. "You can ask someone if you want. To the dance, I mean."

"Yeah," Hart said. "But I don't wanna."

"Do you wanna help on a dance committee?" Ivy asked. "You were at the meeting, weren't you? What task team are you on?"

"Not sure yet," he said.

"Why don't you help with decorations, Hart? You could help hang up stuff. I bet you'd be really good. That's the committee I'm on."

Madison thought she saw Ivy press her leg against Hart's leg, but she wasn't so sure. Were there rules about that? Hart's knee looked a little jumpy.

He cleared his throat. "Did you say decorations? Well . . . that sounds kinda . . . well . . . not for me. Thanks anyway."

"You could do the scary hallway, Hart. That's an important job."

"I guess—look—"

"Please," Ivy begged. "Pretty, pretty, *pretty* please."

Madison knew Poison Ivy was using her whole bag of tricks to get Hart on her side. She even smelled like flowered perfume. Ivy knew 101 ways to get boys to do things. She'd say *anything* to get what she wanted.

"Okay, okay," Hart said. "I guess I could be on a decoration committee. Just cool out, all right? I gotta do this science now."

Madison couldn't hear the rest of what was being said—only that Ivy laughed. And Hart laughed right back.

Was he laughing at her or with her?

And there was his knee, still bouncing up and down like a jackhammer. Was he nervous? Having a seizure? Madison dreaded the thought that Hart was actually in the middle of liking Poison Ivy Daly right there in front of Mr. Stein and everyone else in science class. Madison couldn't take her eyes off that leg.

"Hey! What are *you* looking at?" Ivy snarled. She'd caught Madison staring. She *always* caught Madison staring. Ivy flipped her red hair and leaned in. "It's rude to stare, you know. You're being *rude*, Madison."

But Hart's legs were still moving—*bounce, bounce, bounce.*

Madison secretly wished he would just fall off his stool.

Chapter 5

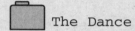 The Dance

Rude Awakening: This Halloween is
turning into Shalloween.

They should put warning labels on
people. Since Ivy joined the decorating
team, the Halloween dance is doomed. She
sits in our meetings with her pink cell
phone sticking out of her bag and her nose
stuck up in the air and I could just
scream! Anytime anyone said anything, she
was like, "I don't think that's a good
idea."

Not only that, but I saw her outside the
cafeteria (she didn't see me) talking to
this cute boy, Nick, about helping with the
dance. She wanted to know if he had a date.
A DATE?

There's no dating! This dance is for
EVERYONE, not just couples. Right???
    I wonder why Hart hasn't called me
Finnster in a long time. Has he forgotten?
I know I hate it when he calls me that,
but I kinda miss it.

Madison hit SAVE and looked up to see the clock
on top of Mrs. Wing's filing cabinets.

It was two forty-eight.

She had twelve minutes to go before the last bell
of the day rang. Today was one of the most antici-
pated soccer games of the school season—the one
scheduled against Far Hills' biggest rival school,
Dunn Manor. Madison was meeting Aimee down at
the lockers right after the final bell. Most of the seventh grade would be in attendance, screaming and
rooting for their favorite infielders. They wanted to
cheer the loudest. Aimee was even skipping her
dance troupe practice for today's game.

It had been a hugely successful soccer season for
Fiona and the rest of the Far Hills Rangers. The
entire team was touted as an early contender for
the district championships, and today's match was
supposed to be closer than close. The only minor
problem was the rain. The Far Hills soccer field
would be a little muddy, since it had been drizzling
all day. Madison didn't mind, but Aimee was obsessing about her hair frizzing.

"Bummer! I can't believe it's raining." Aimee

groaned, opening her locker. Inside she had a mirror glued to the door. She combed her hair and applied a dab of all-natural lip gloss. She extended the container to Madison. "Try some."

Madison shook her head. "Since when do you wear makeup?"

"Gloss is not *really* considered makeup," Aimee said. "Besides, this company doesn't test on animals. So it's cool. And it tastes like candy."

Madison stuck her finger into the little pot of gloss. It was better than the strawberry kiwi smooch stuff she'd used in the past. She smacked her lips. They did shimmer. And they tasted like purple lollipops.

Aimee brushed her blond hair some more. Madison just laughed. "What's the point, Aimee We're just going to get wet anyhow."

Madison adjusted her own ponytail and Aimee closed her locker. Dozens upon dozens of students, parents, and teachers were moving out the front doors down to the soccer field.

Even with the light rain, seventh, eighth *and* ninth graders showed up. Most kids ignored the drizzle, but parents sat holding umbrellas. The game hadn't started yet. Players from both teams were milling about on the field.

Madison flailed her arms to catch Fiona's attention, but Fiona didn't see. She was in the middle of putting on her shin guards. Madison pulled her hand down quickly so no one would spot her waving to someone who wasn't waving back.

"Go, Far Hills! Go, Fiona!" Aimee screeched. She would have danced around, too, but it was very damp and cramped where they were sitting. Instead she just twirled her hips and screamed.

Aimee's screeches and moves were as embarrassing to Madison as her own waving incident. Every time Aimee said something or did something, Madison was sure kids turned around to stare. She wanted to dive under the bleachers—and run back to her locker.

"Look! There's Egg and Chet!" Aimee yelled their names. *"EGG! CHET!"*

They didn't hear. They were down closer to the field, talking to a couple of seventh-grade girls. Chet had his hands in his pockets, and one girl was tugging on his sleeve. Madison couldn't hear them but she knew exactly what they were talking about. It was like the Ivy-and-Hart conversation in science class.

Madison wished that she could learn to flirt like Ivy and the girls who were talking to Egg and Chet.

The Rangers were huddled in a semicircle by the sideline bench. The opposing team, the Mallards, did the same, arms locked, shirts dripping wet. The only difference between the two huddles was that the Rangers were outfitted in blue and white while the Mallards were sporting red-and-gold uniforms. Girls

53

from both teams had mud on their legs even though they hadn't started the game yet.

Whooooooooooooo!

Someone blew a whistle and a roar exploded from below. Both sides were clapping as they took the field. Everyone in the stands clapped, too. Fiona and the rest of the Rangers looked superconfident. There weren't very many cheers for Dunn Manor, just a small group of boys and girls closer to the bottom of the bleachers. Madison saw someone's dad holding a yellow sign that said WE'RE NOT DUNN UNTIL WE BEAT FAR HILLS!

Madison felt a surge of irresistible energy being there. Soon she was cheering as loudly as Aimee.

"Go, Rangers," everyone shrieked together. "Go! Go! Go!"

By now Egg, Drew, and Chet had found Madison and Aimee in the stands. They pushed their way up to their rows.

"Yo!" Egg screamed. "This is so awesome, right? Better than those middle-school games."

Egg and Drew whistled the kind of whistle where they stuck their two fingers into their mouths. It was way louder than the plain old pucker whistle that Madison was trying.

Chet screamed, and everyone looked down onto the soccer field in time to see a Mallard take off with the ball. But there was no shot at goal.

Not yet. But Fiona was on the move.

"There she goes!" Chet screamed. It was funny, Madison thought, to see him looking so happy, almost proud, at what his sister was doing. In spite of the fact that he was the most annoying part of her life, Chet and Fiona were so totally bonded. Madison couldn't imagine what it would be like to have a twin.

Fiona raced up and down the soccer field in the spitting rain. She got her chance to kick on goal—but missed. The crowd sighed together.

That's when Madison saw Hart. He was wearing a Far Hills sweatshirt. He never looked up, so he had no idea Madison was there, but she kept her eyes glued on him. She scanned the area around him, but no Ivy.

"Madison, isn't this the best?" Aimee squealed. "I came to soccer games before with my brothers, and it was never like this."

Everyone around them took a deep breath at the exact same time.

"Ahhhh!"

The crowd howled as the Rangers jumped around on the field. There was a penalty and an off-side kick. The crowd waited. The clock ticked. Fiona kicked.

"*Goal!*"

The ball flew right into the goal net. She was a star! The Mallards' goalie collapsed into the mud. She looked madder than mad.

"*Woooooooo!*" Aimee jumped up and started to

55

do a wave, only no one else followed. This time Madison didn't care.

By the time the soccer game ended, the Rangers were the hands-down winners with a score of 2–0. Fiona and another wing named Daisy Espinoza had scored the game-winning goals. Teammates slapped each other's backs and said, "Good game, good game, good game." Madison could hear them from where she was sitting. This victory meant the team would go on to the district championships, the first time in twelve years for Far Hills.

Madison and Aimee hurried down the bleachers to find Fiona.

"You won the game!" Madison said the moment she spied her soccer star friend.

"Thanks for coming," Fiona said. Her blue-and-white shirt was soaked through. "Hey, you guys, have you seen my mother? She was supposed to come, too."

"Great job!" Mrs. Waters said, appearing out of nowhere. She hugged Fiona tight. Chet was right behind, ready to give his sister a high five.

Everyone was shivering and laughing at the same time. The coach came up to congratulate Mrs. Waters on her daughter's success.

"Nice kicking," Chet said.

Fiona couldn't stop grinning. She looked so happy doing what she did best. It was the same look Aimee had after dance recitals.

"So are you girls coming to our Halloween sleep-over tomorrow?" Mrs. Waters asked.

Chet laughed. "Girl party! Maybe I should invite some guys over, Ma."

"Chet Waters!" Mrs. Waters said. "Why don't you just go help Fiona get her stuff over to the car?"

"He's not going to be there." Fiona leaned in to whisper to Aimee and Madison. "My brother is such a geek."

"We're definitely coming." Aimee grinned. "I would never miss a sleepover. It's really nice of you to have us over, Mrs. Waters. Thank you."

"I can't wait," Madison said. "Hope it's not a dark and stormy night or anything like that."

"Like today!" Mrs. Waters laughed.

Madison looked upward and drops pelted down onto her face. She stuck out her tongue and swallowed a little bit of rain, cool and warm at the same time.

"Why don't I give you girls a ride home?" Mrs. Waters said, trying in vain to hold her umbrella out over Madison and Aimee. The rain was coming down harder now. Everyone ran to the Waterses' minivan.

Madison saw Hart again as she was running, but he didn't see her. Actually, she saw Egg and Drew standing there, too, but she didn't wave like she'd done with Fiona earlier in the afternoon. One non-returned wave was enough for one day. It would be twice as mortifying if Hart was the one who didn't wave back.

"Race ya!" Aimee said to Fiona as they approached the minivan. She leaped over a puddle gracefully, as only a dancer could.

"Last one there is a rotten—" Fiona was already halfway to the car.

Madison stayed back and walked more slowly alongside Mrs. Waters. She was afraid that if she ran, she might fall and land right on her wet behind, right in the middle of the deepest puddle.

Madison didn't want to risk any more embarrassing episodes around Hart Jones—or anyone else.

After a Chinese takeout dinner with Mom, Madison logged on to bigfishbowl.com home page. The writing contest deadline was fast approaching, and she needed to get some work done on her story.

If only she had some ideas.

```
Enter the Caught in the Web Contest
TODAY!
First Prize: Your Story on the Web
plus a mystery game (valued at
$25)!
```

The site flashed brighter and faster than she'd remembered. Fortunately the contest deadline had been extended by a couple of days. That made her breathe easier. It gave her more time to make her story scary. She needed all the time she could get.

While online, her Insta-Message box blinked. It was Bigwheels!

They met in GOFISHY, their favorite chat room.

```
<Bigwheels>: Ur online!
<MadFinn>: Didja get my EMSG?
<Bigwheels>: Y
<MadFinn>: ggg
<Bigwheels>: Howz dance comitee
<Bigwheels>: committee (sorry)
<MadFinn>: ok. SHE'S still around
    but whatever
<Bigwheels>: who?
<MadFinn>: IVY MY ENEMY
<Bigwheels>: IC
<MadFinn>: :>(
<Bigwheels>: Howz Hart?
<MadFinn>: He's :-9
<Bigwheels>: I wish I had a BF
<MadFinn>: Wait a minute, he's NO
    WAY my BF
<MadFinn>: N e way, I have to
    forget him, I think my chances
    are like NONE
<Bigwheels>: Don't say that! I've
    never met you F2F but I bet ur
    cool and pretty
<MadFinn>: Whatever—he likes HER I
    know
<Bigwheels>: Other fish in the sea
    then
```

\<MadFinn\>: Like on bigFISHbowl? LOL
\<Bigwheels\>: ;-]
\<MadFinn\>: Are you entering that
    contest on the home page of this
    site
\<Bigwheels\>: Huh?
\<MadFinn\>: CAUGHT IN THE WEB
\<Bigwheels\>: No u asked me that
    already
\<MadFinn\>: Oh I am
\<Bigwheels\>: What's ur story gonna
    be? I can't write stories only
    poems I think should I write a
    poem?
\<MadFinn\>: I want to write something
    scary
\<Bigwheels\>: Why don't you write
    about that GIRL who's ur enemy @
    school she sounds scary
\<MadFinn\>: Good idea!!! Or I could
    write about my life . . . LOL
\<Bigwheels\>: Yeah IMO real life is
    the scariest thing
\<MadFinn\>: :-0
\<Bigwheels\>: Good nite
\<MadFinn\>: Sleep tight!
\<Bigwheels\>: *poof*

"You want gravy on that?" the lunch lady, Gilda Z, asked, ladle in one hand and giant fork in the other.

Madison stared down at her tray. Was this mystery meat moving?

Gilda slopped on gravy. Most landed on the tray, not the plate. "Next!" she cried.

Madison moved along. She peered over her shoulder and saw Hart standing a few kids back. He was peeling a banana. For a split second, she pretended not to notice him. But it was too late.

"Hey, Finnster!" he called out. He'd spotted her. Even though she suddenly felt nervous to talk to him, she also felt relieved to hear his nickname for her.

"Hart? H-h-h-hey," Madison replied. Her lips quivered like Jell-O. Crushes can make a person speak gibberish sometimes. Madison was so crushed out.

"What's on the menu today?" Hart asked. He glanced down at Madison's plate. "Whoa, that meat loaf looks sick."

Madison's helping of meat loaf didn't look like real meat because it was absolutely the wrong color. The gravy didn't help. Gray-vee. It had a weird brown crust, too.

"Oh . . . not so bad with ketchup, maybe?" Madison smiled nervously. She wanted to say the right things in front of Hart. But all she could do was defend her lunch.

Hart made a loud "yeeeeech" noise. "You have more guts than me, Finnster. I'm having a bologna sandwich today." He cut ahead and moved down the line.

For dessert, Madison grabbed a cupcake with orange frosting. It was decorated like a jack-o-lantern on the top with chocolate chips for eyes. She asked Hart if he wanted one, too. He didn't.

"Um . . . do you want to sit at our table in the back?" Madison asked. She tried to say it casually, but it came out kind of forced. "Sit. Table. The orange one." She gestured like an orangutan who had just learned language.

Hart shrugged. "Yeah. Egg's there already. I can see him. Sure."

She followed him to the back of the cafeteria,

past the table where Poison Ivy and her drones were sitting.

"Hey, Hart," Ivy said.

He gave Ivy one of those guy nods and kept right on walking. She looked surprised. So was Madison.

Madison held her breath. She didn't want to do anything stupid like burst into a merry chorus of "nah-nah-nah-nah-nahs." She didn't dare look back.

When they reached the orange table, Hart stuck out his hand and Egg slapped it. The table was three-quarters full: Egg, Drew, Aimee, Fiona, Chet, and a few floaters at the other end. Hart squeezed in at the opposite end from Madison. Sadly, there would be no accidental knee knocking over lunch.

"How could you get that meat loaf, Maddie?" Aimee asked as soon as Madison had put down her tray. "It looks dead."

Everyone else leaned in to look. Apparently no one had gotten the lunch selection except for Madison.

"Do you even know what's in that?" Aimee stuck out her tongue. "I thought you liked animals."

"I didn't really think about it," Madison said, sticking her fork in it. The fork stood straight up. She threw a napkin over the whole thing. "I'll just eat yogurt, then."

Hart and Chet were laughing. Madison hoped it wasn't at her. She opened the yogurt container.

"Did you see the new posters for the Halloween dance?" Fiona asked. "I am so excited. Señora is calling it Cobwebs and Creeps."

"What is that supposed to be? Our theme?" Madison asked aloud. "I didn't know we had a theme."

"That's because you're too busy getting gross loaf," Egg said. Drew snort-laughed and the rest of the boys started laughing, too.

"Who's going dressed as what for Halloween?" Aimee asked the table.

Egg grinned. "A rapper. Totally."

"You should go as Jimmie J, Egg," Hart said. "Ladies' man."

Jimmie J was a heartthrob from a popular boy band. Madison never understood why he made girls swoon. He had such hairy arms.

"Why stop at Jimmie J, Egg? You should go as the *whole* band," Aimee teased. "But then again, you can't sing at all, so . . . maybe not . . ."

"Not!" Egg chuckled. "Very funny, Aim."

"Is everyone going trick or treating this year?" Chet asked. "Fiona and I always went when we lived in California, but I thought maybe this year was the year when we stopped. . . ."

"Stopped? Why wouldn't we go?" Drew said quickly.

Egg grinned. "Yeah. Somewhere out there is a bucket of candy with my name on it."

"I want *lots* of candy," Fiona declared.

"Last year I had an entire trashbagful of candy and it lasted through February," Hart said. "February! It's my own personal record."

"Man, I ate all my candy in only two days," Egg said. "And then I was dog sick for like a week."

Madison nodded. "I remember."

"I hate it when candy gets stale," Aimee complained. "I had to throw most of my candy out."

"What are you talking about, Aimee? You don't even eat candy," Drew said.

Aimee shrugged and took a bite of carrot.

"Don't you guys think we're a little old to go trick-or-treating?" Madison said. "I mean, I don't wanna sound like I'm a—"

"PARTY POOPER!" Egg yelled.

Aimee slapped Egg's shoulder. "I'm with you, Maddie," she said.

"Hey! I like trick-or-treating," Fiona said. "We're not too old!"

"Are you saying we have to stop trick-or-treating just because we're in junior high?" Egg said. "I intend to do it for as long as I possibly can. And after that, even."

"We have to wear costumes for the Halloween dance. Why not use 'em again to get good candy?" Drew said.

"Hey, know what? If I can't be a rapper, I wanna

65

dress up like a mummy," Egg said. "For my costume, I mean. For the dance."

"A mummy is *in* a wrapper. That's practically the same thing, right?" Drew laughed at his own lame joke.

"What if we all went trick-or-treating together?" Chet said. "Maybe we could go as a TV family or something. Like the Simpsons."

"I love them!" Madison said enthusiastically.

"What did you dress up as last year, Maddie?" Drew asked.

Madison thought for a moment. "I dunno," she mumbled.

Dressing up for Halloween always stressed out Madison.

"I think I'm going to dress up as a boxer this year," Chet said. "Or a martian. Yeah. Something freaky."

Fiona groaned. "You would. "

"I'm going to go to the dance as a ballerina," Aimee said. She picked at a lettuce leaf on her plate. Aimee was becoming the kind of person who counted peas before she ate them.

"Ballerina? Like that's a big surprise." Egg made a face.

"You should go as a wizard," Drew said to Hart. "You have the cape and hat from *The Wiz*, right?"

"Yeah, I do," Hart said. "Maybe I should go as a wizard."

"You were great as the wizard," Fiona said. "And you could do tricks at the dance. You're really good at tricks, Hart."

Egg sneered. "Magic, shmagic. I'm gonna be a ninja. What about you, Fiona?"

"I wanna be a hula dancer."

"Hula girl, whoa!" Egg teased. "You got a grass skirt?"

Fiona smiled at him and tilted her head slightly to the side. She'd been crushing on him for weeks, so she didn't mind his teasing one bit.

"Why don't you lend her *your* grass skirt, Egg!" Chet said, laughing.

Egg made a face.

"Remember when Egg dressed up like a doctor for Halloween?" Aimee asked the table.

Madison rolled her eyes. "That was like a million Halloweens ago—"

"When we were *six*—" Aimee said.

"And Egg got into a yelling match with these nasty kids walking down the street and—"

"Yeah, yeah, and I got picked off by an egg on the Fourth Street overpass." Egg shook his head. "Get to the point, Maddie. I got hit with an egg, so that's when you started calling me Egg. Thanks a lot."

"At least it wasn't toilet paper." Hart laughed. "T.P. would be a worse nickname."

The table snickered.

Madison looked up at the lunchroom clock. The bell was about to sound. She saw Ivy getting up a few tables away, probably heading for the girls' bathroom. Ivy looked right over at Madison and the rest of the orange table with a mean, hard stare. Madison was glad that Hart wasn't watching.

What tricks did Poison Ivy have up her Boop-Dee-Doop sleeves now?

Fiona, Aimee, and Madison got up to return their trays.

"Hey, Maddie, have you entered that fishbowl contest yet?" Fiona asked.

"Huh? Not yet." Madison shook her head.

"I've been going online a lot more," Aimee told her girlfriends.

"You have?" Fiona replied. She swallowed her last bite of chocolate pudding.

"Since I got my screen name, anyway," Aimee said. "It's fun going into those chat rooms. You were right."

Fiona and Madison smiled at Aimee. Finally she was getting wired.

"But I'm still a newbie." Aimee sighed.

"Don't worry," Fiona said, rubbing her friend's shoulder. "Hey, did you both ask your moms about going to the mall Saturday before our sleep-over?"

"Yes!" Madison chirped. "Mom said as long as my room is clean. Which means yes."

"My mother said yes, too. She even said she'd take us! She needs to go to the health food outlet and run some other errands."

"This is going to be so cool." Fiona grinned.

Going to the mall was an event. Not only did it mean trying on and perhaps even buying clothes, it also meant eating tacos at the food court, being parent-free, and spying on cute boys across the atrium or on the escalators. The three girls started making a list of what stores they would visit.

"So now that you're online, are you going to enter the Caught in the Web contest?" Madison asked.

"Nah," Aimee said. "I'm just not a good writer like you, Maddie."

"Me neither," Fiona said.

"Well, thanks, but the truth is, I'm a little stuck for ideas," Madison finally admitted. "Do you think you could help?"

"Write about ghosts," Fiona said. "Ghosts are the traditional—"

"Duh! Ghosts aren't scary enough anymore, Fiona," Aimee interrupted. "How about zombies? They're like ghosts, only they *eat* people. Now, that's scary."

"And yucky." Madison laughed. "Once upon a time there was a flesh-eating zombie named Aimee. . . ."

"Why don't you ask my brother for a good

69

idea?" Fiona suggested as they returned to the orange table. "I mean, Chet's a big, fat, lazy zombie!"

The girls laughed loudly. Chet turned around when he heard his name, but he hadn't caught the insult.

Brrrrring.

The lunchroom bell finally rang. All the boys bolted out of the cafeteria without saying good-bye to the girls. It was the usual routine. The girls headed for the door.

Madison walked out slowly, waiting for a flash of brilliance. She was so impatient. She needed a perfect story idea right now.

What was scarier: today's meat loaf or Poison Ivy?

Phinnie was waiting behind the front door when Madison came home that afternoon. He pounced on her with his scratchy claws. She had to take him for a long walk. Mom was busy writing.

Madison looped around the neighborhood and wandered over to Ridge Road. Without even thinking, she turned down Fiona's block. Phin liked this street because so many other dogs lived nearby. His little pug nose was snorting and sniffling at each tree. Madison couldn't imagine what it would be like to smell so many things at one time.

She looked around at houses on the street, mostly old Victorians with front porches and wide front

70

yards. There was no one else around moving—no cars, no people, not even another dog.

As they passed Fiona's house, Madison glanced up. She thought about how last year Fiona and her family didn't live there. So much had changed.

Madison stopped short and yanked back on Phinnie's leash. Even though Fiona's family had repainted, restored, and added on to the side of the old house, it still reminded Madison of stories she'd once heard about the family who used to live there. People always said the old Martin place was haunted.

"Rowrrrooo!" Phinnie barked and tugged, and Madison nearly fell over. She pulled back on the leash, but he still took off down the street to say hello to a neighbor's poodle.

Madison glanced back at the house and then quickly ran after Phin.

Chapter 7

 Caught in the Web

IT WAS A DARK AND STORMY NIGHT. THE
HOUSE WAS DEAD QUIET, EXCEPT FOR . . .
`Aaaaaaaaaaaaaaaaaaaa!`

Madison stared at the monitor, stuck. Her finger was pressing the *a* key over and over again. She remembered something her English teacher told her once about letting ideas go. Mr. Gibbons said to just "keep writing no matter what lands on the page." So she wrote whatever came into her head.

```
Here I am on bigfishbowl and I'm frozen.
Like a big fish stick.
```

Ick. It wasn't exactly the beginning of the scary story Madison was looking for. It was late Saturday morning, and Madison could hear Mom grinding coffee downstairs. The whole house smelled like hazelnuts.

Madison pulled her laptop over to her bed and lay down on her stomach to type. She was tired and wanted to surf the Net a little before going to the mall with Fiona and Aimee.

"Are you kidding me?" Mom shouted, walking into her room. "Look at this mess!"

Madison looked up from her laptop, surprised. "Mom!"

Her mother picked up a pile of clothes from near the doorway and dumped it in a wicker hamper a few feet away.

"Maddie, Aimee's mom will be here in a little while! Look at this *mess*! I said no mall until you clean your room—and I meant it!"

"But, Mom . . . I was just . . ." She closed the laptop lid and jumped up.

"I don't want to hear any excuses, Madison Finn. Pick up, get dressed, and get downstairs. And put that computer away! You have ten minutes."

Mom shut the bedroom door behind her.

Madison knew what to expect when she finally did head downstairs. In addition to a lecture about putting dirty clothes away and keeping her room clean, Madison would also get a minilecture on the perils of "computer overuse."

Quickly Madison cleaned up. She pushed some papers under the bed and shoved sneakers and shoes into the already overflowing closet. She couldn't miss going to the mall with friends—and without Mom. Besides, after shopping at the mall, she was going right over to Fiona's house for their spooky sleepover. She definitely couldn't miss that!

Madison stuffed some clean underwear, her Lisa Simpson nightshirt, jeans, and a sweatshirt for tomorrow into her bag.

Luckily Mrs. Gillespie was a few minutes late. It gave Madison more time to straighten up all her piles and make her bed neater. She even picked up Phin's toys off the floor.

When Mrs. Gillespie honked the car horn, Madison had passed the clean room test. She ran out to meet her friends.

Aimee and Fiona were bursting with energy when Madison climbed into the car, bouncing on the seats like they'd eaten way too much sugar.

The mall was crowded when they got there. Before Mrs. Gillespie scooted off to run her own errands, she told the girls to meet back at the North Fountain by four o'clock sharp.

As Aimee's mom walked away, the three friends bolted for Chez Moi—a casual boutique with faded denim skirts and lace-up boots in the window. Aimee wanted to try on what the mannequins were wearing. Madison wanted to head toward the back of the store, where the hair scrunchies and jewelry were. Fiona stopped and took a camouflage shirt off the rack.

"For the warrior look," she said, laughing. "Tarzan-ella."

Aimee grabbed it out of her hand and hung it back up. She pulled out a cropped T-shirt with sequins on the top that spelled FOXY, the same shirt the mannequin had been wearing

"I like this one, don't you?" Aimee asked.

"My mother would never let me get that," Fiona said.

"Well, your mom isn't here and neither is mine. Try it on," Aimee said, pressing it into Fiona's hand and taking one for herself and Madison. They scurried over to the changing rooms.

Fiona came out and modeled the T-shirt. Madison could see muscles in Fiona's stomach, from soccer, probably. Aimee had them, too, from dance. The shirt fit Fiona perfectly everywhere else, too.

"You try it on now, Maddie," Fiona said, excited. She grabbed Madison's arm and dragged her into the dressing room.

Madison slipped the shirt over her head. It looked okay around the middle even if Madison's belly was softer looking, but the shirt hung down lower than it had on Fiona. Madison wondered why.

"How's it look?" Aimee asked through the dressing room curtain. "Let's see!"

Madison stood sideways and backways and front-ways in front of the mirror. The lights in the dressing room made her skin look almost green. She also thought the word FOXY was dumb. And there was absolutely nothing filling it out on top. Not like Fiona. Madison whipped the top off and stepped back out in her own loose shirt.

"It's not me. You should get it, though, Fiona. It looked so good on you."

"Ha! You're kidding, right? My dad wouldn't let me out of the house in this." Fiona put the top back on the rack. "Aimee's the one who should get it."

Aimee shrugged. "I don't have any allowance money left."

A salesperson meandered over toward them, so the friends turned to dash. They left Chez Moi and went to check out some other stores.

It was over an hour before Madison, Fiona, or Aimee saw even one person they recognized, which was strange, considering malls were the number-one place to see and be seen. Madison was especially surprised she didn't spy Poison Ivy anywhere.

Passing the food court, Madison saw Egg's sister, Mariah, sitting with friends. She could see the glimmer of Mariah's eyebrow ring. Her now black-dyed hair was wrapped in a polka-dotted bandanna.

She was all the way across the food court, so Madison couldn't yell. She wasn't sure if Mariah had seen her, anyway. Madison wanted to walk over and say hello, but Aimee wouldn't budge.

"You don't wanna do that, Maddie," Aimee said.

Madison looked puzzled. "Why not? Mariah is so nice. And she's your friend, too."

"She's all of our friends, Aimee," Fiona added.

"You guys!" Aimee moaned. "I know from my brothers that freshmen like her cannot be bothered to talk to lowly seventh graders like us except far away from school property, and the mall doesn't count. Besides, she's with boys from the high school, which makes it that much worse. It would just be too, too embarrassing, okay? Can we just not do this?"

"Those are high school boys?" Fiona gasped. The boys dressed all in black like Mariah. "They're not very cute, are they? I thought high school boys were hotter than that."

"It's just Mariah," Madison argued. "She'd be happy to say hello."

"Maddie," Aimee moaned.

"Okay, okay, *fine*," Madison said. As she turned to walk away, Madison looked over once more, only this time Mariah spotted her. She waved. Madison felt her heart leap a little. Mariah *was* a friend—and not just some too-cool freshman. Mariah's boyfriends didn't wave, but that was okay.

"See?" Madison nudged Aimee, who saw the wave, too.

They both waved back. Mariah went back to eating french fries.

"I guess I was wrong," Aimee said sheepishly as they wandered away.

"I guess," Madison said. She didn't want to make Aimee feel bad, even if she *had* been wrong.

"Look over there!" Fiona yelled all of a sudden. She spotted the big sign that read PARTY TOWN. It was a supermarket for cheap Halloween stuff: costumes, makeup, decorations, and props in one-stop shopping.

The first costume they saw was on display at the front of the store. It was a cavewoman outfit. "We probably couldn't wear that at school," Madison said, joking around.

"It would make my butt look big, too, I think." Aimee laughed.

"Your butt!" Fiona laughed. "Aimee, you barely have a butt."

Aimee twisted around to see what her behind looked like. "I do too."

"Yeah, whatever," Madison grumbled. She hated it when Aimee acted fat.

Fiona ran to the back of the store and pulled a grass skirt and green tights from one shelf. She'd decided to borrow one of her mom's Hawaiian short-sleeved shirts and tie it up at the waist. She could wear her braids up, too, with flowers, in her hair. The party store had silk flowers, and she picked out purple, yellow, and coral ones.

Aimee already had most of her ballerina costume at home, so she didn't need to get anything. She found some pink ribbon to wrap into braids and a bun on top of her head.

"This ribbon will totally match my new lipstick shade: Think Pink," Aimee said, admiring the bright color.

Still unable to find a costume, Madison picked through the mask sections, tried on wigs in every length and color, and even put on a Dr. Seuss *Cat in the Hat* hat. It was too big and floppy, though, and kept sliding down her head. Plus it made her think of the first-grade play. She wanted to look older, not younger. She wanted to look like junior high, not elementary school.

Aimee and Fiona bought their stuff, and the three of them went off to meet Mrs. Gillespie at the fountain. Aimee and Fiona opened their bags to show Mrs. Gillespie the costumes. Aimee's mother gave Madison a tight squeeze and whispered, "I'm sure you'll come up with a great costume in no time, Madison."

Madison got quieter than quiet. Was Mrs. Gillespie right? She racked her brain for great costume ideas . . . story ideas . . . over-thinking, as usual.

In the car, Aimee and Fiona were talking about

the stars of the newest teen movie, *Breaking Up Is Easy*, which was showing in the Mall-Plex theater.

"Can we go see that, Mom?" Aimee asked.

"When they change the rating from PG-13, you can," Mrs. Gillespie said with a chuckle. "Either that or when you're thirteen."

Aimee huffed. Sometimes it was such a drag to be twelve and not thirteen.

As they pulled into the Waterses' driveway, Madison twisted her head up and sideways to peer out the car window up at the attic windows. They looked dark and spooky.

Mrs. Waters raved about Fiona's grass skirt and Aimee's ribbons.

Then she put her arm around Madison. "I'm sure you'll think up a great costume, Madison," she said.

Madison smiled, but inside she wondered why everyone kept saying that.

Mrs. Waters made hot chocolate and topped their steaming mugs with squirts of whipped cream. Then the girls moved into the den and sat on a big, comfy couch.

"I like cocoa with those teeny marshmallows more than this," Fiona said. "But my mom got the plain kind. Sorry."

"No biggie." Madison nodded, taking a careful sip.

"I think we should tell ghost stories or something scary," Aimee said, pretending to shudder.

"Yeah." Fiona laughed a little. "Ghosts are okay to talk about. As long as we don't have any in this house."

Madison looked at her friend. "Well, you could."

Fiona looked her squarely in the eye. "What are you talking about, Maddie?"

"Just that . . . well . . . there could be a ghost here," Madison said. "Like in the attic or somewhere."

"Are you for real?" Aimee snorted. She looked like she would fall off the couch.

"I haven't gone up to the attic since we moved into the house," Fiona said.

All of a sudden Aimee jumped off the couch. *"Oh my God!"* she shrieked. "I know who the ghost is! Maddie, remember the people who used to live in this house? You know who I mean!"

Madison hugged her knees to her chest. "You mean the Martins?" she said.

"What are you talking about?" Fiona asked. "What Martins?"

"The Martins were this family who used to live here," Aimee explained. "I used to think their whole story was just a rumor. But maybe *not!*"

"You mean there's really a ghost story about . . ." Fiona took a deep breath. "About this house? *My* house?"

Aimee squealed. "This is *so* cool." The girls huddled closer together, and Madison told the whole story.

81

"The way the story goes is that the Martin family had this dance party one night and Mrs. Martin came up into the attic to get a ball gown or something. She wanted to look especially beautiful for the dance. Anyway, she was looking around and she went into this big chest, looking for the dress. And she was trying it on and posing in front of the mirror and—"

Madison stopped herself.

"Are you guys sure you want to hear this?" she said.

"Yes, yes, *yes!*" Aimee yelled.

Fiona gulped. "Go on."

"Well, a lot of time passed. The rumor is that Mr. Martin started to get worried about his wife after an hour or so. She hadn't come back downstairs. So he went up to look for her. Up into the attic."

"Into *my* attic?" Fiona said. "You're positive?"

Madison nodded.

"Isn't this the spookiest? I love it!" Aimee said.

"So Mr. Martin went looking for his wife and couldn't find her anywhere. They couldn't figure out what happened. The whole town of Far Hills sent out a search party, and they looked all over the house and neighborhood for his missing wife. They found nothing."

"Tell her the next part, Maddie," Aimee said. "Fiona, the next part is the best—"

"Many years later, Mr. Martin died. Everyone said

he died of a broken heart. So his family moved out of the house. And when they were moving, someone found the old chest. It was sealed shut, but they pried it open and inside . . ."

Fiona covered her ears. "*What?* Don't tell me it was the—"

"Say it!" Aimee cheered.

"Inside the chest was . . . *Mrs. Martin!*" Madison screamed.

Fiona looked absolutely horrified.

"Or her skeleton, anyway. Some people think that Mrs. Martin had tried on the dress and then decided to hide in the trunk to surprise her husband and it closed on her, knocking her unconscious and latching shut. She never regained consciousness. Or even if she had, the chest didn't have a safety latch inside. She was trapped forever. And ever."

Aimee had her hand over her mouth, acting a little dramatic, as usual. "Poor Mrs. Martin stuck in a trunk! Isn't that great!"

Fiona gasped.

"I mean, it's awful . . ." Aimee whispered, "that she died and all that, but—"

"No way!" Fiona said. "This did not happen in our attic."

Madison nodded. "It could be true."

"Let's go look!" Aimee said. "Right now."

"I should have brought my lucky charm bracelet with me tonight. I could use it," Madison said. She was shivering a little. "I think you need a little luck to catch a ghost."

Madison, who was very superstitious, had collected many pieces of "lucky" jewelry so far in her life. She usually wore all her lucky rings (one on each finger), but she had taken some of them off earlier in the day. Tonight she only had on her turquoise ring from a shop in New Mexico, a present from Dad after some business trip; her evil eye ring (not an actual eyeball, but close); and her loopy interlocked silver friendship ring. Aimee had the same one, only she'd lost hers right after they bought them last year.

"Okay, I don't care what you say, we have to stop

talking about this ghost thing right now!" Fiona yelped. She was half giggling, but Madison could tell how spooked Fiona had gotten. "Look, there are no ghosts in my house. My family has been here for like five months and we haven't seen anything or heard anything. You guys are scaring me. Cut it out."

"Let's go sit in the other room," Madison suggested. "We can talk about other stuff."

"You know what? Maybe the ghost is here because of the dance," Aimee said, skipping into the living room. The prospect of what might be hiding in the attic was getting her more excited by the minute. When she got excited, she danced. "I think the ghost is here because Mrs. Martin died during a dance—and we're about to have a dance. You think? That's a pretty strong connection. . . ."

"Gee, that could be true," Madison said aloud. "It makes some kind of sense. And it is Halloween . . ."

"Maddie, this makes *no* sense!" Fiona said. "Ghosts make no sense! They aren't real and there are no ghosts in my house."

"Fiona, don't you think we should just look for Mrs. Martin?" Aimee suggested. "We're all here together tonight. It's perfect! We should go right up to the attic and introduce ourselves."

While Aimee was on a mission to ghost hunt, Fiona was ready to make like a ghost and disappear. Madison had to do something.

"Aimee, why don't we just talk about something

else and forget about Mrs. Martin and her dress for a while?" Madison said lightheartedly. "It is Fiona's party."

Aimee looked at Madison and then at Fiona, a little flustered. "I'm sorry. I didn't mean to get so carried away. I promise I won't talk about the ghost anymore."

In a teeny voice Fiona said, "Thanks, Aimee."

The girls brought their hot chocolate mugs to the kitchen for refills and then raced up to Fiona's bedroom. Aimee flopped on the bed and looked over at Fiona's massive Beanie Baby collection. She liked the pink Millennium Bear the best.

Madison scanned Fiona's shelves and yanked down an old yearbook. The cover was red with gold foil, the colors of Fiona's old school in California. Half the pages had the corners turned down and someone had written in Magic Marker on the back cover, *Thanks for a fun year!* Fiona showed them all photographs of her old friends.

"I have to show you guys something else," Fiona said, leaning under her bed to get a huge box. Inside was every copy of *Sports Illustrated for Kids.* She had a plastic folder filled with articles and photos of Mia Hamm, the U.S. women's soccer team star. "She's my idol."

Aimee rolled onto the floor. "Did I tell you that I saw Mrs. Wing and her husband in the school lobby yesterday?" she said.

"What? No!" Fiona giggled. "What does he look like?"

"He's really tall and very cute!" Aimee squealed. "He had on dark glasses."

"I've seen pictures in the computer lab. How tall is he?" Madison asked.

Aimee shrugged. "Tall, tall. And cute. She is soooo lucky."

"Do you really think he's a spy?" Madison asked.

"A spy?" Aimee cracked up. "Where did you hear that one?"

"From you," Madison said, grinning at Aimee.

"Maybe he is," Fiona said. "Maybe he's under-cover."

"In Far Hills?" Madison asked.

"*Deep* undercover," Fiona replied.

For a split second Madison considered the idea that Mr. Wing, Spy King, might make a good subject for the bigfishbowl.com story contest. Maybe he was a covert operative for the junior high school confed-eration, caught in an *international* web . . . of intrigue!

Aimee's stomach grumbled and the friends burst into laughter.

"Let's get another snack," Fiona said. The girls headed back into the kitchen for microwave popcorn.

"I still can't stop thinking about poor Mrs. Martin," Aimee said in a low voice. "How claustro-phobic."

Fiona, who was sitting on the edge of the counter, threw a dishtowel at Aimee.

"Hey!" Aimee said. "What was that for?"

"I told you not to bring up the ghost!" Fiona said. "Mentioning a ghost on the way home from school or even in the middle of a dark graveyard is okay. But talking about one above my bedroom isn't."

"Aimee, you promised!" Madison said.

"I know! I'm sorry. I won't talk about her," Aimee said. "But the thing is . . . What if we have a séance and see if the ghost answers? Then we'll know if Mrs. Martin is really here."

"Now?" Fiona said. "A séance?"

"Let's do something other than sit around and eat," Aimee said. "Come on, Fiona, don't be scared. We'll all be there."

"Can't we just talk about boys and other people from school instead?" Fiona asked.

"How about Ivy? She's pretty scary, isn't she?" Madison chuckled.

"No! You have to do this séance with me," Aimee said. "Let's go into the bathroom."

"What?" Madison laughed. "The bathroom? Aimee, you're crazy."

"I'm serious," Aimee said. "I told you ghosts are *serious*. Let's go into the hall bathroom. Is that okay, Fiona?"

She nodded reluctantly, and the three of them

squeezed in and shut the door. Madison turned the lights down real low.

"Maddie, you have to turn out the lights *completely* or it doesn't work," Aimee said.

The small bathroom went black except for the hall light glowing under the bottom of the bathroom door.

"This is so freaky," Madison said. "Now *I'm* scared."

"Do we have to do this in the *dark*?" Fiona's voice was barely audible.

"Here's what we have to do. Face the mirror together. Then we'll see it," Aimee said. As their eyes slowly adjusted to the dark, murky reflections appeared before them.

"See what?" Madison asked.

"The ghost. Look, I did this with my brother Billy once. Just wait and watch," Aimee tried to assure them.

A minute went by.

And then another minute after that. It was getting warm.

Brrrrrrrrrreeeeeeeeeeep!

Fiona's digital watch beeped. The noise almost sent the trio crashing into the shower.

"Whoa!" Aimee screamed.

"What?" Fiona and Madison said at the same time.

"Look! Did you see that?" Aimee asked, pointing at the mirror. "Look! *That.*"

"What?" Madison said, looking closer. "Is it Mrs. Martin?"

"I have such a bad feeling about this," Fiona said.

There was a knock at the door and all three girls screamed at once.

"What are you doing in there?" a voice said from the hallway. "Is everyone all right?"

Aimee clicked on the bathroom light and the room glowed white.

Fiona turned the knob and opened the door. It wasn't Mrs. Martin. It was Mrs. Waters.

"Mom!" Fiona cried. She grabbed her mother's arm.

"Fiona?" Mrs. Waters said. "Why were you three in the bathroom together in the dark? Is something wrong?"

Aimee and Madison started giggling. They couldn't help themselves.

"Why on earth would you girls lock yourselves in a bathroom?" Mrs. Waters asked again. "You could have gotten hurt with all of you stuck inside here like this."

"Mrs. Waters, do you believe in ghosts?" Aimee asked the question no one else had the nerve to ask.

Mrs. Waters thought for a moment. "Well, I don't know, Aimee. Depends on my mood. If I were in a deserted old castle, maybe. Right now, *no*."

"Mom, have you ever been up to our attic?" Fiona asked.

Mrs. Waters shook her head. "Only once or twice. It's mostly empty. Why do you ask? Do we have ghosts living up there?"

"Well . . ." Fiona started to say.

"Madison and I think there is a high probability and likelihood that ghosts are here at your house," Aimee said. She sounded like one of those TV investigators.

"Mrs. Waters, did you said the attic is *mostly* empty?" Madison asked. "What do you mean by 'mostly'?"

"Mostly empty except for a few boxes and pipes . . . and there's an old chest. . . ."

"*Aaaaaaaaaaaaaaaaaaaaaaaaaaaaaaah!*" all three girls screamed at once—*again*.

"*Girls!*" Mrs. Waters covered her ears. "Stop that screaming."

"We have to go check it out for ourselves!" Aimee shrieked. She asked Mrs. Waters nicely. "Can we go up into the attic? Can we? Can we?"

"Aimee, I really don't think you girls should be going up there exploring. I don't know how safe it is. And besides . . ."

"Please, Mom." Fiona spoke up. She wasn't sure she really wanted to come face-to-face with a ghost, but she also didn't want to spend the rest of the night imagining what *might* be up there.

Mrs. Waters still wasn't sure. "I just don't know, dear."

Aimee started pleading again. "We—but—Mrs. Waters—please—"

She could be very convincing when she wrinkled up her face and opened her eyes as wide as quarters. Madison thought the whole thing was pretty funny.

"Mommy, it's a matter of life or death," Fiona said.

"Life or *death*?" Mrs. Waters gasped, laughing. "Fiona Jane Waters, don't be ridiculous."

Madison finally butted in. "Mrs. Waters, there really could be a ghost up there. You see, there's an old neighborhood legend about the attic in this house. . . ." Madison explained the whole thing all over again.

"You girls have some imaginations," Mrs. Waters said. "I supposed I should be impressed. Old attics usually have a lot of secrets—but ghosts?"

"Please," Fiona begged one last time.

"Well . . . I don't think you'll find much of any-thing, but . . . okay. Okay, you can go up there. Do you three promise me you will be careful?"

They all nodded.

"Let me go get the big flashlight, then." Mrs. Waters disappeared out the door.

For some reason they were still all standing in the teeny bathroom, which now felt even more cramped and hotter than before.

Fiona sighed. "Let's go back to my bedroom and make a plan."

"I bet this wasn't what you had in mind when you invited us over," Aimee joked.

"Yeah. I thought we'd be painting our toenails by now," Madison said.

"We can do that stuff later," Aimee said. "This is better. Isn't it? I'm so glad your mom said yes."

"This is fun," Madison said. "I can't believe we actually told the truth about the ghost. I thought it would make her more worried."

"She doesn't believe in ghosts," Fiona said. "She watches sci-fi movies all the time and never gets scared. Besides, even if Mrs. Martin came out, she could probably kick her butt."

Madison laughed. "Well, that's good, I guess."

"I told you ghosts could be anywhere, right?" Aimee said. "And now we're going to see a real, live one. Right here in this house."

Chapter 9

The stairway up to the Waterses' attic didn't seem old or scary at all. Someone had redone the steps, so it wasn't too treacherous to climb. Madison led the way, followed by Aimee and then Fiona.

"This isn't so scary," Aimee said as she stepped up.

"Speak for yourself, Aim," Fiona said.

"We'll have great stories to tell at the school dance next week, won't we?" Madison said. She reached the top of the pull-down wooden stairs and poked her head up first.

"Wow," Madison said, finally reaching the attic space. Her friends climbed in after her. They all looked around and saw an enormous chest.

"Oh my God!" Aimee screamed. "Mrs. Martin!"

"Girls!" Mrs. Waters called up to them from downstairs. "I don't want you up there too long, make it quick!"

Madison poked her head through the opening just a little bit. "We're only going to be here for a split second, I promise, Mrs. Waters. Right down after that."

The friends walked over to where the chest had been shoved into place. It was obvious no one had moved it for ages. It was a big sea chest with chains and buckles on it.

"Maddie, it looks like the one you described in the story," Aimee said.

"And it's big enough for a person." Fiona gulped.

The chest was enormous and covered in dust, nicks, cobwebs, scratches, dents, and other signs of a long, long life. On the side were carved the initials F.D.M. Everyone seemed to recognize what the letter *M* stood for.

Martin.

"This is crazy," Aimee said, a little breathless.

After a moment, their eyes adjusted to the darkness some more. Fiona found a single lightbulb cord and pulled. The whole room lit up. The chest and the rest of the attic were covered in an inch-thick layer of dust.

"Madison!" Aimee cried out when the room brightened. "Watch out!"

Madison felt something on her face. Something sticky. She was snarled in a thick spiderweb.

"How disgusting," Fiona said, trying to peel pieces of web off Madison's shirt and hair.

"Grosser than gross," Madison groaned. She'd have to reconsider her love of spiders and all things creepy-crawly after this.

"Let's go back downstairs," Fiona said, turning away. "We saw the chest. The ghost isn't around. Okay?"

"We haven't even opened it!" Aimee said.

"You guys seem to forget one very important thing," Fiona said. "I live here."

"Isn't that a better reason for wanting to see what's in this?" Madison asked. "Just in case . . ."

"In case *what*?" Fiona asked.

Aimee was already kneeling down, trying to open the latch. "Drat," she wailed. "It's locked."

"I'm going back downstairs." Fiona turned again to walk away from her friends. "I don't wanna see this Martin lady or anything else that's inside that chest. I'm going back to have another cup of hot chocolate even if it doesn't have little baby marsh-mallows in it."

Aimee struggled with the bolt. "Dean showed me once how to pick a lock."

"Really?" Fiona stopped short, incredulous. "Your brother picks locks?"

"Whatever," Aimee said. She took a clip from

her hair and worked the lock. "They do this on TV."

Fiona looked at Madison. Madison shrugged. Aimee liked to exaggerate, but she really seemed to know what she was doing.

"Try this," Fiona said, handing her a piece of scraggly metal from the floor of the attic.

"Weren't you leaving?" Madison asked.

"Maybe," Fiona shrugged and stayed put.

"Is this against the law? I mean, opening someone else's chest?" Madison asked.

"Got it!" Aimee smiled and tossed the metal piece aside. Madison was shocked. Upon closer inspection Madison noticed that the lock had not, in fact, been picked. The whole contraption was rusted and had broken open.

"Now, everyone, on the count of three," Aimee said. "We'll open it together."

"One . . ."

"Two . . ."

"*Three!*" Madison sneezed on the count. There was a lot of dust up in this attic. The lid popped open. Fiona shrieked.

"*Oh my God!*" Aimee yelled.

It was empty.

"*What a gyp!*" Aimee yelled again.

"Where did Mrs. Martin go?" Madison asked aloud.

Fiona looked all around them. "Did she fly out, maybe? Ghosts do that, don't they?"

"She's a sneaky one, that ghost," Madison teased.

"Was she even here?" Aimee asked. "I mean, come on."

"What did we really expect to see?" Madison asked. "A skeleton?"

Fiona shuddered. "She's still here. I bet she's watching us. Right now . . ."

"Girls!" Fiona's mother called from downstairs.

"Ahhhhh!" This time Aimee was the one who jumped.

"Did someone fall? I thought I heard a loud noise. Girls?"

Aimee clutched her chest. "It's just your mother."

Madison started to laugh. They all did.

"Don't worry, Mom." Fiona giggled. "Don't worry. We're just—"

"Scaring ourselves silly," Aimee said.

They all climbed back downstairs, giggling all the way. "Dinner is ready, girls," Mrs. Waters said. She closed the attic door and hustled the friends into the kitchen.

After dinner the trio headed back into Fiona's bedroom. Aimee offered to French-braid Madison's hair, and Fiona tried her new Frosted Grape nail polish.

"Maybe instead of a hula dancer I should go as a witch to the school dance," Fiona said. "I could put white in my black hair. Something to look weird. It gets all frizzy when I let my braids out."

"It looks so cool down," Aimee said.

"A little nappy," Fiona said, "but I like it this way."

Fiona looked so good all the time—and even more with her hair down. Madison figured that every seventh-grade boy would be asking her to dance next week. Fiona was a perfect combination of pretty and smart and athletic.

"So where's Chet tonight?" Aimee asked.

Fiona explained that Chet was staying over at Hart's house with Egg and Drew. Madison wondered what they were doing. Were they talking about *girls*?

"It's like *Night of the Twin Sleepovers*," Madison joked.

"*Night at Haunted House*, you mean," Aimee added.

Fiona grimaced. "No more ghosts!" She sat back to admire her perfectly painted toes.

"Is Chet going to the dance?" Madison asked, putting some Frosted Grape on her own toes.

Fiona shrugged. "Probably. But he won't dance or anything. Chet's scared of girls. He likes to act cool, but he's a real chicken."

"I've never danced with a boy," Madison admitted aloud.

"Really?" Fiona said.

Aimee got quiet all of a sudden. "Me neither," she said.

"What are you talking about?" Madison said. "All you do is dance."

"Not the kind we're talking about, though. Not real dancing. Not with a real boy that I like or anything. What about you, Fiona?"

She shrugged. "Yeah, I had a boyfriend in California and we—"

Squeeeeeeeeeak.

"What was that?" Madison asked. "Did you guys hear that? Right above us?"

Fiona, who'd been sitting sprawled on her own bed, grabbed a pillow and pushed herself up against the wall. "I don't know. Did you hear it?"

Squeeeeeeeeeak.

"Heard it," Aimee said as the noise repeated itself. "Twice."

"It's Ma-Ma-Mrs. Martin!" Fiona stuttered, scared.

"No way!" Madison said. *"No way."*

The three girls dove under the quilt on top of Fiona's bed and vowed never to come out until they had a surefire plan on how to deal with the situation.

"It could just be the floor up there," Madison said.

"Yeah, with the sound of a ghost walking on it!" Aimee said.

"Isn't there any nice way we can ask her to leave my house?" Fiona said.

"Wait! Did you bring the Ouija board, Aimee? That might work," Madison suggested.

"You really want to try talking to this ghost again?" Fiona cried.

"Yes!" Aimee said. She bounded off to get the Ouija board from her overnight bag.

Fiona's room was covered with a plush green carpet. The trio sat down on it like they were setting up some kind of ghost picnic.

"Now, you have to take this seriously," Aimee warned the other two as she opened the box and the board. "No laughing in the middle of it like before."

"Who's laughing?" Madison said, checking out the plastic pointer. Aimee called it the planchette, but to Madison it looked like the little plastic holder found in the center of a takeout pizza.

"Hey, Maddie." Fiona leaned over and picked a string off Madison's shirt. "You still have spiderweb on you. Which is now probably on my bed, thank you very much."

"Sorry," Madison said. "Okay, what question do we wanna ask?"

Aimee clucked her tongue. "We want to ask about Mrs. Martin. Why is she here? Something like that. We want to know about the ghost."

The Ouija "Mystifying Oracle" board looked ominous. It was a special edition that Aimee's mother bought. At the upper-left corner was the word *yes*.

In the upper-right corner was the word *no*. At the center were all the letters of the alphabet, the numerals one through nine, and then on the bottom were two more words: *good* and *bye*. Aimee turned the lights down lower and the board glowed.

"Again with the lights?" Fiona said. "Jeepers."

"Let's start with something simple," Aimee suggested, putting her fingertips on the pointer. "I'll ask. 'Will I be a dancer when I grow up?'"

"That's the question we're asking?" Madison asked, incredulous.

"For now. Like a test."

Fiona giggled. "What does your dancing have to do with ghosts, Aimee?"

"Okay, fine. You ask the question, then." Aimee backed away from the board. She handed the planchette to Madison.

"We need to concentrate," Madison suggested.

"I thought you always made fun of this stuff," Aimee said.

"That was before I saw Fiona's attic," Madison said.

The three girls closed their eyes tightly and placed the pointer back onto the Ouija board.

"Is Mrs. Martin in this house?" Madison asked.

Fiona freaked out as their fingers moved across the board. The planchette pointed to *yes*.

"Did you guys press it that way on purpose?" she asked.

Madison and Aimee shook their heads no.

"Is Mrs. Martin unhappy?" Aimee asked.

The second answer was *no*.

"Well, is she haunting my house?" Fiona asked.

The third question spelled something out very slowly.

"*M-a-c-h-k-l?*" Fiona asked. "What's that supposed to be?"

"The first two letters are *ma* like Martin," Madison said.

"The last two letters look like *kl*. It could be like kill," Aimee said. "Maybe Mrs. Martin is trying to tell us that she was killed."

"So then what's *ch* for?" Fiona said. "Chocolate? Hot chocolate!"

They all laughed and collapsed onto the carpet. Aimee put the game away. Even ghost hunts could get boring.

"Hey, let's go online," Fiona suggested.

They went back downstairs into the den to log on to the computer. Fiona booted up the computer and logged on to bigfishbowl.com.

On-screen, skeleton fish were swimming around inside the home page fishbowl with little bubbles over their fish heads: BOO! OOH! NOO! They looked so cute. Aimee started pointing and naming them after horror movie characters like Dracula and Swamp Thing. She called one "The Wolf-Fish."

At the top of the home page was the banner

invitation to enter the Caught in the Web contest. There was a countdown clock in a sidebar to show the deadline fast approaching. Madison bit her lip. With all the ghostly excitement, she'd nearly forgotten about the contest.

She had to come up with an idea for her story!

Fiona didn't pay attention to all the flashing stuff at the top of the page. She ignored the contest and skipped right over the skeleton fish—clicking into a chat area called "Girls Only." Madison caught her breath when she saw the roster of members chatting there.

Bigwheels was at the top of the list.

Madison couldn't believe it. She'd already lied to Aimee about her keypal once. She didn't want to have to do it again. Did Aimee recognize the name? Would she ask about it?

Zzzzzzzzzzap!

Suddenly the room flashed and then went black. *Bigwheels* and everything else on-screen was gone. It got so quiet. The chugging sound of the refrigerator had turned off with everything else.

"Fiona, your computer exploded," Aimee said, sitting there in the dark.

"I think the power just blew. Like in the wires or something," Fiona said. "It usually only happens during a thunderstorm."

"That's weird," Madison said. "It's not raining out."

"Girls!" It didn't long for Mrs. Waters to come into the kitchen with the enormous flashlight. She lit some candles on the counter. "Is everyone okay in here?"

"The computer just went poof, Mrs. Waters," Aimee said.

"So weird," Madison said again.

"Mommy, what happened?" Fiona asked.

"It's just an old house. I have to flip the circuit breakers down in the basement. I'll be right back. Will you girls be okay up here without me?"

"We're okay as long as Mrs. Martin doesn't come back," Fiona said.

"Who?" Mrs. Waters asked. "Who's Mrs. Martin?"

"A friend," Madison said.

The three friends looked at each other and smiled.

"I see," Mrs. Waters said, walking toward the basement stairs. As she turned around, her eyes lit up with candlelight. She looked like a character from a horror movie going off to the dungeon.

"Don't worry about us," Aimee called after her, laughing nervously. "We'll be right here. Unless we see a . . ."

Fiona punched her jokingly. "Nooooo! The minute the power goes back on, we're doing beauty stuff. *No more ghosts.*"

"Okay! And we'll have a pillow fight, too." Aimee fake-punched her back.

Madison held up her hands and stretched them out to make shapes from shadows on the wall. She used her thumb and the rest of her fingers to make a "duck" quack its bill open and shut. Aimee made a bird flap its wings.

Three minutes later, the power kicked back in and everything in the kitchen surged on at once. The refrigerator hummed. Everyone cheered. Mrs. Waters came back upstairs.

Madison felt a surge, too—inside herself.

Thanks to Mrs. Martin and her best friends and the power outage, she suddenly had the most wonderful, frightful idea.

It was an idea that just might win her the Caught in the Web contest.

Chapter 10

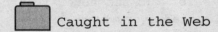 Caught in the Web

Rude Awakening: You can do *anything* once the ghost is clear.

Just sent in my story. Fingers crossed. I hope I win!

Aimee said the story is superscary, and she's pretty much of a ghost expert, especially after our sleepover at Fiona's house.

Fiona, of course, won't read the story. She says it's so close to the truth. That scares her. I don't really mind. But I will make her read it if I win, that's for sure.

Mom liked it, too, a lot. She says I should mail one to Gramma Helen. I need to send it to Dad and Bigwheels, too. Still

haven't told Aimee about my keypal yet.
I'll do it soon.

Madison attached a copy of the story to her file. She printed out one to mail to Gramma.

The Secret of the Old Trunk
by MadFinn@bigfishbowl.com
IT WAS A DARK AND STORMY NIGHT. THE HOUSE WAS DEAD QUIET, EXCEPT FOR the sound of leaves and rain on the roof. An old man stared at a picture on the wall. It was his wife. Her name was Ivy. Ivy had disappeared many years before. She had gone up to the attic before her wedding day to get an old blue dress in an old trunk. That was what she said. But she never returned. Her husband-to-be looked everywhere for her but found nothing. He didn't look in the chest, though. It was sealed shut.
Years went by.
One summer, the man's niece came to stay with him. Her name was Ivy, after the aunt she never knew. She found a photo album with pictures of Ivy and asked a lot of questions. The old man didn't like her being so nosy. She asked if she could go into the attic one day, and he said no, it was off-limits. But she went anyway.
When she got up there, she saw a trunk. It was very late at night, so she tried to be as quiet as a mouse. She had a skeleton key in her pocket to open the trunk. It worked and the lid cracked open.
There was an awful, terrible smell. She

raised the lid a little more. Then she heard footsteps behind her.

"Go ahead and open it," the voice said. She knew it was the old man. He said, "Open it," three times.

She trembled and quaked.

"I SAID, OPEN IT!" the man screamed at her.

The girl pushed open the lid, covering her nose and eyes as she did. She gasped with fear.

"Look inside," the man said.

And so the girl did. She leaned over and peered in.

"OH!" the girl screamed when she saw what was inside.

It was a blue dress!

The man put his hand on his niece's shoulder and squeezed tight.

"I keep this here," the man said in a low voice. "In case my dear Ivy wants to wear it . . . to her GHOST ball!"

"Maddie!" Mom called from downstairs all of a sudden. "Telephone!"

Madison closed the file and went to get the call. Dad wanted to know if Saturday's sleepover had been a success. Madison told him about the power outage, the ghost, the Ouija board, *and* being scared silly.

"Hey, Maddie, what happened to the ghost who went to a school dance?" Dad asked on the phone.

"I don't know, Dad. *What?*" Madison said.

"It had a *wail* of a time!" Dad chuckled.

"Daaaaad!" Madison was the one wailing.

"Do you have a costume for Friday's dance yet?" he asked.

"No," Madison moaned. "Aimee's going to be a ballerina, Fiona's a hula girl. Everyone else's costumes are so cool."

"I'll bet your mother can help you think of something. Why don't you ask her?" Dad said.

"I want to do this myself," Madison said.

After hanging up, Madison dragged herself back upstairs into her closet. She had to start thinking now. Was there a costume hiding inside? She thought about dressing like a hobo, but that wouldn't be original enough. Online she'd seen a T-shirt with a Halloween message that read: THIS IS MY HALLOWEEN COSTUME. Madison thought making a shirt like that would be hysterical, but it wasn't creative enough for a dance.

She went to check out Mom's closet. A blue dress in the corner caught her eye. She could go as Mrs. Martin! But being an invisible ghost wasn't such a great idea for the dance either. She needed people to notice her—especially people like Hart.

Then a caftan dress from a trip to Greece caught Madison's attention. It was a little big, but Madison liked the way it looked. It was a burnt orange color. She tried it on over her jeans.

Mom loved the dress and said Madison could use some other props to go with it for a costume.

Madison thought about who she was dressing up to be. She remembered reading *D'Aulaires' Book of Greek Myths* from school. She loved Greek heroes and heroines. Madison decided she would be Aphrodite, goddess of love. She didn't want to be a ballerina or hula girl or anything that would be perceived as ordinary. Besides, dressing up as a goddess of love meant her odds for capturing Hart's attention were probably increased.

Not that she had a clue what to do if she ever *did* get him to notice her.

There were still four more days left before the dance, which meant four more days of worrying. But school got busier than busy that week for Madison.

It was the end of marking period and teachers were tallying first-term reports. This meant they were also giving quizzes and tests and essays and *everything* else. Madison had to spend more time on homework and less time on files and ghost hunts. She'd clocked in some extra time with Mrs. Wing and the school Web site, too.

Fiona was super busy, too. The Rangers had won each of their district play-off games. Now they were the team to beat in the entire league. Fiona was happy about it, but all the time devoted to soccer meant less time for Halloween dance committee meetings.

Madison missed seeing Fiona at meetings. Aimee

had even missed one afternoon because of dance practice.

Even when Fiona and Aimee were there, they were busy planning for the food or music. Madison had to decorate the gymnasium and cafeteria alone alongside Poison Ivy. And the enemy was as bossy as ever.

"What are *you* doing?" Ivy asked Madison, waltzing over with her hands on her hips. She was wearing a short green dress that looked like tie-dye and clunky black shoes, looking as perfect as ever. She'd been putting up balloons across the back wall.

Madison looked down at the giant package of gauzy web material she was holding. She'd been given the responsibility today of hanging it from the ceiling to the floor in one corner of the room. She had to make a spider's web. Her brain buzzed with the idea that maybe, just like in *Charlotte's Web*, she could stretch the gauze so the web had an actual word at its center. Madison imagined a fake web with the word *DANCE* inside.

"Uh . . . I'm making a spider's web," Madison said. "And I have black construction paper spiders and other bugs to put in the middle."

"Oh, *really*?" Ivy snickered. "Well, I guess it looks like a web."

"What are you doing?" Madison asked.

"I put up signs for the bathrooms and balloons and other things," Ivy said. "Let me see that Web stuff that you're doing."

Madison couldn't believe that Ivy's motives for helping were good ones, but she agreed to let her help with the web. Working together, they could get the gauze stretched out in half the time.

"Why don't you attach it up to the wall there?" Ivy pointed. "I'll hang on to the gauze here." They'd only been at it a few moments, and already Ivy was up to her old tricks.

But Madison agreed it was a good idea, so she leaned over toward the wall. She stretched up with some of the gauze and stretched and . . .

Ooops!

Madison fell right into the wall. Even worse, she fell right into the gauze, causing it to detach. A big piece floated to the floor. She was wrapped in webbing and she couldn't get out.

Ivy roared. She almost looked like she'd turn purple, she was laughing so hard. Soon enough, everyone else heard, too, and they dashed over to see what was the matter. Even Señora Diaz was laughing a little bit as she helped detach Madison from the webbing. Aimee and Egg rushed over from the kitchen and covered their mouths so they wouldn't explode with laughter, too.

"*Oh!*" Aimee cried. "Are you okay Maddie?"

Madison wasn't laughing *at all*. She looked at everyone's faces, including her best friends'. Her stomach went flip-flop. She wanted to run.

But she was caught in the web.

Chapter 11

"Let me see you!" Mom cried. She snapped pictures of Madison in her costume from all angles. "Oh, I'm so happy that you thought of this outfit."

Mom had called up another one of her buddies from Budge Films, where she worked, and arranged to borrow a scepter from the props department. It was made of papier mâché, so it was light enough to carry. Madison made a crown from tinfoil that she spray-painted gold with Mom's help. She also found some junk jewelry in a drawer in Mom's room.

"You look like a real goddess, honey bear," Mom said. She put down the camera so she could adjust Madison's up 'do. Little ringlets fell down her blushed cheeks.

"Oh, Mom." Madison sighed. "Please just take the picture."

"Just stand still, Aphrodite." Dad spoke up. He was standing in the hallway, waiting to drive Madison over to the Halloween dance.

"Thank you, Jeff, for being here," Mom said.

Madison felt weird hearing Mom say Dad's name nicely like that. All three of the Finns were back in the Finn living room together. It was like old times; even Phinnie could tell the difference. The pug was chasing his little curlicue tail and snorting. Dad picked up the dog to calm him down, but Phin wriggled right out of Dad's grip.

Moments later, after several more pictures and kisses and oohs and ahhs, Madison and Dad were in the car. She took a mental inventory: scepter, crown, lip gloss. . . .

The dance started in twenty minutes.

Now that she was all dressed up, she wanted to stay looking pretty during the dance. Would boys notice her—especially one boy in particular? It was Madison's first *real* dance, and she just wanted to be there already! The anticipation made her dizzy. Madison barely said two more words to Dad the whole drive over.

The Far Hills Junior High School parking lot was a madhouse.

One kid dressed up as a giant eyeball in a tuxedo almost fell over and someone had to lead him into the main doors. Madison saw witches, werewolves, and about four ninjas. Egg would be mad about that. He was hoping to be one of a kind. There were hockey players, ghosts, and pop singers. One group of friends had all dressed like an alien family.

Even teachers and chaperones were costumed. Madison chuckled when she saw her substitute science teacher show up as none other than Frankenstein himself—bolts and all.

"Have a great time," Dad said, leaning out the window of the car to kiss his daughter good-bye.

"Okay, Dad." Madison waved him off. "Okay. Bye."

"We'll have dinner when I get back from Boston."

"Okay, Dad," Madison repeated, backing away from his car. "Have a nice trip."

Madison stumbled up the curb. She was the one having the nice trip.

"Be careful," Dad said, pulling away. "And don't forget to have fun!"

Madison wiggled inside her caftan and adjusted her crown. She took a deep breath and walked carefully into the school lobby.

"You're here!" Aimee squealed. She twirled over in her ballerina outfit, followed by her brother Roger.

"You look sooooo good," Aimee said. "Who did your hair like that?"

"Mom," Madison mumbled. "You look good, too. Where's Fiona?"

"She's not here yet," Aimee said.

"Hey, Roger," Madison said to Aimee's brother. "You're a chaperone?"

"Yup. That's me. You've got a nice costume," he added. "Roman goddess of the Halloween dance, eh?"

Madison blushed under her blush. Roger smiled back.

"Hello, all," Fiona said, walking in the front door. She had on a Hawaiian shirt plus a grass skirt and about ten plastic leis around her neck. Chet was standing behind her on the way in, but he didn't stick around. He just stuck his hand up for a quick wave and dashed into the gym.

"Who's Chet supposed to be?" Aimee asked.

"A martian." Fiona laughed. "What else? Didn't you see those little bobbling antenna things on his head?"

The school had a security guard posted at the doorway to the school and again to the cafeteria and gym. They wanted to be careful to check students' bags to make sure no one brought anything inside they weren't supposed to bring.

Madison (a.k.a. Aphrodite), Aimee (a.k.a. Ballerina), and Fiona (a.k.a. Hula Girl) approached the doors to the gym, bristling with excitement. Over by the music booth, Madison saw Mrs. Wing dressed for a masquerade ball. She wore a purple dress and a paper mask that just covered her eyes with purple feathers. Standing next to Mrs. Wing was a man in a rubber mask and doctor's scrubs. Madison assumed he was Mr. Wing.

"This is one of my students," she said to her husband as Madison walked over. "This is Madison Finn and—you're Fiona and Aimee, right? I'd like you to meet my husband, Dr. Bryan Wing."

"Who are you supposed to be?" Aimee asked Dr. Wing.

Everyone laughed when he said, "Wolf-Doctor."

"Have a nice time tonight, Madison," Mrs. Wing said. "See you around."

"All our decorations look so cool," Aimee said, whirling in her ballet slippers as they walked into the main part of the gymnasium. "The balloons look good, and that web in the corner really came out nice, Maddie."

"Yeah, even though I fell in it," Madison grumbled.

"It's Egg and Drew!" Fiona pointed across the gym. Egg was in his best ninja gear. Drew had on jeans and a Mets baseball shirt.

"You call that a real costume?" Aimee said to Drew.

"Sure. I'm a Met," Drew replied. "Hey, Maddie. Nice costume."

"Who are you, Maddie?" Egg asked. "Queen of the World?"

"Shut up, Egg. You're only like the tenth ninja I've seen tonight," Madison said.

Madison noticed that he seemed unusually inter-ested in Fiona's grass skirt. "Can you see through that thing?" he asked her. Fiona giggled.

Aimee rolled her eyes at Madison and whispered, "He's such a geek sometimes."

"*Hart!*" Drew yelled across the gym to his cousin. "*Over here!*"

Madison felt her legs get weak. *Hart?* He was on his way over.

"Yo!" Hart gave all the guys high fives. He was dressed up like a wizard, just like he said he would be. He looked even better than he had looked when he played the Wizard in *The Wiz* at school.

Hart told Aimee he liked her costume, and she twirled around for him. He smiled at Madison, too, but didn't say anything more than, "Hey, Finnster," just like always. He got distracted when some ninth-grade DJ turned on the music.

"I'm hungry," Hart said.

"Yeah, let's go check out the food," Egg said.

"See you guys later," Drew said. The boys walked away together toward the snack table.

Madison clutched her papier-mâché scepter tight. Hart hadn't said anything about *her* costume. She had this weird, empty feeling inside. Everyone else said she looked beautiful. Why hadn't *he* noticed?

"Let's go dance." Fiona goofed around, moving her hula-skirted hips to the music.

Aimee grabbed her arm. "We can't dance *yet*. It's too early."

"What?" Madison said. "Who says it's too early?"

"Trust me, it is. Let's just stand here for a while. See? Kids are still walking in. You have to act mellow at first. Then you dance."

Madison usually didn't question Aimee's logic on such matters.

"Look!" Aimee blurted. She was staring at the door to the gym.

Poison Ivy Daly walked through. She had on a red leotard, red tights, red skirt, red shoes, and red scarf, and she had attached a red tail to her behind and red horns to her head.

"She's a devil!" Aimee snorted. "No way. I can't believe she would come dressed like that."

"Me neither," Fiona said, slack jawed.

Madison *could* believe it. The leotard and tights accentuated Ivy's thin body, and everyone stared. She was followed into the room by her drones, Rose and Joanie, who had on boring outfits and too much makeup. They were supposed to be backup singers, according to Aimee. She'd heard them talking about their costumes the day before.

Ivy scanned the room, but she didn't see Madison, Aimee, or Fiona. She did, however, see Hart right away and walked toward the food table.

Madison watched her parade across the Halloween dance floor along with every boy in the room—even eighth and ninth graders. All eyes were on her, just the way Ivy wanted it.

"Just forget her, Maddie. Let's stand in the center of the room," Aimee suggested.

From the center of the room, Madison had a better view of the food table and Hart. She saw Ivy standing near him. At one point he even reached up and touched the horns on the top of her head. No one was really dancing yet, either, just like Aimee had said. There was an unspoken code about what to do and not to do here. Every moment counted.

Eat. Talk. Be seen.

Dance later.

Madison saw another one of her friends from class, Lindsay Frost, across the room. Lindsay was dressed all in black and was holding her mask by her side. She'd come to the dance as a gorilla. Madison wanted to go say hello, but for some reason she didn't. Lindsay was over near the wall, talking to some boys Madison didn't really know too well.

Girls and boys were segregated everywhere you looked, chatting among themselves. Kids were split into cliques and grades. Madison didn't even recognize half the people in the room. Of course, almost everyone was in costume.

Aimee's brother Roger had been right. This was initiation night. Big time.

"Attention, please," a voice crackled over the loudspeaker. "Welcome to the Halloween dance."

One boy made a fart noise and some other boys cheered.

Señora Diaz stood up on the podium. She was the voice behind the microphone. Madison couldn't see Egg from where she was standing, but she imagined he was squirming in his shoes right about now. He got so embarrassed whenever he and his mother were at the same school events.

"As you know," Señora continued, "we have lots of activities going on this evening. And many helpful people here making sure the dance goes well. Please give a round of applause for your family and teachers who have come out to help us tonight—dressed in costumes, no less."

Kids in the room clapped loudly.

"And to the seventh-grade students on the dance committee who helped with the very important decoration and food and music. Let's give them a round of applause. . . ."

Someone whistled. The clapping got louder. Even the eighth and ninth graders were clapping thank-you.

"*Gracias!*" Señora's voice continued. "Now, we have a line forming for the scary hallway at the far end of the gym. If possible, let's keep the screaming contained to that area tonight, *sí*? We'd like everyone to have a chance inside at least once, so please don't get out and get right back on line. Finally, some eighth and ninth graders will be judging seventh graders in a costume contest throughout the night. Everyone have a *great time!*"

The clapping started up again. So did the music.

"I love this song!" Aimee shrieked. It was hip-hop. She started bending and twisting her body to the music.

"Aimee, you said not to dance yet," Madison said.

"Yeah, but that was like ten minutes ago. It's fine now."

"Yeah!" Fiona shrugged and swiveled in her grass skirt again.

Music pounded over the speakers. A few teachers grimaced at the noise, but it kept right on blaring.

Madison bounced up and down, up and down, from her knees only. She couldn't do much more since the caftan didn't allow for a lot of movement. She straightened out her crown and waved her arm into the air once in a while.

Just like that, Aphrodite was dancing.

Chapter 12

Chet ran over to Fiona on the dance floor, whispering something. He was laughing hysterically. Fiona motioned to Aimee and Madison to walk over to the food table.

"Chet says Tommy Kwong put something in the food," Fiona said. "Let's go see for ourselves."

Floating in the giant fruit punch bowl were plastic flies. Even funnier than the floating flies was the fact that Tommy himself was dressed up like some kind of a bug, wearing a hat with pipe-cleaner and pom-pom antennae on top.

"Hey, Finnster!" Hart came up from behind and nearly scared the crown off Madison. "What's up?"

"Oh! Hart, hey," Madison said. She turned sideways in the caftan and almost lost her balance. "Whoa!"

Hart grabbed her elbow.

"Thanks. This dress is so long, you know, it's hard to . . ." Madison's voice drifted off.

"Cool costume. Who are you supposed to be?" Hart asked, adjusting his own wizard cap.

"Um . . . well . . ." Madison thought for a moment. He'd noticed her outfit finally, but she couldn't very well tell the crush of her life that she was Aphrodite, goddess of love. And she didn't have a backup answer.

"I know!" Hart suddenly said. "You're like a walking Greek myth."

"Well, I'm a Roman or Greek mythical character," Madison said politely. "Take your pick."

"Hercules!" he joked.

"Umm . . . I don't think so," Madison said.

"What's that thing?" Hart pointed to her neck.

Madison reached up and felt her neck. She was sweating. A bead of sweat was trickling down her back. Of course, Hart hadn't been pointing to sweat. He was talking about her necklace.

"Is it real gold?" he asked.

Madison chuckled. "*Not.* My mom got it from some movie friend of hers. Sometimes it's pretty convenient having a mom who has access to weird things like costume jewelry. You know?"

"Yeah, I guess. I don't really wear jewelry."

He laughed and Madison squirmed a little.

"Maddie!" Aimee skipped over toward them. "We have to dance to this song. Hart, get Egg and Drew to come dance."

Pretty soon, Aimee, Fiona, Madison, Hart, Egg, Chet, and Drew were out on the dance floor along with dozens of other Far Hills students. Everyone was twisting and shaking together.

It was one of those songs where everyone is supposed to do the same motions at the same time. During a slower part in the song, everyone sinks down, down, down to the floor and then jumps back up again.

Madison was bouncing in her caftan and waving her arms like before. She lifted the bottom of her dress up a little so she could move her legs more during the song's faster parts. It was hard doing everything at the same time, though. Right next to her, Hart moved up and down to the rhythm the best he could, too.

Madison could not believe that she was dancing right next to Hart Jones.

He was so cute!

After a while, the music slowed down and everyone started to sink toward the floor. Madison followed along, happy for the slowed-down pace. She listened close because she knew that in the next part of the song, everyone was supposed to get back up again.

Madison believed with all her heart that if she

jumped up at the perfect, timed moment, Hart would be impressed.

The music pumped a steady beat. Madison held her breath and then . . .

Jump!

She jumped up so fast—and didn't trip on the hem of her long caftan!

The only problem was that when she jumped, no one else did.

She stood there, upright, staring down at an ocean of costumed faces. Everyone stared back. Hart stared back. Three seconds went by.

It felt like slo-mo eternity.

Waaaaaaaaaaaaaaaaaaah!

Some kid across the room screamed as he leaped into the air on the proper beat. Everyone was knocking around and shaking bodies upright again. Aimee spun in a few twirls.

Madison felt hot all over. She stopped dancing right then and there—and made a beeline for the punch with flies.

Ivy was standing there next to the drink table. "Like your costume, Madison," she said when Madison sped over, breathless.

Madison didn't believe her, of course. "Yeah— you too," Madison said.

"I made my costume, you know," Ivy bragged. "I figured that being a devil was fun, so I sewed this together." She was talking about the teeny skirt wrapped around her waist.

"Mmmm-uh-huh," Madison replied, taking a bite of a potato chip from the bowl next to her. She nibbled on the edge of the chip so it would last longer.

"You guys were all dancing as a group," Ivy said. "How cute."

Madison wanted to say, Didn't see you dancing, but instead she nodded and said, "Mmmm-uh-huh," again.

"This music really stinks, right?" Ivy complained. "Total disaster."

"Aren't you supposed to be a little more positive?" Madison asked. "Seeing as how you're our seventh-grade class president and all?"

Before Ivy could snap back with some clever answer, Aimee rushed up. "Where did you go?" she asked Madison. "I turned around and you vanished."

"I was thirsty. This costume is hot," Madison said.

"Later," Ivy said, snapping her gum. "I'm going to go dance." Ivy walked directly over toward the boys. Madison watched her stand next to Hart. She started talking to him, smiling and flipping her hair, leaning in because the music was loud. Hart didn't seem *that* interested, but Ivy kept pushing herself up against him. She turned around once and caught Madison's eye—and smiled.

Madison never knew a smile could feel like a punch in the gut.

Eventually the music died down a little and a

slower song came on. Madison figured at that point, Hart would stop dancing altogether. Maybe, in the utterly fantastic world of her imagination, Hart would ask *Madison* to dance.

But he didn't do either of those things. He danced with *Ivy*.

Madison's eyes were on them as they rocked back and forth to a pop song that she didn't like one bit.

"Check them out," Chet said, motioning to the dance floor. He was looking for a drink at the table.

Madison just shook her head, not looking. She didn't want to see any more.

"I can't believe they're dancing together," Chet said. "I really didn't know Egg liked my sister."

"Your sister? Wha?" Madison looked up and did a double take.

It wasn't Hart and Ivy Chet was watching. Egg and Fiona were the ones dancing together. Egg even had one of Fiona's leis around his neck. They weren't standing that close, but close enough so they were swaying back and forth to the same rhythm. Close enough to be holding hands, too, but Madison couldn't see if they were doing that.

Madison spun around to see if Hart and Ivy were dancing together. But they had disappeared. There was no wizard hat or her fire-red costume anywhere in the room. Aimee was also missing! Madison felt her pulse race.

"My wife tells me you're a whiz at computers,"

Dr. Wing said, walking right up to Madison. He had removed his wolf-doctor mask to get a drink of fruit punch.

"Oh," Madison said, startled to see him. Aimee was right. He was very cute.

"You help her with the Web site. That's hard work," Dr. Wing said.

"I guess." Madison caught herself staring with nothing to talk to him about. She fished for information. "What kind of doctor are you, Dr. Wing?"

He smiled. "I'm a wolf-doctor, remember?"

Madison chuckled. "No, really. What do you do for a job?"

"I'm serious!" he said. "Well, some people call me a veterinarian."

Madison gasped. Mrs. Wing's husband was a vet? She couldn't believe it. Madison had dozens . . . no, *hundreds* . . . of questions.

"I love animals!" Madison blurted.

"Well, me too." Dr. Wing smiled.

"I mean, I think I would be a good vet someday," Madison explained. "I don't know how you become one, but I love animals more than anything on the planet. Really and truly."

Dr. Wing grinned. He told Madison about an injured bird that had come to his office that morning. Just then, Poison Ivy fluttered by. She and her drones gave Madison a meaner-than-mean look.

"I have to go," Madison said abruptly, shaken by

the look. She wanted to find Fiona and Aimee. "Nice meeting you," Madison added.

Dr. Wing reached out to shake Madison's hand. "Anytime you want to, come around my office. We have a boarding, grooming, and pet adoption shelter attached to our building."

"Far Hills Animal Shelter? You're in charge of that place?" Madison said in disbelief. She knew exactly where he worked. It was where Aimee's family had adopted their basset hound, Blossom.

"Maddie!" Aimee came by again and grabbed Madison's wrist. "Sorry, Dr. Wing, I need her now."

"Aimee, did you know that Dr. Wing is a vet? Isn't that awesome? I just—"

"Come on!" Aimee pulled her over to a row of chairs and sat down.

"Let go of me." Madison rubbed her hand. "You're acting so weird."

"I saw Fiona and Egg dancing together," Aimee said.

"I saw them, too. Where were you, anyway? I was looking for you everywhere."

"Maddie! I was dancing with Egg and Fiona. That's why I'm so weirded out. We were goofing off together and then all of a sudden, Egg grabbed one of the leis off Fiona's neck."

"And . . . ?" Madison probed for more details. Had he held her hand? Grabbed her arm? Touched her head?

"I mean, for Egg to do that is like . . . a major *whoa*."

"It's just a dance, Aim," Madison said. "You said so yourself that a lot can happen here. You said our entire seventh-grade existence could be made by this dance. That's what you said."

"What does that have to do with Fiona and Egg?" Aimee asked.

"Maybe they like each other," Madison replied. She wanted to hear Fiona's side of the story before jumping to any conclusions.

"You're right, I guess," Aimee said, hanging her head. "I know you're right. It's just weird to me. Egg is like another brother, and I can't think of him that way."

"What way?" Madison said.

"Like a boy." Aimee shook her head.

"Everything's getting weird this year," Madison said.

Aimee lifted up her head. "Speak of the devil," she said, laughing, because Ivy really was dressed as a red devil tonight. "It's Miss Weird herself."

Poison Ivy walked right past Aimee and Madison and out the doors toward the bathrooms. Hart was right behind her.

"Hey, Finnster," Hart said.

"Hey, yourself. How—how's the dance going?" Madison asked, stuttering a little. She was so surprised to see him stop.

"Have you been in the scary hallway yet?" he asked them.

"Scary hallway? I went a little while ago," Aimee said. She'd gone in with some of her dance friends when Madison had been talking with Dr. Wing.

"You went, Aim? I haven't gone yet," Madison said. "Is it good?"

"I haven't gone, either! You wanna go with me?" Hart asked. "The line looks pretty short now."

Madison shrugged. "Okay. I guess."

Aimee didn't even suspect anything. She said she'd be fine with Fiona, Egg, Chet, and some other friends.

Madison and Hart went off to get on the line— alone. At least they were alone for five seconds.

That's when the red devil appeared—back from the bathroom already.

"Hey, Hart," Ivy said, talking right to him. "Oh, hello, Madison."

Hart was gearing up for some serious screaming inside the scary hallway. "Chet said overall it's kind of lame," he confessed. "But I say maybe it's fun to go through and try to scare the people who are already in there. Right?"

"We're gonna be scaring people?" Ivy asked.

Madison piped up. "Ivy, he just said that. . . ."

"Um, excuse me. If I needed a dictionary, I'd go to the library, thank you."

Madison bit her lip. "Like you *ever* go to the library," she said under her breath.

Hart turned to both girls and said, "This is so cool."

"I know," Ivy said, sliding up in line right next to him. They weren't holding hands or anything, but they were practically touching.

"Welcome to Scary Hallway!" a voice from behind a rubber mask croaked. Madison could tell it was Mr. Gibbons from the deep voice. "Aha!" he cried. "Look who we have here . . . more unwitting seventh graders to pass through the scary hallway . . . ha, ha, ha, ha!"

"Let's go, the line's moving," Ivy said to the kid who was standing in front of her, even though he was in another grade.

"You okay, Finnster?" Hart leaned back and whispered. "This looks pretty dorky now that we're actually here. I imagined something a lot different."

"I know what you mean," Madison said. She grinned and hoped in some secret way, underneath it all, he was talking about Ivy.

"C'mon!" Ivy said, yanking Hart inside, leaving Madison a step behind.

Madison growled to herself. They were gone. In a Halloween world, Madison was dealt the same thing every year: tricks after tireless tricks.

Chapter 13

"Eeeeeeeeeeeek!" someone screamed in Madison's ear.

She screamed back even louder, almost keeling over in her Aphrodite dress.

Welcome to Scary Hallway.

Maneuvering in her caftan had been tough on the dance floor. It was even more difficult in this space. Plus it was hard to see where she was going. Madison felt so uncomfortable.

Up ahead of her, she heard Hart's whisper.

"You still there, Finnster?" he said.

"Yeah," Madison said. Where else would she be?

To her left, some kid with a rubber ax in his head leaned over and said, "Help me." He had fake blood oozing out of his mouth.

"Gross," Madison mumbled.

Another boy had one of those plastic fake hands that moved. "Here, let me give you a hand," he said, cackling. Madison laughed. The hand was one of the objects she and the other members of the committee had collected for the decorations. He must have lifted it off a table.

"Finnster!" Hart whispered again. "You there?"

"Yes!" she said again, but she really couldn't see anything now.

There were no scary people in her path for a few feet. Now the scary hallway was more like being blindfolded. Curtains folded in around her body as she walked farther along through the maze.

"Hart?" Madison whispered, coming to a sudden stop. She froze. Was someone there? She turned around but didn't see or hear anyone. "Hart?"

"Hart!" Ivy's voice boomed somewhere up ahead. "Don't go. Hold my hand!"

"I want to suck your blooooood!" Some girl with vampire fangs swooped over. She reached out and grabbed Madison's caftan.

"Don't touch me!" Madison screeched, stumbling backward. Now things were getting scarier.

Behind her somewhere, a group of kids started to scream. Not just little *eeeks* however. These were big, fat, *loud* screams—the kind to break an eardrum. They were just goofing around, but it was very annoying.

136

All of a sudden one of the kids inside the hallway was right up at Madison's back. He started to push. Madison was jostled.

"Move," the boy said.

Madison snapped, "I *can't* move."

When she said that, he pushed back a second time, much harder. "I said *move*," he yelled. Everyone was yelling. Madison felt hotter than hot.

She got her balance only to have him shove her a third time. And with that push, Madison went flying for real—dress, crown, scepter, and all.

Flying into Hart, that is. Much to her surprise, she had been jostled right over to the scary hallway exit.

Madison fell through the curtain opening and landed, hard. On top of Hart.

Hart got up first and then reached out to help Madison onto her feet. Taking his hand, Madison stood up, teetering. He had a warm, pink, sweaty hand, but she didn't mind. This was the hand she had hoped and prayed and crossed her fingers that she might hold at the dance.

Of course, the holding only lasted a split second. The moment Madison was back on two feet and Hart shook himself off, the hand was history. And not so long after that, the dance was history, too.

Fiona, Aimee, and Madison logged on to bigfish-bowl.com later that night so they could keep talking about the dance even after it was over. No one wanted the fun to end. They met up in a Friday night, private chat room called LYLAS, which meant "Love Ya Like a Sister."

<MadFinn>: I almost got stuck in
    SCARY hallway
<Wetwinz>: Some kid threw up in
    there I heard
<MadFinn>: No
<Wetwinz>: J/K
<BalletGrl>: So is Tommy getting
    expelled or what?
<MadFinn>: IDGI what's his prob?
    BOYS STINK!!!
<BalletGrl>: What's the deal with u
    and EGG, Fiona?
<Wetwinz>: :-)
<MadFinn>: It's cool if u like him
<BalletGrl>: I guess
<Wetwinz>: Can you believe who won
    the costume awards?
<Wetwinz>: That guy who was an
    eyeball in a tuxedo and got first
    was cool. He's in ninth grade.
<BalletGrl>: I liked the second-
    prize guy who dressed as all the
    characters from Scooby Doo.
<MadFinn>: Third place was funny.
    Bride of Frankenstein was cool.
<Wetwinz>: She was dancing with
    Frankenstein!

\<Wetwinz\>: Did you dance w/n e one
  Maddie
\<BalletGrl\>: No she didn't
\<MadFinn\>: Yes I did sorta
\<Wetwinz\>: WHO
\<MadFinn\>: No one 4get it!
\<Wetwinz\>: WHO????????
\<BalletGrl\>: I'm getting tired.
\<Wetwinz\>: LYLAS
\<MadFinn\>: LYLAS (2)
\<BalletGrl\>: I need a chat room
  dictionary!
\<BalletGrl\>: It's getting late
  almost 1030 whoa
\<Wetwinz\>: I have 2 go 2
\<MadFinn\>: Nooooo! stay
\<BalletGrl\>: Lets hang out
  tomorrow
\<Wetwinz\>: I have soccer
  remember?
\<BalletGrl\>: Oh yah
\<MadFinn\>: OH yah it's the
  CHAMPIONSHIPS!!!
\<Wetwinz\>: Yup I am PSYCHED
\<MadFinn\>: See u tomorrow
\<Wetwinz\>: *poof*
\<BalletGrl\>: Where did she go?
\<MadFinn\>: she logged off, aim.
\<BalletGrl\>: ok C U L8R bye
\<MadFinn\>: WAIT!!
\<BalletGrl\>: what

<MadFinn>: i have to tell you
    something ELSE
<BalletGrl>: what
<MadFinn>: Remember when we were
    @ my dad's & u saw that
    insta-message from someone named
    Bigwheels?
<BalletGrl>: No.
<MadFinn>: Oh.
<BalletGrl>: Huh?
<MadFinn>: well u did see an
    insta-message & the thing is that
    i did know who Bigwheels was.
    She's my keypal.
<BalletGrl>: Kewl
<MadFinn>: wait a minute u don't
    care?
<BalletGrl>: I wanna have online
    friends, too. Maybe I'll meet
    someone else who does ballet. U
    know?
<MadFinn>: u REALLY don't care?
    Really and truly?
<BalletGrl>: truly
<MadFinn>: Aim ur the best!!!
<BalletGrl>: C u at the game!

Madison said good-bye and logged off bigfish-
bowl.com. She was a teeny bit disappointed that
she hadn't won any of the costume prizes from
the dance, but neither had Ivy. That was some

consolation. Besides, what mattered most of all now was that she (1) had spent half the night with her crush (and her heart was happy), (2) spent major time with her BFFs, and (3) *finally* admitted the truth to Aimee about Bigwheels's existence.

Although it was very late after the chat, Madison still didn't feel tired. She stayed online and decided to write Bigwheels an e-mail.

She owed her one. So much had happened.

```
From: MadFinn
To: Bigwheels
Subject: Dances and Other News
Date: Fri 27 Oct 1:36 PM
Long time, no write.

Just got back fm. my school dance &
I am blissed out.

I danced w/him. Yes, THE him I have
been talking about since school
started. He came dressed as a
wizard. I had on this dumb costume.
I went as a goddess.

Anyway, how r u? How r ur parents
doing these days? I think about
you whenever I see my mom & dad
together. This is because my
parents (u know this) are divorced.
I think about your family.
```

How was your school dance? Write
back real soon.

XOXOXO Yours till the pumpkin pies,

MadFinn

P.S. Did you ever enter that
contest on bigfishbowl? I think
they will be sending winners
soon. I ended up liking my
story. Did you ever write that
poem?

After Madison sent the e-mail to her online
friend, she finally changed into pajamas. After
crawling out of Aphrodite's caftan, Madison combed
the curls out of her hair, too. They were tangled
where Mom had spritzed too much hair spray. She
washed the blush off her face.

But she still wasn't so sleepy. Madison turned the
computer back on.

 Scary

This past week in English, Mr. Gibbons
wrote on the board: Don't be afraid to
scare yourself. Half the class was like,
"WHAT??!"

He does that a lot, writes things we may
not understand. Asks us to talk. So it got
me thinking about a list of the things that

scare me. I thought of 8 so far.

What am I afraid of?

1. The dark
2. Failing
3. Being left out
4. Ghosts like Mrs. Martin
5. Really big zits
6. Dancing badly
7. Kissing a boy
8. Horror movies

Rude Awakening: Sometimes you have to dance the fright away! Amazingly, I tried dancing tonight. And even though my dress was too long, it worked. I felt less self-conscious and way less scared.

Am I gonna be scared of seventh grade forever???

I'M AFRAID NOT!

Ha ha ha.

Chapter 14

Saturday morning Madison woke up extra early so she could write in her files and clean up her room for real. She'd fake-cleaned it for Mom's benefit, but now the mess was beginning to grow and multiply once again.

Sweatpants and a training bra trailed out of the hamper.

Papers, files, and notebooks poked out from under the bed.

Even Madison's desk overflowed with magazines, schoolbooks, and two half-empty glasses of apple juice she forgot to bring back to the kitchen.

Madison checked her e-mailbox to see if she'd received any messages from bigfishbowl.com since last night. She was addicted to checking e-mails, especially when she was secretly hoping for a message back from Bigwheels *and* an update on the Caught in the Web contest. The results were supposed to have come in by now.

Her mailbox was flashing!

Madison grabbed at the edges of her desk and clicked the buttons to open her e-mailbox. Just as she'd hoped, there was a brand-new message from Bigwheels waiting there with a poem attachment.

```
From: Bigwheels
To: MadFinn
Subject: Re: Dances and Other News
Date: Sat 28 Oct 8:36 AM
I didn't make it to my school's
Halloween dance, but it sounds like
u had a great time. Congrats.
I am sitting here after school and
my mom just made me the yummiest
pumpkin cake. I am so happy cuz it
is my absolute favorite. Did you
decide to go trick-or-treating or
no? I think you said no but I can't
remember.

I wrote a poem BTW. Here you go
even if it is kinda silly. It was
for my class and I thought it might
make u laugh.

    Happy Halloween
    There once was a pumpkin on a farm
```

Who didn't like the other gourds.
The pumpkin reached one vine out
   like an arm
And spoke a few funny words.
"Halloween isn't fun without
   friends,"
the pumpkin said from his stem.
"My friends are all cut off down
   to the ends,"
And sure enough someone had
   picked them.
When you spend Halloween carving
   one
Remember what some pumpkins say,
Be with your friends and have fun
On a special Halloween day!!!

They haven't posted the winners yet
4 that contest. How did you do? I
bet you won it. FC!!! (That's
fingers crossed). I have this
feeling. N e way, write back soon.

Yours till the wind blows,

Bigwheels

**Madison was becoming more and more con-
vinced that Bigwheels was *her* twin—not like Fiona
and Chet—but close.**

As she shut down the Bigwheels message,

Madison noticed her mailbox indicator flashing again. There was another message—and this one was from the bigfishbowl.com Web site! Madison held her breath and opened the document.

She read it aloud slowly to Phinnie, even though he wasn't paying much attention. He'd recurled up into a furry ball at her feet.

From: webmaster@bigfishbowl.com
To: Members Only
Subject: Caught in the Web Contest
Winners
Date: Sat 28 Oct 8:34 AM
Happy Halloween!

The big fins at bigfishbowl.com
asked YOU to write us a mystery
for Halloween. Your stories were
FRIGHTFULLY good. We received
over three hundred entries.
Thanks to everyone who wrote
stories!

The stories below will be posted
in their entirety starting on
HALLOWEEN.

Thanks for entering! And
congratulations to the winners.

And here's the top winners' list:

GRAND PRIZE: Blood and More, by QuakeKing21
RUNNERS-UP: Bat Breath, by PcenloveXO
Revenge of the Slugs, by LoriGirl
The Slayer, by Mariohottie
The Secret of the Old Trunk, by MadFinn

"I can't believe it!" Madison shouted when she saw her name on the screen. "Mom! Mom! I won! Come here!"

"Rowrooooo!" Phin awoke with a howl. *"Rowrooooo!"*

Madison had been selected as a runner-up. Phinnie barked his approval and jumped up for scritches on his back. Mom, hearing the racket, came into the bedroom to see what all the fuss was about.

"You won?" she cried.

"Well, I got a runner-up prize," Madison said, pulling Phinnie into her lap.

"Honey bear, that's fantastic!" Mom said sweetly, and patted Madison on the head. "We have to celebrate! Right now. Oh, I'm so proud of you, Maddie."

Madison felt all tingly inside. She was proud of herself, too. Although the Ivy drama had momentarily threatened to ruin seventh grade and the school dance for her, Madison was finding out that she could still have a very happy Halloween. Madison and Phinnie followed Mom into the kitchen, where she warmed up a special loaf of the pumpkin bread Madison loved.

"This is just turning into the best Halloween ever," Madison said, pouring herself a bowl of Lightly Honeyed Oaty-Os, too. Phin curled up by the dishwasher.

"Why is that, Maddie?" Mom buttered the slices of pumpkin bread.

"It just is." Madison took one bite and smiled.

Madison leaned over to feed Phin a corner of the pumpkin bread. He licked his chops for more.

"You know, I never won anything before, Mom," she said. "And I feel so happy right now. I really can't explain what I'm feeling."

Mom smiled. "It won't be the last time you win something, I promise you that."

Madison thanked Mom and went back upstairs to get dressed. She tried calling Aimee to tell her about the contest, but the Gillespie phone lines were busy. One of Aimee's brothers was always hogging the phone. She'd tell Aimee and everyone else about it later when they met up at the school soccer game.

Today was the *big* game everyone had been waiting for. The Rangers were up against the other most winning team in the district, the Cobras. The game was being hosted at Far Hills Junior High.

Aimee was going to the game straight from a private ballet lesson in the morning, so Madison walked to school by herself. As she crossed the parking lot and headed around back to the field,

Madison glanced at purple-and-orange posters taped to the doors of the school building.

SOMETHING TO SCREAM ABOUT!

She laughed. The whole week had been a scream. A little piece of her wished she could be back at the dance again.

"Maddie!" Drew was running to the soccer field, too.

"Hey!" Madison said. "I just found out I won a writing Web contest. Well, I got runner-up."

"Congratulations," Drew said.

They walked over to the bleachers. Egg was sitting there, goofing around with Chet and another friend, Dan. Egg's sister, Mariah, was sitting there, too, with some of her older friends in black, the same ones Madison had seen at the mall food court the weekend before.

The stands were filling quickly with seventh, eighth, and ninth graders. Parents held up painted signs that read GO RANGERS! Everyone had on jackets and scarves to keep the wind away. The air was crisp, and smelled like leaves.

One side of the bleachers seemed to hold mostly Cobra fans, but no one was arguing or anything about which team was better—*yet*. Madison felt overwhelmed by the color, noise, and feelings in the pit of her stomach.

She really belonged. This was her school.

Mr. and Mrs. Waters were sitting down in front, sipping cups of coffee. Fiona, tying her laces, had her knee up on the bottom step of the bleachers. When she turned and saw Madison come across the field, she broke into a giant grin. "Maddie! You're here! That is so great!"

Fiona threw her arms around her friend. Madison hugged right back.

"Where's Aimee?" Fiona asked. Then she remembered about the ballet lesson. Aimee would be coming later, close to the first whistle.

"So I gotta go," Fiona blurted. "Thanks for coming! See you after the game!" She hugged Madison one last time and then ran over to her team's huddle for warm-ups and pep talks.

"Hey, Maddie," Mariah said, waving. She turned to the guy on her left and said, "This is Karl." Karl nodded in Madison's direction.

"Hey, howyadoing?" he said. She smiled and wondered if maybe he was cuter than she and Aimee and Fiona first thought at the mall.

"So how was the Halloween dance?" Mariah asked Madison discreetly.

"Fine. I went as Aphrodite," Madison whispered back.

"Ooooh," Mariah teased. "Goddess of love!" Luckily no one but Karl heard her say that. He didn't seem to care about anything they said.

"I didn't see you there," Madison said.

Mariah shrugged. "Nah, I blew it off. Karl and I went to the movies. But I'm glad you had a nice time. I bet you looked good."

Madison lowered her head, a little embarrassed. She turned to watch Fiona take practice kicks out on the field.

"Where's Hart?" Chet asked Egg. Madison turned to hear the answer.

"He is way sick," Drew replied. Since he and Hart were cousins, their mothers had spoken that morning.

"Sick?" Madison said.

"*Way* sick. Like throwing up."

"Ewwww, gross me," Egg said. "Maybe he ate the flies in that punch last night."

Drew and Chet both snorted.

"So I guess he's not coming to the game, then?" Madison asked.

"There's Aimee!" Chet cried. "She looks like Barney!"

Aimee was running up the side of the field with a purple duffel bag. She had on a purple sweatshirt and leggings, too.

Madison stood up so Aimee would see where they were sitting.

"Hiya, everyone!" Aimee said, sitting down on the edge of the bleachers. "I am so wiped out. We had a guest at our ballet lesson this morning. We had to do these exercises over and over—"

"Yeah, Aimee, like we care about your ballet lesson," Egg cracked.

"Egg!" Madison cracked back. "And like we care about anything you have to say, either."

"Thanks, Maddie." Aimee smiled.

"That's cool that you take private lessons," Chet said. Drew agreed.

Aimee smiled back at them. She sneered at Egg.

"May I have your attention, please!" someone yelled from the soccer field. It was one of the referees speaking into a portable loudspeaker system. *"Your attention, please!"*

"Go, Cobras!" someone on the other side of the bleachers screeched.

"Welcome to the Far Hills district championship."

Madison scanned the playing field for Fiona. She was jogging in place, chatting with teammates, eating an orange. She was getting set to win. Madison knew that this would be a special day in the history of the seventh grade.

"Say cheese!" Mrs. Waters said, pointing a camera up toward the bleachers. She snapped a photo of Egg, Chet, Drew, Dan, Madison, Aimee, Mariah, Karl, and whoever else could squeeze into the photo.

"Now, let us introduce our teams!"

"Rangers *rule!*" a group of girls yelled out a few rows behind Madison and her friends. Everyone cheered.

When Fiona came out onto the field, the

applause soared. Madison clapped as hard as she possibly could. Aimee was screaming at the top of her lungs. Chet, Drew, and Egg were yelling, "Woo woo," like dogs.

"Rangers rock! Rangers shake! Go, Fiona! No more snake!" Madison and Aimee had planned a special cheer in Fiona's honor.

"That's pretty good, Maddie," Egg said.

Madison grinned.

"And don't forget we want everyone to play fair!" the loudspeaker voice boomed. A coach recited rules from the junior high school soccer bible. Strict rules about sportsmanship needed to be followed down on the field. While the rules were being read, Fiona stuck her arm up and waved to everyone in the stands. Mrs. Waters snapped more pictures.

"Go, Fiona!" Aimee and Madison yelled at the same time. They cheered so much throughout the game. They were hoarse at the end.

With two minutes left in the game, the score was tied 3–3. A halfback kicked the ball over to Fiona at the right wing position. She took off down the field.

"Go! Go! Go!"

It sounded like everyone in the stands was cheering at the same time, even Karl.

No one was following her down the field. The goalie appeared panicked, jumping from foot to foot, side to side.

"She's gonna make a goal, I know it!" Aimee screeched.

"Go, Fiona!" Chet called out.

Fiona got within yards of the goal, and it looked like she was going to make a kick in, when all of a sudden she surprised everyone.

She kicked the ball to the side. She passed it to one of her teammates, Daisy Espinoza

And Daisy kicked it right in.

"*Score!*"

The Cobra goalie didn't know what happened until it was too !ate.

"We won!" Aimee yelled right in Madison's ear. They were jumping up and down and the bleachers were shaking. Aimee threw her arms around Madison.

Down on the field, Fiona and Daisy ran over to each other, arms in the air. They embraced. Madison felt a surge of excitement. The rest of the team ran up, too, and slapped Fiona on the back.

"My sister rocks!" Chet said. He dropped his cool exterior for two seconds to bask in Fiona's soccer skills. The fact that Fiona was a star on the team only made everything else that much sweeter for Madison and her friends.

Madison smiled to herself. The only ghosts in Far Hills now were fading memories of elementary school.

Seventh grade had many more treats in store. Madison could feel it in her Halloween bones.

Mad Chat Words:

9	Yummy
<:-	Stupid question
;-]	Smirking
EMSG	E-mail message
F2F	Face-to-face
BF	Best friend or Boyfriend
FC	Fingers crossed
<ggg>	Grin
LYLAS	Love ya like a sister
LYLAS (2)	Love ya like a sister x 2/twice
4get it	Forget it
Cuz	Because
N e way	Anyway

Madison's Computer Tip:

I've been getting weird e-mails from people I don't know. Egg and Drew told me that sometimes strangers send viruses and gross stuff over the Internet. You could download something bad onto your computer and not even realize it. **Never download files from unknown senders.** Even if I'm really, really curious, I always ask my parents first or I just delete it.

Visit Madison at www.madisonfinn.com

Book #4: *Caught in the Web*

Super Quiz

Now that you've read the story . . . how much do you *really* know about Madison and her friends?

1. Which author is Madison's English class reading at the start of the story?
   a. William Shakespeare
   b. Edgar Allan Poe
   c. J. K. Rowling

2. What does the winner of the bigfishbowl.com mystery-writing contest win?
   a. A trip to an amusement park
   b. A fish tank
   c. The posting of her story on the Web site and a mystery game

3. What's the punch line of Madison's dad's joke that goes: What do you put on a Halloween sundae?
   a. Whipped scream
   b. Ghost toast
   c. Scary sauce

4. What does Egg's mother, Señora Diaz, do for a living?
   a. She teaches Spanish at another school.
   b. She teaches Spanish at Far Hills Junior High.
   c. She is a dance instructor.

5. What is the name of the family that used to live in Fiona Waters's house?
   a. The Mellons
   b. The Martins
   c. The Miltons

6. What special equipment does Drew's family have at their home?
   a. A tractor
   b. A toy oven
   c. A recording studio

7. What color is Ivy's cell phone?
   a. Pink
   b. Purple
   c. Frosted white

8. Where do Madison and her dad go to get pumpkins?
   a. Far Hills Farm
   b. Funny Farm
   c. Peterson's Farm

9. What is mega squash?
   a. The super zucchini Madison sees at a farm
   b. The name of a character on Madison's favorite TV show
   c. A wrestling move that Egg teaches Madison

10. Which city does Madison's dad visit for business?
    a. Atlanta
    b. Boston
    c. Charleston

11. When the girls go shopping at the mall, Madison tries on a T-shirt. What does it say?
    a. HOT STUFF
    b. YOU GO, GIRL
    c. FOXY

12. How did Egg get his nickname?
    a. He ate a lot of scrambled eggs and threw up.
    b. Someone threw an egg at him on Halloween.
    c. He has a birthmark on his arm shaped like a fried egg.

13. Which female sports star is Fiona's idol?
    a. Mia Hamm
    b. Lisa Leslie
    c. Anna Kournikova

14. Where is the skeleton in Fiona's attic supposed to be?
    a. Behind a large wooden door
    b. Inside a closet
    c. Inside an old trunk

15. What happens when the lights go out in Fiona's kitchen?
    a. Madison trips over a chair.
    b. Madison gets an idea for her story.
    c. Madison scares Aimee with a loud "Boo!"

16. Who is the dance-task-team leader for the Halloween school dance?
    a. Ivy Daly
    b. Madison Finn
    c. Aimee Gillespie

17. What game do the girls play at the sleep-over—that scares them *a lot*?
    a. Ouija board
    b. I Never
    c. Lights Out

18. What is the title of Madison's Halloween story?
    a. "The Secret Haunted House"
    b. "The Secret of the Old Trunk"
    c. "The Secret of the Skeleton"

19. What is Chet's Halloween costume for the dance?
    a. A spotted dog
    b. A ballplayer for the New York Mets
    c. A Martian

20. What is Fiona's Halloween costume for the dance?
    a. A hula girl
    b. A dancing girl
    c. A soccer player

21. What is Hart's Halloween costume for the dance?
    a. A ghost
    b. A wizard
    c. A ballplayer for the New York Mets

22. What is Egg's Halloween costume for the dance?
    a. A ballplayer for the New York Mets
    b. A ballerina
    c. A ninja

23. What is Poison Ivy's Halloween costume for the dance?
    a. Aphrodite, the Greek goddess of love
    b. A red devil
    c. A princess

24. What is Madison's Halloween costume for the dance?
    a. Aphrodite
    b. A hula girl
    c. A princess

25. What do the purple posters outside the school say?
    a. Something to Scream About!
    b. No Shirt, No Shoes, No Service
    c. Keep Out, Students!

26. While setting the auditorium up for the dance, what happens to Madison?
    a. She falls into a bucket of apples.
    b. She falls into the fake cobwebs.
    c. She falls on Ivy and ruins Ivy's dress.

27. Which of these things *does not* scare Madison?
    a. Being left out
    b. Horror movies
    c. Tuna salad

28. What does Bigwheels write about in her Halloween poem to Madison?
    a. Pumpkins
    b. Ghouls
    c. Spiders

29. When Aimee shows up for the soccer game, what color is she wearing?
    a. Bright pink (like a flower)
    b. Purple (like Barney)
    c. Yellow (like the sun)

30. What story wins the Halloween writing contest?
    a. "Blood and More" by QuakeKing21
    b. "Revenge of the Slugs" by LoriGirl
    c. "Bat Breath" by PcenloveXO

31. What new gadget does Madison's dad get in this book?
    a. A digital camera
    b. A new iPod
    c. A waterproof wristwatch

32. What does Stephanie do for a living?
    a. Computer sales
    b. Automobile repair
    c. Interior decorating

33. Where did Madison's dad first meet Stephanie?
    a. At the beach
    b. At an amusement park
    c. At a technology conference

34. What good news does Bigwheels get in this book?
    a. Her parents are getting back together.
    b. Her favorite singer is coming to town.
    c. Her pet terrier is having puppies.

35. What color does Mariah Diaz dye her hair in this book?
    a. Purple
    b. Light brown
    c. Black

36. What type of makeup does Aimee start to wear in this book?
    a. Green eye shadow
    b. Fingernail polish
    c. All-natural lip gloss

37. What was the last time the Far Hills girls' soccer team won the district championship?
    a. Twenty years ago
    b. Twelve years ago
    c. Fifty years ago

38. What is the name of the substitute teacher for Mr. Danehy's science class?
    a. Mr. Burnes
    b. Mr. Stein
    c. Mrs. King

39. What phrase does Mr. Gibbons write on the blackboard?
   a. "Go for the gold."
   b. "It is what it is."
   c. "Don't be afraid to scare yourself."

40. Which of the following people has an eyebrow ring?
   a. Mariah Diaz
   b. Lindsay Frost
   c. Madison Finn

Answers:
1b, 2c, 3a, 4b, 5b, 6c, 7a, 8c, 9a, 10b, 11c, 12b, 13a,
14c, 15b, 16c, 17a, 18b, 19c, 20a, 21b, 22c, 23b, 24a,
25a, 26b, 27c, 28a, 29b, 30a, 31a, 32a, 33c, 34a, 35c,
36c, 37b, 38b, 39c, 40a

How well do you know Maddie?

36–40 correct: You might as well pack your bags and move to Far Hills, because you are a *Madison Finn* fanatic!

30–35 correct: You could totally be Madison's BFF, because you know her inside out!

26–29 correct: You think Maddie's pretty cool, and you'd have fun hanging out with her.

20–25 correct: You know a few things about Madison, and you're interested in finding out more about her.

19 or fewer correct: You didn't quite catch all those details about Maddie, but don't worry—there's still lots of time to learn.

Mad Chat Match

Match the following Mad Chat words with their correct meanings.

9	Love ya like a sister x 2/twice
<:-	Yummy
;-]	Fingers crossed
EMSG	Because
F2F	Stupid question
BF	Forget it
FC	Love ya like a sister
<ggg>	Best friend or boyfriend
LYLAS	Smirking
LYLAS(2)	Face to face
4get it	Grin
Cuz	Anyway
N e way	E-mail message

See page 170 for answers.

Pop Quiz!

What is Madison's astrological sign? Fill in the blanks below and arrange the circled letters at the bottom to find the answer.

Ⓞ _ _ _ is Maddie's pet pug.

Madison used to be friends with Ⓞ _ _ .

Fiona's last name is _ _ _ _ _ Ⓞ .

Ⓞ _ _ _ is Fiona's twin brother.

Walter Diaz is better known as Ⓞ _ _ .

Hart's last name is _ _ _ _ Ⓞ .

Answer:

Ⓞ Ⓞ Ⓞ Ⓞ Ⓞ Ⓞ
_ _ _ _ _ _

See next page for answers.

Mad Chat Match Answers

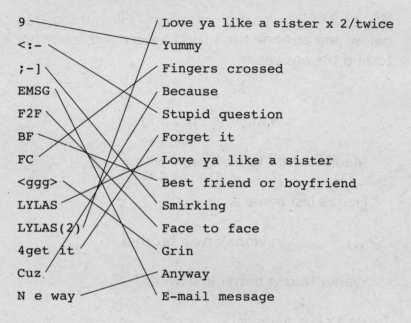

9	Love ya like a sister x 2/twice
<:-	Yummy
;-]	Fingers crossed
EMSG	Because
F2F	Stupid question
BF	Forget it
FC	Love ya like a sister
<ggg>	Best friend or boyfriend
LYLAS	Smirking
LYLAS(2)	Face to face
4get it	Grin
Cuz	Anyway
N e way	E-mail message

Pop Quiz Answers
What is Madison's astrological sign?

ⓅH I N is Maddie's pet pug.
Madison used to be friends withⒾV Y.
Fiona's last name is W A T E RⓈ.
ⒸH E T is Fiona's twin brother.
Walter Diaz is better known asⒺG G.
Hart's last name is J O N EⓈ.

Answer: Madison's astrological sign is PISCES.

Thanks for Nothing

For Crawford with thanks for *everything*

In memory of CB and Bogie

"Nooooooo!" Madison covered her face with her hands and peeked through her fingers.

This e-mail was bad news.

```
From: GoGramma
To: MadFinn
Subject: Thanksgiving
Date: Sat 11 Nov 7:56 AM
```
I am so very sorry, Maddie, but
I won't be coming to your house
for Thanksgiving. My hip problem
is back, and I'm not traveling
anywhere. Your aunt Angie is
spending the holiday with your uncle
Bob's family, so our traditional

visit is on hold until next year.
Don't be sad. I will miss you and
Phin very much. At least we can
talk online now. I finally have the
hang of this e-mail.

How did your report card go? How is
your friend Aimee? Write me another
letter.

Love, Gramma

Madison groaned as she reread the message for the third time. When Gramma Helen didn't like something, she would say, "Maddie, that is for the birds." That was exactly how Madison felt right now. Only this Thanksgiving was going to be "for the turkeys."

How could Gramma not come to Far Hills? Madison deleted the yucky message.

For the past twelve years, Madison's parents had hosted a major feast every Thanksgiving. Mom's mom, Gramma Helen, and Mom's sister, Aunt Angie, and her husband, Uncle Bob, would travel on the plane from Chicago to New York. Dad's brother, Uncle Rick, would even come from Canada with his wife, Violet, even though Canadians celebrate their Thanksgiving in October.

The Finn house had been the epicenter of everyone's Thanksgiving universe for as long as Madison could remember.

Mom always decorated the house with paper turkeys and gourds and pumpkins and spice candles. All of the town guests slept on sleeper sofas around the house—except for Gramma. Madison gave up her bedroom for Gramma. But she didn't mind. Madison loved having the house full of people . . . and so did Phin, Madison's pug. He loved all the extra attention.

Thanksgiving morning meant sleeping in, watching the Macy's parade on TV, and eating way too much good food. Dad wore an extra-large poofy white hat and called himself the house superchef. Madison was his unofficial chef-ette. She got up at five in the morning to help him make the best corn-bread stuffing on the planet.

But not this year.

This year Dad wouldn't be in the Finn kitchen, thanks to the big D—D for divorce. And thanks to Gramma's bad hip and Aunt Angie and Uncle Bob's changed plans, there would be no out-of-town visitors. There wouldn't even be turkey on Madison's dinner table. Unfortunately, Mom was a vegetarian who wanted to save the turkeys, not baste them.

Madison had visions of eating a Thanksgiving bean burrito and tofu stuffing with cranberry sauce this year.

Phin was curled up in a ball on the floor, snoring, oblivious to the change in holiday plans. Would he miss the Thanksgiving attention even more than

Madison would? He'd surely miss turkey scraps tossed under the table.

"Maddie, did you call me? Do you need something?" Mom rushed upstairs and found Madison curled up on her plastic purple chair in the center of her room. "I heard you scream and . . . hey! What's that look on your face?"

Madison pouted. "Gramma can't come to Thanksgiving." She leaned over to pet Phin's ears. He made a snuffling noise.

"She e-mailed you, huh?" Mom frowned. "She said she would."

Madison could tell from Mom's tone of voice that she knew about the change in plans already.

"I'm sorry, honey bear," Mom added. "Gramma wanted to tell you herself. I know how disappointed you must—"

"Thanksgiving STINKS." Madison crossed her arms. "Can't we go to Chicago to see everyone?"

"I told you I have work commitments that week. I'm so sorry, Maddie. Really I am. Next year we can—"

"Next year?" Madison said. "What about this year?"

"This year will be just the two of us. Is that so bad?" Mom chuckled, trying to make light of the situation. But Madison wasn't laughing back.

"I knew everything would be ruined when I saw a black cat yesterday," Madison moaned. She believed that it was terrible luck for a person to walk under ladders or cross a black cat's path. Bad Thanksgiving luck had definitely found her.

"But we'll have fun together!" Mom said with a big smile. "Won't we?"

"I guess." Madison shrugged.

Mom took a deep breath.

"What's Aimee doing for Thanksgiving?"

"Having a normal day. Her family isn't divorced," Madison snapped.

The moment she'd said the words, Madison knew how hurtful they sounded. She reached for Mom's arm.

"I didn't mean that." Madison gulped. "I am so sorry, Mom."

Mom threw her arms around Madison's shoulders and squeezed. "I'm sorry, too. I know our new arrangements take some getting used to. But Angie and Bob will come next year. So will Gramma."

As Mom hugged, Madison felt all her feelings swell up inside like she would burst. But she held back from crying.

"Let's just make the best of it, okay, Maddie?" Mom said, gently smoothing the top of Madison's head.

Madison nodded. She didn't really have a choice. Whether she liked it or not, certain rules about holidays had been set up in the Finns' divorce arrangements. The judge had ruled that Mom and Dad swap Madison from holiday to holiday. This year, Mom got

Thanksgiving. Next year, Dad would.

The back-and-forth between Mom and Dad made Madison dizzier than dizzy on a regular basis. Holidays, however, were proving to be the worst. In this family tug-of-war, Madison Finn was *definitely* all pulled out.

The doorbell zinged. Madison leaped up and dashed downstairs to get the door.

Aimee was standing on the back porch, arms waving in the air, her dog Blossom's tail thwacking against the sliding doors. From inside, Phin started panting, he was so happy to see his doggy girlfriend through the glass.

"What are you doing here, Aim? I was just gonna call you!" Madison said as she opened the doors. Blossom dashed inside and ran off with Phin.

Aimee struck a pose with her hands up in the air. She was wearing a brand-new yellow winter parka.

"Whaddya think?" she asked. "I ordered it online from Boop-Dee-Doop. Well, my mother did. We ordered it on her credit card. My first Internet purchase ever."

Madison shook her head. "Cool color."

"It's called Lemon Drop," Aimee said.

"It's nice. But in case you hadn't noticed, Aimee, it's like fifty degrees outside."

Aimee pulled the jacket off. "I know. I know. But I just couldn't wait to show you. That's why I came over."

Madison decided to make it a special occasion. She took out the blender to make yellow fruit smoothies in honor of the jacket. Making smoothies was one of Madison's favorite things to do.

"Put extra banana in mine," Aimee requested.

They watched the blender go.

"I just found out my gramma isn't coming for Thanksgiving," Madison said, adding ice into the machine.

"Bummer." Aimee sighed.

"Yeah." Madison sighed back. She poured the smoothie into a glass. "So what's happening at your house for the holiday?"

Aimee shrugged and took a big slurp. "Mom is making some kind of health food dinner, as usual. My brothers begged for turkey, so we're having one of those, too. You know the drill."

"Uh-huh. The drill."

Aimee looked at Madison sideways. "Is something wrong, Maddie?"

"I wish that I had the usual drill for Thanksgiving."

"Yeah, you have to spend Thanksgiving without your dad," Aimee said. "That's stinky."

"Without my dad. Without my gramma," Madison said. "Without *everyone*. It's just gonna be Mom and me. And two people can't have a real Thanksgiving alone together."

"Why don't you guys go to Chicago?" Aimee asked.

"Mom's work." Madison sighed again. "Some project she has to do. I wish I were you or Fiona. She gets to go all the way to California for Thanksgiving."

Fiona Waters was Madison and Aimee's brand-new seventh-grade best friend. She'd moved to Far Hills from California over the summer with her twin brother, Chet.

"Fiona said her gramps has a great big swimming pool out there." Aimee giggled. "They'll be swimming on Thanksgiving! Now *that's* weird."

Aimee twirled around. She danced when she wanted to cheer her friends up, and Madison looked like she could use some cheering.

Madison cracked a smile.

"So are you gonna do that extra-credit project in social studies?" Aimee asked, waving her arms in a circle over her head.

Social studies was the one class Madison, Aimee, and Fiona had together. Their teacher, Mrs. Belden, had a reputation for being one of the toughest teachers in junior high—but she always gave kids a chance to do extra-credit projects. She said hard work was good, but it was just as important to have fun.

"I don't get why she calls it extra credit when *everyone* has to do it," Madison moaned. "And why do we all have to pair up?"

"I don't know. But we could do our project together. We can make a turkey or something."

"A turkey?" Madison exclaimed. "Like what? A turkey sandwich?"

Aimee laughed. "Sure. Let's make a mini-replica of the first Thanksgiving dinner with little drumsticks and corn on the cobs. . . ."

"Hey, what time is it?" Madison asked all of a sudden.

Outside, the sun was dipping down in the sky. It cast the entire room in an orange glow.

Aimee looked at her yellow wristwatch. She had watchbands to color-coordinate with each outfit, including her new parka. "Wow, it's almost five o'clock. Already four-thirty."

"It's getting late. Let's take the dogs out," Madison squealed. "Blossom! Phin!"

Blossom came running with Phin. They were panting like crazy.

"Wanna go OUT?" Madison said. Aimee laughed and grabbed the leashes.

It was fun to walk the dogs together. Madison and Aimee liked to think that their dogs were best friends, just like them.

When Madison returned home, Mom was perched on the sofa, watching edited reels from one of her documentary films.

"I'm going up to my room," Madison announced.

Mom didn't flinch.

"I'm going up to my room," Madison announced again, louder this time.

"Okay. Dinner's in an hour," Mom said, waving her off. "And clean that mess. And finish your homework."

Madison made a face, only Mom didn't see it. Mom sounded like a recorded message: do this, clean that.

Once upstairs, Madison consciously decided not to pick *anything* up. She crawled over her enormous pile of clothes and pile of files and collapsed into her purple chair. There were much better things to do than clean her room! She powered up her laptop.

Madison had only intended to log on, send an e-mail back to Gramma, and log off. But once online, she got *way* distracted from those tasks. She surfed around and went to the home page for bigfishbowl.com. There was a new feature advertised on a flashing yellow banner across the top.

Just Fishing Around! The Ultimate Search Engine!

Madison typed in the word *dog* for fun, just to see what a search on her favorite subject might turn up. Madison was pleasantly surprised to see 3,412 possible matches and started reading. Links were underlined.

<u>**Dog** Owner's Guide: Welcome to **Dog**</u>
Owner's Guide
If you have a **dog**, want a **dog**, or
love **dog**s, you've come to the right
place for all kinds of information

about living with and loving **dog**s.
Includes **Dog** Screen Saver, more.

Dog Emporium Online
Flea collars, heartworm pills, soft
beds, chew toys, rawhide . . .
everything discounted for your
family **dog**.

Dog of the Day—Sign Yours Up Now
Tell us about your special **dog**. Is
your bichon frise funny? Does your
weimaraner whine? Winners daily!

Madison added a few more words to the search
to find dog links closer to home. She typed in DOG,
FAR HILLS, NEW YORK—separated by the required
commas. A familiar name popped up.
Madison knew this vet!

Far Hills Animal Shelter, Clinic,
Dog Boarding
Welcome from Bryan Wing, DVM, and
staff. Full service, referrals, **dog**
boarding, Tales of Homeless Pets,
Breed Tips, **dog** grooming care.
Volunteers needed!

Dr. Wing was married to Madison's computer
teacher, Mrs. Wing. This was the direct link for Dr.
Wing's Web site.
On the site's home page there was a photograph

of a basset hound that looked just like Aimee's dog, Blossom. That dissolved slowly into a photo of a yellow Labrador retriever (who was really more cream colored than yellow) and a teeny dachshund named Rosebud. More flashing type at the bottom of the screen read: *Come and visit our offices!* There was a teeny photograph of Dr. Wing and a short letter underneath that.

Welcome to Far Hills Animal Shelter and Clinic! We're glad you've stopped into the section of our "virtual" animal shelter. For ten years, my team has been dedicated to pet rescue and care in Far Hills. Working with shelters, veterinarians, and other concerned businesses, we hope to eliminate our homeless pet problem and care for sick and abandoned animals in our area. Won't you please become a volunteer and help out?

"Rooooowowf!" Phin barked. He was curled up into a ball by the base of Madison's purple chair. Madison scratched Phin's head.

The idea of helping out at the animal shelter seemed so exciting. Maybe this year's Thanksgiving didn't have to be for the turkeys after all? Maybe this Thanksgiving could be for the *dogs* instead?

Phin would *definitely* love that.

Chapter 2

 Animals

Mom thinks I should still be taking flute lessons, but I am soooo over the musical instrument thing. I am going to be an animal volunteer. That makes more sense, since I have loved animals my entire life.

Here is a list of all the pets that I have had:

1. Sea monkeys in a plastic jar.
2. Goldfish named Peanut Butter and Jelly because one was yellow and the other was sort of purple.
3. Ick, my cat. I named him that because he threw up fur balls a lot.
4. Phinnie, the best dog ever. I love my pug better than any pet!

My biggest wish in life would be to live
on a farm or near a zoo or in the apartment
over Wink's pet shop in Far Hills so I
could see more animals all the time and
Phin would have more animals to play with.
I wonder what the shelter will be like? Dr.
Wing's Web site says they take care of sick
animals and do "animal rescue." I wonder if
that's some kind of animal SWAT team?

Rude Awakening: It's a dog-meet-dog
world and I want to be part of it RIGHT
NOW.

"What a wonderful idea, Maddie," Mom said
when Madison told her about the Far Hills Animal
Shelter. "I'm happy that you want to volunteer—
especially at Thanksgiving time. And it's only a short
ride over there. We can drive over today to check it
out."

As Mom drove them to the clinic downtown,
Madison could feel her entire body humming.
*Would the animals at the clinic like her? Would she
like the animals? What would Dr. Wing say when he
saw her?*

Madison fussed and twisted in the car's front
seat. The belt felt so snug. She couldn't stay still. This
ride was taking forever!

"Well, there's the clinic," Mom announced. "At
last!"

She pointed to a squat-looking, pink cement

building with an iron gate and planters filled with mums out front. A teeny neon sign blinked HOSPITAL under a bigger, painted, wood sign that bore the clinic's name: FAR HILLS ANIMAL SHELTER.

"Maddie, are you going to just sit there or are we going inside?" Mom teased. Madison led the way as they got out of the car.

"It looks nice from the outside, right, Mom?" Madison said as she approached the clinic slowly. Each stepping-stone was shaped like a dog bone.

"Doggies everywhere," Mom said, pointing out photos of different dog breeds on a poster in the clinic window. "Phin sure would be jealous."

"Hiya!" chirped a blond woman wearing a white lab coat and a purple T-shirt. The shirt read I'M FOR FUR-FREE. She introduced herself as Eileen and stood behind the front desk like she guarded the place.

"Hi," Madison said. "I'm looking for Dr. Wing—"

"Pet problems?" Eileen interrupted. "Well, we can help you. We got all sorts of pets here. In all shapes and sizes."

"We're not looking for a pet or bringing in a pet," Mom said. "My daughter would like to volunteer. She goes to Far Hills Junior High, and she says she saw your Web—"

"Volunteer? Well, sure!" Eileen said. "Why don't you have a seat and I can help you both in just a sec." She stepped into a back room.

The front door of the clinic opened with a gust of

air, and a bearded bald man came inside with a parrot on his shoulder. He took a seat by the door across from a woman who was holding an empty leash. Madison saw little animal hairs all over the woman's clothes.

Pets always leave their mark on people, Madison thought. She looked down at the chew marks at the edge of her own sneaker.

"Heeere's Gidget!" Eileen reappeared in the waiting room holding a teeny, yipping white dog. The animal made a jump for its owner, trembling and shedding more onto her black sweater.

"Come here, Gidgie-widgie, come here," the owner cooed. The white dog looked happier than happy.

Next Eileen turned to the bearded man. "So, Mr. Walsh, it looks like Rose is losing some feathers again."

Eileen stroked the top of the parrot's head, and it nipped at her fingers. But she didn't seem to mind.

"Rosie is losing as many feathers as I'm losing hair," the old man said. "And I swear I've been feeding her that special seed you told me about."

Rose squawked as Eileen took her back into the examining room. "We'll have you all fixed up in a jiffy, Rosie. Not to worry. And you shouldn't worry, either, Mr. Walsh."

Madison wondered what was behind the door that everyone seemed to disappear behind. As usual, questions streamed into her mind like floodwater.

Were there several different kinds of examining rooms?

Did the clinic have an operating room, too?

Where did the animals live and stay?

Were there cages and fish tanks and fenced-in pens?

And where was Dr. Wing?

Madison stood up and craned her neck to see if she could catch a look in back. Eileen was taking longer than she said.

Meanwhile Mom was hardly noticing any of the dog or parrot activity in the waiting room. Ever since she'd begun development of her latest film project, she did work every chance she got—even in the middle of a veterinarian's waiting room. She was busy checking work messages on her cell phone.

Madison counted red linoleum squares on the floor. She could see where dog paws and cat pads and other pet footprints had left their mark.

Eileen returned in a flurry. "So, here are the forms to fill out," she said.

Being only twelve, Madison needed special parental permission to volunteer. Mom adjusted her cell phone on her ear and scanned the forms for a place to sign. She put her name on the line under Madison's own signature.

Finally Madison handed the pages to Eileen. "Are you a doctor too, like Dr. Wing?" Madison asked.

Eileen winked. "More like an animal nurse. I help Dr. Wing with almost everything. And I run this place on weekends. We're open mostly for emergencies and walk-ins."

"If I volunteer, will I be helping you with animal rescue?" Madison asked.

"Oh," Eileen gasped. "You'll be helping in all sorts of ways around here."

Eileen glanced over the pages to make sure everything was signed. Suddenly she looked up and smiled. "Well, I'll be. You're Madison. Madison Finn?"

"Yeah." Madison smiled nervously. She thought something was filled out wrong. Why was Eileen saying her name that way?

"From Far Hills Junior High—you said that, didn't you? I get the connection." Eileen slapped her forehead. "You see, my son is also—"

Suddenly a boy walked into the waiting room.

"Madison?"

"Dan?" Madison wrinkled her brow. It was Dan Ginsburg from school. He hung around with Madison's guy friends, Egg Diaz, Drew Maxwell, Chet Waters, and even Hart Jones. Dan was the guy who ate everyone's dessert at lunch when they didn't want it. In fifth grade, all the kids in middle school called him Pork-O, but they stopped doing it when he got way bigger than them. He was taller and wider than anyone in seventh grade.

"It is you!" Dan said, supersurprised. "No way!"

"So you two know each other?" Eileen smiled.

"Your son helps out here, too. Well, isn't that nice," Mom said, tucking her cell phone away. She seemed relieved to know that Madison wouldn't be the only twelve-year-old being a veterinarian's helper. Dan extended his hand to shake Mom's.

"Hi, Mrs. Finn," Dan said.

"This boy's a regular Dr. Dolittle, if you ask me," Eileen said.

Dan looked mortified. "Ma, do you have to—"

"Dan, I didn't know you liked animals," Madison said. "I mean, that's so cool. I love animals more than—how come you never said anything?"

"I don't know." Dan seemed flustered. "I never thought about it. I've been coming here since I was little."

"Cool," Madison said. She was genuinely impressed.

After a few more words about forms and schedules, arrangements were made for Madison to officially come back and help out at the clinic Tuesday after school. Dan said he'd be there, too.

Madison and Mom thanked Eileen and said good-bye. The door jingled as they exited, and Madison grinned to herself at the bell's tinkling. It was like a joyful ringing to mark the beginning of this new adventure. She'd be helping animals as often as she could.

Suddenly she felt less jumpy. Not only was she a real volunteer, but she even knew someone who already worked here. She couldn't wait to tell everyone. Dad would be prouder than proud. And Aimee and Fiona would think the clinic was really cool.

On the way home, Mom stopped to pick up pizza dinner. Mom was famous for picking up takeout. Tonight Madison wouldn't have to add to her Scary Dinner file. Sometimes when Mom felt like cooking, it was more than scary.

"Well, I guess you were right, Maddie. Maybe volunteering does beat flute lessons," Mom said on the car ride home. "You have a great smile on your face! I wish I had a camera. And Dan seems very nice. Wasn't he the Lion in *The Wiz*?"

Madison flashed a grin and nodded.

"Who knows, Maddie?" Mom added. "Maybe you're destined to be a vet yourself someday."

"Well," Madison mused, "I could be a vet . . . or I could be a computer programmer . . . or maybe a writer. I know I want to be famous, that's a definite."

"You'll be a vet on some weekday afternoons, anyway," Mom said, turning into their driveway. "Right now, I'd like you to take Phin for a walk. Okay?"

"Okay!" Madison hopped out of the car and skipped up the front porch steps.

"WOOOOOOOOOORRRRF!" Phin snorted a combination hello and sneeze as Madison came inside.

The dog jumped up and sniffed Madison's hands and legs and jacket and sneakers.

"Phinnie!" Madison said, leaning down to greet him. "What are you doing?"

Phin smelled something. He smelled *everything*. Was it the pizza they'd picked up on the way home? Or the Far Hills Animal Shelter all over Madison's clothes and skin? He licked her legs all over.

"Run!" Madison squealed, making a dash for the kitchen. After much petting and a handful of dog treats, Phin finally calmed down enough to go for his walk. They made their usual loop around Blueberry Street before dinner.

Madison ate a giant slice of pizza and then headed straight for her bedroom. It was getting late, and she still had science reading and math homework. She also needed to send an e-mail to Bigwheels, her online keypal.

As she logged on to bigfishbowl.com, Madison was still wired with excitement from her trip to the Far Hills Animal Shelter.

```
From: MadFinn
To: Bigwheels
Subject: BIG NEWS for Bigwheels
Date: Sun 12 Nov 5:23 PM
Do you like animals? Do you have a
pet? I know I asked you that but I
forget. I am bouncing off the
```

walla-wallas because my mom says I
can volunteer at this animal
clinic in our town. Have you ever
volunteered for anything? I can't
concentrate and I have to study,
too. Where r u?

Please write back soon.

Yours till the puppy loves,

MadFinn

P.S. Attached is a picture of my
dog, by the way. His name is Phin
and he's a pug. Isn't he cute?
<<Attachment: PHINNIE.jpg>>

**Just as Madison was about to log offline again,
Aimee sent her an Insta-Message.**

<BalletGrl>: hey I tried calling you
<MadFinn>: mom is on the line with
   clients
<BalletGrl>: how wuz the vet
<MadFinn>: sooo many 3:]
<BalletGrl>: huh
<MadFinn>: DOGS
<BalletGrl>: I get it. Meet me B4
   school tomorrow
<MadFinn>: xtra credit in SS???

```
<BalletGrl>: TOTALLY C U
<MadFinn>: woof!
<BalletGrl>: *poof*
```

Tomorrow was back to school, but Madison couldn't get her mind off the animal shelter. She'd rather spend time with dogs than Pilgrims. Maybe she and Aimee could combine the two?

Suddenly she got a silly idea.

Maybe they could do an extra-credit report on dogs that crossed on the Mayflower?

Dad would have a good laugh at that one.

Monday morning Madison went to the school lobby to put her canned tomatoes in the large donation box. Egg and Fiona had just done the same thing.

"There must be five cans of yellow waxed beans in there," Egg said.

Madison laughed. "And a can of pinto beans, too. What are those?"

"It's like a vegetable graveyard," Fiona said.

Students and teachers were asked to bring canned food from home just before Thanksgiving. The cans would be given to the homeless and other needy people in the Far Hills community.

"GOOD MORNING, STUDENTS," a voice suddenly boomed from the loudspeaker, which just happened to be on the wall near Egg's head. Egg faked a sudden eardrum injury. Madison and Fiona chuckled.

"STUDENT COUNCIL MEETINGS WILL BE HELD THIS AFTERNOON IN THE ASSEMBLY," Principal Bernard said. "AND YOUR ESTEEMED CLASS PRESIDENTS WILL BE TAKING THE NAMES OF VOLUNTEERS FOR OUR ANNUAL TURKEY TROT AT THESE MEETINGS . . . AND PLEASE DON'T FORGET THE CAN DROP IN THE LOBBY. . . ."

November was a busier-than-busy month at school. While the can drive was about helping the homeless, the Turkey Trot was a short running race for students to raise money for the Far Hills Senior Center. Everywhere kids went, someone at school wanted them to give time, give cans, or give thanks.

"Why don't they just give it a rest?" Egg snapped. "Like we don't have enough to do."

"Did Principal Bernard say 'esteemed' class president? That's a joke." Fiona snickered. "Since Ivy was elected, I don't think she's done much of anything."

Madison just shrugged. Ivy Daly was their enemy number one, appropriately nicknamed Poison Ivy, but Madison wasn't in the mood to talk about her. Madison had more important things on her mind.

"Hey, Finnster!" a voice called from across the lobby. Madison turned to say hello. She knew it was Hart Jones. He'd nicknamed her Finnster years ago and it stuck. She didn't like it very much, but somehow the way Hart said it made it seem beautiful. She was crushing on Hart big time, so when she did greet him, Madison did it very carefully.

"Oh . . . hey . . ." she said, tossing her head as casually as she could. Whenever she saw Hart's brown tousled hair and wide smile, Madison could feel her own heart thumping inside her chest.

"What's going on?" Hart asked.

Madison pretended to look for a book in her orange book bag. "Just going to class. What about you?"

DUH! Madison wanted to run as soon as she had asked that dopey question. Of course he was going to class. Where else would Hart be headed in *school*?

Egg interrupted them with a hard tug on Hart's shirt. "Hey, man, I gotta show you something. Let's go."

"See you later, Finnster," Hart said, letting himself be dragged away.

Egg and Hart had become fast friends along with Drew and Chet. They liked to travel in a pack.

"I totally love your outfit, Maddie. Did I say that already?" Fiona giggled. Madison was wearing a denim skirt and a purple T-shirt with little flowers embroidered around the neckline.

"Thanks," Madison replied. "I like your shirt, too."

"Where's Aimee?" Fiona asked.

"Probably dancing," Madison said.

Aimee sometimes took ballet private lessons in the morning before school. She was determined to be a ballerina or some kind of professional dancer when she got older, so she went to private lessons in addition to her afternoon practices for Dance Troupe. Sometimes Aimee would have to get late passes to morning classes if her ballet lessons interfered. She often made dance her number-one priority.

As the first round of bells rang, Madison said good-bye to Fiona and went to Mrs. Wing's classroom. Egg and Drew weren't there yet.

"Madison!" Mrs. Wing said, smiling from ear to ear. "My husband told me you'll be volunteering at the Far Hills clinic. I think that's terrific."

Madison felt herself blush a little bit. "He told you? But he wasn't even there when I visited."

"He goes in late on Sundays to prepare for the coming week. He saw your name on the sign-up sheets." Mrs. Wing leaned down closer to Madison. "That's a very fine thing you're doing, you know. The animals need so much attention. Good for you!"

Madison blushed a little bit more at the compliments.

Brrrrrrrring.

As the second round of bells clanged, Egg and Drew appeared suddenly at the classroom door and scurried over to two empty seats near Madison.

Egg leaned over to Drew and whispered, "Whoa. Mrs. Wing looks pretty today."

Madison couldn't believe Egg had developed a crush on Mrs. Wing when seventh grade began—and that it still hadn't fizzled. He couldn't get the goofy stare off his face whenever he was inside her classroom.

"Today we'll be learning the basics of PowerPoint programs," Mrs. Wing said. "Who can tell me what that is?"

The class was noisy, so she clapped to get everyone's attention. The satin scarf over Mrs. Wing's shoulders made a soft swoosh with each clap. The painted scarf, with autumn leaves in brown, orange, and yellow, sounded like a rustle of *real* leaves.

Egg was right, Madison thought, staring at the scarf. Mrs. Wing was so pretty. She even had a cool husband. She had a perfect life. *Perfect.*

Madison wished her family were close to perfect like that.

By the time social studies rolled around in the afternoon, Madison was all ready with a tentative outline for her extra assignment with Aimee. They had planned it out during lunch, and they were both really excited.

Unfortunately, Mrs. Belden, their social studies teacher, wasn't as enthusiastic. She had a cough and a cold and was crankier than cranky.

Rat-a-tat-a-tat-a-tat.

Mrs. Belden tapped the edge of her desk with a plastic ruler to get everyone's attention.

"As you know, I'm proposing extra-credit projects with a holiday theme."

A wave of whispers flooded the room as Mrs.

Belden pulled down a map of the original thirteen colonies and pointed to Massachusetts.

"This is Plimoth," she said. "P-l-i-m-o-t-h, as they spelled it back then."

Egg and Drew were chattering. Madison felt certain they'd agreed in advance to be partners.

Fiona was across the room talking to her soccer buddy, Daisy. The circle of friends had agreed ahead of time that if Madison and Aimee partnered, Fiona and Daisy would do the same. That way no one would feel left out.

Madison glanced around the room, to see who else might pair off together. She guessed that Ivy and one of her drones would be partners. Rose Thorn and Phony Joanie were always right by Ivy's side.

Mrs. Belden kept talking over all the distractions and noise. "Class! Now listen up. I want you to do these projects in pairs. I think that if we can work together better as a group, we may begin to have a little more discipline about our work. You all have loads of great ideas, so it should be fun working together."

Hart raised his hand. "So can we pick our extra-credit partners?" he asked.

Aimee and Madison looked at each other with a smile, and then Mrs. Belden shook her head no.

Madison's stomach did a 180-degree flip-flop. Aimee's hand shot into the air.

Mrs. Belden kept right on talking.

"Actually, Hart, the topic of your project will be up to you, but pairs working together will be chosen by me. This isn't really a voluntary thing, either. I've decided everyone must do the extra credit. And yes, that includes you, Ben."

Ben Buckley, the smartest kid in the room and probably in the entire school, didn't look happy with that news.

Madison's jaw dropped. She scribbled in the margin of her notebook: MAYBE U WILL STILL BE MY PARTNER?

Aimee wrote in the margin of her notebook: HOPE SO.

Mrs. Belden read from a list of names and pointed to different student pairs-to-be. Fiona and Daisy were matched up first. Madison felt more hopeful that Aimee would be her partner.

Next Ivy was matched up with Drew. Everyone giggled out loud. The thought of a boy-and-girl pair—especially *that* pair—was so funny. Drew looked especially embarrassed. Poison Ivy looked . . . well, disgusted. Then again, Madison always thought she looked that way.

"Hart Jones and Dan Ginsburg." Mrs. Belden read the next pair off her list. The two boys smiled and high-fived on the other side of the room.

Madison kept up hope that she and Aimee would be paired.

"Madison Finn." Mrs. Belden read her name off the list, and Madison took a huge breath. "Your partner will be . . ."

Madison listened closer than close.

". . . Walter Diaz," Mrs. Belden said.

Madison gulped. *Egg*? She'd been matched up with her closest guy friend? Was that a bad thing or a good thing? She couldn't decide.

Aimee punched Madison on the shoulder. "You're soooo lucky," Aimee whispered. "Now who am I gonna get?"

The answer came a moment later.

"Aimee Gillespie, I'd like you to work with Ben Buckley."

Aimee tried not to look appalled. Madison knew she was. Ben was *way* obnoxious. With his super-snobby attitude, he would have been a much better partner for Poison Ivy.

"I'm so bummed," Madison moaned as soon as class had ended. She and Fiona and Aimee went to their lockers. "I'm bummed that we won't be partners, Aim."

"Well, Ben may be superstrange, but at least he's supersmart, too," Aimee said. "That'll make up for his personality, won't it?"

"All that really and truly matters is that we didn't get the Princess of Evil," Madison whispered, motioning to Ivy, who just happened to be walking past at that very moment. The three friends stared.

"Uh, can I help you?" Ivy snarled, nose in the air. She made a face and walked on by with Rose Thorn and Phony Joanie.

"Maddie!" Egg yelled. He ran up to the girls. "How cool is this? We got matched. I have a great idea already. You are gonna be so glad you got me."

Madison wasn't surprised that Egg acted a little full of himself. She knew he would want to be the one in charge. "I have things totally under control," he said.

"You do?" Madison asked. "But we haven't even decided what we're doing."

Aimee rolled her eyes. "You're like . . . a total turkey, Egg."

"But turkey's okay, since it is Thanksgiving," Madison said, grinning.

Egg laughed. "Very funny, Maddie. Just hilarious," he said.

As they packed up their bags to head home, Madison tried to adjust her outlook on the entire situation. "I think we'll be great," Madison said.

Egg pushed her shoulder. "Hey, I'll e-mail you later, okay?" He ran off to find Chet.

Madison noticed Fiona staring at Egg when he disappeared around the corner. Everyone knew Fiona had a mega-crush on him. Madison wondered if maybe Egg liked Fiona more than he admitted, too.

Later that afternoon, Madison went online to find ideas for her extra-credit project with Egg. She checked her e-mailbox and was surprised to find it full of messages.

FROM	SUBJECT
✉ Boop-Dee-Doop	special offers
✉ Bigfishbowl	SANDWICH POLL
✉ JeffFinn	ANOTHER JOKE!!
✉ FHC	Welcome!

Boop-Dee-Doop announced 10 percent off all merchandise, which was great news, since Madison was saving up her allowance for a pair of flared jeans with a low waist and patches on the back.

Bigfishbowl.com was announcing the results of their Sandwich Day poll. They always celebrated obscure holidays that no one ever really heard of. Sandwich Day was November 3. The yummiest sandwich according to the bigfishbowl.com poll takers was peanut butter and jelly. Hamburgers came in a close second.

Next Madison read the e-mail from JeffFinn, aka Dad. Madison knew that he would probably send her at least one joke a day until Thanksgiving.

From: JeffFinn
To: MadFinn
Subject: ANOTHER JOKE!!
Date: Mon 13 Nov 4:23 PM

If April showers bring May flowers, what do May flowers bring?

33

Guess this and I'll take you to dinner.

I love you,

Dad

Madison groaned. Didn't Dad realize he'd been telling her that same joke since she was four years old? The answer was "Pilgrims," of course. *Duh!*

She was about to click DELETE but stopped herself. Dad hadn't mentioned anything in his note about Thanksgiving dinner. She reread it.

Madison secretly wished that Dad would protest all the divorce rules so they could all have a big old turkey dinner together. But Dad never protested much of anything.

The only e-mail remaining took Madison by surprise. The Far Hills Clinic (FHC) had sent Madison a welcome letter.

From: FHC
To: MadFinn
Subject: Welcome!
Date: Mon 13 Nov 4:08 PM
Woof! We're so happy to welcome you, Madison Finn, to our Far Hills family of volunteers. Thanks to people like you, we can provide

care and help for animals in our
community. That's something to bark
about! We look forward to seeing
you on your first day. If you have
not signed up yet, please call
Eileen Ginsburg at the clinic—she'll
be pleased to put you on our
schedule.

Thank you,

Dr. Bryan Wing
and all the animals at FHC

Although the family parts of Thanksgiving
between Mom and Dad still needed a little sorting
out, the school parts seemed to be working out
well—and this e-mail indicated that the volunteering would be good fun, too. Gramma Helen would
say, "Don't count your turkeys before they're
hatched."

But these days, Madison Finn wanted to count on
everything.

Chapter 4

"Well, hiya!" Eileen said when Madison walked into the clinic on the next day. "Are you ready to work?"

Madison could feel her face flush. *Ready?* She was readier than ready to meet and help each and every animal.

Eileen showed her to a back room where the cages were kept. Barks, squawks, growls, and whines came from every direction. There were mostly dogs doing all the talking, but Madison spotted a few other critters and birds who had something to say. A tabby cat was curled up in the corner of one cage with a cast on his leg. He couldn't stop meowing.

"Poor Freddie. Wounded in a cat fight," Eileen said, stroking Fred's ears through the cage door. "He's under a little medication. That's why his eyes are all glassy and he's so talkative. We'll keep him sedated for a day or two until he has a chance to start healing."

Eileen introduced Madison to other staff members and showed her around the clinic. Madison learned that the clinic "emergency room" was where the veterinarian on call would help an animal recover until its wounds healed. Like right now. Sometimes the animal brought in would be a family pet. But most of the time, the clinic dealt with strays and unwanted animals from the community.

Madison felt sad when she discovered just how many different animals were abandoned in Far Hills—even sweet cats like Fred.

Dr. Wing stepped into the room. He smiled at Madison and went over to the cage where the yellow Labrador retriever named Spanky lay awake, but breathing heavily. The dog had an anxiety disorder, so the doctor had given him a sedative to calm his nerves.

"Hey, Dr. Wing," Madison said when he looked up. He looked a little different from the last time Madison had seen him, at the seventh-grade dance. There he had been wearing a costume.

"Hi, Madison," Dr. Wing said. "Have you met the other volunteers?"

"Other volunteers?" Madison repeated. Was there a whole crowd of people squished together in the back?

"We have a lot of people doing different duties around here. You'll meet them all at some point," Dr. Wing explained.

Eileen pressed against the small of Madison's back and pushed her gently. "Next stop, kennel room. Here we go, Madison."

Madison's five senses were overwhelmed once again as they passed into the new area. A woman with a red beehive hairdo and a lab coat with a tag that read STAFF smiled. The air smelled like wet dog.

As they passed into the place Eileen called the kennel, Madison eyed medicine cabinets crammed with jars and bottles, Technicolor posters of animal anatomy, a bulletin board covered with Polaroid photographs of posed pets, and overflowing barrels of kibble. It was impossible to see, smell, or hear everything at once.

Half the cages were filled with dogs in assorted shapes and sizes. Some had scars on their fur and skin. Some were fast asleep, others just scared. Many barked at the slightest human movement. A home-made sign over the row of cages read DOG POUND—TAKE ME HOME!

Dan was in the corner with an older man he called Mr. Wollensky.

Mr. Wollensky smiled. "Have you met our fam-il-eee?" he asked with a thick Russian accent. The dogs howled as he spritzed the hose around their cages.

"Madison, help me move some of these dogs. We have to wash out their cages," Dan said, opening a cage door. A wirehaired dog was huddled, shaking, in a corner.

"Awww, she's so cute," Madison said, biting her lip as she tentatively moved toward the cage. She let the dog sniff her hand first, since she didn't know if these dogs were friendly or not.

"Hello, Pepper." Dan laughed. "Dr. Wing lets me name puppies sometimes when they come in nameless. I named her that because she made me sneeze." Dan petted her head. "You can take Pepper out if you want."

"Awww." Madison smiled at the pup. "Don't be scared." She helped lift Pepper out of the cage and into a small pen to play with rubber chew toys until her cage was washed out.

Mr. Wollensky sprayed the hose more, and Madison got a little wet. It was fun to be helping out immediately after she arrived.

"Eileen?" Dr. Wing poked his head into the back room. "Dan, have you seen your mother? I need her help."

Dan dashed off to find his mother. Madison wondered if Dan got to sit in on the medical examinations. He'd been working at the Far Hills Animal Shelter and Clinic since he was five. Madison had only been here for five minutes.

Madison reached down and picked up Pepper, who licked her face. "You're a cutie pie, Pep."

"Yip!" Pepper said, as if she understood.

While Mr. Wollensky continued to hose down the dog area, Madison helped transfer other dogs one by one into the waiting pen and then back into their cages. She read signs on their cages that listed their names, date of arrival, and medical condition if any.

Blinky, arrived October 15, abandoned, eye infection.

Blinky looked like he was crying nonstop, which Madison assumed accounted for his name. He lay there like a sack, breathing deep, paws crossed. Madison looked real close to make sure he was alive.

"That is sickie dog," Mr. Wollensky said.

"Huh? What kind of dog is Blinky?" Madison asked.

He leaned in and adjusted his hearing aid. "I say sickie dog. Yes?"

Madison had trouble understanding Mr. Wollensky. His hearing problem and Russian accent made it hard to communicate with him. But he was very gentle. Mr. Wollensky seemed to love animals as much as Madison did.

Mr. Wollensky reached out for Madison's arm. "You no touch these dog," he cautioned her. "Bad dog."

Pavlov, arrived September 30, neglected. Handle with care. Bites.

Pavlov growled from behind the bars. Mr. Wollensky explained in broken English about how he'd named this particular dog Pavlov after a *Russian* doctor who conducted special kinds of science experiments. Dr. Pavlov was a man who tested whether a ringing a bell could trigger a hunger response in his dog. It worked. Since then, conditioned responses were called Pavlovian responses.

Madison could barely understand what else Mr. Wollensky was saying, but she decided he was very nice. He introduced Madison to the remaining animals in cages, including a cat named Whisky that was going bald, a bulldog that was waiting to be spayed, and a hyperactive puppy named Kazoo.

"No become too attached," Mr. Wollensky said. "Then you be sad when dog go."

Madison told him getting attached wouldn't be a problem.

"I already have a dog," she explained to Mr. Wollensky. He just smiled and nodded and smiled. Madison figured he didn't understand a word she was saying.

The clock on the kennel-room wall said it was almost time to head home, so Madison used the office phone to call Mom for her ride.

Mom wasn't really talkative on the way home or even during dinner—take-out Chinese. She asked Madison to help fold laundry down in the basement, so they went downstairs together.

"Tell me again about the cute dogs," Mom said after a few rounds of fold-the-bedsheets-and-towels.

Madison perked up. "Mom, I think volunteering was the smartest thing I've ever done. Ever."

Mom sighed. "You do a lot of smart things, honey bear."

Phinnie came clinking down the stairs. Madison and Mom turned to look at him. As he reached the bottom, he sat there a little lopsided, tongue hanging out, snorting like mad.

Mom sighed again. "Oh, I wish Thanksgiving could be different this year, sweetheart, I really do."

"We—we don't have to talk about that," Madison stammered. "You seem sad."

"The whole arrangement has been on my mind since Sunday. You seemed so disappointed with it just being us two for dinner," Mom said. "I didn't know what to say to you. I feel bad about it."

Madison couldn't believe her mom was being so honest.

"I'm so NOT disappointed, Mom," Madison said, lying through her teeth.

Mom shrugged. "Well . . . to tell you the truth, Maddie, I am. I'm a little disappointed. I miss the family the way it was. I miss my family."

Together, in silence, they folded one last fitted sheet, and then Madison went upstairs to go to sleep. Before she changed into her pajamas, Madison booted up her computer for an e-mail check, quietly so Mom wouldn't hear.

Two e-mails flashed. Both came from real friends.

The first one distracted Madison a little from everything Mom had been talking about. It was from Egg, and his spelling was as bad as ever.

From: Eggaway
To: MadFinn
Subject: CLASS PROJECT
Date: Tues 7 Nov 7:31 PM

I have been thinkin about the
project Mrs. Belden & thinkweshould
do something about pligrims maybe.
Like build a model. I found cool
Websits that have infoand pictures.
What do u think? LMK. Bye!!!

**Bigwheels got in touch, too. Madison was so
relieved.**

From: Bigwheels
To: MadFinn
Subject: Gobble gobble
Date: Tues 14 Nov 9:18 PM

You are way better at writing than
me. The answer to your question is
YES about Thanksgiving. We have
sooooo many peeps for dinner. We live
in a small house, so Mom and Dad and
my aunts and uncles and us kids rent
a hotel space for dinner. It is so
weird. I think that last yr. there
were like 86 of us. I didn't even
know them all and I'm related to
them!!! My sisters were freaked, too.
It makes you claustrophobic (did I
spell that right?)

Don't worry about your Thanksgiving because it will work out no matter where you are. We should be super thankful, right? You don't need lots of people. Besides you have ME!!!

Yours till the turkey gobbles,

Bigwheels

p.s. Tell more about the animal shelter in ur next e-mail

Bigwheels was right. Madison closed her laptop and decided right then and there that she had to stop worrying about being alone with Mom on Thanksgiving. She had to stop worrying, period. The divorce had happened, and there was nothing to be done about it. No matter how hard she wished, nothing could bring Dad and Mom back together.

Madison suddenly thought about all the animals in the shelter, woofing and sniffling and giving her kisses. They seemed so lost and needy without their own families. Madison wondered: if she couldn't change things with Mom and Dad, maybe she could help the animals instead?

Closing her eyes to sleep, Madison's whole body warmed to the idea. She drifted to sleep counting . . . not sheep, but puppies.

Puppies and puppies and more puppies . . .

Chapter 5

Between fourth and fifth period Madison met Aimee and Fiona in the second-floor girls' bathroom. Since they didn't always have class together, they'd try to steal some time in between classes, away from teachers and everyone else. They liked sneaking even just a few minutes of gossip and giggles.

Today Fiona was complaining a little about her social studies partner, Daisy Espinoza.

"She's amazing at soccer," Fiona said. "But she's really not very good at this whole project thing."

Aimee shrugged and leaned into the bathroom mirror. Madison watched her intently. Aimee was touching up her lip gloss.

"What do you guys think?" Fiona asked. "Should I ask to switch partners?"

"I don't think you can," Madison moaned.

"Otherwise I would have done it already."

"That's not true," Aimee said all of a sudden. "You got Egg as a partner. He's a good match."

"Yeah, well . . ." Madison shrugged.

"Egg is soooo cute," Fiona grinned. "I mean . . . well, you know what I mean. . . ." She looked embarrassed all of a sudden.

"Yeah, whatever you say, Fiona." Madison laughed a little because she knew all about Fiona's supercrush. Fiona acted so goofy whenever Egg's name was even mentioned.

Madison hopped up to sit on the radiator next to the sinks. Thankfully, the heat wasn't turned on full. A bell went off. They had three minutes before the next class period.

Aimee pinched her cheeks to make them pinker. She didn't take her eyes off her reflection.

"Do you guys think Ben Buckley is cute?" Aimee asked softly.

Madison covered her mouth so she wouldn't gasp with laughter, but she started to giggle.

Fiona bit her lip. "Are you serious?"

Aimee swirled around and asked her friends, "Why are you looking at me like that? Okay, I know Ben's obnoxious, but . . ."

Before she could say another word, the bathroom door was flung open. Poison Ivy Daly and her drones buzzed inside. But Ivy stopped short when she saw Madison, Aimee, and Fiona.

By now, Madison was giggling *out loud*. Ivy was taken aback.

"Oh, I didn't know this bathroom was dirty," Ivy snarled, and turned on one heel as she led the way out the door.

"What's *that* supposed to mean?" Fiona said, acting a little spacey.

Madison made a face and stuck out her tongue behind Ivy's back.

"When are you leaving for California, Fiona?" Aimee asked, as if the interruption had never happened.

Fiona beamed and reapplied her own lip gloss. "We leave in a week. I'm already packed."

"Can you smuggle me in your luggage?" Madison joked.

Fiona offered Madison some gloss. It was called Shimmer, but Madison didn't want any. She'd only chew it off, like she always chewed off lipstick and nail polish.

The second warning bell rang. They had to hurry.

As they exited the bathroom, the three girls almost smacked right into Hart and Dan, who were rushing off to class, too.

"Whoa," Hart said, avoiding the collision. "Hey, Finnster . . ."

Madison's cheeks turned red and hot. But they didn't talk. No one wanted to be late for class.

Concentrating seemed pointless after that. All

Madison could think of was the way Hart's brown hair looked when they had bumped into each other, the way it was swept over to the side, the way it curled near his neck. No matter how hard she tried to think about math equations, it was Hart and his hairdo that kept popping into her head.

Since Mom was busy working on film edits this week, she'd asked Fiona's dad to give Madison a ride to and from the animal clinic. Mr. Waters agreed. It was on the way to Chet's karate class, which made it convenient for everyone.

While sitting in the Waterses' car, Madison stayed silent in the backseat while Chet and his dad talked sports. Chet looked like a miniature version of his father.

"I can't remember if you told me this or not. Are you playing on any teams, Maddie?" Mr. Waters asked. She *had* told him before, but she didn't mind repeating it.

"No teams," Madison confessed. "I work on the school Web site and now I have the volunteering."

"Well, that's certainly a lot to do," Mr. Waters said. He gave Chet a sidelong glance. "Why don't you stop playing video games and try volunteering?"

"Dad," Chet mumbled.

The Far Hills Animal Shelter and Clinic appeared at the top of a steep road, and Mr. Waters pulled up in front.

"Thanks, Mr. Waters!" Madison said as she jumped out. "Bye, Chet!"

Inside the waiting room, chaos reigned. Big dogs sniffed little dogs while shivering cats extended claws and hissed from inside their kitty carryalls. One boy held on to a box so tightly his knuckles had turned white.

Doctor Wing read a name from his chart, and the white-knuckled boy jumped up.

"The python won't eat," the boy said loudly. Madison shuddered to think of the clammy snake curled up inside the box. She'd seen big snakes last summer on her trip to Brazil with Mom, and they gave her the jeebies.

Peeling the box gently from the boy's grasp, Dr. Wing disappeared into an examining room.

"Hello?" Madison chirped over the front counter. An elderly woman was helping Eileen behind the counter. As she turned around, Madison could read Eileen's T-shirt today: LEMUR ALONE! SAVE THE RAIN FOREST! Madison wondered how many shelves Eileen probably needed to keep her shirt collection in order. On Tuesday, she had admitted to having ninety-four T-shirts.

Madison followed Eileen into a paneled office just off the waiting room. Dan was sitting there behind a computer terminal. Madison plopped down into the one empty chair next to him.

"Hey," he said without turning from the monitor.

"Dan's going to show you how to keep updates on the animals in the shelter and clinic, Maddie. We

49

log all our information onto this database. Okay, hon? See you in an hour or so," she said, winking and shutting the door behind her.

Dan punched a few more keys to pause the screen. "This is like control central for the clinic. It's way cool."

"I thought volunteers just fed and watered the animals," Madison said.

"Being a volunteer here means all kinds of stuff. I figured you might like doing the computer work, since you're so good at it. Dr. Wing said something to my mother, too. He knows you help with the school Web site," Dan said.

Madison was impressed that they would have considered that. She still wanted to know when she'd be doing some big-time animal rescuing, but she didn't want to ask too many questions.

Dan stuffed half a doughnut into his mouth and wiped the corners with his sleeve. "Okay," he mumbled, still chewing. "You gotta enter the password here. It's *Falcon* this week. Dr. Wing changes it all the time."

"*Falcon*. Got it," Madison said, watching his every move. "You have . . . uh . . . jelly on your face, Dan." She giggled.

Dan blushed and grabbed another napkin.

They proceeded to the main directory of the database, which included descriptions and photos of the animals who had been brought into the shelter for rescue. It also featured a running tally of supplies for the animals and the animal clinic, a roster of volunteers and their schedules, and much more.

"Hey, that's me!" Madison said when she saw her name as she scrolled down a page. It said: *After school, schedule permitting.* Most junior high and high school students had the same notation.

Dan pointed to a list of supplies and explained to Madison how to add and subtract information based on what was being used in the veterinary office. If Madison used up a bin of kibble, she needed to enter that one bag of kibble was used on the computer.

"My mom set it up so we'd keep track. It saves her time," Dan explained. "It's cool being responsible for stuff, ya know?"

"I know what you mean," Madison said, eyes fixed on the screen.

Dan pulled up another page with the special form the clinic would fill out if a dog got sick.

"If you're checking on a dog or cat or whatever and they look sick, just look at this and you know what questions to ask. Like, 'Does the animal have difficulty keeping food down?' You can fill this out here, hit send, and blam! Dr. Wing gets it in his e-mailbox. Coolness, right?"

"Cool," Madison said. "What's that page?" She pointed to another document named Waiting Lists & Foster Care.

"The clinic is pretty small, so Dr. Wing can't take in all the animals. So sometimes people in Far Hills give animals foster homes."

One by one, they went over other basic procedures. Madison suddenly understood why having volunteers was so important. There was a lot going on behind the scenes. For every yelping pup in the kennel room, there was a sick cat on an examination table. For every person who wanted to adopt a stray, there were three strays that couldn't find a home.

She watched Dan closely. Most kids at school thought of Dan as the overweight kid who only wanted brownies and never played sports. In reality, he knew about computers and animals of all kinds. Madison decided right there that Dan Ginsburg was cooler than cool.

"Ya know, I want to be a vet when I grow up," Dan said.

"I would love to be a vet, too," Madison said. "Or maybe a movie producer like my mom."

"You could make movies about animals," Dan said. "Like *Jaws*."

"*Jaws?*" Madison gasped. She knew that was the scary movie about a man-eating shark.

Dan chuckled to himself. "Just kidding."

After working on the database some more, Dan and Madison were on their way to becoming friends. It seemed funny to have so much in common with a boy, but Madison was thankful for it.

"DR. WING!"

There was a sudden shout coming from the waiting room. Dan recognized his mom's voice, and they jumped up to see what was the matter.

Eileen was kneeling on the steps near the door. In her arms she was cradling a small dog, trembling and whining. Her fur was all matted and dirty. Her sad eyes were wet with tears. It looked like she had burns on her coat and tail, too. Madison wanted to look away. The dog was obviously hurting.

"Oh, man," Dan groaned.

"Dan." Eileen shot him a look.

Dr. Wing rushed up. "Another one, huh?" he said to Eileen. She nodded and sighed. The dog whined a little louder as more people gathered.

Dan whispered to Madison, "Sometimes people abandon their dogs right here, right on the clinic steps."

"People just leave the dogs alone here?" Madison asked.

Dr. Wing and Eileen brought the abandoned animal into an examining room to see what damage had been done. The dog needed a bath and medicine right away. It was a mixed breed, called a schnoodle. The name was a perfect fit for the miniature dog's mix of schnauzer and poodle. Dr. Wing checked the dog's temperature, breaths per minute, and heart rate. Everything was racing.

"Gums are swollen," Dr. Wing said, checking

inside the dog's mouth. "Needs hydration."

Dan whispered to Madison, "Most dogs that come in off the street haven't eaten, and they're all dehydrated."

"Irregular breathing," Eileen said aloud, stroking the dog's coat.

"Let's get an IV over here," Dr. Wing said.

Madison gawked. It was like an emergency-room TV show, only with animals.

"You two need to go back to the other room now," Eileen said gently, shutting the door.

Dan shook his head. "I've seen that happen so many times."

"It's so sad," Madison said. "What will you name this one, Dan?"

"Good question. Hmmm . . ." Dan thought for a moment.

"She looks like the color of cinnamon," Madison said. "And sweet, like cinnamon sugar."

"Sugar! I like *that*. Mom will, too," Dan said.

In the back of the clinic, there was an office that was decorated more like a bedroom or a den. That was where Dr. Wing or someone on his staff would sometimes stay overnight if they were worried about an animal. Tonight the doctor was staying there himself to watch the new arrival.

Everyone wanted to make sure Sugar the schnoodle made it safely through the night.

Madison wished she could stay over, too.

Chapter 6

 The **Mayflower**

Whew. I was afraid Egg would forget our
meeting for social studies, but he didn't.
He was just LATE. We finally picked our
project (the **Mayflower**) for Mrs. Belden's
class. Wow! He had so many great ideas
about building this model of the actual
Mayflower ship and putting it onto
PowerPoint. I hate to say that I never
expected him to be good at this kind of
thing, but he is good. Wicked good.

Egg really and truly needs this project
to raise his social studies grade, so the
pressure's on. I already printed a list off
a Web site that explains how the real ship
was built back in its day. Materials I
think we need so far: poster board,

clear-dry glue, board chips for the boat.
   Sometimes I think I'm doing my
extra-credit project with a PARTNER with a
missing PART! LOL. But he did say he was
sorry for being late twice. I guess I'll
get over being annoyed eventually.

When Madison couldn't think about the extra
credit anymore, she opened the file on the disk with
her English essay instead. She could finish typing on
the library and media center computer. This was such
a quiet spot! She had to rush, however, so she could
still go downstairs to meet Fiona after soccer practice.
Mr. Waters was taking Madison to the Far Hills Animal
Shelter and Clinic again this afternoon. This family
was becoming her regular ride for her extra trips to
the clinic. Madison had explained to Mom about the
sick schnoodle and how much she wanted to be with
her. As long as Madison got her work done, Mom said
she could go more than once a week.

   "Hop in, Maddie," Mr. Waters said.

   "Is Fiona around?" Madison asked, poking her
head inside the front seat. She saw Fiona's soccer
bag inside the minivan.

   Mr. Waters shook his head. "Around the corner.
Get in and we'll ride over there," he said, helping
push her backpack between the seat and the floor.
Madison slid the door shut behind her.

   "Fiona went to get her brother," Mr. Waters said,
driving around to the other side of school.

There, by the entrance and exit to the boys' gym, Fiona was waving and waiting with Chet. Next to them, sitting on his propped-up backpack, was Egg.

Madison waved. Egg smiled.

"Hey, partner," he joked as he got into the backseat behind Madison.

"Whatever," Madison quipped. "When you're not *late*, anyway . . ."

"Cut me a break, will ya?" Egg said.

"Hey, Maddie!" Fiona said, sliding open the door and jumping inside.

Chet rode up in front next to Mr. Waters.

"You're like a limo service, Dad," Fiona quipped. The truth was that Mr. Waters worked half days at the office and half days at home, so he could afford to get out afternoons for chauffeuring duties.

Madison twisted around to see Egg. "Why are you here, anyway?"

"Secret mission," Egg cracked.

"Yeah, secret mission to eliminate annoying twin sisters . . ." Chet started to say. Fiona slugged him on the shoulder.

"And friends of twin sisters," Egg added.

Madison shot him a look.

"Now, now. Settle down, kids," Mr. Waters said. He changed the subject. "So how was practice, Fiona?"

"Fine."

"What's your coach got planned for a winning season?"

"I don't know," Fiona said because she didn't feel like being interrogated. "Dad, can we get ice cream?"

"Oh yeah, Dad. Can we?" Chet asked.

While Fiona and Chet pleaded for an ice cream detour, Madison gazed out the minivan window . . . far, far away as she could. Outside, Far Hills was in the process of relandscaping parks and repaving its main thoroughfare. One part of the downtown area had a dog run so owners could go give their dogs exercise. As they passed by, she counted five or six dogs chasing Frisbees in clouds of dirt. Before Madison realized it, they'd arrived at the clinic.

"Here we are!" Mr. Waters announced as they pulled up in front. As Madison got out of the car, Fiona and Chet waved, but Egg made a funny face. She wasn't sure why. He really could be *so* annoying.

"Good-bye!" Madison skipped away.

They drove off.

"Hellooooo?" Madison called out when she walked into the clinic. She didn't hear any people or animals right away. "Eileen? Dan? Dr. Wing?"

Madison walked into the office first. Dan wasn't around. She could hear Dr. Wing and a nurse in one of the examination rooms. Madison checked the animal cages. Most of the dogs were calm and quiet. Mr. Wollensky was back there today, grooming one of the Yorkie terriers who had been staying at the clinic for a while. Madison greeted them both and proceeded to read the charts in front of some of the other cages.

Blinky, arrived October 15, abandoned, eyes healing.

Blinky blinked and panted hello. Madison could tell he was getting much better. So were the dogs in connecting cages.

Pavlov, arrived September 30, neglected. Handle with care.

Pavlov was lying there, chest still heaving with uneasy rhythms. He wasn't hurt on the outside. Pavlov was hurt on the inside. Madison imagined how much he'd suffered before getting to this place. It made her so sad.

Then she came to Sugar the schnoodle's cage.

Since Sugar had been discovered, Dr. Wing and Eileen had taken extra-special care of her. Her coat looked shinier now. Most of the tangles were combed out. Without the scabs and matted fur, Sugar looked more like a spunky dog—rather than just a mess.

Sugar stuck her nose right up to the cage door and sniffed. When Madison put her finger a little closer, Sugar licked it gently.

"Hello, Sugar," Madison said. "Schnoodle-oodleeee-oh." The dog cowered a little, but still came back to investigate Madison's scent.

"WHO are you talking to?" Dan asked, walking into the back area. "You sound like a yodeler."

"Dan!" Madison jumped, a little taken off guard. "I didn't know you were here!"

"So who are you talking to?"

"Just the schnoodle. She's so pretty today," Madison said. "I'm glad I named her Sugar."

"Yeah, she looks way better than before," Dan said, slinging his backpack onto the floor and walking over to the cages. "You were in pretty bad shape before, but now you're one hot dog."

Madison groaned. "That's so lame, Dan."

"It was funny! Come on!" Dan snickered. He stuck his fingertips under Sugar's nose and she licked them.

"What happened to her?" Madison asked. "Do you think she was abused?"

Dan nodded. "My mom says so. We get all kinds of dogs here with problems like burns from cigarettes, broken bones, and not being fed. People can be so mean. I don't get it. How could you be mean to an animal?"

Madison's heart sank. She couldn't believe it, either. As the afternoon went on, Madison found herself drawn to Sugar's cage more than the cages of any other dogs. This schnauzer-poodle loved all the attention.

"I'm a little surprised at how quickly she's recovering, to tell ya the truth," Dan's mother said when she saw Madison and Sugar together. "Usually these dogs need time before they cling on to ya. You must have something special, Maddie."

"She's the one who's special," Madison said.

"Yup, this one seems to have a bond with you," Eileen said. "You're turning into a special volunteer in only a short time. I'm impressed, and so is Dr. Wing."

Madison dropped her head, a little self-conscious from the sudden attention. She scratched the top of Sugar's head.

"Well, I mean it," Eileen said. "Right away you were a natural at this, and we're very lucky to have you be a part of our little Far Hills Animal Clinic family."

"Thanks, Eileen," Madison said softly. She looked at Eileen's T-shirt, which read LOVE A PET, LOVE A VET.

Madison felt loved, too.

When Madison came home, she sprawled on the bed to check her e-mail. She loved the way Sugar had nuzzled, snuggled, and *needed* Madison. Bigwheels would love hearing all about it.

Phin tried to climb onto the bed, but she shooed him away.

"I'm busy right now, Phinnie," Madison cooed.

Phin barked and got down on all fours like he would pounce. This pug wanted to play. But then he gave up and crawled under Madison's desk.

There was only one message. It was from Dad.

From: JeffFinn
To: MadFinn
Subject: Let's Talk
Date: Thurs 16 Nov 5:03 PM

Honey bear, we need to talk soon. I tried leaving a message, but tell your mother the machine is broken. I know you are at the animal hospital. I hope that is fun. Please call me tonight when you get in.

A joke for you: What do you get when you cross a turkey and an octopus? Ha ha.

I'll tell you the answer when you call!

Love you,

Dad

Madison shut off the computer and dashed downstairs to the living room. She checked the answering machine, which was blinking frantically. She dialed Dad's number.

What did Dad have to tell her that he couldn't say in e-mail?

Dad would never put important things in e-mail. He liked to talk about things in person, or at least on the phone.

"Hey, sweetie," Dad whispered as he picked up the phone. "How's my little girl?" He always called her that, much to Madison's dismay. She thought of herself as slightly more sophisticated, especially since junior high began.

"What's up with you, Dad?" Madison asked back. "By the way, the answer to your riddle is you get a lot of drumsticks when you cross an octopus and a turkey!"

Dad laughed. Then he told her about work being busy as ever. He had purchased a new wok for his kitchen.

"I was thinking about making stir-fry turkey this Thanksgiving," Dad said.

"Very funny, Dad," Madison replied, half laughing.

He followed up with another joke. "Hey, Maddie, why was the turkey included as a member of the band?"

"What band?" Madison groaned. "Okay. Why?"

"Because he had all the drumsticks." Dad laughed out loud. "Get it?"

It was maybe the dumbest joke Dad had told in the longest time, but suddenly Madison felt choked up. She wasn't sure if she got teary with the mention of Thanksgiving, or if she had a sudden surge of missing Dad, since he hadn't been around much lately.

"I really wish we could—" Madison swallowed

the words. "I wish we could spend Thanksgiving together, Dad."

Dad got silent on the other end of the phone line. "Gee, Maddie—"

Madison interrupted. "Oh, forget I said that. That was so dumb."

"No. What's going on? Is something bugging you?" Dad asked.

"You mean besides homework and my friend Egg?" Madison blurted, trying to shift gears and change the subject.

"Huh? You lost me," Dad said.

Madison took a deep breath. "I miss you, Dad. So much."

She could hear him take a deep breath through the phone, too. "I know," Dad said. "I know you do."

"So why can't I spend Thanksgiving with you—and your family?" Madison asked.

"My family? What? Madison, we've been over this. The lawyers' arrangement says—"

"I don't care what it says," Madison cried. "I don't want to spend Thanksgiving in this house if YOU can't be here. Thanksgiving is supposed to be a family holiday, and I don't want to spend Thanksgiving alone with no one but Mom because . . . I just don't want to. I don't."

Dad took another loud breath. "Madison?" he asked sweetly.

Madison was afraid of what he might say. She'd let all her feelings come tumbling out at once. They'd taken her by surprise.

"Why don't we talk about it at dinner tomorrow night," Dad said, trying to change the subject. "And about that dinner . . ."

Madison gulped. "Yeah?"

"I was going to bring Stephanie," Dad said.

Madison was silent.

Dad quickly recovered. "Unless you don't want me to. I mean, it can just be you and me alone, Maddie. You tell me."

But Madison didn't quibble. She agreed to have dinner with them both. It was hard to have anything but good feelings for Dad's girlfriend when she always came with a little present for Madison like flea-market earrings made from glass and asked lots of fun questions about school and boys and life in general. Stephanie seemed so interested in what Madison thought and believed. She was pretty, too, with perfect fingernails.

"Hey!" Mom walked in, carrying an armful of groceries. "Who's on the phone?"

"No one," Madison fibbed, covering the receiver. Then she admitted the truth. "Just Dad."

"Oh," Mom said, walking into the kitchen. Madison could hear her pushing vegetables into the refrigerator bins.

"Bye, Dad," Madison said into the phone quickly.

"I have to go help Mom make dinner. She just got home."

Mom asked her to help boil water for the ziti while she cut up lettuce and tomatoes for salad.

"I was talking to Dad about Thanksgiving," Madison said, filling a pot.

"Oh," Mom replied. "Does he have plans?"

Madison put water on the stove and added a little olive oil to separate the boiling pasta. It was a trick Gramma had shown her. "Actually, he didn't really talk about Thanksgiving."

Madison wasn't sure why she lied, but she did.

"Oh," Mom said for a third time. "Well, I'm sure he'll be spending it with that girlfriend of his."

"Her name is Stephanie," Madison added. She could tell when Mom didn't want to talk. Whenever she "forgot" someone's name, it meant the subject should be changed.

"So where's Phin?" Mom asked. "We should walk him before supper."

"Phin?" Madison whirled around, half expecting to find him by her feet, but the pug wasn't there. "I dunno. I saw him a while ago. . . ."

"He's been acting funny lately. Have you noticed?" Mom said. She had been taking Phin for long walks during the afternoons when Madison went to volunteer at the shelter.

"I haven't noticed anything," Madison said.

"It's probably nothing." Mom shook her head.

"He's probably just a little jealous. You're giving all your attention to the other dogs now."

Madison giggled. "Mom, don't be ridiculous. Phinnie doesn't know what I'm doing."

The phone rang again and Madison grabbed it. "House of Finn," she cried into the receiver spontaneously. She looked across at Mom, who was chuckling a little now, too. Lately they'd been goofing around when answering the phone. One night Mom had picked it up and said, "Finn Land." They almost fell on the floor, laughing so hard.

But Egg was the one on the phone, and he didn't get what was funny at all.

"House of what?" Egg said.

"Oh, it's you." Madison faked a growl.

"What is your problem, Maddie?" he asked. "You can't still be mad about me being late. I said sorry like a hundred times already."

"You said sorry twice. That is not a hundred times," Madison said.

She and Egg bickered some more. Ten minutes later, they came to an agreement to meet the next day after school to talk about the *Mayflower*. They'd meet in Mrs. Wing's computer lab so they could use the Internet. No one would bother them.

"Don't forget, Egg, please be on time. I don't want to wait around forever," Madison said.

"Yeah, yeah, I KNOW," he grumbled.

Madison tried to soften the tone a little bit. "This

project will be awesome—I know it," she said reas-
suringly.

"Of course it will!" Egg said. He sounded encour-
aged, so she hung up the phone and sat down to
dinner.

"Is this a little sticky, or is it me?" Mom asked
when she tasted dinner. "We'll keep practicing,
right, honey bear?"

The pasta was overcooked, but Madison ate two
helpings.

Right before bed, Madison powered up her laptop.

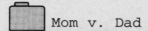 Mom v. Dad

Rude Awakening: It's hard to be fair
and square when you feel like part of a
triangle.

Am I being fair to Mom? She is trying so
hard to make dinners and to be nice letting
me volunteer and taking Phin for walks. Do
I say thank you and please enough? I made
this whole huge deal about wanting to
spend Thanksgiving with Dad and now . . .
everything is different. I just want to
have turkey on Thanksgiving and to make
them both happy. Am I making Mom sad? Is
Dad sad? How am I supposed to be?

Madison hit SAVE and logged on to bigfish-
bowl.com. She was in search of a friend—and a little

perspective. Bigwheels was online! She Insta-Messaged her keypal, hoping for some wiser-than-wise advice.

```
<Bigwheels>: hi there
<MadFinn>: what r u doing up???
  Ur online!
<Bigwheels>: Im bored w/homewk
<MadFinn>: HELP
<Bigwheels>: my teachers gave a
  really hard assignment
<MadFinn>: u work all the time
<Bigwheels>: IYSS
<MadFinn>: I don't mean in a bad
  way
<Bigwheels>: :>)
<MadFinn>: E2EG I wrote to ask
  advice about my parents
<Bigwheels>: what is wrong are they
  fighting
<MadFinn>: What will I do at
  Thanksgiving with Mom it's a big
  mess
<Bigwheels>: so don't have dinner
  w/Mom
<MadFinn>: but I will hurt her
  feelings if I don't
<Bigwheels>: no u won't, he is ur
  Dad she will understand that is
  her job right?
<MadFinn>: yeah but she'll be alone
```

```
<Bigwheels>: so don't WORRY
<MadFinn>: thanx for ur help
<Bigwheels>: what r u doing 4 ur
    project in school u never told me
<MadFinn>: top secret :-#
<Bigwheels>: LOL I have a project
    too BTW
<MadFinn>: really??
<Bigwheels>: I am writing a paper
    on Wampanoag Indians
<MadFinn>: have you ever been to an
    Indian reservation
<Bigwheels>: no but I have read a
    lot of bks
<MadFinn>: ZZZZZZZZZZZZZ
<Bigwheels>: r u bored?
<MadFinn>: no just sleepy THANKS
    sooo much 4 ur help
<Bigwheels>: sweet dreams
```

Madison logged off her computer and got under the covers. She pictured herself walking Phin and Sugar and Pavlov and Blinky and the rest of the dogs at the same time. She was pulling their leashes and laughing in the November breeze.

This wasn't just any dream.

It was a sweeter-than-sweet dream.

Chapter 7

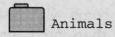 Animals

Rude Awakening: The not-so-dreamy thing about dreams is that you wake up.

I would rather spend more time with animals than anyone else these days.

Today I had a yucky quiz in math that I was 100 percent unprepared for! Grrrr. I should have studied harder and I wish I'd studied harder BUT I haven't had time. I have been going to the clinic more than once a week. I have to make time to study more. I don't want Mom to tell me that I have to stop going to the clinic!

Animals understand me way better than Mom and Dad do. Better than anyone.

Madison checked the clock in Mrs. Wing's classroom and then saved the update to her Animals file. It was a Friday afternoon, and Madison and Egg had made specific arrangements to discuss their extra-credit social studies project. Here. Now.

Where was he?

Madison glanced through the pile of books she'd borrowed from the library. They were stacked on the desk in front of her. One book was a retelling of the entire *Mayflower* journey with reenactment photos. Another book included a complete list of passengers. A Thanksgiving craft workbook even had instructions on making a diorama of the actual *Mayflower* ship.

Madison hoped Egg would come with inspired Thanksgiving ideas of his own that could complement hers. That's what being partners was all about.

Where was he?

By three-thirty, Egg still hadn't arrived—and Madison got a sinking feeling . . . like *she* was sunk. She bent down to grab her orange bag. As she sat up, she saw Egg walking into the computer lab, humming. *Humming?* He didn't seem the least bit concerned.

Madison glared.

"Hey," he said. Then he noticed the look on her face. "What's your problem?" he asked.

Madison stuffed the books into her bag.

"What is it?" Egg asked, taking a seat right next to her. "Is this because I'm late? What time is it? Three o'clock?"

Madison laughed a loud "HA!" and zipped her bag. "Yes, Egg, you are late," she said simply. "Later than late. It's three-thirty-five."

He grabbed her arm. "I lost track of time. Really."

"Well, I'm asking Mrs. Belden for a new partner," Madison said a little dramatically. "I'm asking tomorrow before class."

"Maddie, don't be like that." Egg hung his head. "I said I was sorry and you're dropping me?"

"How can you just forget that we're supposed to meet?"

"I'm so sorry, Maddie. I didn't forget completely."

Madison slung her book bag over her shoulder. "Well, I don't know. That's what you always say."

"Please. We'll do the project. I swear I won't ever be late again," Egg pleaded. "PLEASE?"

Madison put her bag back on the desk. "You mean it?" she said.

Egg nodded. "Cross my heart and stick a needle in my—"

"Yeah, yeah," she said. "But this really is the last time, Egg."

They took seats at the study table in the corner of Mrs. Wing's classroom and opened their notebooks. Madison yanked a small pile of *Mayflower* books and her notebook out of her orange bag.

Egg just sat there, rolling a pencil between his fingers.

He hadn't brought *any* backup materials.

"Wait a minute. You said you were bringing books." Madison tried to remain as calm as possible, but it was getting harder to do that.

"I never said that," Egg replied quickly, a little defensive.

"Yes, you did!" Madison said. "Egg, are you for real?"

Egg rolled his eyes. "I NEVER said that I was bringing any books. *Really.*"

"Thanks for nothing," Madison said under her breath. She stood up, put the books into her bag, and got ready to go for real this time.

Egg followed her out of the classroom into the hallway, but when she continued to ignore him, he turned on his heel and left.

A moment later, Fiona appeared at the lockers. She'd stayed late for indoor soccer practice.

"Weren't you meeting Egg after school?" Fiona asked. She always wanted the inside information on Egg's every move.

Right now the last person Madison wanted to talk about was Egg.

"I absolutely refuse to even say his name," Madison snapped, walking fast. Fiona hustled alongside her.

"What's wrong?" Fiona said. "Are you mad

about something? Are you mad at me?"

Madison stopped. She apologized by giving Fiona a quick hug. She hadn't meant to snap. Everything this Thanksgiving season was leaving Madison extra stressed.

"I'm sorry," Madison said. "I'm just feeling a little stressed out. How was soccer?"

"I got two goals in our scrimmage. I like indoor almost as much as outdoor soccer."

"You wanna walk home together?" Madison asked. She was ready to leave school—and the Egg incident—far behind her. It felt better walking home with a BFF like Fiona.

"Maddie, what's up with you and Dan?" Fiona asked. "I meant to ask you in school today. I see you guys together a lot lately."

Madison laughed. "Me and Dan? What do you mean?"

"Aimee and I were wondering if maybe you like him," Fiona said. "You've been hanging out with him at the clinic all week. And he's always talking about you, too."

"What? I don't like Dan *that* way," Madison said. "He's like a brother."

"He's not like MY brother." Fiona smiled. "But that's a good thing. . . ."

"How's your project coming along with Daisy for social studies?" Madison asked.

Fiona started babbling about how she and Daisy

were planning an amazing oral report on Sarah Hale. Sarah Hale was a woman who spoke up about the values of Thanksgiving during the Civil War. She helped convince President Abraham Lincoln to declare it a national holiday.

"I think I might dress up like Sarah Hale and Daisy might dress up like Abe Lincoln. We're not sure yet. It's been so much fun."

"You're kidding, right?" Madison moaned.

"And we're going to read part of Lincoln's Thanksgiving Proclamation from the war, too. I almost forgot that part," Fiona added.

Madison waved good-bye when they got to Fiona's house. Walking away, she buttoned up her coat a little because the air was crisp. It was hard to believe that November was more than halfway over.

Much to her surprise, Dad was waiting in the driveway, arms folded, when Madison wandered up.

"I know we said five," he said. "But I decided to come by early."

Madison looked at her watch. "An *hour* early?" she exclaimed.

"Why don't *you* run inside and get yourself together," he said softly. "I'll wait out here."

"Why don't you just come inside and wait, Daddy? Mom won't mind. She's so busy working, anyway."

Cautiously Dad approached the front door, trying to catch a glimpse of whatever might await him inside. He hardly ever came back into 5 Blueberry Street anymore. The Big D was like a big roadblock.

Mom opened the door wide. "Hello, there," she said. Phin squiggled out and went right for Dad, who leaned down to scratch the top of his coarse fur head.

"Hello, Frannie," Dad said in a soft voice.

Mom opened the door wider and tried to smile. She ushered him inside.

Even though Mom and Dad were acting perfectly nice to each other, Madison felt all awkward when they were in a room together. She never knew what to say.

"I have to change," Madison blurted.

Dad smiled. "Good idea."

"Yes, we like our child dressed when she leaves the house," Mom said.

Madison shrugged and dashed upstairs. She could hear Mom and Dad still chuckling moments afterward. It was strange to have them together in the house.

Quickly she ransacked her closet and pulled out her jean skirt with the purple patches and slipped into a pale yellow sweater and dark grape-colored clogs. She piled her hair into a purple clip and put on her moonstone earrings and moonstone ring, too. It was her special, lucky jewelry she'd gotten from Dad *and* Mom on separate occasions.

Phinnie was in the bedroom with Madison when

she got ready, but he didn't scurry over to her for kisses like he normally did. He lay on the floor, paws stretched out in front, eyes glazed over. He looked sad, Madison thought. She patted him on the head.

"Phinnie, what's the matter?" she asked.

He rolled over onto his back and sat up, nuzzling her free hand.

"I have to go, Phinnie," Madison said, standing herself. "I'm sorry. I have to go to dinner with Dad."

Phin lay back down in the exact same spot. Madison headed slowly back downstairs.

Mom and Dad were standing in the hallway, in almost the exact same positions they'd been in when Madison charged up the stairs. They were talking about the weather.

Madison reappeared, taking two steps at a time. "I'm ready to go!" She waved to Mom with a big grin. "See you later."

"Have a nice time, honey bear," Mom said, kissing Madison's cheek. "Good-bye, Jeffrey."

Dad said good-bye and then put his arm around Madison as they walked back to the car.

"You look very pretty this evening, Maddie," he said. As usual, he noticed when she was trying to wear something special. "Especially the earrings," he added, winking.

"Dad . . . why do you and Mom always argue?" Madison asked as they drove away.

Dad seemed confused. "Argue? What are you

talking about? We were talking about the Weather Channel."

"Well, it's just so weird when you guys are together now," Madison said.

"What are you talking about, Maddie? You know real arguing. That's what your mother and I used to do every day when we were—"

"I know," Madison cut him off. "But the thing is, Dad, it all feels the same to me. It's just too weird the way you talk—about the dumbest things in the world."

"We're just being polite, Maddie," Dad said. "Neither of us wants any more conflicts, believe me. You have to stop worrying. It has nothing to do with you."

Madison really wanted to believe him, but she just wasn't sure.

When they arrived at the restaurant, Stephanie met them in the lounge by a big grand piano. A man with a salt-and-pepper beard was growling some song about love.

"You look gorgeous!" Stephanie said, leaning down to give Madison a squeeze. "Love that purple skirt!"

Madison blushed a little and mumbled, "Thank you."

"Let's get our table, shall we, ladies?" Dad said, grinning. He had pep in his step as he led them over to the maitre d's station.

"This is an elegant restaurant, Jeff," Stephanie cooed during appetizers. She kept kissing his cheek, but Madison didn't mind as much as usual.

"Did you cut your hair?" Madison asked Stephanie. It was newly set into a bob of brown curls that rested just on her shoulders.

Stephanie threw back her head and all the curls bounced like on some shampoo commercial. "Do you like it?"

"You look gorgeous!" Madison teased. "You do. Really and truly."

As dinner passed, Madison felt very comfortable with Dad and Stephanie, more than she ever had before. She began to wonder about Thanksgiving. Maybe she should be spending it with *them*?

Madison wanted to find the right moment to bring up the subject, but then Dad started talking about Thanksgiving on his own. It was almost as if Madison had willed him to bring up the subject.

"Stephanie was asking me about our holiday plans, Madison," he said. "Now, I know that you are supposed to spend Thanksgiving with your mother."

"Yeah?" Madison said.

"Your dad and I wondered if maybe you'd spend it with us instead?" Stephanie asked.

She didn't know how to respond. Even though she'd been thinking about that very thing, she was taken by surprise. She awkwardly picked at a leaf of lettuce on her plate.

"I know we have to ask your mom and all that," Dad said. "And we're not asking you to choose or anything. I just got to thinking when we talked the other day. . . ."

"Would your mom mind?" Stephanie asked, trying to catch Madison's eye.

"What do you think, Maddie?" Dad asked.

Madison took a long pause before answering. "Well . . ." she started to say.

"No pressure," Dad said.

Stephanie spoke up. "He's right, Maddie. It's just a suggestion."

Madison took time to think about it. Dozens of thoughts whizzed through her mind, thoughts about Gramma Helen's busted hip and stuffing and cranberry sauce and what her best friends would be doing on Thanksgiving day—like Fiona's going to California and Aimee's hanging around the house, watching football.

How should she respond to Dad and Stephanie's question? She didn't know what to do. Say yes? The words wouldn't come.

Madison felt like such a turkey.

81

Chapter 8

 Important Decisions

Rude Awakening: To go or not to go? That is the question.

Tonight at dinner everything changed inside my head. I want to go with Dad and Stephanie, but I don't want to leave Mom all alone for Thanksgiving. What am I supposed to do?

Mom was waiting for me in the living room when I walked in tonight and I said something dorky about how I ate pork chops for dinner. That was all I could say.

And there she was sitting on the sofa, pulling out all our old Thanksgiving decorations, like this funny-looking cornucopia I made in kindergarten, and all I can think about was how sad I feel this year. How can I help decorate if I don't want to be here?

    I really and truly want to be with Dad.

    That's my decision. Better get to sleep.

The next morning at breakfast, Mom was *still* pulling out Thanksgiving decorations. Inside an old, ratty shopping bag she'd rediscovered orange and brown grosgrain ribbons and cardboard turkeys with tears along the edges and faded spots where they'd been used over the years.

"I pulled this down from the attic," Mom said, smiling. "Turkeys, pumpkins, you know the stuff we always put up when you were a kid."

Madison took a big swallow of cereal. "Mn-hhuhh," she said, chewing and nodding at the same time. "Mn-hhuhh, I know."

"Can you believe we still have this?" Mom said, pulling a plastic Pilgrim out of the bag. One foot was almost eaten off.

Phin got up on his hind legs when he saw the chewed-up Pilgrim and started to growl. Madison nearly spit out her mouthful of cereal.

"He's still mad at it?" she asked.

The plastic Pilgrim had been a decoration that was part of a Plymouth Rock set Dad bought when Phin was just a puppy. He had been afraid of the set at first, but then he'd munched on each plastic figure one by one. The Pilgrim Mom was holding was the only one rescued from the bunch.

83

"Grrrrrrrrrrrrrrrrrooooof!" Phinnie yapped again. "Rowrrororooo!"

Mom and Madison started to laugh. It felt so good to laugh.

"Phinnie," Madison said, grabbing for his collar. But he didn't pay attention. He scooted over and jumped onto Mom's lap instead.

"Hey, there, wiggler," Mom teased, scratching his head.

Madison slurped down the rest of her cereal. Putting up decorations was not what she wanted to do, but the idea of telling Mom the truth about Dad's invitation was something she wanted to do even *less*. What was there to celebrate? She thought of the devastated look on Mom's face when the Thanksgiving truth was revealed: Madison wanted to spend Thanksgiving with Dad. This decision was final . . . right?

Mom's work phone rang, and she went into the office. Phin followed her inside with his nose in the air. Normally he would have stayed close to Madison and begged for a cookie.

"Phinnie?" Madison watched the dog follow Mom. She sighed and went upstairs to open a brand-new file on her laptop.

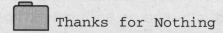 Thanks for Nothing

Rude Awakening: I've decided to quit Thanksgiving cold turkey.

First of all, I'm mad at Egg. And Mom
and Dad are about to get really mad at each
other because of me. Even Phin is moping
around! What do I have to be thankful for?

Thanksgiving should be way easier than
it is. Why do I feel a whole lot of thanks
for NOTHING? YUCK.

**As Madison hit SAVE, a brand new e-message
marked *priority* popped up on the screen. It had a
red exclamation point next to it, which meant "read
me now."**

From: Bigwheels
To: MadFinn
Subject: NOW IT'S UR TURN!
Date: Sat 18 Nov 9:25 AM
How is the animal shelter? What
kinds of dogs are there? Other
animals, too?

I have a funny story to tell. I
ALMOST CAME TO NEW YORK for
Thanksgiving! Instead of our big
family thing we almost decided to go
visit my other grandma on the East
Coast. What if we came there? I
wonder if you and I would ever be
able to meet F2F. My mom says
someday we will. She knows all about
you BTW. Does ur mom know about me?

It's so funny b/c usually you write
and say I miss you b/c I am the
lame one who hasn't e-mailed. But
now it's me who misses you like
you're a new part of my family or
something.

Where r u?

Yours till the autumn leaves,

Bigwheels

P.S. Whatever happened to your
crush? Write back soon. I'm waiting.

Since the note had just been sent, Madison typed
back an Insta-Message quickly, hoping to catch her
buddy online. "Bigwheels, where are you?" she
asked aloud, typing as fast as her fingers would go.
She scanned the alphabetical list of names in the
bigfishbowl.com waiting room.

```
Amazing23
andrew_mac
AngelFace
Bethiscool
BryanSarah
Email_BOY
f2f2f2f2f
Jessica_01
LittleKevin
MARKIEhockey
```

Nowhere!

Madison's keypal had vanished as quickly as she'd arrived. Madison reread Bigwheels's e-mail and thought about everything she'd said. Then she went back to the Thanks for Nothing file and reread everything *she'd* said.

There had to be a better way to see things.

Madison just didn't know where to look.

She clicked back to Bigwheels's original e-mail and punched REPLY.

```
From: MadFinn
To: Bigwheels
Subject: Re: NOW IT'S UR TURN!
Date: Sat 18 Nov 10:06 AM
```
I can't believe you aren't coming to NY. I wonder if we ever really will meet. That is so weird. I wish sometimes that you lived next door.

The social studies project is better, I guess. My partner isn't taking it as seriously as me, but I think we'll be ok. I wish my family felt more ok, though. What is your family really like? And I mean all the time and not just on Thanksgiving. You know how sometimes people act so different during the holidays? At least my family does. What do you talk about with your family?

BTW my volunteering @ the clinic is awesome. I am soooo close already to this one dog I named Sugar. She is a mixed breed and very friendly. It tickles when she gives me kisses on the hand.

Please write again soon.

Yours till the pork chops (because I had those for dinner last night),

MadFinn

p.s. I still think my crush likes this other girl who happens to be my enemy @ school. I told you that, right? I don't know for sure. Bye!

Late on Saturday afternoon, after walking Phin around the block and working for an hour on a school essay, Madison headed over to the animal shelter and clinic with Mom.

The sky was beginning to cloud up like rain was on the way. Madison brought her raincoat and umbrella just in case. She was always prepared for bad weather, even drizzle. Madison liked to be prepared for as many things as possible.

"I'll pick you up later on," Mom said before driving off. "In a couple of hours, okay?"

"Thanks, Mom," Madison said. "See you later."

Eileen was sitting at the front desk of the clinic with a juice bottle and an empty stare. She seemed tired today, but her shirt read I'M FELINE GREAT! It had an image of a giant, fluffy gray cat and a logo for the National Pet Adoption Service.

Madison walked up to the counter and grabbed the visitor and volunteer sign-in sheet. Dan's name was signed for the morning, which meant he was around somewhere. He was probably in the back, taking care of Sugar the schnoodle or some other pup. She went back to search for him

"Madison," Eileen called after her. "I have to check in with Dr. Wing. Would you please go in back and help Mr. Wollensky with the cages?"

Madison started to walk away.

"Don't forget, it's the weekend," Eileen called after her. "So we don't have many appointments. It should be quiet around here. We just need to feed everyone. I'll be back in a jiffy."

As Eileen hustled out a side door, Madison looked for Mr. Wollensky and Sugar.

She glanced at the cages of animals lined against the wall. The dogs stared back. All of a sudden one howled. Then *all* the dogs started howling in unison.

"Hey!" Madison called out to them. "Shhh! Stop that!"

Then they howled a little louder—even Sugar.

Mr. Wollensky started to laugh. "They have something important to say, yes?"

"I wish they would stop."

Madison begged the animals, "Shhh! Please? Pretty please?" As if they understood a single word she was saying!

"HOWWWWWWWOOOOOOOOOO," Sugar wailed at the fluorescent light on the ceiling. She wouldn't stop baying.

Mr. Wollensky decided a feeding was probably in order. Maybe one cup each of Happy-Gro Kibble would quiet them? Madison tried to help him by grabbing an oversized container of food from the shelf. She started to measure the kibble out very, very slowly until—

CRASH!

The giant bag of dog food split open and Kibble went streaming all over the floor. Madison stared as kibble rolled under counters and into corners of the room. She threw her hands up with despair.

Mr. Wollensky laughed again. "Oh, my! What mess!"

The dogs kept right on howling.

"Is everything okay in here?" A nurse from the front desk came back to the kennel area. She looked worried.

Mr. Wollensky had everything under control in moments. The dogs stopped howling, too, and started eating. "Everything good," he said, waving the nurse back to the front. "We under control."

Madison collapsed onto a nearby chair and put

her head in her hands. "That was a close call," she told herself. Suddenly she felt a wet nose on her hand.

"You have a friend who wants to play," Mr. Wollensky said, handing Sugar's leash to Madison.

Sugar *was* a new friend, Madison thought. Sugar prodded Madison with her paw like she wanted to be picked up.

"What are you doing?" Madison asked, petting the dog's wiry-haired head. Madison stood up and stepped back to play. Unfortunately, she slipped right down, losing her balance on loose kibble that was still on the floor.

PLUNK!

Madison sat there on the floor in a kibble dust daze, a squiggling, wiggling schnoodle jumping on top.

Mr. Wollensky laughed at the sight of her.

"Hey, Mad-i-son!" Dan yelled, coming back into the kennel room. "What are you doing on the floor?"

"Madison! Is everything okay?" Eileen asked, walking in behind him. "Mr. Wollensky, what happened here?"

"She's crying," Dan said to his mom.

But of course Madison wasn't *crying*. Madison was laughing—hard. Sugar's dog kisses *really* tickled.

"We are fine now," Mr. Wollensky said to Eileen. "Madison and I are cleaning up."

Madison smiled at Mr. Wollensky.

"Your mom just called," Eileen said. "She won't be back in time to pick you up, so I'll be giving you a ride home."

But Eileen would do better than just drive Madison home. She offered to stop off at Freeze Palace for ice cream on the way.

While Eileen dashed to the supermarket, Madison and Dan waited outside Freeze Palace. They ate their ice cream on the curb.

"It's cold out today," Madison said.

"There is *never* a bad time for ice cream!" Dan laughed.

Madison walked on the curb like it was a balance beam. Dan tried, too, but he lost his balance. His ice cream scoop plopped into the gutter.

"Aw, no!" Dan cried, looking at his empty cone. "Good-bye, chocolate chips."

A man was walking a giant sheepdog in front of the store.

"Nice dog," Dan said to the owner as he bent down to pet it. When Madison petted the dog, he slobbered all over her arm.

"Look out!" Dan cried. He pointed to her opposite hand, but it was too late. All the dog petting had Madison off balance, too. And now her ice cream had dropped off, too.

"Whoopsie," she said, giggling.

Dan shook his head. "Way to go."

The sheepdog was happy about the accident, however. He was licking the ice cream off the ground.

Madison and Dan laughed. Madison was glad she and Dan were friends.

his ergroup was happy about the project, however. He was in and the ice cream off the bounce?

Madison and Diaz learned. Madison was also in and Parr's the friend

Chapter 9

Sunday morning Madison got up earlier than usual for a weekend. She had the social studies project on the brain. Today she and Egg had to finish their extra-credit project. *Finally.*

Madison had been collecting a file and notebook of project ideas for almost a week. She'd found a list on the Web that showed the names of all 104 *Mayflower* passengers from 1620. She had read up about storms at sea and sickness on the plantation. There was a separate list of crew members and ship passengers, some of whom had survived and others who had perished.

After eating breakfast, Mom drove Madison over to the Diaz house. It had been Madison's idea to meet there. That way Egg wouldn't be late and he'd *definitely* show up.

When Madison rang the doorbell, it took a moment for anyone to answer. She later found Egg's grandmother, Abuela; his aunt, Tía Ana; his older sister, Mariah; and his mom sitting in the kitchen, reading the paper and talking.

Egg's house was different than Madison's in so many ways. It was smaller in size, but his place was packed with people.

"Hola! Cómo estás?" Señora Diaz chirped when Madison arrived. She poured a tall glass of juice. "Walter *está arriba.*"

Señora Diaz taught Spanish at Far Hills Junior High and always tried to get Madison to practice her Spanish.

"Por favor, siéntate!" Abuela said to Madison, asking her to sit. Abuela had known Madison ever since she had been a little girl. Madison always loved to hear her tell stories.

"Buenos días, Abuela," Madison said, taking a seat. She searched her mind for the right Spanish words.

"Qué linda eres!" Abuela cried. Madison had no idea what she had said. Just then Egg came into the kitchen.

"What did she say?" Madison giggled.

"Abuela says you're pretty," Egg said.

Madison smiled. "Oh." She could tell that just saying those words made Egg a little bit embarrassed.

"*Cómo está escuela?*" Abuela asked Madison. She wanted to hear about school.

"Come on, Abuela, Madison and I have to go," Egg said, wanting to leave the kitchen.

Madison ate a small cookie from a basket on the table and racked her brain for a way to say that it was good. The only phrase she could remember was, "*Dónde está la policía?*" from last week's Spanish class. But no one wanted to find the police, so she said nothing. She and Egg went to his room to practice the extra-credit presentation.

In a terrarium near a large window, Gato puffed out his pink lizard throat as if to say hello. Egg's pet gecko, Gato, was named for the word *cat* in Spanish. Madison always thought it was funny that Egg would name one animal after another. She liked the fact that he had an unusual pet, though.

"So let me show you what I've got up on the computer," Egg said, punching a few keys. "I've been working on this all weekend."

"Whoa." Madison's jaw dropped as the screen came into focus.

Egg had taken the flat model of the *Mayflower* and turned it into a three-dimensional object on-screen. Madison was thrilled. He downloaded the images so they could put them into a special presentation for class.

"Wow, you can see all the rooms inside," she said, admiring it. "Do you think this should be our

96

whole presentation? I thought we could hand out fact sheets, too. It's always good to pass around something."

"Oh," Egg said. "You think so?"

Madison let him scan through a few more pages.

"See?" Egg pointed to the page. "It has three main masts and a poop deck that's very high up. The middle part of the ship is curved really low into the water."

Madison glanced at the computer screen and cross-referenced it with other reading materials on the *Mayflower* she brought along.

"It says here that the ship was called a 'wet ship' because it was mostly in the water. I didn't know that, did you?" Madison asked.

"Huh?" Egg was too busy moving objects around on-screen to be paying any kind of real attention to what Madison was saying.

"Did you know that the place where passengers slept was called the 'tween decks?" Madison asked. "Cool, huh?"

For twenty minutes, Egg and Madison pored through books and searched on the Internet for more ideas on what to write about.

"Maybe we can make a real ship to show in class," Madison said.

"That would be so lame," Egg whined. He thought only something on the computer would knock everyone's socks off.

"What if we brought materials and everyone could watch the computer and then make their own *Mayflower*?" Madison suggested. "Then we'd have both."

"You want this to be an arts-and-crafts project?" he asked. "Maddie, we need to be high-tech. Paste is for first graders."

"No, no," Madison said. She shook her head no. "What about the Pilgrims? They weren't high-tech." Madison wanted to say that sometimes she *liked* making collages and crafts and what was wrong with that?

"Fine, we can make a poster, too," Egg finally agreed.

But they were interrupted all of a sudden.

"WALTER!" Egg's mother's voice bellowed from the other room. "You have another guest!"

Egg ran down the stairs.

Madison heard Egg greet Drew. She could hear Drew explain that he'd just been working on his social studies project over at Ivy Daly's house. She cringed at the thought.

Drew came into Egg's bedroom and flopped onto a chair. "Hey, Maddie, what's up?"

"Um . . . Egg?" Madison asked. "What about our meeting? We just started. Why is Drew here?"

"Well, I guess we'll have to finish up later," Egg said.

"Huh? Later?" Madison felt a little knot of anger work its way up her throat. "What do you mean, 'later'?" she asked. "Can't *Drew* come back *later*?"

"Can't we just finish tomorrow?" Egg asked.

Drew didn't say much of anything.

"What about today, Egg? We've been planning this for almost a week," Madison said. "You promised."

Drew interrupted. "Hey, I can come over another time. You guys are working on the extra-credit thing."

"Nah, we were mostly done," Egg said.

The rising anger knot was now lodged in Madison's throat. She could feel her whole body flush, like when she got embarrassed—only worse.

"Egg, you promised," she repeated.

She wanted to run.

"I promised not to forget any more meetings. This isn't forgetting. It isn't the same thing."

"Fine, then I guess I'll go," Madison said abruptly. She quickly gathered her books and stuffed loose papers into her orange messenger's bag.

"Why don't you stay and play Wrestle Showdown on the computer? You wanna?" Egg asked. "We can do team play since there's three of us."

"No," she said firmly. "E-mail me later. We don't have a lot of time to work on it anymore."

"I know, I know," Egg said, already a little distracted. He was loading the wrestling computer game and setting up the joysticks.

"Hey, Maddie," Drew asked her on the way out. "What's the deal with you and Dan?"

"Huh?" Madison stopped short. She made a face. "What are you talking about?"

"Ivy was just saying some stuff when I was at her house. . ." Drew said.

"Saying *what*?" Madison wrinkled her nose.

"Nothing. Forget I said it," Drew said.

Madison had no idea what Drew was talking about. She scurried out, passing by the kitchen where Abuela, Señora Diaz, and Tía Ana sipped coffees.

"Madison, you just got here! Where is Walter?" Señora Diaz called out.

"Egg is with Drew. We're going to finish later," Madison explained. She smiled at Egg's family. "See you later. I mean, *adiós*."

"*Adiós!*" Egg's grandmother cried.

Madison lifted the bag of *Mayflower* books over her shoulder and walked toward home. It weighed more than usual, so she took slower steps. There was no big rush to get anywhere right now.

As her house came into view, Madison squinted. Dad's car was in the driveway, which seemed strange, since she wasn't meeting him for dinner or any special occasion.

Madison crept toward the front porch entrance. She'd sneak up the stoop and take them by surprise. What were they saying? The living-room window was cracked open, so Madison could hear voices clearly on the porch without being seen by anyone. She crouched down and listened to Mom and Dad talking. This time, they weren't just chatting about the weather.

Mom and Dad were discussing Thanksgiving. Mom was telling Dad how she wanted to let Madison go with him and Stephanie, since that seemed to be what Madison wanted. Madison listened real close.

She could not believe her ears.

Madison couldn't remember a recent time when they'd ever been this nice while talking about the Big D and Madison—or any subject, for that matter.

"What will you do for the holiday, then?" Dad asked Mom. "I don't think you should have to be alone, Frannie."

Mom quickly said that it didn't matter and the most important thing was for Madison to be happy. Eventually Dad agreed with reluctance.

"We'll leave it up to Madison," he said. "She can decide what *she* wants for Thanksgiving."

Suddenly, from the other side of the porch, Phinnie appeared. Madison smiled at him from afar and then he came over, wiggling. Unfortunately, he wiggled over while making the loudest snorts ever. Madison tried to move backward, but *then* she lost her balance.

The weight shifted in Madison's bag, and the heaviness of all those books sent her toppling. It was her second fall in two days! Madison felt like Queen of the Klutzes.

Phin ran away. And then Dad heard. He leaned into the screen to see Madison lying on the porch.

"Maddie?" he cried out through the screen. "What are you doing out there?"

Madison sat up. "Just hanging out, Dad. What are you doing in there?"

Mom had made her way outside by then. She extended a hand to pull her daughter upright again. She helped Madison pick up her bag, too.

"Hi, Mom," Madison said softly. "What's going on?"

Mom crossed her arms. "Why don't you come inside so we can all talk."

All week, Maddie had worked herself up into a tizzy about the change in family plans for the holiday. But now Madison knew Thanksgiving would *really* never be the same again. Seventh grade was bringing big changes not only at school. It was making bigger-than-big changes at home.

And Madison was right smack-dab in the middle of it all.

Chapter 10

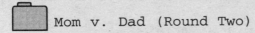 Mom v. Dad (Round Two)

Two weird things about dealing with parents who have had the Big D:

1. When they ask, "What do YOU want?" something is wrong. They don't know what to do. It's better to play dumb.
2. Do not eavesdrop while kneeling (very painful).

Mom and Dad expect ME to decide about Thanksgiving? It seems totally unfair, since they're the grown-ups and I'm the kid. This is like a tug-of-war and I never liked stupid tug-of-war! At second-grade field day we played that game and I fell in the mud.

My head hurts just thinking about all this stuff.

Bigfishbowl.com was busy on Sunday night. Madison went online to find her keypal or maybe even her BFFs. Bigwheels would have something encouraging to say. But Madison ended up in the middle of a three-way chat with Aimee and Fiona instead.

<MadFinn>: AIMEE!!!!!!
<BalletGrl>: I found this wicked
    cool ballet chat room I've been
    here like 2 hrs.
<MadFinn>: is Fiona online 2?
<Wetwinz>: hi
<MadFinn>: EGG is sooooooo lame you
    guys
<BalletGrl>: what now
<MadFinn>:   :-< he blew me off
<Wetwinz>: ur ss project? I thought
    u met @ his house
<BalletGrl>: WAI
<Wetwinz>: u guys always say stuff
    about him stop!
<MadFinn>: what did u do today
<Wetwinz>: Dad made the plane
    reservations for Thanksgiving.
    We're leaving a day early so I
    get to miss school that Wed.
    before. California here I come.
<BalletGrl>: you are so lucky
<MadFinn>: I am spending it w/Dad
    now

104

```
<BalletGrl>: ???????
<MadFinn>: and Stephanie. Mom said I
  could.
<Wetwinz>: that's kewl
<MadFinn>: is it weird to leave Mom
  alone though?
<BalletGrl>: Yup I think so YES
<Wetwinz>: maybe
<MadFinn>: I wanna DTRT
<Wetwinz>: Do the right thing! yeah
<BalletGrl>: I have to finish
  homework I've been on the
  computer for a long time bye!
<Wetwinz>: Daisy and I finished our
  extra credit we're doing Pilgrims
<MadFinn>: u guys what should I
  do????
<BalletGrl>: NOTHING ha ha ha ha ha
<BalletGrl>: <k>
<Wetwinz>: peace out
```

Before Madison logged off, her mailbox blinked
with three messages.

FROM	SUBJECT
✉ GoGramma	RECIPES
✉ Eggaway	Project
✉ Dantheman	SUGAR

First Madison saw a note with attachments from
Gramma Helen in Chicago.

From: GoGramma
To: MadFinn
Subject: RECIPES
Date: Sun 19 Nov 5:28 PM

Hello, there. I miss you very much.
But your aunt is taking very good
care of me here.

Since you will be spending
Thanksgiving with your mother, I
thought you might like to make
some of my favorite recipes for
dinner.

Your uncle here showed me how to
attach a file to this message, so I
hope that works. Write again and
tell me all about your other
classes.

The volunteering job sounds like
fun, too.

Love, Gramma

<<Attachment: FruitTerrine.doc>>
<<Attachment: GrammaStuffing.doc>>
<<Attachment: SweetPotatoPie.doc>>

The second e-mail was from Egg.

From: Eggaway
To: MadFinn
Subject: Project
Date: Sun 19 Nov 5:33 PM

U R gonna be so psyched. I added
these noises to the *Mayflower*
presentation. Now when you put the
mouse on the ship, you can hear
seagulls and water noises and surf.
Mariah helped out. Hope that's OK.
BFN.

**The final message was from Dan Ginsburg, and
he'd marked it high priority.**

Priority: HIGH
From: Dantheman
To: MadFinn
Subject: SUGAR
Date: Sun 19 Nov 6:09 PM

My mom just told me that Sugar was
sick and might need surgery. Will
you be coming to the clinic
tomorrow? I know u said u might
show up. I think Sugar would like
to see a friend. C U in school.

**Sugar the schnoodle was sick? The pooch was
alone in the world, without a family to love and
protect her. Madison knew Dr. Wing was the best**

veterinarian in Far Hills, but Madison was sadder than sad about Sugar.

She grabbed her math notebook and plopped down in her plastic purple chair. She wanted to catch up on studying so she'd be able to go to the clinic tomorrow after school. Sugar would need her.

Monday morning Madison was still feeling a little sad. She looked everywhere to find Dan before homeroom, but the halls were too busy to track him down. Science class at the end of the day couldn't come soon enough. She'd see Dan there.

The science lab room was abuzz with chatter. Mr. Danehy wasn't always great at keeping order in the classroom.

Madison heard the whispers but didn't think much of it at first. Then she looked up to find an entire row of kids staring. *Staring* right at her.

Shifting in her chair, Madison tried to act casual. But people were still staring, and she didn't know why.

"Hey, Finnster," Hart said. He was sitting a stool away. "What's the deal?"

Madison was *utterly* perplexed. "The *deal*?"

But Hart didn't answer. This time, it was her lab partner, Poison Ivy Daly, who spoke up.

"Everyone says you and Dan Ginsburg are going out."

"What?" Madison blurted. "Everyone *who*?"

"You know." Ivy snapped her gum. *"Everyone."*

"You're kidding, right?" Madison said. But "everyone" was still staring. And now everyone was talking.

Mr. Danehy smacked his palm on the chalkboard at the front of the room.

"Enough! Silence!" he commanded.

Everyone hushed, even Madison. She was squirming in her seat.

Ivy started to laugh. Then her drones, Rose and Joan, laughed.

Mr. Danehy waved his hand in the air. "Just what is so funny, Miss Daly?"

Ivy sucked her laughs back in. "Nothing, Mr. Danehy."

Madison bowed her head and made a wish that by some magic scientific power, Mr. Danehy would force Ivy out of her chair and out into the hallway.

She looked around.

Had everyone heard Ivy's rumor?

Madison's stomach lurched. Had Hart Jones even heard the gossip? What did her crush think?

"What's the matter, Madison?" Ivy taunted in a low voice from where she was sitting. "You didn't think anyone saw you on your ice cream date? I saw you and your boyfriend, Dan."

Madison looked around the room again. Dan was across the room. He smiled in her direction.

"He's not my boyfriend," Madison snapped. Her

face was red-hot. Embarrassment and anger boiled inside like lava ready to burst. "He's my FRIEND," she said firmly, glaring at Ivy. "Not that YOU know anything about having a real friend."

Ivy didn't answer. She just tossed her head. "Don't get so huffy, Madison."

After class, Madison rushed out the door. She went directly to Mrs. Wing's classroom, where she was supposed to meet Egg.

"Hi," Madison said quietly. "Egg, can I ask you something?"

"Look at *this*!" he showed Madison some of the extra-special effects he'd added to the computer. The cursor was a Pilgrim hat.

"Egg . . . did you hear anything weird lately? About me?" Madison asked.

"Huh? What?" Egg shook his head.

Madison shrugged. "Nothing. I just heard this rumor in science class and . . . well . . . about me and Dan. . . ."

Egg laughed out loud. "Are you joking?"

"So you didn't hear Ivy Daly spreading any rumors?" Madison asked a second time, just to be sure.

"Ivy Daly is a dork," Egg said. "Don't worry about it. No one ever believes her, anyway."

Madison smiled. "Thanks, Egg. I'm really sorry for being upset."

"That's okay," Egg said. "But before we practice, tell me what are we going to say again? You're way better than me at presenting."

The next half hour they reviewed facts and planned who would say what during the presentation. Then they went upstairs to the media center. The librarian, Mr. Books, let Egg print out a few pages with the color laser printer. He'd downloaded pictures of cartoon Pilgrims, and Madison and Egg glued the pictures on their poster of the *Mayflower*.

Their run-through went *perfectly*.

Madison felt very thankful to have Egg as her friend—and social studies partner.

She started a brand-new file when she got home.

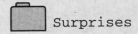 Surprises

Surprises can be awful. Like the Dan gossip. How would Ivy have seen me and Dan having an ice cream cone? But surprises can be good.
1. After a week of yucky work, Egg turned up to meet me and was 100 percent prepared. Our presentation is going to be the BEST. He has special effects on the computer. He's so good at that stuff. He even added MUSIC! We worked on the construction of the paper Mayflower together. I did lots of the work on that—even added glitter glue even if it's not a real Pilgrim kind of thing.

2. Sugar doesn't need surgery! Dan called
   to tell me that she is just going
   through shock or something after being
   rescued. I can't wait to see her this
   week.

   Any day now I'm expecting some kind of a
surprise from Mom and Dad. They are mostly
acting cool around me, but I don't know.
How do they really feel about me going with
Dad? Am I hurting Mom's feelings by picking
him? Are they going to start all that
arguing again?
   There is still something not right about
the whole thing. Life after the big D is
one surprise I can never seem to figure
out.

Chapter 11

When Madison's alarm went off, she stayed under the covers. Her insides felt fluttery, like she was on a ride at the amusement park. She definitely didn't want to risk eating breakfast.

Today were the extra-credit presentations.

She hoped that Egg wouldn't be late . . . or forget. She wondered if Egg was nervous right now, too.

"It's almost eight!" Mom yelled from downstairs. "You better be out of that bed!"

Madison leaped up. "Drat! Drat!"

Now she was *late*.

Rushing around wasn't the way Madison had hoped to spend the morning before her presentation. But here she was, frantically pulling on socks and sneakers and combing her hair. Even more ominous was the rain that started to pour outside. She tied her hair back into a ponytail to avoid a bad case of the frizzies.

"You're going to do fine," Mom reassured her. "I'll drive you over to school today. The rain looks very bad."

The car ride made Madison a little queasy. The orange juice Mom had made her drink was sloshing inside her empty tummy. Mom told her to take deep breaths and to relax.

Madison arrived at school a little damp, but on time. But Egg wasn't there.

All through homeroom, Madison watched the door. But no Egg.

Egg still hadn't appeared at the end of homeroom. Madison thought maybe he would go straight to Mrs. Belden's classroom.

Madison sat down next to Fiona and Daisy. They looked so funny because they had dressed up in "period" costumes. Daisy wore a ratty-looking black beard and a cardboard top hat she'd obviously stapled together quickly with black construction paper. Fiona wore her hair in two braids on either side of her head.

"So you guys are Abe Lincoln and *who*?" Aimee asked them.

"You'll see," Fiona said, acting mysterious. "I can't believe you forgot already. I told you last week."

"What is the soccer ball for?" Ben the brainiac asked.

"Oh," Daisy said. "The ball is just from morning practice. I forgot to put it into my locker."

"Ohhhh," Ben rolled his eyes.

"What's your report on?" Daisy asked Ben and Aimee.

"We're doing a report on Native Americans," Ben said.

"Wampanoog," Aimee added.

"Wampanoag," he corrected her. "Sounds like frog. You better get it right in class."

Aimee laughed. "You better not tell me what to do, Ben." She tapped his shoulder and tossed her hair a little.

Ben turned pink. "Uh-huh."

Madison chuckled. Maybe Aimee really did have a crush on Ben.

Once more, Madison searched the halls for Egg, but he was still nowhere to be seen.

Madison's stomach was doing super-duper loop de loops. In thirty seconds the bell was going to ring. *Where was Egg?*

Madison knew that Mrs. Belden always shut the door tight and didn't approve of latecomers. Her skin felt all clammy with the anticipation. First she had been rushing. Now she was waiting.

"Are you okay?" Poison Ivy said to Madison. "You look a little sick. Is that sweat?"

Madison wiped her brow with one sleeve and pursed her lips. "Did you say something?" she said to Ivy. Madison was in no mood for Ivy's poisonous comments today.

Ivy turned back to Drew. "What's her problem?" she asked him. But Drew didn't say a word.

Madison looked at the clock. "Do you know where Egg is?" she whispered to Drew.

"No, I dunno where he is."

Brrrrrrring!

"Looks like someone has a problem," Ivy taunted. Her drones giggled from a few rows back.

Madison shot Ivy a glare. "Looks like you're the one with a problem, Ivy," she whispered back to her enemy.

Drew laughed. Ivy was speechless.

Madison watched the classroom door. Mrs. Belden was about to close it. She had her fingers on the knob, even. But then Egg appeared!

Mrs. Belden grinned and motioned Madison over.

"What happened to you?" Madison whispered to Egg. He pulled her aside, and Madison expected to hear a long list of reasons why Egg was later than late. She expected to hear: "The entire project got mangled and I was trying to re-sort it on my computer," or, "I deleted the *Mayflower* program by mistake," or, "I'm sick as a dog and I don't want to do this."

But that wasn't what Egg said at all.

"I'm sorry, Maddie. I was just nervous. I wanted to check the whole program again just to make sure it worked, so I went up to the media center and . . ."

"Forget about it," Madison said. "We're good to go."

Madison could feel her heart beating. For whatever reason, the simple extra-credit report had become all-important for Madison. This was about more than the *Mayflower* and grades. This was about her and Egg working together.

"Hey, Maddie," Egg whispered. "I gotta show you something."

Egg showed her the giant, color poster of the *Mayflower* they had made together. Egg had pasted more smaller pictures and labels onto the different areas Madison had laid out. She'd talked about adding more detail, but they hadn't had enough time.

"What is THAT?" Madison asked.

"I added more stuff, like you wanted."

"Wow." Madison was stunned. She hadn't even known he was paying attention to anything she'd said the whole time they'd been working together on the project. "You did all that last night?"

"I know you wanted this to be really special. Besides, my sister helped me."

Madison was happier than happy. "It is so cool."

"I think you were right about having something to pass around and show in class. And I have my laptop inside all ready for the PowerPoint," Egg said.

Mrs. Belden stuck her head out into the hallway. "Why don't you two go first so you can pass out your materials and then sit down to watch the others."

Egg and Madison walked into the class with the homemade *and* computerized *Mayflower*s. Ivy was staring. Rose was staring. Drew was staring. *Everyone* had all eyes on them. Going first was the worst. Madison could feel her heart thump. But this kind of staring was different than in science class. This was the good kind. Egg handed out the fact sheets Madison had typed up.

"Should I start?" she nervously asked.

Mrs. Belden nodded.

Madison's dad told her she should begin the presentation with a joke. Madison knew the perfect one.

"If April showers bring May flowers, what do *May flowers* bring?"

"Pilgrims!" Dan shouted from the back.

"Like we don't all know that joke already." Ivy grunted. "Come on."

"Miss Daly, that is unnecessary," Mrs. Belden said.

Ivy crossed her legs with a huff. "Sorry."

Madison continued. "Egg and I have created a model of the *Mayflower*, a ship that brought the Pilgrims to the New World. We found out some interesting facts about the *Mayflower*."

"There were lots of trading ships at the time that were also called the *Mayflower*," Egg said.

"And this ship wasn't meant to carry passengers," Madison added. "Originally. But people squeezed into the area with livestock and guns in between decks."

Everyone gathered around the computer while Egg and Madison explained. It took a little longer than five minutes, but Mrs. Belden seemed very impressed.

"That was an excellent example of teamwork," she told the class. "You two get a gold star for organization."

Madison and Egg beamed. They had been greater-than-great partners, better than expected. Madison had worried for nothing. Egg had come through! After some polite applause, they sat down on the side of the room. Aimee leaned over and whispered, "Way to go." Fiona smiled at Madison, too. She was proud.

Fiona and Daisy presented next. Unfortunately, their extra-credit project had a few loose ends—and nothing seemed to work out right. Fiona's costume ripped, Daisy lost her place *six* times while reading the Thanksgiving Proclamation, and they sometimes talked so quickly that no one could understand a single word.

But Mrs. Belden was generous with her compliments. "Very creative, girls," she said when they sat down again. "I like the costumes and the narration of Sarah Hale, Fiona."

Fiona sank into her seat again, eyes on the floor.

Aimee and Ben gave the most embarrassing presentation of the morning. Aimee looked a little lost, which was very unlike the dancing, showy presenter she could be. Madison wondered if maybe, just maybe, Aimee's crushing on Ben was the reason. Madison was getting pretty good at crush detecting. She'd never seen Aimee so distracted by someone.

Mrs. Belden had to cut off Ben when he talked for too long about Samoset and Squanto, the Native Americans who had helped the Pilgrims in Plymouth. Aimee stood by, flashing pictures and maps.

"Well done," Mrs. Belden interrupted. "I think we all agree that was quite a history lesson, Ben and Aimee."

As soon as they were finished, Poison Ivy and Drew were called up to present their extra credit. Both Drew and Ivy were dressed like Pilgrims. Ivy passed around a basket with corn bread in it and talked about how women Pilgrims had no say but did all the work. She even claimed to be a direct descendant of Pilgrims on the *Mayflower*.

"You never told me that," Drew suddenly blurted.

"Shhh," Ivy hissed, and kept right on talking.

Mrs. Belden interrupted. "Is this true, Ivy? That's a big thing."

"Ummm . . . well . . . not really. But aren't we all related? I mean, what's the big deal?"

The class got very quiet. Ivy shifted from foot to foot. Drew had a blank stare on his face.

Mrs. Belden spoke up. "Please continue, Ivy."

But she didn't say a word. Poison Ivy Daly looked like she was about to hyperventilate.

Some kid in the back of the classroom moved, and his chair squeaked. That's when Drew started to laugh. It wasn't a teeny giggle, but a big snorting laugh. And it was supercontagious.

Even Mrs. Belden had to cover her mouth so she wouldn't laugh.

Ivy glanced around the room. "May I please be excused?" she asked, and ran out into the hall.

A few moments later, Ivy returned to class with Mrs. Belden. She looked like she was sniffling, but her lip gloss looked perfect. When Ivy walked past Madison to go back to her seat, Madison couldn't help but smile a little. It served her right for starting a rumor about her and Dan. Being in the spotlight wasn't always so great—even for Ivy Daly.

Then Dan and Hart were the next ones up to present.

Once they reached the front of the classroom, both boys slipped trash bags over their bodies with a cutout hole for their heads. The bags had colored paper feathers, and they each wore backward base-ball caps with more feathers taped to the brims.

"Today we would like to do our extra-credit project to a song," Hart joked.

Everyone snickered.

"Yeah," Dan continued. "Called 'The Turkey Pokey.'"

Everyone laughed out LOUD.

"You put your right wing in, you put your left wing out, you do the turkey pokey and you turn yourself around." It was sung to the tune of the regular "Hokey Pokey." Mrs. Belden was smiling to herself the whole time the boys were singing.

The turkey getup was Dan's idea. He wanted to celebrate the bird that—in his words—"got wicked gypped every Thanksgiving." Dan had a true animal-lover side to his personality. Meanwhile Hart decided it would be funny to dress up and "talk turkey," too. They presented random facts about turkey symbolism and turkeys from other cultures and explained how Native Americans turned turkey feathers into beautiful cloaks.

"This was a highly original presentation, boys," Mrs. Belden said as the bell rang. Extra credit had been a lot more fun than anyone expected.

That night, Madison sent Egg an e-mail message.

```
From: MadFinn
To: Eggaway
Subject: MAYFLOWER PRESENTATION
Date: Tues 21 Nov 4:52 PM
We had the best presentation. You
are so awesome and I am soooooo
sorry for not believing we could do
```

it. Thanks 4 all ur work, Egg. BTW:
my mom says she wants to see it
sometime, so maybe you can come
over? I hope we r still good
friends. TTFN. <:>== (p.s. That's a
symbol for a turkey ha ha!!)

Madison noticed she had another e-mail in the box. It was from Dad, and he'd sent it to Stephanie, too. It looked serious.

From: JeffFinn
To: MadFinn
Cc: Stephie8
Subject: Thanksgiving Feast
Date: Tues 21 Nov 5:02 PM
Maddie, I wanted to call to talk to
you, but the phone has been busy,
so I sent this instead. We need to
talk about Thanksgiving again. I
want to make sure you know
everything because we have some big
plans. Things have changed a little.
But I know you will love it.

Stephanie's family has kindly
extended an invitation to their home
in Texas, and I would like to go
with her and bring you along. Isn't
that exciting? You've never been to
Texas before! What do you think? We

123

would have so much fun. Stephanie
has an enormous family with lots of
kids your age.

Call me soon so we can talk. I love
you!

Madison reread the e-mail and caught her
breath. No, she'd never been to Texas before. And
she didn't want to go now.
She didn't want to go *ever*.

Chapter 12

"Time for school," Mom said, tugging the comforter off Madison's bed.

"No," Madison said, curling back into her pillows.

Mom sat on the edge of the bed. "Would you please talk to me? What is going on?"

Madison hadn't said anything last night to Mom about Thanksgiving because she figured Dad would. But Dad probably knew Mom wasn't going to like the arrangement one bit.

Thanksgiving was tomorrow. It was enough to make someone want to stay under the covers forever.

How would Madison break the news to Mom about Texas?

"Mom," Madison said quietly. "Can we talk?"

Mom frowned. "Is something wrong, honey

bear? Are you sick? You haven't really been yourself for the last—"

"I don't want to spend Thanksgiving with Dad!" Madison blurted.

Mom leaned backward with a quizzical look on her face. "We've been through this already, Maddie. It's really okay with me. I understand. Being in this house will be hard over the holiday."

"You don't get it, Mom," Madison insisted.

"What don't I get?"

"Spending Thanksgiving with Dad doesn't mean being with him only. It means spending it with Stephanie, too."

Mom stroked Madison's forehead. "You like her, Maddie. She's a nice person."

"You still don't get it. It means being with Stephanie and everyone in her family. And I don't want Thanksgiving with her family, and that's where Dad's going. He wants me to fly to Texas to be with him. Ugh."

This was definitely news to Mom. But she kept her cool.

"I see." Mom nodded. "Well, Maddie, I think Dad is trying to make you feel included. And I think Stephanie has a big family. Dad probably thought you'd enjoy an adventure. You were very vocal about not wanting to stay in this house or even in Far Hills. Remember?"

Madison nodded. She was the one who had

started the Thanksgiving tug-of-war. Madison had made such a big deal, and now here she was going back to the original plan.

"Have you told your father how you feel?" Mom asked.

"Not exactly," Madison shrugged. "He'll be mad at me."

Mom laughed. "Maddie, your dad won't get mad at you. I think you need to call him. Come on. We have time before school. You need to do this now."

Madison dialed Dad's house.

Dad was silent at first, and Madison got worried about what he might say next.

"I'm sorry, sweetheart," he finally said. "I had no intention of putting you in the middle of this. I guess we just all want to be with you. I think you should stay at home with Mom, and I'll see you when we get back. How does that sound?"

Madison felt warm all over. Once again, Dad had said exactly the right thing to make her feel better.

When she hung up the phone, Mom leaned in for a giant hug.

"So does this mean it's just you and me again?" Mom asked.

Madison just smiled.

The day was a lot brighter. And it wasn't just that the rain had stopped. Madison hadn't realized just how much the whole Thanksgiving decision-making process had been clouding her days. Now that things were settled, she was feeling much better.

On the way to her first class, she caught a glimpse of herself in a display cabinet outside the history department. She smoothed her ponytail down in the glass reflection.

It took her a few moments before she even noticed the display on Thanksgiving. Around the borders of the glass window were acorns and pumpkins. Different teachers had posted artwork and papers. But in the center of the entire display was the *Mayflower* poster Madison and Egg had created together.

There she was—right there in the middle of everything. Extra credit turned into extra recognition. Madison felt really proud.

The second bell rang, and Madison caught up with Aimee and Fiona. "Where have you been?" Aimee asked. "I looked for you on the way to school. You haven't been walking much this week, have you?"

"Mom gave me a ride again," Madison said. She didn't feel like going into more detail about Thanksgiving and Mom and Dad and everything else that got messed up. Aimee didn't ask any more questions.

Later in the day, Mom surprised Madison by picking her up and driving over to the clinic. Dan hitched a ride with them, too.

Eileen was busy working at the front desk in a new T-shirt that read BE A VEGETARIAN.

Madison and Dan went into the paneled office and entered data into the database. Then they joined Eileen and a few other volunteers to hang special decorations. Madison hung up one poster that read SAVE THE TURKEYS. Eileen even hung up a funny turkey mobile with a moving turkey wattle (the icky red jiggly thing under a turkey's chin).

"I saw a wild turkey last week," Dan said as he hung up a turkey poster. "It was so big. I wonder if someone got him for the holiday?"

"You mean . . . ate him?" Madison laughed.

They both made an "eeeeeew" noise and laughed some more.

"I am so glad I came to volunteer here, Dan," Madison said. "I know that sounds really sappy, but I am. And I'm glad we got to be better friends."

"Yeah," Dan said. "It's been cool having you around. The animals really like you."

"Thanks." Madison reached out and petted Sugar's paw. it was dangling out of her cage. "Is that what you think, Sugar?"

The schnoodle made a low noise that Madison took as a qualified "yes" to her question.

Dan grabbed a few leashes off the Peg-Board at the side of the room.

"Hey," he said, tossing a leash to Madison. "Let's take her for a walk. I'll get some of the others."

Madison put on her scarf and her jacket. She gently lifted Sugar out of a cage and hooked on her leash. Dan let out some of the other animals, too: the yellow Labrador retriever, a miniature dachshund, a Jack Russell terrier, and a Yorkie terrier.

They walked up and down in front of the clinic a few times and then crossed over to walk on the other side of the street.

"HELP!" Madison laughed as the dogs swarmed around her. The leashes were getting tangled quickly.

Dan laughed, too. "This would make a funny picture."

"Good thing no one has a camera," Madison said.

They walked around the block. Dan wasn't talking too much. Madison didn't know why.

"What do you guys do for Thanksgiving?" Madison asked.

He shrugged. "You mean me and my mom?"

"Yeah," Madison said.

"This is a weird time of year. My dad died around this time two years ago."

Madison was amazed at how honest Dan was being, like they'd been friends forever and ever.

She took a breath. "I'm so sorry."

"Yeah, me too." Dan smiled. "He was a cool guy."

"Did he like animals, too?" Madison asked, leaning down to pet the top of Sugar's head.

Dan thought for a minute. "Yeah, I guess so. We always had pets. I remember this duck that lived in our yard."

Madison wanted to ask more questions about Dan's dad, but she didn't know how. She started asking about his mom instead.

"Your mom is so cool," Madison said. "Especially the T-shirts she wears."

"Yeah," Dan said. "She has a ton of them, right?"

When they walked back inside the clinic from exercising the dogs, Eileen was hanging a red-and-orange streamer across the waiting area. It really brightened up the place.

Madison packed up her stuff and wished Dan and his mom a happy holiday. Her own mom was waiting in the car outside.

That night, Madison wrote a quick e-mail to Dan, thanking him for being so nice at the clinic. It was Thanksgiving, after all. She figured that was a good thing to do. Madison found some other e-mails waiting for her.

FROM	SUBJECT
✉ Wetwinz	We're Here!!!!
✉ Bigwheels	Turkeys

One was from Fiona. She had left that morning on a flight to California.

From: Wetwinz
To: MadFinn, BalletGrl
Subject: We're here!!!!
Date: Wed 22 Nov 1:11 PM

I miss u guys already! Boo hoo. Our flight was totally packed with kids. I babysat a little for this one woman's little girl. She was sooooo adorable.

Oh no, I left my favorite dress @ home but NBD, I'll live, I guess. Mom said maybe we can shop today for something new.

It's not that warm here like beach weather, but the sun is shining and it's way different than Far Hills. I've already seen my BFF from here and I ran into this old boyfriend who is a year older. His name is Julio. You would freak, he is so cute. He has a new girlfriend, though—oh, well.

N e way, I am going with Chet to the mall and we're hanging with his old crowd of friends. I wish you guys could be here. I hope you have a happy Thanksgiving. . . .

Love and smooches fm. me! Xoxoxoox

p.s. Howz Egg? LOL say hello to him
& Drew 4 me.

p.p.s. Let's go to bigfishbowl and
IM each other soon.

Madison grinned at the screen and pressed SAVE.
That message was a keeper. She was just as thrilled
to see a short and sweet note from Bigwheels, too.

From: Bigwheels
To: MadFinn
Subject: Turkeys
Date: Wed 22 Nov 11:52 AM
Long time, no write? I know you've
been busy, but I miss our notes.
Please send news about anything.
Have you ever heard this quote: If
you want to soar with the eagles,
you have to put up with a lot of
turkeys. LOL.

I thought you or your dad would
like that one.

We're having dinner with both sets
of grandparents, my parents, my
sister and brother, and loads of
aunts and uncles and cousins. I
think I told you. Anyway, I'm nervous
to see some of my other cousins

because they can be really snotty to me. I don't know why. I would never treat someone that way. Would you?

Thanks for being my friend at Thanksgiving!

Yours till the potatoes mash,

Bigwheels

After reading both e-mails three times each, Madison went immediately into her files. She had started the year unsure about her friends, but here they were all around her. It was ridiculous to think that she had a whole lot of thanks for *nothing*. Right now, her life was chock-full as Madison's kindergarten cornucopia Mom had displayed atop the mantel. She was bursting.

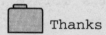 Thanks

Rude Awakening: Good things are like grapes. They come in bunches.

I had a long talk with Dad today about spending Thanksgiving with Mom. He was very cool about it. So now I am actually looking forward to being alone together. I don't need a million people around to eat turkey.

Mom and I are going to make the pie and stuffing tomorrow. No more surprises!

Things couldn't be yummier.

Chapter 13

Madison rolled over and opened her eyes, thinking it was later than it was. Outside was still dark, just beginning to lighten up. The trees were moving in the wind outside her window.

She sat up and put on slippers and shuffled down the hall to her mother's bedroom. Phinnie was sprawled on top of Mom's bed, eyes glistening in the half dark. She climbed up and kissed Mom's cheek.

"Happy Thanksgiving, Mom," Madison said.

Bleary-eyed, Mom awoke with a start. "Maddie, you scared me half to death. I was in the middle of a dream."

They lay in bed and talked about Mom's dream and about Thanksgivings long ago, like the time when Mom had to be rushed to the emergency room for slicing her finger while cooking.

"I remember that was really gross," Madison said. "There was blood all over the counter."

"It always looks worse than it is," Mom said. She smiled all of a sudden, and Madison felt self-conscious.

"What? What are you looking at?" Madison said.

"You. You look so pretty in this light."

Madison made a face. "You mean I look pretty in the dark?"

They laughed and got out of bed.

Mom spent the morning speaking with international clients as she'd been doing all week. They faxed notes to her and important contracts. Mom's latest project for Budge Films was taking up so much time. Madison wondered why anyone would have to work on Thanksgiving since it was a holiday. Then she remembered that it was only a holiday in America, so everyone else in the world had to show up at work the usual time and place.

Madison figured she'd get a head start working on dinner in the kitchen. She took out the peeler and started peeling carrots into a big bowl. She made a feeble attempt at skinning the sweet potatoes, too, but they were so tough and hard to peel. She needed Mom's help for those.

While Mom worked, Madison also watched some television, like the Macy's Thanksgiving parade. When she had been younger, Mom and Dad would sometimes take her into New York City to watch people blow up the giant balloons and floats on the night before the parade started. It was magic to see Big Bird and Spiderman get inflated into enormous, building-sized balloons.

Today Madison watched the balloons on TV only. She curled up into a little ball under Gramma's afghan on the sofa and counted the number of baton twirlers in every marching band. Next year, Madison would have to ask to go back to the city and watch the parade in person. She didn't think Mom would go for it, but it couldn't hurt to ask.

As she was lying on the sofa, Phinnie walked by Madison. She called out for him to come over and snuzzle, but he walked right on by. *Again.* Now Madison was starting to take it personally. Or maybe the dog was sick? She worried a little, but not enough to get up and take Phin's temperature or pet his little nose to see if it was warm when it was supposed to be cold and wet. Instead Madison curled deeper into the couch pillows.

Mom came back into the living room after noontime and announced that her work was completed.

"Let's call your gramma!" she suggested, grabbing the phone and squeezing in next to Madison on the couch. They dialed the number.

"Hello, there." Gramma's voice came across loud and clear.

"Hey, Mother," Mom said. "It's me and Maddie. We called to say hello. How's the turkey in Chicago?"

"Turkey's been in the oven since seven. Angie and Bob are coming over later today."

"Mother, I really am sorry we couldn't make it there. We miss you."

When it was her turn to speak, Madison grabbed the phone from her mom and shouted into the receiver. "Warm hugs from me, Gramma," Madison said. "And Phinnie, too."

Gramma chuckled. "What did you say, dear?" she asked. Madison realized she'd taken out her hearing aid. "You're finished with who?"

"Oh, nothing, Gramma. We made all your recipes today. Thank you for them. The stuffing is yummy."

"That's fantastic. Well, I love you, Maddie, dear," Gramma said. "Did you hear me?"

"Loud and clear," Madison said. "Let me put Mom back on the phone, okay?"

No sooner had the call to Chicago ended than the phone rang again. Madison hoped inside her heart when she picked up the phone that it would be a certain person—and it was.

"DADDY!" she screeched into the receiver.

He was gushing all over the place about missing Madison. He told her that Texas just wasn't the same without her. The night before, he and Stephanie had been to a steer auction near the family ranch.

"Stephanie lived on a ranch?" Madison asked.

"Yup," Dad said. "I am now an official cowboy, so watch out."

Madison laughed.

"Honey, Stephanie was here a moment ago," Dad continued. "She wanted me to wish you a happy Thanksgiving, okay?"

Madison felt a twinge of sadness because good-byes with Dad were always the hardest, no matter where she was or what she was doing. Even on the telephone.

With family phone calls out of the way, the dinner preparations started for real around one o'clock. All the vegetables—including sweet potatoes—had been peeled. Madison had mixed the stuffing's dry ingredients into a bowl. Mom came along and helped pull everything together the best she could.

Mom wasn't a great cook, but she didn't mind experimenting. Mostly, she was a bad cook not because she was untalented—it was more like she was too busy. Her job took up so much of her time.

An hour into the cooking frenzy, everything seemed to be going along great. The food was all cooking inside the oven, and Madison and Mom went into the den to watch a little more television.

As soon as Mom and Madison snuggled into the couch, the kitchen smoke alarm went off and they both jumped clear out of their seats. The small drippings from Gramma's sweet potato pie had set off a burnt, smoky bomb inside the kitchen. The whole kitchen smelled like burning sugar, a funny, sweet smell that made Madison a little queasy.

"The pie is ruined," Madison said as she carefully pulled on pot holders and rested it on a pie sheet. It was all black and burned around the edges, but Mom set it aside for a special dessert anyhow.

Dingdong.

Madison turned around toward the kitchen sliding door. Aimee was standing outside with a wrapped package, twirling around. "Brrrrrrr!" she said as Madison pulled open the sliding door. "Happy Nonturkey Day!"

Mom laughed.

"You're still in your pajamas!" Aimee gasped. "I had to get ready early because people were coming over."

"We're just hanging out," Madison said, catching the corner of Mom's eye.

"You are so lucky, Maddie. I wish I could have a mellow Thanksgiving like you. I have to be stuck at home with my dumb brothers, who are so annoying," Aimee wailed. "All they do is watch football."

"I like football," Madison said.

"Then you hang out with them. I just want to go to the movies or something," Aimee said. She put a small tinfoil package up on the countertop. "My mom said to give you guys this. It's a loaf of her macrobiotic apple bread. It's made with honey and oats or something."

"That's very nice, Aimee. Thank your mom for us both."

"Well, back to my family!" Aimee announced with flair. She twirled her arms into the air. "Ta da! Now you see me, now you—"

She jumped back out the same way she came.

"Call me later!" Aimee yelled through the glass sliding door. She made a goofy face and vanished.

Dinner was half burnt and half cold, but *all* fun. Madison and Mom couldn't believe that they had actually made any meal as elaborate as Thanksgiving dinner, complete with a Jell-O mold and a bowl of homemade stuffing.

"Does this taste funny to you?" Madison asked when she took a bite of stuffing.

Mom grinned. "Probably." She took a pinch of the stuffing and put it under the table. "Here, Phinnie! Mom has something for you."

They both burst into laughter.

Dessert, they decided, would be saved for later in the evening. Mom said they'd have some time to digest first. She seemed to have a plan about the whole day. Together they washed up the dishes and played a game of Scrabble.

Around seven-thirty, the doorbell rang.

"Who could that be?" Mom asked.

Madison shrugged. She had no clue. "Maybe it's Aimee again? Or Egg?"

Dingdong.

It rang a second time, and neither Mom nor Madison moved.

"Are you going to get it?" Mom asked.

Madison begrudgingly got up. She looked down at herself. She hadn't changed out of her pajamas since the morning. She looked like a mess.

"Mom, if it's a boy . . . even just Egg . . . I can't let him see me. . . ."

Mom grinned. "Okay, I'll get the door."

Madison rushed into the small half bathroom downstairs to see what she looked like *exactly*. Her hair was looking a little flyaway, but her pj's looked surprisingly presentable. Only the bear claw slippers that Madison had on her feet looked ridiculous.

"Who is it, Mom?" Madison said as she walked back into the living room.

Madison screamed. "Oh, wow!"

Standing in the doorway was a bunch of orange Mylar balloons with art of cartoon turkeys on each one. Through the balloons, a strange man peeked at Madison and grinned.

"Special delivery for Madison Finn," he said.

Madison squealed. "That's me!"

Mom helped Madsion grab the balloon bunch from the man and signed for them. Madison laughed when she saw what the deliveryman looked like. He was wearing a turkey costume!

Phin loved the balloons even more than Madison. He started running around the house. He even slammed into the side of the chairs as he skidded down the hallway. He was that excited.

"Rowrooooo!" he yelped.

"Read the card," Mom said, pulling the small blue envelope from the bunch of balloon strings.

Madison opened the card so fast, it almost ripped.

> For Maddie
> With love and drumsticks
> From Dad and Stephanie

"Isn't that nice," Mom said.

Madison nodded. "This whole Thanksgiving is nice, Mom."

Mom disappeared into the kitchen and brought out a big tray with Gramma Helen's sweet potato pie, milk, tea, and some cookies, too.

"The pie looks a little crispy," Madison said. It was scorched around the edges.

"Well, I'm not a super cook yet, but I'm working on it, honey bear," Mom said. "We can cut around the burned parts."

Madison smiled. She had made the right decision about Thanksgiving. She *could* have her turkey and pie *and* eat it, too. And surprises never seemed to end. . . .

Chapter 14

The next morning Madison was so hungry, she took a bite of cold sweet potato pie before she even had breakfast.

She could barely wait to tell Aimee about everything that had happened, but Aimee and her brothers weren't around, so she left a voice message to call back. Aimee was probably over at her father's bookstore, Book Web.

Madison got ready for the clinic. Mom said that she could spend the day there.

Sugar the schnoodle was waiting!

Eileen was busy working on some files and paperwork at the front of the clinic when Madison walked in with a spring in her step.

"Hiya!" She waved. Eileen just nodded back a

silent hello. Today her T-shirt said HAVE YOU HUGGED YOUR DOG TODAY?

Hugging Phin was one of Madison's favorite things. And she'd been thinking about hugging Sugar all morning long, too.

Dan wasn't around today. Madison remembered that he had gone for the weekend to his cousin's place in Connecticut. He wouldn't be back until after school break was over.

The only person in the back was Dr. Wing. He was standing in front of the cages.

"Hi!" Madison said as she bounced into the room.

Dr. Wing smiled. "Happy day-after-Thanksgiving. Aren't we chipper?"

"TOTALLY!" Madison said. She went immediately to Sugar's cage. "Is it okay if I walk—hey—wait a minute—"

Madison looked into every cage.

"Sugar? Where's the schnoodle? Oh no, please don't tell me she's sick again!"

Dr. Wing shook his head. "No, nothing like that."

"Where is she?" Madison asked. "Where's Sugar?"

"A nice family from the east side of Far Hills came in and adopted her," the doctor explained. "They'd been considering it, and I guess they made a final decision over the holiday. Isn't that great?"

Madison froze.

All the giddiness that had been swirling inside turned to pure defeat.

Sugar was gone?

"Madison," Dr. Wing said. "What's wrong?"

She shook her head. "I just didn't expect this. Not today."

"Well, it's a great thing. Sugar was a very sad puppy, and now she has a loving, caring family. If that isn't the Thanksgiving spirit, I don't know what is," he said.

"I know, but—" Madison wanted to cry, but she took a deep breath. "It's a surprise, that's all."

"I'm sure Sugar will be very happy with her new family arrangements, Madison. Don't worry."

She had to admit that Sugar being adopted was a good thing. Many times abused and neglected dogs with scars and personality problems had hard times finding new homes. That's what Eileen and Dan had said. Madison wanted Sugar to have a happy home forever.

But it was still hard looking at Sugar's empty cage.

She hadn't even had a chance to say good-bye.

"She is gone now," Mr. Wollensky said. He was there to volunteer today, too. "You look very sad, Madison."

Madison sighed. "I just didn't expect to come here and find her gone like this."

"Is hard to let go, yes?" Mr. Wollensky asked.

Madison watched as he opened up the cage and took out the messy newspapers that were lying across the bottom. Madision watched as Mr. Wollensky cleaned away the only things that were left from Sugar's stay at Far Hills Clinic. Bit by bit, all traces of her were taken away.

Now Madison *really* wanted to cry.

"You feel Sugar in *here*, yes?" Mr. Wollensky pointed to his heart. Madison felt a lump in her throat. She did feel Sugar. She missed the schnoodle so much that she couldn't even find the words to describe it. It was an ache—inside.

"Once I had a dog here I wanted to adopt for my own."

"Like Sugar?" Madison said. She had wished that the schnoodle could have been her dog. "What happened?" Madison asked.

"It was not meant to be. This dog ended up with family who could take good care of him. Family's very important."

Madison nodded. She understood. Sugar had a family now, and family, no matter how big or small, was important. Madison thanked Mr. Wollensky and grabbed her coat.

Madison decided to walk home, even though it was a very long walk. A woman across the road was walking a dog that looked familiar. She approached the woman and bent down to pet the dog.

"He's a pug," the woman said. "I hate it when kids call him Squashed-Up Nose and things like that."

Madison smiled. "I know. I have a pug, too."

Suddenly it hit her: she had a pug, too. She already had a dog who she loved more than anything in the whole wide world. And he wasn't going *anywhere*. Madison realized that she hadn't walked Phin in days.

She needed to see Phin—now. She needed to pet his coarse fur, hear his little snuffle, and watch his curlicue tail wiggle.

Soon she was running down the block, running toward home. She'd left her gloves in her orange bag, so her fingertips were like icicles. But she ran faster until she reached the porch at home.

"Phinnie!" Madison gasped a little as she walked back into the house. "Phinnie, where are you?"

Mom appeared in the doorway. "What's going on? I thought you were over at the clinic. You were going to call me to come pick you up. . . ."

Madison was looking all over the front hall. "Mom, where's Phin? Have you seen him? I need to see Phin."

"Hold it, hold it. Shhhhh. Follow me." Mom tiptoed into the den. There, on the den couch, Phin had curled into the tightest ball and was snoring away.

Madison watched him quietly for a few

moments, but then she couldn't contain herself. "Phinnie!" Madison yelled.

He awoke with a snort, and she threw herself over his little pug body.

"Roowwrorooooo!" he yelped right back at her.

Madison lifted Phin into her arms like a baby and carried him upstairs into her bedroom.

"I missed you sooooo much," she cooed in Phin's ears. He licked the tip of her nose and panted. Madison didn't even mind his doggy breath.

With Phin still in her lap, Madison logged on to her laptop computer. She had a special destination in mind, a place she'd discovered a long time ago. Madison plugged a few words into the bigfishbowl search engine, and up popped the address she was looking for.

<u>Dog</u> of the Day—Sign Yours Up Now
Tell us about your special **dog**. Is your bichon frise funny? Does your weimaraner whine? Winners daily!

She accessed her photo files and pulled up her favorite shot of Phin. She'd taken it last summer in the backyard. He was standing in tall grass, and the sunlight was hitting his back in just the right places.

"Rowwwroooo!" Phin pushed his snorty nose into her side and wiggled back and forth. He knew how cute he looked.

Madison filled in the Web site form with her dog's full name, Phineas T. Finn, and a few lines about why she loved him.

Phin doesn't mind my messy room. He loves me when I'm sad or happy. And he gives the best hugs in the world. Some people say he looks funny, but I don't think so. Phin is a true member of my family.

Almost immediately, Madison got a return e-mail to inform her that the Dog of the Day submission had been received and would be processed.

"You're my family, Phinnie!" Madison kissed his little ears, and he squirmed. Sooner than soon, he would be making his big Web debut.

Madison opened a blank e-mail and started to write a note to Gramma. She wondered if their Thanksgiving dinner had turned out as nicely as hers had turned out with Mom.

From: MadFinn
To: GoGramma
Subject: I MISS YOU!!!
Date: Fri 24 Nov 1:13 PM

Your sweet potato pie recipe was awesome, Gramma, even if we did burn it a little. Thank you for that. Of course I missed you more than anything. I had no one to play Crazy Eights with me.

I got a good extra-credit grade in social studies. The teacher gave me and Egg both an A+. She said that we were great partners. I was so nervous, but it's funny how things work out.

I was afraid that if Thanksgiving wasn't the way it always had been that I would be so sad. But change was okay. In the end it was A-okay. Our family is still here. I'm still here, too.

I hope I do get to visit you soon. Mom says maybe she'll let me go to Chicago next summer. I will keep my fingers crossed so I can go.

Thanks for being the best gramma in the universe. Thanks for listening. Thanks for *everything*.

Yours till the pumpkin pies,

Maddie

xoxox

Madison hit SEND. The message went *poof*. As Madison logged off the laptop, Phin jumped off her lap and onto her bed.

"I'll be right back, Phinnie," Madison said, getting up and tiptoeing out of the room. She found Mom downstairs at her own computer.

"Mom?" Madison said as she came into the room. She assumed Mom was doing something work related.

"Come take a look at this, Maddie," Mom said with a big grin.

Madison went over to the desk, and without even thinking, she sat right in Mom's lap. She hadn't sat there in years. It felt good to sit there again.

On the monitor, Madison saw that Mom had made a collage of different photographs from their family. There was a picture of Madison as a little baby. There was a shot of Madison, Mom, and Dad holding a stuffed turkey. There was a close-up shot of Gramma and Madison making a pie together.

"Oh, wow! That's the first sweet potato pie she ever showed me how to make!" Madison said.

"See?" Mom said. "Everyone's still here. Our family isn't going *anywhere*, honey bear."

"I love you," Madison said.

"I love you more," Mom said, winking.

Madison sighed. She knew no family was perfect, but she couldn't help but think that *her* family came about as close as a person could get.

It was perfect for *her*. That's what mattered most.

Mad Chat Words:

3:]	Doggy
:-#-	My lips are sealed
>:-<	I am angrier than angry
<:>==	Turkey
woof	Woof (what did you think?)
LMK	Let me know
WAI	What an idiot!
E2EG	Ear-to-ear grin
DTRT	Do the right thing
NBD	No big deal
IYSS	If you say so
BFN	Bye for now

Madison's Computer Tip:

The Internet can be so helpful with school projects. I search the Web for information on subjects like my Thanksgiving presentation with Egg. The only problem with getting information online, however, is that I need to make sure my facts come from the right places. **Double-check any information you might get online, because not all Web sites have accurate facts.** I usually go to Web sites like museums, libraries, or other big organizations when I look up information for school reports.

Visit Madison at www.madisonfinn.com

Book #5: *Thanks for Nothing*

Super Quiz

Now that you've read the story . . . how much do you *really* know about Madison and her friends?

1. Why can't Gramma Helen come to Far Hills for Thanksgiving?
   a. She forgot to buy a plane ticket.
   b. She doesn't eat turkey.
   c. She has a bad hip.

2. What is the name of Aimee's basset hound?
   a. Bubbles
   b. Blossom
   c. Buttercup

3. What is so special about Aimee's new winter parka?
    a. It's the perfect color—Lemon Drop.
    b. It's lined with fleece.
    c. It's the same one Nikki, the singer, wore in her video.

4. What is the one class that Madison, Aimee, and Fiona have together?
    a. Science
    b. English
    c. Social Studies

5. And who is their teacher in that class?
    a. Mrs. Belden
    b. Mrs. Wing
    c. Mr. Danehy

6. Which one of the following was *not* a former pet of Madison Finn's?
    a. Silly Puddy, the goldfish
    b. Ick, the cat
    c. Sea monkeys

7. Which other kid from school works at the animal clinic in Far Hills?
    a. Drew Maxwell
    b. Dan Ginsburg
    c. Ivy Daly

8. Who runs the animal clinic?
   a. Dr. Wing
   b. Mrs. Wing
   c. Professor L. Wing

9. Who is the older clinic volunteer with the Russian accent?
   a. Mr. Wollensky
   b. Mr. Tzaichofsky
   c. Mr. Romanov

10. Which smart guy does Aimee have a teeny crush on?
    a. Drew Maxwell
    b. Tommy Kwong
    c. Ben Buckley

11. What always happens when Madison wears lip gloss?
    a. She gets spots on her sleeve.
    b. She chews it off.
    c. She gets kissed.

12. Who is Fiona's partner for the school Thanksgiving project?
    a. Daisy Espinoza
    b. Madison Finn
    c. Walter "Egg" Diaz

13. What or whom does Fiona pick for the subject of her project?
    a. The *Mayflower*
    b. Sarah Hale
    c. Turkey farmers

14. What does Madison choose for her project topic?
    a. The *Mayflower*
    b. The Titanic
    c. Turkey sandwiches

15. Who is Madison's project partner?
    a. Aimee Gillespie
    b. Hart Jones
    c. Egg Diaz

16. What is the name of Madison's dad's girl-friend?
    a. Samantha
    b. Stephanie
    c. Sally Mae

17. What does Madison's dad's girlfriend ask Madison to do?
    a. Join them for Thanksgiving dinner
    b. Keep a secret about her past
    c. Never call Dad again

18. Egg's pet, Gato, is what kind of animal?
    a. A dog
    b. A gecko
    c. A hamster

19. Gramma sends Madison an e-mail with recipes, including Fruit Terrine, Stuffing, and what else?
    a. Turkey gravy
    b. Sweet-potato pie
    c. Pumpkin pie

20. Who or what is Sugar?
    a. A sick pet at the clinic
    b. Madison's favorite rock singer
    c. The name of a teen magazine Madison reads with her friends

21. What evil rumor does Poison Ivy start to spread?
    a. The rumor that Madison and Egg are having a big fight
    b. The rumor that Madison failed her last math test
    c. The rumor that Madison and Dan are an item

22. How does Madison start her school Thanksgiving presentation?
     a. By tap dancing
     b. By serving pretzels with mustard
     c. By telling a joke

23. Who is Ivy Daly's project partner?
     a. Lindsay Frost
     b. Drew Maxwell
     c. Suresh Dhir

24. Which routine do Dan and Hart do for their
presentation?
     a. The Turkey Pokey
     b. The Stuffing Stuffer
     c. The Turkey Lurkey

25. Which state does Madison's dad's girlfriend
come from?
     a. Wyoming
     b. Montana
     c. Texas

26. What does Madison receive from her dad at
Thanksgiving?
     a. A chocolate turkey
     b. A bouquet of balloons
     c. A cranberry compote

27. Who is Egg's older sister?
    a. Mariah
    b. Carrie
    c. Wendy

28. Where does Fiona go for Thanksgiving?
    a. Her cousin Martha's, in New Jersey
    b. Back to California
    c. Nowhere. She stays in Far Hills.

29. Who wears a T-shirt that reads: *Lemur Alone! Save the Rainforest!*?
    a. Mrs. Wing
    b. Dan Ginsburg
    c. Eileen Ginsburg

30. What does this symbol mean: <:>== ?
    a. Turkey
    b. Stand back.
    c. I lost my arm and I can't find it.

31. What is the name of the search engine that Madison uses?
    a. Gaggle
    b. Yoohoo
    c. Just Fishing Around

32. What online store does Aimee visit to shop for clothes?
    a. My Closet
    b. Fashion Central
    c. Boop-Dee-Doop

33. What special effect does Egg add to the social studies project?
    a. Music
    b. Neon lights
    c. Volcanic sparks

34. Where do Aunt Angie and Uncle Bob live?
    a. Houston
    b. Chicago
    c. Paris

35. What kind of lessons does Madison's mom want her to take?
    a. Flute lessons
    b. Skydiving lessons
    c. Singing lessons

36. What group of people is Bigwheels writing a paper on?
    a. The Wampanoag Indians
    b. The *Mayflower* pilgrims
    c. The British royal family

37. Where does Fiona go to spend Thanksgiving?
    a. Chicago
    b. California
    c. Paris

38. What is the name of the old boyfriend Fiona runs into?
    a Dominic
    b. Richard
    c. Julio

39. What game does Madison like to play with her Gramma Helen at Thanksgiving?
    a. Crazy Eights
    b. Monopoly
    c. Hide-and-seek

40. What is Aimee's favorite chat room on bigfishbowl.com?
    a. The fashion chat room
    b. The ballet chat room
    c. The pet-owners' chat room

Answers:

1c, 2b, 3a, 4c, 5a, 6a, 7b, 8a, 9a, 10c, 11b, 12a, 13b, 14a, 15c, 16b, 17a, 18b, 19b, 20a, 21c, 22c, 23b, 24a, 25c, 26b, 27a, 28b, 29c, 30a, 31c, 32c, 33a, 34b, 35a, 36a, 37b, 38c, 39a, 40b

How well do you know Maddie?

36–40 correct: You might as well pack your bags and move to Far Hills, because you are a *Madison Finn* fanatic!

30–35 correct: You could totally be Madison's BFF, because you know her inside out!

26–29 correct: You think Maddie's pretty cool, and you'd have fun hanging out with her.

20–25 correct: You know a few things about Madison, and you're interested in finding out more about her.

19 or fewer correct: You didn't quite catch all those details about Maddie, but don't worry—there's still lots of time to learn.

Mad Chat Match

Match the following Mad Chat words with their correct meanings.

3:]	Bye for now
:-#-	If you say so
>:-<	Let me know
<:>==	What an idiot!
woof	No big deal
LMK	Ear-to-ear grin
WAI	My lips are sealed
E2EG	Do the right thing
DTRT	Turkey
NBD	I am angrier than angry
IYSS	Woof (what did you think?)
BFN	Doggy

See page 169 for answers.

Madison's Mega Word Search

   See if you can find all the characters from the Madison Finn series in this puzzle. Search for names backward, forward, up, down, and diagonally. When you have finished, the remaining letters (in order) will spell out a secret message. Happy searching!
   Search for names in capital letters only.

AIMEE	GRAMMA
(Mrs.) BELDEN	HART
BEN	IVY
(Principal) BERNARD	JEFF
CHET	JOAN
DAN	LINDSAY
(Mr.) DANEHY	MADISON
DREW	PHINNIE
FIONA	ROSE
FRANCINE	STEPHANIE
(Mr.) GIBBONS	WALTER
(Assistant Principal) GOODE	(Mrs.) WING

D T H S N O B B I G B
A S T E P H A N I E E
N A N W A L T E R D R
E R O S E K C P S O N
H A Y F T R A H F O A
Y M O V R R D I E G R
N M A D I S O N E T D
E A A A D N G N I W I
D R N N A O J I G T H
L G I A I M E E S B O
E Y A S D N I L F O K
B E N I C N A R F F !

Secret Message:

___ ___ ___ ___ ___ ___ ___   ___ ___ ___

___ ___ ___ ___ ___ ___ ___ ___   ___ ___

___ ___ ___ ___ !

See next page for answers.

Word Search Answers

Secret Message:

THANKS FOR
READING THIS
BOOK!

Mad Chat Match Answers

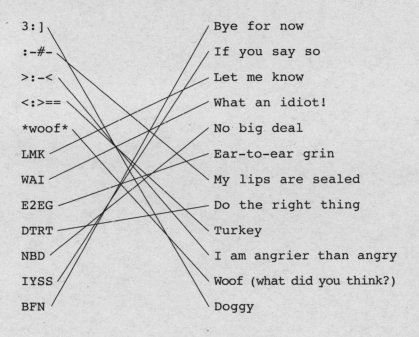

3:]

:-#-

>:-<

<:>==

woof

LMK

WAI

E2EG

DTRT

NBD

IYSS

BFN

Bye for now

If you say so

Let me know

What an idiot!

No big deal

Ear-to-ear grin

My lips are sealed

Do the right thing

Turkey

I am angrier than angry

Woof (what did you think?)

Doggy

From the Files of

Madison Finn

Lost and Found

For Emma Silverman-Keates, Emily Remmers, and Maija Fiedelholtz—three future Madisons who sparkle with life and joy

No matter how hard she shoved, Madison couldn't squeeze all her stuff into the teeny green gym locker. She had hated gym class from the moment seventh grade started. Before the winter holidays, Madison's gym class was scheduled in the afternoon. Now, gym was in the morning, first period on Mondays.

The worst part was wearing the dreaded gym uniform. Its ugly blue polyester gym shorts made Madison's legs itch, and a too tight, white T-shirt with a blue Far Hills Junior High logo was not exactly the most flattering fashion statement. And wearing that shirt meant wearing a bra, even though Madison didn't have much to fill it out.

And even *worse* than wearing a scary,

see-through T-shirt was the fact that Hart Jones would see her looking that way. Hart, Madison's big crush at school, just happened to be in her same gym section. He would see her wearing the ugly outfit.

Madison had to stop herself from over-thinking immediately. She sighed and took a seat on the small benches between locker banks. *Hart Jones.* Just the idea of him made her feel faint. Or was that because the locker room smelled like wet rubber floor mats and soccer balls?

She pulled her sweater over her head and wriggled into her T-shirt. Then she carefully yanked off her stockings and tugged on the polyester shorts under her wool skirt. They felt snugger than snug, and her legs prickled with goose bumps from the chilly air.

The locker area wasn't very full, so no one had seen her change. That was a major relief. Madison was standing alone in her row. Madison's homeroom had been dismissed early. Sometimes homeroom teachers let certain groups out earlier than others. However, neither of her best friends, Aimee or Fiona, had arrived from her homeroom yet.

Madison heard whispering in the next locker bank but didn't think much of it at first. Then she heard someone say *her* name.

"I can't believe I still have Madison Finn as my partner," the person grumbled with a huff.

Madison knew the voice. It was Poison Ivy Daly, her mortal enemy.

Ivy was speaking about their science lab. Mr. Danehy had assigned Madison and Ivy as lab partners. He obviously didn't know how much they didn't get along.

"Just ignore her," Ivy's friend Rose advised. "What's the big deal?"

Madison stood on top of the bench, leaning into the lockers, to hear whatever more she could hear. Ivy was talking to her drones, Rose Thorn and Phony Joanie. Madison knew they might say not-so-nice stuff, but she still wanted to hear it. Unfortunately, the juicy eavesdropping stopped there. Madison's name wasn't mentioned again. They moved on to talking about hair. Ivy always wore her perfect red hair in perfect red clips.

As Madison stepped off the bench, the room got very quiet. Madison was surprised to see someone standing in the space between the locker banks. It was Ivy. And she was staring right at Madison.

"Hello, Madison," Ivy said curtly. "I didn't know you were in here."

"Yeah, well . . ." Madison mumbled. She turned back to the green locker.

Madison wondered if, even for a fleeting second, Ivy felt a smidge guilty about gossiping without knowing who was nearby. But clearly Ivy felt nothing of the sort. She just *stared*. Madison felt Ivy's eyes watching her.

Rose and Joanie appeared from around the corner, too.

"Nice shorts," Joanie snapped to Madison. She was always snappy.

Madison felt her entire body shrink when Joanie said the words, however. *Nice shorts.* Ivy, Rose, and Joanie were wearing their shorts baggy and longer. They made the uniform look good. But Madison stood there in gym shorts one size too small.

"'Scuse me!" Aimee Gillespie said, appearing from nowhere and sliding past the others into Madison's locker bank. Best friends have a way of showing up just at the right time. "Hey, Maddie!" she chirped.

Ivy raised one eyebrow at Aimee's entrance and walked away to find a mirror. Her drones followed.

"What was that about?" Aimee asked Madison.

Madison sat down on the bench again. Her shorts felt tighter than ever now. "These." She pointed to them.

"Huh?" Aimee shrugged. "Not everyone got the new shorts, I don't think. It doesn't really matter, does—"

"*New* shorts?" Madison asked incredulously. "*What* new shorts?"

Aimee explained that a letter had been mailed home with an order form for a new style of gym shorts. The administration had received complaints about the sizes being too small for a lot of girls. They were offering a new style.

"I never knew," Madison said. Her mom must

have thrown out the mail without reading it. She did that sometimes.

"But you look great in those shorts," Aimee said. "You have nice legs."

"Thanks," Madison said. Maybe the shorts weren't so bad after all.

Fiona appeared with a flounce and a smile. "Helloooooo! Did you guys have a good weekend?"

She'd already changed into her gym uniform, pulling off her clothes to reveal the shorts underneath her pants. Fiona said it was easier to change that way. Of course she had on the loose shorts.

"Where did you get those?" Madison asked her.

"I don't know," Fiona admitted, a little spaced out. She sneezed. "They're more comfy than the other ones."

Madison would have to ask Mom to order her a pair of those.

"GIRLS!" A booming voice echoed into the locker room. Coach Hammond blew her whistle for emphasis. "LET'S GO! LET'S GO! INTO THE GYM!"

She wasn't as mean as a drill sergeant, but Coach Hammond was strict about starting class on time, lining up in perfect rows, and playing fair.

Madison hid behind Aimee and Fiona as they shuffled into the main part of the gym. She was happier than happy to see a few other girls wearing the shorter, snugger shorts.

"OKAY!" Coach Hammond yelled. She yelled

5

even when she was standing nose to nose with a student. "TODAY WE HAVE PHYSICAL FITNESS TESTING! HEADS UP!"

Aimee turned to Madison. "This stinks. It's Monday morning. Who tests your physical fitness on Monday?"

"Yeah." Fiona sniffled. Then she sneezed three times in a row.

Madison sat down on the floor between her friends, pretending to listen and watch Coach Hammond. But her eyes were wandering over to Hart. He was looking hunky, lying on his side across from them, whispering to Chet Waters, his new best friend and Fiona's twin brother.

"UPSY DAISY, BOYS AND GIRLS," Coach Hammond commanded. "EVERYONE UP AND INTO NEAT ROWS, PLEASE. WE NEED TO TEST YOUR AGILITY AND SPEED."

Coach didn't call it a race against each other, but kids pretended like it was. Everyone in the first row was paired up with someone in the second row.

Boys mostly paired with boys, except for Fiona and Chet, who led off the rows. They wanted to race each other for the obvious reason.

Coach Hammond didn't hear their friendly exchange.

"Eat my dust," Chet whispered to his sister.

Fiona smirked. "You—ah-ah . . . *choo*!" she said, sneezing again. "You *wish*."

6

Coach Hammond explained that the task was to run up and down the length of the gym three times, then weave through the orange cones at the side of the room and run three more times up and back in the gym.

"I'm tired just thinking about that," moaned Hart. He was standing right behind Madison.

"ON YOUR MARK, GET SET . . . GO!" Coach Hammond blew the whistle, and Fiona and Chet took off for the other side of the gym.

Madison couldn't exactly remember what she had to do during past fitness tests in middle school, but they had certainly never been like this. Kids were cheering on other kids, like it was a sporting event.

"Go! Go! GO!"

As Fiona made the turn to come back toward the group the second time, she tripped and fell to the floor.

"Ahhhhh!" a bunch of girls, including Madison, screamed.

Coach Hammond shooed them away and helped Fiona to her feet.

Fiona rubbed her elbows, which had slammed into the floor. She started to cough. "I feel hot, Coach."

She was *burning* hot, as it turned out. So the feverish Fiona was sent to the nurse. She waved to Madison and Aimee as she left the gym.

I hope she's really okay, Madison thought.

"LET'S GET BACK IN LINE, BOYS AND GIRLS,"

Coach Hammond ordered. Everyone obeyed. The paired-off test subjects started up again.

Years of ballerina twirls helped Aimee to pass the fitness test easily. She was fast *and* graceful. Her running companion was some girl Madison only knew a little. The girl had to stop halfway through the test to take a big puff from her inhaler. She was one of two asthmatics in the class, but she still passed the test.

Most kids passed. When their turns came, boys and girls sped up and down the gym without even breaking a sweat.

Madison always knew she was good at running, or at least she was good at running *away*. But right there in the heat of the moment, she was losing her nerve. She had a fear that she would be the one to *not* pass. She'd be the one who fell into a sweaty, lumpy pile.

She looked over to see who'd be racing by her side. It was Ivy, who made a face.

Madison leaned over to retie her sneaker. Out of the corner of her eye, she caught Hart looking her way, too. She thought he was smiling a little.

"Hey, Finnster," he called out.

Some kids giggled at the nickname.

Madison gulped.

"ON YOUR MARK, GET SET . . ."

As soon as Coach Hammond screeched "GO," Madison was off and zipping across the gym. She didn't pay attention to how fast Ivy was going.

She turned at the first wall and never looked back. Even when an orange cone got knocked over in the middle of the test, Madison ran on. She huffed and puffed as she finished up. . . .

"IT'S A TIE!" Coach Hammond wailed.

Madison looked over at Ivy as they walked over to the sidelines, expecting her to grimace or pout or make her poisonous sneer.

But Ivy *smiled* instead.

"That was wicked hard," Ivy said, breathing heavily. She walked away.

Madison shook her head and adjusted her shorts to make them a little bit longer. Seventh grade could be wicked hard.

"I hope Fiona's not really, really sick," Aimee whispered to Madison as they changed back into their school clothes in the locker room after gym ended. "Oh my God, what if she is really, really sick?"

"She isn't," Madison said, hoping that her friend was okay. She pulled on her stockings leg by leg. "Nurse Shim probably already called her mom."

"Let's call her later," Aimee suggested.

Madison grabbed her things out of the teeny green gym locker and climbed the stairs up toward the computer center. Her math textbook felt heavier than heavy inside her bag. Madison had a giant exam coming up the next day; she had barely reviewed the first half of the chapter.

When Madison walked into Mrs. Wing's classroom, she found her favorite teacher sitting at her desk. She was looking out the window at the dark, blue-gray sky.

"Looks like stormy weather," Mrs. Wing said softly, her glass-bead earrings jingling as she turned her head to face Madison. "Looks like snow."

Madison sat down at her desk. "Cool!"

Mrs. Wing chuckled. "I don't like this cold. Winter is my least-favorite season. Brrrr." She faked a dramatic shiver.

"Mrs. Wing, do I need to come after school today to help with the Web site?" Madison asked, changing the subject. She had signed on to help as an assistant school cybrarian, which meant inputting polls, answering questions, helping to keep the school data, and more. Lately extra-credit homework and volunteering at the Far Hills Animal Shelter took preference over the Web, but Madison wanted to start working on the computer more.

"I was speaking with Walter about helping with the data entry," Mrs. Wing said. "And Drew, too. There's always room for helpers."

Walter Diaz, otherwise known as Egg, was Madison's best guy friend. And Drew Maxwell was Egg's best friend and therefore Madison's friend, too, by association. Not only were the two boys into computers as much as (if not more than) Madison, but they had their own Web page development in

10

progress. Madison wanted to build her own site one day, too.

"So what are we adding to the site?" Madison asked Mrs. Wing.

Mrs. Wing smiled. "I want to add a Winter Wonderland section with news about hockey games and winter festivals and everything else going on inside and outside the school."

"What's up, Maddie?" Egg called out as he strolled into the computer lab. "What are you doing here so early?"

The second-period bell rang, and Drew walked into class along with everyone else. "Hey, Maddie," he said, sliding into a desk and giving her a wave.

While Mrs. Wing got the rest of the class settled, Egg talked nonstop about his new skates.

"I just got these killer hockey skates," he boasted. One of Egg's greatest goals in life was to play for the New York Rangers hockey team. "I can't wait to try them out. They're black with silver stripes on the side."

"Like racing stripes," Drew quipped. "You wearing them tomorrow?"

"What's tomorrow?" Madison asked.

Egg gasped like he'd just been punched. "Oh, man! You don't know about it? A whole bunch of kids are going down to the Lake Wannalotta after school tomorrow."

"Who set this up?" Madison asked.

"Me and Chet. Didn't we tell you?" Egg replied.

"No." Madison rolled her eyes. "Anyway, I don't see what the big deal is with skating."

"What planet are you from?" Egg asked. "Skating is *way* cool."

"My cousin used to be a hockey skating champion at his old middle school," Drew said. "That was definitely way cool."

"Your cousin?" Madison asked. "You mean Hart?"

Drew nodded.

"So . . . is Hart going to be skating, then, too?" Madison asked.

"Of course, Maddie," Egg cracked. "Everyone is going. You can't miss it."

Madison looked down at her desk and sucked in her breath. She didn't know how to skate very well, a fact that never seemed to matter before, but now it mattered a lot. She chewed on the inside of her lip and thought about her options. Could she just skip the whole skating scene without attracting too much attention? And while she was at it . . . wasn't there a way she could get out of her math test, too?

Egg leaned over and pinched her shoulder before returning to his seat. "You'd better be there," he said. "Or I'll never let you forget it."

Madison just nodded and tried to smile.

Chapter 2

"So, are you ready for your math test?" Aimee asked Madison as they walked home from school that day.

Madison stuck out her tongue like she'd eaten something yucky. "No. Math is my enemy. Do you think I can get out of the test somehow?"

Aimee laughed as she retied her purple wool scarf around her neck. "Yeah, sure. And while you're at it, why don't you get out of your English paper and all your other homework, too? And why don't you find world peace? And then why don't you find a cure for—"

"Ha, ha! Very funny, Aim," Madison said, crinkling her nose with disapproval. As much as Madison loved her BFF, she hated the sarcasm that often came along with Aimee.

Aimee just giggled. "Race ya!" she said, and took off down the block.

The pair ran the shortcut route, dashing through someone's backyard and down a side street. Then they skipped over to Blueberry Street, where they'd both lived since they were babies. The girls were breathless from running in the cold, cold air.

"So, you didn't tell me, what are you wearing to the skating party tomorrow?" Aimee asked, still huffing a little.

Madison frowned. "What do you mean, *party*?"

"No, no, I don't mean party like *that*. I mean . . . well, you know. I'm wearing my lemon-drop ski parka, and I have these great new jeans with embroidery up the sides. I think I might even wear my—"

"Oh," Madison interrupted. "What is a person supposed to wear to a skating thing?"

"What's the matter with you, Maddie?" Aimee asked.

Madison shrugged. "Whatever."

Aimee came to a complete stop. "Something is totally the matter, isn't it? I can tell these things."

"What?" Madison said.

Sometimes best friends could be annoying even when they were trying to help out the most. Aimee was ultrapersistent.

"I have an excellent idea. Why don't you borrow my Fair Isle sweater for skating tomorrow? It was my mom's, and she is a wicked good ice-skater."

"I don't need your mom's sweater, Aim," Madison said. She sighed. "What I need is to learn how to skate."

"You can skate! I remember last year, you—"

"—sat on the side of the ice and clapped for everyone else," Madison finished Aimee's sentence.

"Oh. Yeah." Aimee frowned.

"And the year before that, I pretended I had a sprained ankle. Remember?"

"You mean to tell me it wasn't sprained?" Aimee said.

Madison chuckled. "Aim, it was *your* idea to make up that excuse."

"Oh yeah," Aimee said. "Gee, it was so good, I fell for it."

"Look, I gotta run home," Madison said, smiling her widest smile. She leaned in and hugged her friend. "And I'll probably go to the skating thing, so don't worry."

"Promise me you will go," Aimee demanded, sticking out her pinky for a pinky swear. *"Promise."*

Madison pulled off her green wool gloves to squeeze.

"Hey, Aim, are you gonna call Fiona?" Madison asked before they said their last good-byes. "I wonder if she's feeling any better."

"I'm going to go call her right now. Why don't you go home and we can all go online together?"

15

"That's a great idea," Madison said. She turned toward her house.

"And don't forget your other promise!" Aimee yelled after her.

Madison tossed her head as if to say, "No problem," but inside, she was feeling bad already about the pinky swear. Madison had a sinking feeling she might have to break her promise to Aimee.

As soon as she'd dumped her book bag in the front hallway, Madison said hello to Mom and her cute pug, Phin, who were in the kitchen. Then she bounded upstairs to her bedroom and pulled on her favorite new woolly sock-slippers with monkeys woven on top, the ones Mom gave her for Christmas. When it was this cold outside, Madison liked nothing better than getting as snuggly as she could as soon as she arrived home.

Lying across the bed on her tummy, Madison booted up her computer. She opened a brand-new file.

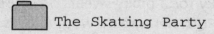 The Skating Party

Once Mom and I watched this movie called
Ice Castles on TV. It was really old, and
it was about a girl and guy who were
professional skaters and then they fell
in love. Even though it was from the
seventies, I loved that movie soooo much.
I wish that could be me, like me and Hart

skating together. Something about that
makes my stomach all fluttery.

   Rude Awakening: Is it a real problem to
go ice skating with someone who makes you .
melt?

After writing a few more pages, Madison closed
the file on skating—for the time being. But she was
still obsessing about the skating. Should she go . . .
or not?

What would Bigwheels do?

Madison plugged in her supersecret online password and logged on to bigfishbowl.com to see if her
keypal Bigwheels was online. She probably wouldn't
be, since she lived in Washington State, which was
all the way across the country. It was three hours
earlier in Bigwheels's world at that very moment,
which meant Bigwheels was in school instead. But
Madison decided e-mail was better than no conversation at all.

From: MadFinn
To: Bigwheels
Subject: Ice-Skating Trauma
Date: Mon 15 Jan 4:03 PM

How is school?

Okay, so I have a very important
question for you: Have you ever
fallen while skating?

Well, I have. On my face,
practically, so ice went up my
nose. And I almost cut my hand on
the blade of an ice skate, too, and
that freaked out my dad. This was
all when I was six or something.
Since then the whole idea of
SKATING freaks me a little bit.

So my dilemma is this skating
thing, and you-know-who will be
there. Should I go and risk
mortification (is that a real
word?). Or should I stay at home
with my dog, Phin, where it's
supersafe? (You know my vote.)

I wish you were online so you could
write back now.

Yours till the ice breakers,

MadFinn

**No sooner had Madison hit SEND than she got an
Insta-Message.**
It wasn't Bigwheels, though. It was Aimee.

<BalletGrl>: So I called Fiona and
    she's soooo sick
<MadFinn>: Oh no

\<BalletGrl\>: She has a fever of like 102

\<MadFinn\>: :-(

\<BalletGrl\>: I talked to Chet & her mom

\<MadFinn\>: Is she going 2 school tomorrow?

\<BalletGrl\>: NO & she can't go sk8ing either

\<MadFinn\>: Is skating off then?

\<BalletGrl\>: (@@)

\<MadFinn\>: Yeah HHOK

\<BalletGrl\>: U r gonna be AWESOME skating ur such a worrywart

\<MadFinn\>: Should I call F now

\<BalletGrl\>: Not tonite she's sleeping her mom said

\<MadFinn\>: R u studying for math now

\<BalletGrl\>: I don't have a test YOU do . . . hello I only said that 2 u like a million times

\<MadFinn\>: Oops :-(

\<BalletGrl\>: W-E

\<MadFinn\>: Do u have dance class Tues?

\<BalletGrl\>: yup pointe 2 hrs after school (grrr)

\<MadFinn\>: C u in the morning?

\<BalletGrl\>: Let's walk 2 school. Bye!

MadFinn: TTFN

Madison turned off her computer just in time to hear Mom call her downstairs for dinner. They were having vegetarian soufflé, only it had "fallen" while inside the oven.

"Is it supposed to look so flat?" Madison asked Mom.

"It doesn't look as nice, but it tastes exactly the same," Mom said, rushing to serve it before it got any flatter.

Madison picked out all the peppers in her piece and took a bite. Surprisingly, the soufflé wasn't that bad tasting at all. Mom's cooking was definitely improving. Since the big D (as in divorce), Mom was trying much harder to be a better chef, a better housekeeper, and a much better organizer.

"So how was school today?" Mom asked.

Madison took another bite and just shook her head. "Mmmmfffine," she mumbled.

"Walter called here earlier, you know. I think you must have been on the computer."

"Egg called?" Madison asked.

"Yes, he told me to remind you to bring your ice skates to school. What's that all about? Since when do you like ice skating?" Mom said.

Madison wanted to scream, but she calmly replied, "I don't."

"So why are you going skating?" Mom asked.

"Just forget it, Mom," Madison answered. "Please."

Mom sat back in her kitchen chair and took a

20

sip of her water. "What's going on, Madison?" she said.

"Huh? Nothing's going on, Mom. Some kids are going skating and asked me to come. What are you smiling at?"

"You make me smile," Mom said quietly.

Madison shook her head. "What's the point of going when I can't skate?"

"Oh, honey bear, you can skate. You can do anything you set your—"

"You just don't understand, Mom," Madison pleaded. "You just don't."

"Well, maybe not," Mom said. "But I was only trying to help."

Madison's heart sank. She could tell that her mom was annoyed. This week they'd already had a few big arguments.

Just yesterday, Dad had called from Denver, where he was visiting on a business trip. He wasn't sure if he was coming back in time for his weekly dinner for Madison. Mom didn't like hearing about that. It upset her that Dad would extend a trip to Denver with his new girlfriend, Stephanie—and change plans on Madison. To make matters worse, Madison defended *Dad*.

Big mistake.

Brrrrrrrrrring.

Mom reached across the kitchen counter to pick up the phone.

"Oh, how are you, Mother?" Mom said, pretending to be chipper. Mom's mom, Gramma Helen, was on the line. "What's new? Oh? Well, nothing much. No, we weren't watching TV. We were just finishing our dinner. Oh? Well, Maddie's right here. Let me get her."

Mom covered the receiver and whispered to Madison, "She's talking a mile a minute. You talk to her."

"Gramma?" Madison squealed when she took the phone.

Gramma squealed right back. She explained how she'd been watching the Weather Channel like she always did from six to six-thirty on weeknights, when she saw something particularly peculiar on the travel report.

"There's a great big mess of a snowstorm headed right for Far Hills!" Gramma exclaimed. "They said the name of the town and everything right there on the TV, would you believe it?"

Madison gasped. "A snowstorm?"

With phone in hand, she wandered over to the bay window in the living room, pressed her warm nose onto the cold window, and looked outside. All she could see were shadows on the porch from streetlights. No snow yet.

"Are you *sure*, Gramma?" Madison asked.

Mom called out from the other room. "She's right! The Weather Channel has a special warning for our area."

After Madison said good-bye to Gramma, she made a secret, secret wish.

"I hope we have a super-snow day tomorrow," she said to herself. "Like the biggest snowstorm ever."

Madison imagined giant white snowdrifts everywhere, with snow that kept falling even when she begged it to stop. No one would be able to go anywhere or do anything.

No school . . .

No math test . . .

And most important . . .

NO skating.

Chapter 3

Brrring! Brrring! Brrring!

Madison opened her eyes. It was so dark.

She couldn't feel her feet because they were buried down under the blankets on her bed. Her entire body was wrapped in the comforter like a mummy, so it took effort to roll over to see her alarm clock. It was 6 A.M.

Phin, who had been nestled on the floor inside the folds of an old blanket, jumped up on the bed. Madison heard her mom talking on the phone but didn't hear exactly what she was saying.

Only the teeniest peek of light was coming in around the edges of her curtains. It was between night and morning, that just-before-dawn time when anything could happen.

"Madison?" Mom whispered from the doorway.

Madison's eyes snapped shut. She pretended to still be asleep.

"Madison?" Mom said, a little louder this time. "I know you can hear me. That was the PTA phone chain. School is canceled today. There's more than a foot of snow on the ground."

"Mo-om?" Madison's voice croaked. Her body tingled. She'd wished for a snow day, and now here it was.

Mom walked over to the bed and sat on the edge. A little more light was beginning to sneak in through the curtains, so Madison could see the soft outline of Mom's face. She was smiling.

"Why don't you sleep in for a little while, honey bear?" Mom said, tucking her in even tighter than before. "Sleep in, and when you get up, we'll make waffles."

Phin was walking around on the bed, with his curlicue tail in motion.

"Yum, waffles," Madison said softly.

Mom kissed the top of her head and grabbed Phin, who was getting frisky like he wanted to go out. "I'm going to walk Phin before it gets any snowier. You close your eyes and go back to dreaming, Maddie."

Unfortunately, the last thing Madison could do right now was sleep. As soon as Mom disappeared with Phin, Madison wriggled out of her mummy wrap and began tossing. The light was getting brighter and brighter because outside was getting whiter and whiter.

Madison jumped up and ran to the window.

Wow!

While she was sleeping, someone had dumped powdered sugar all over the neighborhood—or at least that's what it looked like. No one from the city had plowed or driven on the street yet, so every patch of pavement was covered in white. And snow was still falling.

"Mooooooom!" Madison yelped as she tugged on her jeans and socks. She pulled them on right under her Lisa Simpson nightshirt and then threw a sweater on over that. "Mooooom!"

But Mom didn't answer. She was outside with Phinnie.

Madison went into the back hallway to get her winter snow boots and laced them up tight, put on her green gloves and jacket, wrapped a scarf around her nose and mouth, tugged on her rainbow-striped woolen cap, and opened the front door.

Madison could see one set of people prints (Mom's) and another set of pooch prints (Phin's) going down the path toward the street.

"Mom? Phinnie?" Madison called out. Her voice echoed in the still morning air.

"Quiet, Maddie! Everyone can hear you!" Mom shushed her from up the street, hustling back home. She let go of the leash, and Phin ran as fast as his chubby little body would take him, all the way to Madison.

They wandered around outside for a little while longer, skidding across the soft snow. Madison brushed clumps of white off the tops of bushes. The snow was too soft to make snowballs. It disintegrated in her hands like flour.

Around the neighborhood, people had begun to wake up. Madison could see yellow lights burning in a few windows. The retired fireman who lived across the street was already up, shoveling his driveway. Way off in the distance, Madison could hear the vroom of a plow making its rounds. Soon the powdery street snow would be packed up against the curb.

"I can't believe we don't have school!" Madison said, grinning from ear to ear. She rubbed the bottoms of Phin's paws, which were icy and wet. He was shivering.

"We should go inside," Mom suggested.

Madison followed her up to the house. Along the way, she saw a row of icicles on their porch post and pulled one off. Clutching the icicle made her remember. Sucking on ice was something she used to do all the time in second grade, when she and Ivy Daly were best friends.

Second grade.

That time seemed so long ago from right now.

Madison moved an icicle into her mouth carefully so it wouldn't stick to her lip. She remembered how Ivy once put two small icicles on her lips, letting them stick there and pretending to be a walrus.

Ivy used to be so good at making Madison laugh.

It's a bad storm, folks.

Yes, indeed, up to two feet inland and a foot along the coast.

And we're not done yet!

Expect more snow this afternoon.

Madison flipped the channels to see what other stations were saying about the weather. She couldn't believe this snowstorm had dropped so much snow—and wasn't over yet.

"It's cold out there!" Mom said, moving the boots from a slushy puddle in the hall to the porch. "Let's make some cocoa, too."

"Mmm—yummy," Madison said, nodding. She went to the cupboard and got the hot chocolate and the waffle mix. "Mom, it's almost eight. Do you think it's too early to call Aimee?"

"Not at all. Her father is probably over at the bookstore already," Mom said. She was talking about Book Web, a bookstore and cybercafé that Aimee's parents owned in downtown Far Hills.

Madison dialed, but the Gillespie line was busy.

She tried Fiona's house next, but Mrs. Waters answered and said her daughter was still sleeping. "May I please leave a message?" Madison asked sweetly. Mrs. Waters said Fiona would call as soon as she woke up.

Madison dialed Aimee's house for a second time. It was still busy.

There was a chance that Aimee was online, so Madison dashed upstairs to get her laptop computer. She'd get in touch with her BFF somehow. Madison plugged in the phone jack and dialed up the bigfishbowl.com Web site.

The home page was *swimming* with members.

```
Hotstuff76
Jessica_01
Qtpiegal2
BryanSarah
Peacenluv11
BalletGrl
```

Aimee *was* there! For someone who had only just learned about using computers, Aimee was on the Web more than anyone else Madison knew.

Madison sent a surprise Insta-Message to her friend.

```
<MadFinn>: Hiya!!!
<BalletGrl>: Hi!
<MadFinn>: Can you believe all this
    snowww?
<BalletGrl>: :^D
<MadFinn>: Soooo whassup?
```

```
<BalletGrl>: I have to do shoveling
    with my brothers and then Dad
    asked us all to help @ the store
<MadFinn>: So you can't hang out
<BalletGrl>: Sorry I can't right
    now. Plus my dance lesson was
    canceled, which is a real bummer
<MadFinn>: Is anyone else doing
    stuff
<BalletGrl>: I don't know
<MadFinn>: I know Fiona is still in
    bed:-~(
<BalletGrl>: What r u doing
<MadFinn>: 0 (like the big goose
    egg)
<BalletGrl>: Come to the store then
    w/us
<MadFinn>: Hmmmmm
<BalletGrl>: Well call me there L8R
    then, promise?
<MadFinn>: Ok ok
<BalletGrl>: Gotta run
<BalletGrl>: *poof*
```

After Madison signed out of the conversation,
she returned to the home page to check her e-mail.
But before she could even select the MAIL key, she
was Insta-Messaged again.

```
<Wetwinz>: Hi Maddie
<MadFinn>: Hi Fiona
```

```
<Wetwinz>: I am soooo sick
<MadFinn>: Y r u on the computer I
    thought you were still in bed
<Wetwinz>: My mom doesn't know I'm
    up
<MadFinn>: Whats wrong w/u?
<Wetwinz>: Fever, chills, puking it
    is gross Mom says I have to stay
    in bed until it goes away and I
    have a headache too I'm supposed
    to be under the covers now
<MadFinn>: :>(
<Wetwinz>: Where's Aim today
<MadFinn>: cybercafé
<Wetwinz>: DLTM
<MadFinn>: Yup she's working can u
    believe it
<Wetwinz>: Bummer for a snow day
<MadFinn>: Bigger bummer = being
    sick = you
<Wetwinz>: I'd say come over but I
    don't wanna breathe on you and my
    mom won't let me go out
<MadFinn>: Oh well
<Wetwinz>: 911 my mom is coming
<MadFinn>: Call me 18r
```

Madison saw that she had mail. Maybe she had a note back from Bigwheels.

Bigwheels hadn't written, but there *was* e-mail from Dad.

From: JeffFinn
To: MadFinn
Subject: SNOW
Date: Tues 16 Jan 7:11 AM

What do you get when you cross
Dracula with the snowstorm in Far
Hills? Frostbite!

Hey, sweetheart, I'm here in Denver
with Stephanie. Oh, boy, there's so
much snow there and here, I can't
even get a flight out until tomorrow.
How is it there? How is Phinnie?
He always hated walking in the
snow because his feet got
frozen.

Needless to say, I'm stuck here in
Colorado. I will try to call or
e-mail later on today. As soon as
I get back, I'm taking you out for
dinner and a movie, too. How does
that sound? Write back to me.

Love,
Dad

Madison was a little sad about Dad's not being
able to see her this week, but the joy of the lucky
snow day was taking over.

Nothing could get her down today. Madison was free as a bird. She'd watch a video for starters. Then she'd catch up with her friends later.

"Maddie?" Mom called to her from the other room.

Madison bit her lip. Something in the tone of Mom's voice told her that she wouldn't want to hear what Mom had to say.

"Maddie," Mom said again, appearing at the bedroom door. "There you are! I've been calling you for five minutes."

"I was online," Madison mumbled.

"Well, I got this terrific idea and I need your help."

There was that word Madison dreaded most: *Help.*

"Help for what, Mom?" Madison asked cautiously.

Mom chuckled. "It's nothing bad, so you can get that look off your face. I think it'll be fun. I want you to come up to the attic with me and look around in the old boxes. I need some backup materials for the documentary I'm working on. I can't find some of the paperwork, and I'm sure it's up there."

Madison buried her face into a pillow on her bed and then lifted her head up quickly again. "Help go through boxes? Today?" Madison asked.

Mom crossed her arms and smiled. "Today," she said simply.

Madison knew what that meant.

No escape.

Chapter 4

"When was the last time you were up here?" Madison asked as they entered the attic. It smelled like wet carpet from when there had been a leak last summer.

"Oh, I don't know. I brought up all those cartons that had been sitting in my office. Those over there."

Mom pointed to a few boxes with yellow labels that read BUDGE FILMS, the name of Mom's production company.

"Then what are all *these*?" Madison asked.

She pointed to a mountain of other boxes in all shapes and sizes that were pushed up against one wall. Some were ripped on the sides, and others were covered in dust. No one had touched most of these boxes in years. In the middle of the floor was a half-open box with tinsel coming out. It was their

Christmas ornament box. Mom still hadn't put away all the decorations.

"You know, Fiona's attic isn't this messy, Mom," Madison said.

"Well, Fiona just moved here from California. We've been here for a little while longer."

"I guess," Madison said, shrugging. She looked around some more.

On one wall of the attic, the sun glimmered in through a round window. One of the coolest-looking parts of the house was the attic window. Madison had never really noticed how beautiful it looked until just now.

"So what are we supposed to do?" Madison asked her mother.

"Look for my papers—and whatever else we may find. Our lives are up here, packed in boxes. It's amazing, isn't it?" Mom said, resting her elbow on the corner of an old dresser.

"Hey!" Madison said. She spied the gleam of a lock and pressed her body between two boxes to lift out an old case. "What's this?"

"That must be my old flute," Mom said, taking it from her. "I thought that was thrown out ages ago."

Madison had been playing the flute on and off throughout elementary school. She'd nearly given it up since junior high began and she found herself busier than busy with other work. She hadn't realized that Mom played the flute, too.

"I never knew you played! Can you still play?" Madison asked enthusiastically.

"Oh no!" Mom giggled. "Your father tried to get me started up again a few times when we were first married, but . . ."

Mom stopped midsentence. The phone was ringing downstairs.

"I have to grab that!" Mom said, moving to the attic stairs. "It's my office. You dig around and tell me what else you find up here. I'll probably be a little while if it's my editor on the phone."

"Okay, see ya," Madison said, still holding the dusty flute case. She opened it up and peered inside. The flute had tarnished. It felt cold to the touch. Inside the case, she also found a piece of old sheet music for a song by the Beatles. Madison set the case, flute, and music aside.

She didn't know where to look next. Suddenly the drudgery of an attic "job" seemed exciting to Madison. This was like a magical treasure hunt.

One box read TAX DOCUMENTS. Madison moved that out of the way. Behind it, there was a wooden box with an old phonograph player inside. The lining of the box was moth-eaten, and the player didn't look like it worked, but Madison cranked the handle to see what would happen. Dust flew everywhere. A very thick record turned around and around, but no noise came out.

"No wonder they invented CDs," Madison said, moving to another space in the attic.

There was a shelf of books up against the wall, too. She hadn't seen it at first when she walked inside. The dim light from the round window made it hard to see. Madison saw rows of titles on botany, birds, law, and everything else she could imagine. The covers were dust covered, though, so Madison could barely read the gilded titles.

There was an entire row of books by Louis L'Amour, a western author Madison's grampa Joe had loved to read, before he died. Madison pulled one book off a shelf to see the pages inside. The binding cracked as she opened the book. There was an inscription: *To Joe with all my heart, Helen.*

Madison smiled at the idea of Gramma Helen and Grampa Joe being together, in love. She wished love could last forever and ever. But sometimes it didn't. She knew that now.

Madison wondered if her love for Hart Jones would last forever—or at least as long as seventh grade lasted.

"Madison!" Mom yelled up to her.

Madison rushed over to the attic stairs. *"What?"*

"Honey bear, get down here quick. I just put on the weather, and it says we're supposed to get more snow." Mom was talking frantically. She always made fun when Gramma Helen talked that way, but the truth was that Mom talked faster than fast most of the time.

She told Mom she'd be right down, then she went back to lock up the new-old flute. On her way back out, Madison tripped over a box that was marked BRAZIL, FILMING—NEW. It had a Budge Films yellow label, too.

"Hey, Mom, I think I found your office stuff here," Madison said.

"Okay," Mom yelled back. "Then we'll get it after lunch. You have to come down and see this weather report, though. We've got some kind of cold front headed our way. Wowza. Their map of the United States is covered in clouds."

As Madison entered the kitchen, she could tell Mom was making grilled cheese sandwiches. The kitchen smelled like burned toast.

"We should go get some supplies," Mom said, eyes on the small television set in the kitchen.

"Supplies?" Madison asked. "Are you worried we're going to be buried in snow or something?"

"You never know, and it is definitely—"

"Better to be safe than sorry," Madison interrupted. "That's what Gramma always says."

"So eat up your sandwich and we'll go to the store," Mom said. She disappeared upstairs to put on different clothes and makeup. She usually had to "put on her face" before heading out.

Madison turned the volume back up on the weather alert that the local news show kept replaying. MAJOR STORM WARNING kept scrolling across the bottom of the TV screen. *This was serious.*

As she took a chewy bite of her grilled cheese, Madison once again reflected on the events of the past day.

She had wished for a snowstorm, and a snowstorm had been provided. Now another snowstorm was coming.

Did Madison wish one time too many?

Once again the phone rang. Madison jumped up to answer, which was good since it was a call for her. Aimee was calling from Book Web.

"Oh my God, it is sooooo busy here," Aimee blurted. "No wonder Daddy wanted some help. Even with my brothers and me we're busy. You should really come down and see—"

Aimee hadn't even given Madison a chance to say hello before she started to talk . . . and talk . . . and talk. She did that a lot.

Finally she asked how Madison was doing.

"I'm okay, I guess," Madison replied. "I'm helping my mom out, too, with her work."

"Cool!" Aimee said. "Can you believe all the snow we got? I'm sorry we can't hang out. Maybe later?"

"The weather lady says that there's more on the way," Madison said.

"More?" Aimee yelled, so loudly, Madison had to pull the receiver away from her ear. "Did you say *more*?"

"Yes," Madison said. "And would you stop screeching, please?"

They both laughed.

"The only bad part is that the whole skating thing is canceled," Aimee said. She sighed. "They closed the whole area by the lake because someone drove their car into a ditch near there. That's what my brother Roger said."

"Oh no . . . really?" Madison feigned disappointment. But she could feel her body *hum*. She didn't mind if skating was canceled! That was what she'd been hoping! She tried to mask her excitement, to keep her truer-than-true feelings hidden from everyone else, even her best friend.

But it was hard to fake out her best friend. Aimee already knew the truth.

"Don't act all sad, Maddie! I know you didn't want to go to the lake," Aimee said. "You don't have to pretend like you're bummed out or anything. I know how you feel about skating."

"You . . . *what*?" Madison was embarrassed, but she grinned so wide, Aimee could probably *hear* the grin through the phone line. "You do?"

"Yeah, I do," Aimee said. "And it's okay."

Madison felt so relieved.

No skating—and no secrets from her best friend, either.

Someone asked Aimee to help out in the bookstore, so she had to get off the telephone, but it

40

turned out to be good timing because at that *exact moment* Mom came downstairs.

"Let's hit the road!" she said.

Madison grabbed her rainbow hat and green gloves.

The roads were busier than they'd been earlier that morning, but there were still fewer cars than on a nonsnowy, ordinary day. Mom drove slowly so the car wouldn't slip and slide all over the wet, slushy streets. By the time they pulled into the parking lot near the Far Hills Shoppes, the wind had picked up a little. The sky turned ashen white, like all the color had been sucked right out.

They stopped in at the Tool Box hardware store first. Mom picked up a box of extra-large candles, three new flashlights and extra batteries, and a new shovel. Their old shovel had gotten a big dent in it when Mom tried shoveling that morning and hit a slab of ice.

Afterward they circled over to Stationery Barn, an office-supply outlet. Mom was a sucker for gold paper clips and neon-colored pens. She loved jazzy office accessories so much that whenever she took Madison shopping, they came home with armfuls of notebooks and files and folders they didn't need. Today Mom used "cleaning out the attic boxes" as her excuse to buy new cartons, folders, and special labels for the folders. Madison benefited from the shopping spree. She got a cool pen with a squishy-soft, orange gel grip.

The shops were bustling. Everyone was either standing in line for caffè latte at The Coffee Mill or buying supplies for the storm that was coming their way. All anyone could talk about was the weather. Madison began to fear the worst. What if they were covered with fifteen feet of snow and frozen for an eternity until some future civilization dug them out of the ice?

Across the mall, Madison thought she spied Poison Ivy and Rose Thorn, shopping for clothes, but they disappeared before Madison could find out for sure. She bumped into Dan Ginsburg for real, however. He was looking over the stand that sold baseball hats. Madison was friends with Dan from seventh grade and from the Far Hills Animal Shelter, where she was a volunteer.

"Hey, Maddie!" Dan said, giving her a high five. He was always in a good mood. "My mom was just talking about you this morning. She wants to know if you're coming in next week for the massive winter cleaning."

Dan's mom, Eileen, was a nurse at the animal clinic.

"Yeah, sure, I'm all for cleaning," Madison giggled. "My mom has me cleaning junk out of the attic today."

"Sorry for you!" Dan said.

"Actually, I'm the one who's sorry, Dan. I haven't been around that much. How are all the animals?"

42

Madison had begun her volunteer stint at the clinic by going three times a week, but now she only went once every other week. She wanted very much to get back to more regular visits.

"Maddie, the animals miss you. And that dachshund you liked was adopted, by the way. Did I tell you that?" Dan asked.

Madison had grown attached to many dogs at the clinic, including a miniature dachshund named Rosebud. Now Rosebud had found a new family. Madison felt so happy about that. She wanted all the dogs to find happy homes.

"Any *new* animals?" she asked Dan.

He nodded. They were now boarding a runaway golden retriever, a scruffy beagle, two parrots, and a litter of tabby kittens. He said they'd also fixed up a German shepherd that had gotten hit by a car.

Madison turned away for just a moment to see her mother walking toward them. She waved and wrapped up the conversation with Dan.

It was time to head home again through the snow and ice. One stop at the supermarket for food and they'd be fully armed and ready for the arrival of the next storm.

Later that afternoon, Madison had helped Mom shovel the front steps and sidewalk, and had taken Phin for a stroll around the block. But she felt lost without her friends. Aimee was at the bookstore.

Fiona was sick. No one else had called. Not even Egg.

To fight the boredom, Mom suggested she head back up to the attic, but Madison didn't feel like it anymore. She turned on her laptop instead.

She plugged in the Web site address for the Weather Channel from TV and saw more maps showing snow and clouds and other storm signs. Then she surfed over to bigfishbowl.com, but the server was down, and she couldn't get into any of the chat rooms. She also couldn't access "Ask the Blowfish," a special feature on the site that let members ask questions about life, love, and other junk.

Luckily she didn't log off, however. A moment after she'd read the SERVER UNAVAILABLE message for bigfishbowl.com, Madison's Insta-Message icon flashed.

```
<Eggaway>: Yo, Madfinn!
<MadFinn>: Hey Egg whassup
<Eggaway>: Skymoonsunstars
<MadFinn>: VF
<Eggaway>: We're all meeting 18r @
    the lake
<MadFinn>: Isn't that closed?
<Eggaway>: No whats ur prob? I
    wanna sk8! My new hockey sk8s are
    the best
<MadFinn>: (:>|
<Eggaway>: VVF
```

```
<MadFinn>: When?
<Eggaway>: Like 3 @ the lake
<MadFinn>: I have to get a ride
<Eggaway>: ASK UR MOM
<MadFinn>: Don't yell @ me she's
    working
<Eggaway>: Yo! Maybe Chet's dad can
    drive u
<MadFinn>: Maybe. who's going?
<Eggaway>: Me, Drew, Chet, Hart,
    these other kids Lance and Suresh
<MadFinn>: That's all guys, Egg
<Eggaway>: So?
<MadFinn>: I dunno
<Eggaway>: I think Ivy and Joanie
    may come
<MadFinn>: Oh
<Eggaway>: Hart invited them and
    some other girl who lives next
    door to him, she does real
    skating contests
<MadFinn>: Oh
<Eggaway>: And if it snows today
    again we'll do it later I'll
    e-mail bye!
<MadFinn>: Oh
```

Madison's heart skipped a beat as she clicked offline.

She immediately opened a new page in one of her existing files.

Hart

Rude Awakening: I keep getting cold feet when it comes to Hart. And it's not because I'm standing in the snow.

It's her.

No matter when, where, or what the situation, everyone notices Poison Ivy. And I just know that this afternoon, Hart will be hanging out with her. I feel like it would be torture to go there and see that happen without Aimee or Fiona to back me up. Even though they still don't know about my crush . . . help!

I wish Bigwheels would write back.

Maybe the guys will be too busy skating to notice? Maybe they'll all play hockey and leave her out? I wish.

Madison glanced away from the computer for a moment to collect her thoughts. From where she was sitting in her bedroom, she had a full view of the window looking out on the street. Some kids were sledding on a slope in her neighbors' yard.

She noticed something. Big fat flakes were just starting to fall again onto the windowsill and glass pane.

More snow. *Already!*

Madison smiled to herself. No one would be meeting at three o'clock today . . . and maybe not even tomorrow. She had an extra day or two to prepare herself for skating, Hart, and Ivy.

The second storm was moving in.

Seventh-grade snow days were about to get *really* interesting.

even tomorrow. She had all extra day of two for
prepare herself for skating. Paris and Div
The second storm was moving in
seventh-grade snow they were about to get
really frustration Alien

Chapter 5

"Rowrrooooo!" Phin was standing on Madison's stomach, panting. The clock next to her bed said 8:23 A.M.

Madison leaped out from under the covers and ran to the window. The blanket of snow across Far Hills was at least a foot deeper than the day before—and it was still snowing, snowing, snowing.

She donned her monkey slippers and shuffled down the stairs to breakfast. The smell of pancakes filled the air.

Mom had made a superbatch of silver-dollar cakes. She'd even warmed up syrup in the microwave. Madison felt special. The last time Mom ever did that was for Dad when they were still married. She put fruit slices on top of one pancake for the face: strawberry eyes, banana nose, and orange mouth.

"Mom, you haven't made me smiley pancakes since I was little," Madison said, taking her first enormous bite. "These are so yummy."

Mom sat down at the table. "Isn't this fun, the two of us stuck indoors?"

"Do you think it will ever stop snowing?" Madison asked, taking another big bite of breakfast.

"Doesn't look like it," Mom said, gazing out the kitchen window. "I'm going to get lots of film editing done today, that's for sure. I remember when we had bad storms like this in Chicago, growing up."

The house rattled with the wind.

"Just like that." Mom laughed. "Windy, snowy, really miserable. Your grandmother always sent your aunt Angie and me into the yard to make snow angels. Of course Angie usually beaned me with snow*balls* instead."

Mom told a few more weather-related Chicago stories that made Madison laugh.

When Mom was finished telling stories, Madison called Fiona to see how she was feeling. But she sounded hoarse, so Madison could barely hear her.

"I have a fever of a hundred and one," Fiona said. "I'm all clammy."

"That means the fever is going away, though, right?" Madison asked.

"Mom says I can't even get out of bed. I'm so sick of watching television, and I read my English reading through next week's assignments already," Fiona said.

Madison realized she'd been out of school for a day and a half and she hadn't done any homework yet. She'd have to deal with that later.

"Is Aimee still helping her dad at the store?" Fiona whispered.

"Yeah," Madison said. "But she's not working all of today. We were going to hang out. Can we come over to see you?"

"My mother says I'm still too sick to have visitors." Fiona sighed. "I feel like I'm quarantined from the rest of the planet."

"Well, as soon as she says it's okay, we are totally coming over."

"Is everyone out skating and playing in the snow and all that?" Fiona asked. "My stupid brother won't tell me anything."

"Not really," Madison answered. "Not yet, anyway. The lake was closed yesterday. It's been too stormy."

Fiona giggled a little bit. "I really miss you guys."

"I miss you, too," Madison said. She wanted to tell Fiona all the specifics about the skating party and then the cancellation of the skating party and the rescheduling of the skating party . . . but she decided not to tell her anything. She didn't want Fiona to feel any more "out of it" than she already did. Being sick was the worst feeling in the world, especially when your head felt woozy with cough and cold medicine.

After they said their good-byes, Madison called Aimee. Aimee wasn't going to the bookstore after all. They made a date to walk their dogs in the middle of the blizzard. Madison secretly hoped they could make angels in the snow, too. Just like her mom and Aunt Angie had done when they were her age.

Mom was waiting upstairs in the attic to resume the big clean. She'd torn into a few other boxes and recovered many of the papers she'd been looking for yesterday.

"Do you think you could help me organize some of this information on the computer?" Mom asked Madison. "Like, could we put information on a graph chart together?"

Madison wasn't a hundred percent sure about how to make the perfect graph chart, but she was eager for the computer challenge. She knew that even if she got stuck working on it, she could always ask Mrs. Wing for help. Madison wanted to beef up her computer skills over the next few months so by summer she'd be ready once and for all to start up her very own Web page.

"I can help you, Mom," Madison said. "But can we do it later? I was going to walk Phinnie and go over to Aimee's for a little while."

"Sure. Have fun," Mom said. She was sitting cross-legged in a pile of paper that spread all around her like a puddle. Rubber-banded stacks of slides were piled in between her legs. "I really need to hire an assistant to help me archive these materials."

"I'll help, Mom," Madison said again. "Just later, okay?"

Mom beamed. "You look cute this morning, honey bear. Are you wearing those pajamas over to Aimee's or what?"

Madison made a face and then skipped down into her bedroom. She pulled on a new pair of corduroys with patches on the pockets that had been a Christmas present from Dad's girlfriend, Stephanie. Before leaving her room, she decided to log on to her laptop to see if Egg had sent e-mail with more news on when and where the "new" skating party had been planned.

To her surprise, Madison found her e-mailbox bursting with mail.

FROM	SUBJECT
✉ Eggaway	SK8ING!!!!!
✉ Boop-Dee-Doop	Clearance
✉ JeffFinn	Fw: This is SNOW funny
✉ Webmaster@bigfis	Server Down
✉ Bigwheels	Re: Ice-Skating Trauma

Madison read Egg's note first. He had sent it to a lot of people.

```
From: Eggaway
To: Chet Wetwins; Fiona Wetwinz; Aim
BalletGrl; Rose Rosean16; Ivy
Flowr99; Hart Sk8ingboy; Susie
Peace-peep; Joan JK4ever; Lance
Bossbutt; Suresh Suresh00; Maddie
MadFinn; Dan Dantheman; Drew
W_Wonka7
Subject: SK8ING!!!!!
Date: Wed 17 Jan 10:33 AM
```

```
ok sooo this is the deal we're NOT
meeting today b/c Drew sez the lake
is STILL closed from storm and it's
still snowing n e way. My mom calld
school & she thinks they'll close it
Thursday too so let's mt tomorrow
instead @ 3 at the lake. bye!!!!
```

Madison looked over the list of "to" names on Egg's e-mail to see who was invited skating and who wasn't. Unfortunately, she saw Ivy, Rose, and Joan's e-mail addresses on the list.

But she also saw another e-mail address.

Hart.

Without thinking, Madison selected Sk8ingboy and added it to her own address book. She figured it was good to have, just in case she ever needed to send him e-mail.

Just in case.

Then Madison moved on to the other mail, deleting the Boop-Dee-Doop "special offer" because she knew Mom wouldn't let her get anything, anyway, and deleting the note from bigfishbowl's Webmaster. She knew the server had been down. She didn't need to read about it anymore.

The next message was from Dad, which was very short and sweet.

```
From: JeffFinn
To: MadFinn
Subject: Have You Heard This One?
Date: Wed 17 Jan 12:13 AM
```

```
What do you get when you cross a
witch with a glacier?
A cold spell!

LOL. Thought that was sort of cute.

Miss you, Maddie.

Love,
Dad
```

Dad had told that one at least three or four times already. It was one of his winter "regulars." Luckily the message from Bigwheels wasn't something she'd already heard. Bigwheels had

actually typed the e-mail the day before.

From: Bigwheels
To: MadFinn
Subject: Re: Ice-Skating Trauma
Date: Tues 16 Jan 8:09 PM

School is same as always. My
parents were doing really well
except Dad moved out again for a
temporary separation. Don't ask. I
told my mom I didn't care, but of
course I do.

How do you deal with your parents?

I LOVE SKATING, by the way. I agree
that it can be a little scary. That
sounded so weird that you almost
got cut on a skating blade. But
it's really not so scary on regular
rinks. I used to skate on a lake.
That was way scarier. I remember
those times when I was very little.
I didn't actually skate, but my dad
did, and he carried me. There was
one time the lake ice cracked. Dad
almost fell in.

I can't wait for the Olympics to
start because I want to watch the

ice skaters do triple-Lutz jumps. I
think the ice dancing is my
favorite part. They all look so
romantic dancing on the ice like
that, don't you think?

I don't skate now, but I think you
should. It really doesn't matter if
you fall. Don't worry about your
crush, either. He will NOT fall,
either, and definitely not for that
Ivy girl. She sounds mean. Trust me.

Write back again soon.

Yours till the snow caps,

Bigwheels

Madison looked over at the clock and gasped.
It was way later than she thought.
Aimee was waiting.
She closed her computer down quickly (saving
the Bigwheels message for further reply), grabbed
her coat, and headed out the door.
The weather outside was nippy. More fat
snowflakes were falling, and she stuck out her
tongue to lick one out of the air. It tasted like ice
cream, but that was no surprise to Madison, who
had always believed that snowflakes were naturally

sweetened. She ran to Aimee's in less than five minutes.

"Where have you been?" Aimee said when she opened her door. She was in her slippers and jeans.

"You're not even dressed?" Madison asked.

Aimee twirled around and got into some ballerina poses. "No, I'm not dressed. But I look pretty good, don't I?"

"Quit posing and *get dressed*!" Madison said, exasperated. "Please?"

Aimee burst into laughter and ran inside. Madison followed her.

It took Aimee only half an hour to get on all her gear, and in no time, she and Madison were stomping around in the Gillespie backyard. A little while later, Aimee's brothers Billy and Dean came out to join them for a game of snow Frisbee.

Ker-splat!

As Madison reached to catch the Frisbee, she lost her footing. She fell hat over boots into a snowdrift.

"Nice one, Maddie." Billy snickered.

Aimee rushed over to help her up out of the snow, but Madison was laughing so hard, she couldn't even stand.

"I—can't—get—aaaaaaah—help!" Madison cried as she bent forward and fell back again.

Aimee started to giggle, too.

"Hey, did you see that?" Dean said, looking up at

the sky. He pointed to a cloud. "I swear I just saw a lightning bolt."

"No way," Aimee said, punching him in the side. Her face was flushed pink from running around in the cold air.

Madison finally stood up, patted the snow off her pants and back, and walked over to her friend. "What are you guys looking at?" she asked.

The sky looked ominous, grayer than before. Another bolt of lightning *did* crack against the winter sky. Evening was on its way.

"I've never seen anything like that before," Billy said.

The four stared and stared, as if staring would make another lightning bolt appear. And then, in the middle of all the dark sky, it began to snow once again.

Madison felt wet drops on her eyelashes. She gazed at other snowflakes as they landed on the front of her hand, examining the crystal shapes up close.

"What time is it, Dean?" Madison asked Aimee's brother.

He looked at his digital watch. "Five-oh-six," he said.

Aimee frowned. "You have to go? Already?"

"I have to walk Phinnie!" Madison shook the snow off her green gloves and ran toward home.

Mom was standing on the porch when she got

there, shoveling some of the snow that had collected near the front door.

"Well, look at you, the Snow Queen!" Mom said,
smiling at Madison's approach.

"Very funny, Mom," Madison replied.

"I ordered pizza for dinner tonight," Mom
added. "And Phin has already been for a walk."

"Sounds good," Madison said, heading for the
house.

"And I want you to help me move some of those
boxes in the attic," Mom said. "I discovered a whole
bunch of stuff up there from grade school."

"From *my* grade school?" Madison asked.

"Yes," Mom answered. "Journals, books, even an
old photo album. They're in a box that's half open.
You were so cute back then. . . ."

"What do you mean, 'back then'?" Madison
laughed.

Mom grinned. "You know what I mean, honey
bear."

Madison grinned back and stepped inside the
front hallway. She tugged off the rainbow hat,
which made her hair stick out in a bouquet of static
electricity.

Old photo album?

She couldn't wait to see what Mom was talking
about.

Madison's clothes were sopping wet from the game of snow Frisbee. She hadn't realized it until she went to remove them and had to *peel* her pants off.

The answering machine in the front hall was blinking twice, which meant two calls. She hit the PLAY key. A tinny-sounding voice echoed in the hall.

Message one.

"Maddie? Maddie, are you there? It's Daddy, still in Denver, sweetheart. We're holed up here in the hotel at the airport, waiting for the next available flight. Only problem is that the airport is closed and looks like it might stay closed for another day or so. I miss you, Maddie. Stephanie says hello. Tell your mother I said hi. I'll call again later when I think you might be—"

Beeeeeeeeep. Message two.

"This is Ronnie Dustin at Budge, calling for Fran Finn. Fran, we have a distributor for that Brazil documentary. Give me a call, please, at your earliest convenience. I'm in the LA office."

Madison clicked STOP and then saved the last message. But she deleted the first one, figuring that Mom probably wouldn't need to hear Dad's voice. Her parents were getting along better these days, but Mom still bristled a little bit at the mention of Dad. She tried to be fair, but no matter what Dad ever did to redeem himself, Mom would find something wrong.

None of that mattered to Madison. She loved everything about her dad, even the parts that weren't so perfect, even the horrible jokes. Plus Dad always noticed and complimented Madison on her outfits.

After playing the messages, Madison hopped upstairs to put on sweatpants, her woolly monkey slippers, and an old plaid shirt she'd inherited from Dad. It was so warm.

She turned on her laptop computer and let it warm up, too, before opening another new file.

 Snow Day

Today was the BEST snow day I have ever had in my entire life, and I am not exaggerating one bit.

Secret admission #1: I maybe have a baby crush on Aimee's brothers again (but only a

teeny, tiny one, I swear). They looked
soooo cute today outside her house. We
played Frisbee for an hour or more, and
Aimee was acting kind of dorky, but she
always acts weird around her brothers. I
don't know why.

Secret admission #2: I think I will go
skating at the lake Thursday. I'm getting
up my courage. I'm feeling so HAPPY.

I've never seen so much snow in my whole
life, like I could get lost in all this
snow. Aimee and I made the BEST snow
angels, and it was all powdery for perfect
wings.

Rude Awakening: Getting left out in the
cold can be a good thing. Blizzards are
awesome!

While Madison was online, Phinnie came into her
room and curled up near her feet. She could feel his
warm little pug body. In the next moment, however,
he jumped up and scampered up the attic stairs.

"Phinnie?" Madison turned and called after him.
"Phinnie, are you there?"

"Rowrrooooooo!" Phin called back. Madison
could hear the click-clack-click of his black nails running back and forth in the attic.

She got up quickly to head upstairs, too. Phin
would make a huge mess if he started chewing on
any of the materials Madison and her mother had
left out of boxes.

Madison remembered what Mom had said about the extra items left in one of the open boxes. She took the attic steps by twos and hurried to see what was inside the books and albums.

Once upstairs, Phinnie seemed to calm down. Madison guessed that he'd heard steam in the pipes or a creaking floorboard and gotten jumpy.

The box Mom had mentioned was sitting right by the attic entrance. Madison looked through some of the art projects and pictures. But there was another box that caught Madison's eye.

Madison walked over to the box in the corner of the attic. The box had large red letters that read FRANCINE HOOPER. On top was a rubber-banded pile of old, torn report cards with her Mom's name on them.

The rubber band snapped off in Madison's hand as soon as she reached for it. The cards were chilly from being in storage for so long. Each report card was filled in with so many comments.

Very good writer. Needs improvement on math skills. Suggest extra-credit program for Frannie this summer.

Madison chuckled to herself. Mom had been unsuccessful in math class, too. Just like Madison. Fortunately, summer school hadn't been necessary in Madison's case.

Excellent English papers this term! However, we cannot overlook the fact that Fran needs to get to school on time. Her tardiness has become a problem.

Mom was always late? It seemed funny that Mom would be so angry with Dad for being late when she herself had a problem with lateness on many of the report cards Madison was reading.

Inside the report card box, she discovered news-paper clippings from Mom's school paper, showing Mom taking a jump shot at a basketball game and cramming for finals in a school library.

Next to the report card box, Madison noticed another box marked KEEP OUT! THIS MEANS YOU, MOM AND DAD. Madison recognized the handwriting. She had written it a long time ago. Mom hadn't cracked the seal yet, but Madison did. She found something inside she hadn't seen in years.

Nesting at the top of the box was an old, wooden cigar case covered with decoupage. A long time ago Madison had saved letters, comics, and other special notes in it. Most of the letters and papers had rough edges, torn sides, and broken seals. She'd called this her "secret box."

Opening the box slowly, Madison gasped. She 'd forgotten all this existed! She read and then reread every letter. Her favorite was a note from Gramma Helen, who had written while traveling with Grampa Joe in Europe. Madison had saved the enve-lope because the stamp was so pretty.

She looked deeper inside the mystery carton to see what else lay buried or wrapped in newspapers beneath the cigar box.

First Madison found a yellow diary with a lock from five years before. It had never been written in. The pages were crackly to the touch.

Then she saw a stack of pictures she'd finger painted in kindergarten. They were mostly painted orange. It had been Madison's favorite color back then, too.

On the bottom of the box, she found a photo album, the one with the word SNAPSHOTS spelled out in big, gold letters across the fake leather album cover. She had gotten the book from Aunt Angie for her eighth birthday.

Madison opened the book very slowly in case there was anything stuffed inside. She didn't want things to fall out. Turning the plastic pages made a lot of noise.

On the first spread of photos, Madison saw herself wrapped in a fuzzy yellow blanket, looking more like a chick than a little baby. There were three poses in that outfit, next to a picture of Madison lying with a bare bottom on the living room floor. She had a big grin on her face and a teddy bear in her hand.

Madison turned the page quickly. Baby pictures could be so embarrassing.

The next spread showed Madison sitting high up on her dad's shoulders. He was standing in the yard, watering flowers. In another photo he was barbecuing hot dogs. That was back when Madison's mom still ate meat. She'd been a strict vegetarian for a few years now.

There was a big photo of Mom and Dad seated together on a hammock. They were kissing, in the picture. Madison stopped to look at that photograph a little longer than the others.

She couldn't take her eyes off her parents. They had looked so happy then. In the photo, Madison could barely make out the shadow of a little child on the left side. She realized she was the one standing just outside the photo's frame. She'd been standing there, watching Mom and Dad kiss.

She glanced through the next few pages to find even more shots of Mom, Dad, herself, and other family members:

Gramma Helen putting Madison's hair into braids.

Grampa Joe carrying Madison into the ocean.

Dad pouring soapy water over Madison's head in the tub.

Mom feeding Madison green mushy food.

Madison jumping on her bed.

Page after page, Madison found the baby and then grade school pictures she'd always loved. She looked through them all twice. And then she got to the pictures of second grade.

There was Ivy Daly. *In almost every single one.*

Their best friendship dated back to the beginning of school. Ivy and Madison had been inseparable. They had dressed alike and liked the same things. They had both liked to blow bubbles, climb trees, and plan tea parties for their dolls.

Madison saw photos that showed all of these things.

She saw an Ivy she'd forgotten existed.

She saw the *nice* Ivy she used to know, once upon a time.

Madison plucked one of her favorite photos off the page, a shot of her and Ivy standing with arms wrapped around each other's shoulders, smiling. She would scan the photo to attach it to her Ivy online file.

At the very end, Madison found the last page stuck to the inside back cover of the photo album. She tried carefully to pry it apart, afraid it would rip.

And no sooner had she peeled it apart than something dropped out.

Something Madison *definitely* was not expecting.

Stuck inside the back cover of the album was a yellowing envelope that Madison barely remem-bered sealing. The envelope was stained with age-old, dried fingerprints, and someone had marked it very carefully on the outside.

MADISON FINN & IVY DALY
Do Not Open Until Seventh Grade
That Means NO ONE except US!!!

It was an envelope from second grade. Madison

could remember the day when she and Poison Ivy had torn the paper off a legal pad and signed their names in ink. She remembered Ivy hugging her when they licked the envelope shut and added a "backup" seal of black electrical tape, because that was the only tape they could find.

Madison peered closely at the envelope to see what it said. On the back was a different message:

MADISON FINN & IVY DALY
Friends Forever and Ever and Ever
For OUR eyes ONLY!!!

Ivy had drawn teeny little flowers and borders all over the envelope—and every flower Madison saw sent her mind back to the day when the letter had been written.

Madison *always* thought about the fact that Ivy was her mortal enemy. But she rarely thought about why.

Until now.

She picked up the envelope and read it three times more.

Madison could almost hear the sounds from back then, the time when she and Ivy had their seats next to each other in school, when they always teamed up for dodgeball, and when they vowed to *both* win the Far Hills Little Miss pageant together.

Inside the album were taped together pictures

that showed the sides of Ivy most people in junior high had either forgotten or never known: the funny girl, the sometimes-too-shy girl, and even the scared-of-boys girl.

Once upon a time, Ivy hadn't been poisonous.

"Madison!" a voice yelled from downstairs. "What's going on up there? I called for you twice."

Mom had probably reheated pizza and set the table.

"Come on down! Dinner is ready!" she yelled.

"Okay, Mom," Madison mumbled.

Madison placed her secret cigar box back into the dusty carton, putting the report cards, papers, and other life memorabilia on top of that.

"So what time *is* it?" Madison asked as she bounded down the stairs.

Mom said it was six-thirty, and Madison nearly fell over. "Six-thirty? How did it get to be so late?"

"You were obviously having a good time going through boxes, Maddie. You went up there an hour ago," Mom said. "So what did you find?"

Madison could feel the unopened seventh-grade letter from her and Ivy burning a hole inside her pocket . . . but she said nothing.

She would keep *this* discovery to herself—at least for now.

Chapter 7

From: MadFinn
To: Bigwheels
Subject: Need Your Advice
Date: Wed 17 Jan 7:59 PM

Thanks for cheering me up. I won't
worry about Hart if I can help it,
but that's like asking me not to
eat chocolate. I can't!!!

Right now I am worrying about something else instead. I am staring at
this letter on my bed. It's from
Ivy, only it was written like a
million years ago. Well, it was
written by both of us in second
grade. I'm telling you about it

because I just feel so weird having it. I found it in the attic.

In second grade, Ivy used to be my best friend on the planet. And we spent all our time together, mostly wanting to be as cool as her older sister, Janet. She was five years older and she was the coolest. So when we were in second grade and Janet was in seventh grade, we thought that she got to do the best things. We wrote this list of things WE wanted to do in seventh grade—together! And then we signed it and sealed it and put it away never to be opened until we were in the REAL seventh grade.

That's NOW.

What am I supposed to do with this? I don't like Poison Ivy anymore, and I don't want to share this letter with her, because she doesn't deserve it. But it seems wrong not to share. Know what I mean? After all, we did both make a promise, and we sealed it together. You know I'm superstitious about things. Won't I get seven years bad luck or

71

something if I open it on my own?

What do you think? Should I show it to Ivy? HELP!

As always, I appreciate your advice from far away.

Write soon.

Yours till the mail boxes,

MadFinn

Madison marked her message to Bigwheels with a little red exclamation point for priority mail service. She wanted to know what to do right away.
All at once, her computer bleeped.
And Bigwheels appeared like some kind of Internet fairy godmother.

```
<Bigwheels>: U r online!
  Helllloooo!
<MadFinn>: Did you get my message?
<Bigwheels>: No what messg?
<MadFinn>:
  Aaaaaaaaaaaaaaaaaaaaaaaaaah
<Bigwheels>: Lemme check now . . .
<Bigwheels>: YES! Ok
<MadFinn>: Hello?
<MadFinn>: Hello?
```

<MadFinn>: Bigwheels????????
<Bigwheels>: Wait. I wuz reading it
<MadFinn>: SWDYT
<Bigwheels>: (::)(::)
<MadFinn>: Im crankier than cranky
  what should I do?
<Bigwheels>: U prob should show the
  letter 2 her
<MadFinn>: U think so? Really? Y?
<Bigwheels>: b/c of what u said.
  She was part of it and u made a
  promise together. I believe in
  promises.
<MadFinn>: But she'll probably just
  tear it up or laugh in my face
<Bigwheels>: Or not
<MadFinn>: Why r u so optimissic
<MadFinn>: I mean OPTIMISTIC
<Bigwheels>: Just b/c she is mean u
  don't have 2 be mean right?
<MadFinn>: I guess how do u know so
  much
<Bigwheels>: BTDT
<MadFinn>: Oh
<Bigwheels>: Did u watch the early
  skating trials on TV this week?
<MadFinn>: No ur like a sk8ing
  fanatic aren't u
<Bigwheels>: Not really I just think
  they look so graceful on the ice
  I wish I could do that

<MadFinn>: Me too I'm Queen of the
   Klutzes I swear
<Bigwheels>: So is it still snowing
<MadFinn>: No
<Bigwheels>: So were you skating
   today too or what?
<MadFinn>: No skating b/c Lake
   Wannalotta is closed
<Bigwheels>: I saw on the weather
   that the snow was moving across
   the country. We're supposed to
   get another storm, too.
<MadFinn>: That's kinda cool so we
   have the same weather
<Bigwheels>: Yes
<MadFinn>: Have u written n e poems
   lately?
<Bigwheels>: Not so much I'm working
   on one what about you?
<MadFinn>: NO!!! I gotta run
<Bigwheels>: Write back soon??
<MadFinn>: Yes! thank u
<Bigwheels>: *poof*

**No sooner had Madison exited her Insta-Message
chat with Bigwheels than she got an IM from Fiona.**

<Wetwinz>: Maddie?
<MadFinn>: How r u feeling F?
<Wetwinz>: SICK
<MadFinn>: R u taking medicine?

<Wetwinz>: Yes, I think I'll be
    better by tomorrow
<MadFinn>: What's tomorrow?
<Wetwinz>: Skating
<MadFinn>: Oh well u r sick maybe
    we'll cancel it
<Wetwinz>: LOL no way Egg would
    never do that
<MadFinn>: It could happen he is
    your CRUSH after all
<Wetwinz>: Double LOL
<MadFinn>: I think he likes u 2
<Wetwinz>: Not right now my nose is
    dripping I feel so gross UGH
<MadFinn>: Thanks for sharing
<Wetwinz>: Maybe you & Aim can come
    over sometime soon
<MadFinn>: Is that ok w/ur mom?
<Wetwinz>: I'll ask her maybe
    tomorrow
<MadFinn>: ?4U did u say Hart came
    over to see Chet?
<Wetwinz>: Yes but I only saw him
    for a minute
<MadFinn>: What were they doing?
<Wetwinz>: Why do u care?
<MadFinn>: I don't I just was
    curious that's all
<Wetwinz>: Ya know, I think Hart is
    kinda cute, too
<MadFinn>: Really

<Wetwinz>: Don't you?

Pzzzzzzzzzzzt!

With a loud, sizzling sound, the power zapped off and Madison's laptop computer screen went black.

"Fiona?" Madison said feebly as she hit a few keys and tried to boot up the laptop again. She was able to get the computer running again on her battery, but the Internet connection was lost.

Power, phones, and all connection to the outside world suddenly ended.

And her room was darker than dark.

It was nine-thirty P.M. and the storm had returned, bringing with it one last gust of wind and wet snow.

Madison felt her way over to the window in her bedroom. Streetlights were out, and all the houses on her block were cloaked in darkness. The only light Madison saw was the faint blue glow of her laptop. It cast a hue and threw shadows on her bedroom wall.

"Maddie?" Mom whispered from Madison's bedroom doorway. She was holding a flashlight. "Where's that blue light coming from?"

"My computer. The battery's still charged," Madison replied.

Mom clicked off her flashlight and came over by the window to put her arms around Madison's shoulders. "This has without a doubt been the worst storm I've ever seen here in Far Hills."

"It's global warming, Mom," Madison said. In addition to caring for endangered animals (and *all* animals), Madison had recently become worried about other environmental issues, too.

"First it snows, then it clears up, then it thunders, then the power goes out. Tomorrow it'll probably be seventy degrees and humid." Mom shook her head.

Madison squeezed Mom's forearm. "Look over there!" she said. "It looks like someone else has a flashlight in their house."

"There, too!" Mom said, pointing.

Madison gazed at her mom's face. Although she looked bluish in the light of the bedroom, Mom still looked so pretty. Madison hadn't really stared at her up close like this in a long time. She was too busy doing homework or something else to notice Mom's eyes or lips or the way Mom's hair curled up top.

"What do you say we go downstairs and light a few of those candles we got at the store today?" Mom suggested.

"Sure," Madison said. "Good thing we bought extra supplies."

Phinnie jumped up on Madison with his two paws and prodded her, whining. He wanted some attention, too.

Mom leaned over and scratched the top of Phin's head.

Phin wheezed. His little brown pug eyes rolled into the back of his head.

"Happy dog." Mom laughed.

They turned on the flashlight again and walked slowly down the stairs toward the living room.

A red-and-blue flashing light zoomed past the front windows.

"Must be the electric company," Mom said.

Mom hummed as she lit a few of the fat, vanilla-scented candles. She arranged them on the coffee table. Then she and Madison sat on the couch together without saying much else.

After a few minutes, Mom took Madison's hair out of its elastics and offered to brush it. Now it was Madison's turn to hum. Mom hadn't brushed her hair in years. It felt so good. After only a few moments of hair brushing, Madison fell asleep.

The next thing Madison remembered was waking up in the well-lit living room, curled up under one of Gramma's quilts. Phinnie was asleep under the coffee table, snoring. It was morning.

"Mom?" Madison said, lifting her head off the couch. She could hear the humming and buzzing of appliances in the kitchen, so she knew the power was back on again.

"You conked right out last night, honey bear," Mom said from the doorway to the kitchen. "I sat there as long as I could, but then my arm fell asleep."

"I don't even remember . . ." Madison said, yawning.

"Well, it's Thursday, so you better get a move on," Mom said. "Looks like the snow really has stopped for good. The sun is out, too. I'm assuming you'll be spending the day with friends?"

"Friends?" Madison repeated. She flipped over on the couch to look out the living room window. It was brighter than bright outside. The storm was long gone. She got a sinking feeling in her stomach. Today would definitely be the day when everyone met at the lake to skate.

Madison stuck her head under the quilt and wished for more snow, more time, more *something*!

But it was too late for wishing.

"Madison?" Mom yelled from the kitchen. "Didn't you hear the phone? Come on and answer it. It's Walter."

"Walter?" Madison moaned. She went over to the phone. "Hi, Egg."

"Hey, Maddie!" Egg yelled into the receiver. "We're meeting at eleven at the lake. Be there!"

"Um, Egg, I'm not sure I can go," Madison said.

"Get out of here," he said. "Everyone is going except for Fiona, and you have to be there. You promised."

Madison sighed. "I can't."

"Yeah, whatever. I'll see you at eleven," Egg said. He hung up.

Madison immediately dialed Aimee's number.

"Help!" she said as soon as Aimee picked up the phone. "What am I gonna wear to the lake?"

Aimee laughed. "Relax, Maddie. I'll be right over."

"Why don't you want to wear this?" Aimee suggested. "You always liked my striped ski sweater."

"I just don't know. Stripes make me look fat," Madison said.

"What are you talking about?" Aimee said.

"Look at my hair. It's all static electricity. I can't go out like this."

They were standing inside Madison's bedroom with the closet doors thrown open and half of the closet now on the floor.

Aimee stepped over a pile of shirts and bent down to look through them a second time. "It's just a dumb afternoon skate. Let's not get so freaked out about the whole thing."

"I am! I can't *skate*!" Madison said.

"Okay, okay." Aimee backed off.

Madison rifled through the few items that remained on hangers inside the closet. Then she apologized.

"I'm sorry, Aim. I just don't like the idea of falling on my butt in front of everyone from school—including Poison Ivy. She'll use that against me for years."

Aimee nodded. "Well, maybe. But who cares about her? I thought we decided that we didn't care about what Ivy said or did."

"We don't," Madison blurted.

But what she wanted to do was scream.

Madison wanted to tell Aimee about the sealed letter she'd found in the attic, about how she missed the Ivy she knew in second grade, and about how she suddenly felt weirder than weird about being in Ivy's presence.

"Maddie?" Aimee asked. "How about *this* sweater? I've never seen you wear this one."

She held up one of Madison's newest sweaters, a Christmas present from Mom. It was orange angora, fuzzy all over like a tabby cat.

"Maybe," Madison said. She'd never even put it on.

"It's your favorite color, right?" Aimee said. "Go ahead and try it."

Madison slipped it over her head. It fit snugly, but it was so warm and cozy. "I like this one," Madison said, moving over to look in the full-length mirror.

Aimee picked up a pair of jeans from the floor. "And wear it with these, which won't look weird if you fall on the ice. . . . I mean . . ."

Madison glared at Aimee. "If I *fall*? Thanks a lot, Aim! That's like a whammy. Now I'm destined to fall."

"I—I didn't mean to say that," Aimee stammered. She fell backward onto Madison's bed and started to laugh a little. "You are so paranoid, I swear."

Madison slipped on the jeans. "Well, I guess this looks okay," she said to her reflection.

"It looks fab! Now I have to go home and get dressed," Aimee said. "It's already ten o'clock. Everyone's meeting in an hour."

"Can your brother give us a ride over to the lake?" Madison asked.

"Yeah, someone will. I don't know if Roger or Billy is going to Dad's store today. And my mother has a yoga workshop or something. She left this morning."

"Your mom is so busy," Madison said.

"She said you could come for dinner tonight if you want. We're having tofu lasagna."

"Um, no thanks." Madison bit her lip. "I have plans with Mom already."

Madison couldn't stomach even the idea of eating another all-natural, nut-and-grains-and-tofu meal at Aimee's place. She loved squirrels, but she didn't see the point in eating like one. Besides,

Mom's "scary dinners" of fast food had been fast improving, so eating at home wasn't half bad. Since the Big D, Mom had been trying to work a little bit less and pay a little more attention to meals and housecleaning and other home stuff. And surprisingly, she and Mom were having a lot of fun together during the snow days.

Aimee grabbed her scarf and coat. "Come over and we'll drive to the lake in a little while."

"You didn't say what you're wearing," Madison said.

"My lemon-drop ski parka, what do you think?" Aimee said. "It's been waiting to make its ice-skating debut. And my new jeans with the embroidery up the sides. Oh, Maddie, I planned my outfit like days ago. I could never ever wait until the last minute—I would just lose my mind, you know?"

As Aimee left, Madison looked in the mirror again and smiled. She was calmer than calm now. This was going to be okay. She hung the rest of her clothes back in the closet.

But then, as she was tidying her room, Madison noticed the sealed Ivy letter. She picked it up from her dresser and read the front and back, something she'd done at least fifty times since finding it. Then she turned on her dresser lamp and held the letter up to the light. *Wasn't there any writing she could see through the envelope?* She wanted desperately to know what it said.

"Drat," Madison said to herself. She couldn't see anything except for random scribbles and their names.

Madison sat down on the bed quietly. She wanted to work out a plan to bring the letter to the lake. Ivy had a right to read the letter at the same time as Madison. That was what they had promised each other. Madison needed to find some quiet time with Ivy and pull Ivy away from her evil drones.

Was this letter something that could change Ivy from enemy back into friend? Would it make up for all the yucky things that had been said and done over the past four years? Would they share a good laugh about surviving seventh grade—and even about both liking Hart Jones?

Madison curled up onto a pillow and sighed. A part of her felt like crying, but she didn't understand why. She picked up the phone and dialed Fiona's house, but the machine picked up.

Why did she feel like crying?

Madison sat upright again, determined not to feel anything.

She would give Ivy the letter and then walk away. She would let Ivy decide who should open it. That would be that.

Madison walked back over to the full-length mirror and stared at her reflection once more. "Chill out, Maddie," she told herself. "It's only a dumb letter. It's only a dumb skating party."

Mom happened to walk into the room at that exact moment and heard Madison talking to herself. "You really shouldn't say that, honey bear."

"What?" Madison said, whirling around.

"I don't like hearing you talk that way about yourself or about anyone. You are *not* dumb," Mom said.

"Oh." Madison gulped. "I didn't know you were standing there."

"You are a beautiful young lady. And that sweater looks dreamy on you, if I may say so. Your mother has good taste, right?" Mom said.

Madison nodded. "Yeah. It's just that I get so nervous about doing things I'm not good at. And skating is one of those things. And then there's this boy . . ."

"Boy?" Mom asked. "You mean Egg?"

"What?" Madison said. "Eeew! Yuck! *No!* Someone else."

"You mean someone who's going to be at the lake, too?" Mom asked.

Madison nodded. "So I have to look right. I have to act right. I have to—"

"You have to *be yourself*, sweetie. This boy will like you just fine if you have a good time and be yourself."

"But what is being myself, Mom?" Madison sighed. "I just don't know."

Mom smiled. "Oh, Maddie, I wish I could take all your nerves away. Come here."

Mom hugged Madison. Then she helped her comb her hair so it wouldn't have so much static. The digital clock read 10:52. Madison had to hurry.

"Good luck!" Mom waved good-bye from the porch. Madison waved back and sped over to Aimee's house, trying to avoid ice slicks and slush puddles along the way. She had on her rainbow cap, green gloves, and orange parka and her new orange sweater and jeans.

Most important, the Ivy letter was neatly jammed into the inside pocket of her coat.

Roger, Aimee's oldest brother, drove the girls over to the lake. He had a bad cold and kept sneezing the whole time, so Madison and Aimee huddled in the backseat as far away from the germs as they could get. They didn't want to get sick, the way Fiona had been all week. By the time they passed through the gate marked WELCOME TO LAKE WANNALOTTA, the skating party came into view. Almost everyone else was already there. Madison could see Egg speeding around the lake, showing off his new hockey skates. Drew was following right behind him with his digital camera. Ivy and her drones were huddled by a bench. About a dozen other kids who weren't in the seventh grade were there, too.

"I haven't skated yet this winter! I am so psyched," Aimee said as she leaped out of her family's minivan. Madison wanted to stay in the backseat and go back home with Roger, but she finally did get out, skates in hand.

"Hey, Finnster!" someone yelled.

Hart.

Madison felt her cheeks blush. She wasn't prepared to say hello, so she let Hart do most of the talking. He rushed right over, also carrying his skates in his hands.

"Whatcha been doing during the snowstorm?" he asked, babbling on and on about the weather. Madison couldn't understand why he was talking so fast—or why he was talking *to her*. Out of the corner of her eye, she saw Ivy give a dirty look in her direction.

"We'd better put our skates on," Madison said. She felt warm.

"I knew you'd come," Egg said, walking over to both of them. He was walking on the ground but wearing his skates.

After five minutes, with Aimee's assistance, Madison's skates were tied up and she was ready to hit the ice. Hart was still struggling with one of his laces, which had broken.

"See you out there," Madison said, wobbling over to the ice. There was a splintered wooden deck built on one edge of the lake where people could enter and exit.

Ssssssssssst!

Chet skidded to a stop on the edge of his blades, sending up an ice spray.

"Hey, Maddie!" Chet said. "Fiona said to say hi to you and Aimee. She's almost better. Mom says you guys can come over Sunday if you want. Actually, I think we're gonna have everyone over for hot chocolate."

"Really? Great!" Madison said.

Chet spun around in a circle like some kind of professional skater.

"Where did you learn to do *that*?" Madison asked him. "You're from California."

"So? We skate there, too," Chet said, laughing. "Are you skating or what?"

Madison was about to make up some excuse, but then Egg skated by and pushed Chet. He took off to chase Egg around the ring. Across the ice, they caught up with Drew, Lance, Suresh, and some other kids from school.

"Madison?" Dan Ginsburg was standing right behind her. "I figured you'd be here. Cool."

"Hey, Dan," Madison said, smiling. "Everyone is here."

"Are Ivy and Hart going out or what?" Dan asked.

Madison's mouth dropped open. "Huh?"

"Look over there. I heard he was a good skater, so why is he letting *her* show him how to skate? How dorky is that?" Dan laughed and skated off.

Madison shoved her hands into her pockets. She felt the letter and pulled it out. Maybe I should just rip this up, she thought. But she put it back into her pocket again.

She could see that Ivy was actually grabbing Hart's hand and pulling him along the ice. *She was touching him!* Rose and Joan were following like good drones. Madison looked away.

Across the ice, Aimee was doing some kind of pirouette. Madison was amazed. Aimee was excellent at ballet, skating, and so many other things. Some cute boy was already talking to her on the ice, too.

"Maddie!" Aimee shouted, and waved. "Get out here. It's FUN!"

Madison tentatively stepped out on the ice. Her legs started to slide apart like she'd do a split, but she was able to steady herself quickly. She pushed off with her right foot but couldn't quite push off with her left. This meant that when she tried to skate, all she did was go around in circles.

Aimee came over when she saw Madison wavering on the ice. "Gotcha," Aimee said, sweeping in and putting her arm on Madison's arm.

"Aimee, I can't do this," Madison said. Her knees *and* voice were shaking.

"Yes, you can," Aimee said. She pulled Madison along by the side and then switched over to skating in front. As Aimee skated backward, she pulled Madison along with her.

"Cowabunga!" Egg screamed from the middle of

nowhere. He skated right toward the two girls. Aimee jumped back, but before Madison knew what had hit her, she was lying flat on her back.

"Jerk!" Aimee yelled at Egg as he zipped away, laughing hysterically. She leaned down to help Madison up off the frozen lake. "Are you okay, Maddie?"

"Yeah," Madison said. She could see that almost everyone was staring at her now, like they were waiting for her next round of ice acrobatics.

"You wanna keep skating?" Aimee asked.

They circled the ice once together. "I need to stop for a minute," Madison said. She clung to the edge of the ice, holding on to the railing, while Aimee skated off. Next to her was a girl she'd never met before, who introduced herself as Susie Quinby.

"Where do you go to school?" Madison asked.

"Actually, I go to boarding school. I'm just home on break," Susie said.

"Really?" Madison said. "So where in Far Hills do you live?"

"Well, do you know where Hart Jones lives? I'm his next-door neighbor. And he's the one who invited me here. He's wicked nice."

"Really?" Madison said. For a brief moment, she let go of the railing, which sent her body sliding back into the middle of the lake.

"Madison?" Susie called out.

But in a matter of seconds the damage was done.

Madison Finn felt her body swirl around the ice before landing with a hard smack.

She'd fallen.

And she couldn't get up.

Chapter 9

"Is this yours?" Susie was leaning over Madison, holding the Ivy letter.

Madison finally lifted herself up. The ice was cold on her butt. "Yes, that's mine!" she said, grabbing the letter and shoving it back into her pocket.

"What happened over here?" Egg said, skating up to investigate the fall. "One minute you're gliding over the ice, and the next minute you're— SLAM!"

"Very funny, Egg," Madison moaned, struggling to her feet.

Ivy skated over. "Ouch, that must have hurt." She snickered. Most of the other kids around Madison giggled, too.

"Hey, Finnster," Hart said as he checked in, too.

"HEY, EVERYONE!" Egg cried out from across the ice. "IT'S TIME TO PICK TEAMS!"

"Why do we need to pick teams?" Madison asked aloud.

Drew said, "Ice tag's better that way!"

Everyone skated off toward the middle of the lake to play, but Madison collapsed on a bench instead.

"What are you doing over here?" Aimee asked, joining her on the bench.

"I can't play ice tag," Madison said, making a face. "I'll just watch."

"Then I'll watch, too," Aimee said, sitting.

"GET OUT HERE, AIM! WE NEED YOU!" Egg yelled from the ice.

"Let's just start the game," Ivy complained. "If she wants to sit out, then let her."

"Hey, Finnster!" Hart shouted. He was a little unsteady on his skates, but he threw his arms into the air and glided across the ice. "It's easy! Come on!"

Madison laughed. She shot a look at Ivy. "Okay!" she said cheerily. Aimee grabbed her hand, and together they went out to the middle of the ice.

Ivy stood there frozen, arms crossed, with an angry glare on her face.

Rose skated by Madison and said, "No one is going to pick you for their team if you can't skate, Madison."

Madison was shocked. How could she say some-

94

thing so mean in front of everyone else? But no one else was listening. Not even Aimee.

Should she go back to the bench?

Madison glanced over at Ivy, who had wiggled herself over a little closer to Hart. She looked so pretty. Ivy wore red velvet jeans, a blue turtleneck sweater, and a denim jacket with fleece inside. She was the best-dressed skater on the lake, for sure.

The ice tag captains were Egg and Lance. Egg chose first.

"I PICK MADISON!" Egg yelled at the top of his lungs.

Ivy scoffed. But Madison smiled. Egg was such a good friend sometimes, usually when she least expected it. He came through for her when she needed support the most—like now.

"I choose Aimee," Lance said.

Aimee skated over to his side, making a sad face at Madison. They wouldn't be on the same team, but that was okay. Madison couldn't help but laugh when she realized that out of everyone—boys and girls—she and her BFF were chosen first. That meant something.

The rest of Egg's team worked out to be Chet, Dan, Rose, and Hart. They were up against Lance, Aimee, Ivy, Suresh, Joanie, and Susie. Drew was "official game photographer." He was more into his new Christmas present than skating.

The way it worked was each team chose their

"tagger," and that person sped around the ice, tagging whomever he or she could catch. The goal was to tag people on the opposite team and send them to jail over by the tree.

Madison figured she would get tagged right away, but no one came after her. She stood off to the side, pretending to be invisible while everyone else skated around each other, giggling and screaming. If she stayed under the radar, she'd stay safe. However, as soon as Ivy was It, the attention turned in her direction.

Ivy sped over in Madison's direction, and tagged her out, knocking her down on the ice.

Madison saw Drew snap a digital photo at the exact moment of contact.

Great shot.

Ivy brushed off her hands and skated away. Madison was left alone at the tree, while everyone else seemed miles away.

What she wanted to do was kick off her ice skates and run as fast as she could away from the lake, away from all these people, *away*!

But she didn't have to run. All at once Aimee skated toward her, much to the protests of her teammates.

"Maddie," Aimee whispered. "I'll keep you company."

Madison shook her head. "That's not fair, Aim, you're not out."

A moment later, Hart's neighbor Susie skated over, too. "I saw what that girl did, Madison," Susie said. "I'll get her back for you."

Aimee smiled. "We *both* will."

"But she's on your team," Madison said.

"Maybe," Susie said. "But she isn't very nice. She was totally unfriendly to me until I told her that I live next to Hart."

"WHAT ARE YOU GUYS DOING?" Egg yelled from across the ice.

Ivy yelled, too. "COME ON, AIMEE! SUSIE! GET BACK IN THE GAME!"

Susie and Aimee skated back on the ice, and headed right in Ivy's direction.

"Wait just a minute! I'm on your team," Ivy protested to them both.

"Whoops!" Aimee said as she pretended to trip, skating right into Ivy.

Susie skated at her from the other side. Just then Chet tagged Ivy to send her to jail.

"YOU'RE OUT, IVY!" Egg yelped, laughing.

Ivy looked around in all directions. She didn't know where to go. Rose pointed across the ice at the jail by Madison. But Ivy saw Hart, goofing around with Drew on the other side. She took the long way to the tree, so she could pass by Hart.

Madison watched as Ivy skated full speed right at him. He wasn't really paying attention. He didn't see her coming.

Whooooomp!

The pair crashed to the ice. Everyone took a deep breath.

But then the laughter began—Ivy and Hart laughing. They were lying on top of each other on the ice, laughing like little kids.

Madison wanted to *cry*.

"Now, that is just disgusting," Aimee said, skating over toward Madison. "She is the grossest. And she is so obvious. I could just—"

"Forget it, Aim," Madison said, cutting her off.

Madison noticed Drew over at the crash site, snapping digital photos for the school Web site. She cringed at the thought that there would be a picture of Ivy and Hart on the Web for everyone to see, like they were a "couple" or something.

Madison had made Ivy pay temporarily, but as always, the enemy got the last laugh.

She reached into her pocket for the Ivy letter. It was wrinkled and a little wet from traveling all over the ice today.

"Poison Ivy Daly will never, ever, *ever* see this," Madison told herself. "Not after what she's done here. No way."

After an hour more of ice tag, Madison's toes were beginning to feel like little ice cubes. She sat on a bench, watching everyone else have a good time on the ice. Hart and Ivy skated together, talking and laughing. He didn't call out, "Hey, Finnster!" again during the whole time Madison was sitting on the bench. Ivy insisted on helping Hart skate, and he didn't seem to mind. Madison guessed the boys weren't patient enough with him since he was only a beginner. Or maybe Hart liked Ivy?

Aimee and Susie were practicing spins and turns together. Since Susie had been a competitive skater, she knew so many neat tricks. Aimee seemed thrilled to learn all the new moves. They waved to Madison from the center of the ice, looping their bodies around, making jump spins, and rotating like tops.

Madison was impressed, but she didn't venture out onto the ice to join them. She was content to sit on the bench and freeze. By now, Madison's green gloves had gotten so wet that she could barely feel her fingertips. And her rainbow hat was getting very scratchy around her hairline.

"Hey, everyone!" Chet yelled, skating over by the benches. "I want to invite all you guys over to my house Sunday afternoon!"

"COOL!" Egg yelled.

Lance, Suresh, Dan, and Joanie said they couldn't go.

Madison could see Ivy and Hart and Rose, still skating way out on the lake. They didn't make it back in time to hear Chet's announcement. She wondered if they could go. She hoped *not*.

"So it's like this," Chet continued. "My sister's

been way sick for like a week and she's better now, so we're having this hot chocolate party or whatever you want to call it."

"Hot chocolate *party*?" Susie said. "Delish. Is it okay if I come? I mean, I know I just met you guys."

"Sure," Aimee said.

Madison grinned. "You and Fiona will really like each other," she said.

"I think her brother is pretty cute," Susie said.

Aimee laughed out loud, but Madison looked over and noticed that Chet was smiling a little at Susie, too.

"Do you like any of these boys?" Susie asked.

Aimee laughed even louder. "I don't think so."

"Not really," Madison said, looking around for Hart. "No one here."

"So everyone come over Sunday around one," Chet repeated. "I'll send you guys an e-mail with my address and all that."

Everyone began to disperse. Kids were running around in all directions, looking for mittens, skates, and where their rides had parked. Just as Aimee's brother Roger pulled in, someone threw a snowball and it landed on Roger's windshield.

Madison saw Aimee's dog, Blossom, in the front seat. Blossom poked her big basset hound snout out through the cracked-open window.

"Wowwwwwwffff!" Blossom barked.

Madison raced over to the minivan and petted

Blossom's head. "Hey, Roger," she said. "Aimee's taking off her skates. She'll be here in a sec."

"Snowball fight, eh?" Roger said, chuckling. "Someone's going to get beaned. You better get in the car."

Madison climbed in just in time to see a snowball narrowly miss Aimee's head. She stood up, indignant, and made her own snowball, whirling it toward Drew and Egg.

Within moments, a snowball war had broken out. Chet hurled snow at Aimee, who hurled snow at Lance, who hurled snow at Susie, who tried to hide behind one of the benches.

Drew got socked on the shoulder and yelled at some kid because he feared his new camera would get wet.

At the same time, Ivy, Hart, and Rose were coming off the ice. Madison couldn't believe the way Hart was following Ivy around like a puppy dog. They weren't paying much attention to the snowball fight that had gotten under way, at least not at first. Ivy was talking and tossing her red hair like she always did.

But then Chet sent a snowball flying in their direction. It narrowly missed all three of them.

"Whoa!" Hart yelped. He ducked down so he wouldn't get beaned.

Ivy, on the other hand, didn't duck fast enough.

Sploooch!

A superslick snowball landed right on the side of

her head. Her beautiful red hair turned into a wet mess.

"Oh my God!" Aimee cried from behind the bench. Susie clapped.

Ivy stood there for a moment without moving.

"Are you okay?" Hart said, trying to help her get the ice off her face and shoulder.

"What are you smiling at?" Ivy cried. "Someone intentionally threw that snowball, and you know who you are!"

Hart giggled. "Well, it is just a snowball, Ivy."

Rose giggled at that, too.

"What are *you* laughing at?" Ivy snapped at Rose. "This hurts. You're supposed to be on my side."

"It's just a little red," Rose said. "You'll be okay."
Sploooch!

Another snowball whizzed past and landed on the ice.

"STOP THAT!" Ivy screeched.

By now Aimee noticed Roger's minivan. She said good-bye to Susie and dashed over to the car.

"Hey, Blossom!" Aimee cried, getting into the front seat. Roger backed up and headed out of the Lake Wannalotta parking lot.

"Maddie, did you see that snowball fight?" Aimee asked. "Ivy almost got hit twice!"

"You'll notice I got into the car when the snow started to fly," Madison said.

"Yeah, well, I think that is the funniest thing I

have ever seen. Chet was aiming for Hart, and he hit Ivy! Serves her right! She looked soooo mad!"

Aimee and Madison howled with laughter. Blossom joined in.

Madison was readier than ready to leave behind this long day of skating. Not only had she crashed, bottom down, on the ice, but after everything that happened, she had never shown Ivy the sealed letter. She wasn't able to find five minutes alone to share the letter with Ivy. Should she hide the letter in the attic again and try to forget she'd ever found it?

But she couldn't forget.

As they drove onward, Madison got more excited about getting home to her warm clothes, good eats, and most of all—to her own doggie.

She wanted to give Phinnie a giant pug hug before taking him out for his post-blizzard walk. She'd figure out what to do with the letter . . .

Later.

"Mom!" Madison cried as she walked into the house. "Mom? I'm home from skating." She removed her hat and gloves and headed over to the kitchen for a warm drink.

"Oh, Maddie!" Mom wailed. She came running out from the kitchen, carrying the portable phone. "Oh, Maddie!"

"What?" Madison cried. In a split second all the worst-possible things that could ever happen raced through her mind.

"Oh, Maddie!" Mom kept saying the same thing over and over.

"Is it Dad? Is it Gramma?" Madison asked. "What's wrong?"

"Phinnie!" Mom cried again. "I took him out for a long walk, and when we came back, I must have

left the door open a crack because the next thing I knew, he was gone. He's *gone*!"

Madison fell backward onto the couch. "Gone? That's not possible!"

"I drove around the neighborhood. I was just calling that nice lady Eileen over at the Far Hills Clinic in case someone reports finding a missing pug. Oh, I don't know what else to do."

"Phin is *lost*?" Madison said, still not believing what was happening.

"Not lost, exactly. Oh, I think he ran away. I'm so sorry, honey bear," Mom said. She threw her arms around Madison's shoulders.

Madison broke free and tugged on her rainbow hat again. She grabbed Phin's leash, which was hanging on a hook in the hall. "I have to find him."

"He's never, ever done this before," Mom said. "He has to be somewhere nearby."

Madison raced for the front door. "I'll go look for him. Mom, you stay here in case he comes home."

"I don't want you looking by yourself," Mom said. She looked heartbroken.

"I'll just make a loop around Blueberry Street. I know where he likes to sniff and play. Maybe he headed over to Aimee's to see Blossom?"

"I checked. But you should check again. I'll call over there and let Aimee know you're coming. Maybe she can help you search."

But Madison didn't want any help. She had to find Phinnie on her own.

First she walked their usual short route down Blueberry Street and looping back. She checked all the bushes and areas where Phin loved to sniff most.

"Phinnie!" Madison cried. *"Phinnie!"*

One of their next-door neighbors, a real estate broker named Olga, was out shoveling her driveway. Madison waved and asked if she'd seen Phin, but she hadn't. She offered to drive Madison around, but Madison wanted to walk.

Around the corner from them, Madison checked out what was happening at a small playground with a swing set and monkey bars. Sometimes Phinnie liked to run around and play near there, although they hadn't been since the summer. Three little kids were building a snowman.

"Have you seen a dog?" Madison asked.

"I don't like dogs," one little girl said.

"Oh." Madison didn't know what to say to that. The little kids went back to building their snowman.

She turned onto Ridge Road, where Fiona and Chet lived. There were a bunch of old Victorian homes on this block with big yards and other dogs. She saw Charlie, a Dalmatian, playing in the snow. His owner was on the porch.

"Hello?" Madison called out. "Have you seen my little dog?"

"You're the one with the pug, right?" the man

asked. Madison nodded, and the man said, "Nope. Sorry."

Charlie came over to Madison, wagging his tail. Her heart sank. Was Phin lost for good?

But she kept walking.

At the end of Ridge Road was a small pond. Sometimes Phin would get curious about frogs and the water. But the pond was a sheet of ice, and Madison couldn't see him anywhere in the area.

"Phinnie?" she yelled out. She could feel her voice wavering. Madison was getting sad and frustrated. Phin had never run away before. Why did he pick today to run?

"Madison?" a voice cried from behind her.

It was Rose Thorn. Madison's stomach flip-flopped. The last person she needed to see right now was one of Ivy's drones.

"Hi, Rose," Madison said. She realized that she'd been standing in Rose's backyard.

"What are you doing?" Rose asked.

"I lost my dog," Madison wailed. "My pug, Phinnie."

"Bummer," Rose said. "Where did you lose him?"

"If I knew that . . ." Madison started to say.

"Does he run away a lot?" Rose asked. "My cat runs away, but she always comes back."

"Cats and dogs are different."

"Well, where do you think he ran?" Rose asked.

"I don't know. I thought the park. Then I checked

the pond. And the streets where I usually walk him." Madison sighed. "I don't know. And he doesn't like the cold. His little paws get all frozen, so he can't walk right."

"Do you want help looking for him?" Rose asked.

Madison looked at her with disbelief. "Huh?"

"Let me help you look. If we split up, we can do it faster," Rose said.

Madison wondered why she would have turned down help from one of her biggest supporters, Mom, and now take help from one of her biggest enemies, Rose. But she did.

"Okay," Madison said. "If you really want to help."

Rose went into her house for her hat and gloves, and they continued around the neighborhood together.

Ten minutes later, the pair had looked on four other blocks with no luck.

"Maybe I should just check back at my house," Madison said. Then she saw Mom's car pulling up beside them on the street.

"I couldn't just sit there at home," Mom said. She turned to Rose and said, "I'm Madison's mom. Are you a friend of Maddie's?"

Rose shrugged. "We're in school together. We can't find your dog anywhere. And I have to get home now."

"Thanks, Rose," Madison said. "I mean it."

"I hope you find Phin," Rose said.

"Thanks," Madison said, and waved good-bye.

"Why haven't you ever mentioned Rose before?" Mom asked as Madison climbed into the front seat of the car. "She seems nice."

"Not really," Madison said abruptly. She covered her face with her hands. "Mom, I don't know what I'll do if Phinnie is gone. I'll be sad forever."

They stopped by Aimee's house one more time. Phin wasn't there.

"How long has he been missing now?" Mrs. Gillespie asked.

Madison frowned. "An hour. And it's getting dark."

"Well, I'll get the boys out to help you look," Mrs. Gillespie said. She called for Roger and Billy and asked them to drive around the other sides of the neighborhood while Madison and her mom checked door-to-door.

They must have rung a dozen different doorbells, but no one remembered seeing a little pug.

Phinnie *was* lost.

"Thanks, boys," Mom said to Roger and Billy when she sent them home a while later. She tried to console Madison with a hug, but Madison pulled away.

"We can put up posters around the neighbor-hood. And I'll try calling Eileen again."

As they pulled into the driveway, Madison began

to cry. She couldn't imagine spending a night without her beloved Phin. They got out of the car and headed for the porch.

"Rowrorooooo!"

"Mom?" Madison's eyes widened. "Did you hear that?"

Mom clapped, and they both started running toward the front door. Phin was there, with his curlicue tail wagging as fast as his little bottom could shake.

"*Phinnie!*" Madison screeched. She threw her arms around him and buried her teary face in his coarse fur. "He came home!"

"Thank goodness," Mom said.

Madison lifted Phin up and carried him inside while Mom hurried to call the Gillespies and everyone else who had helped them look for Phin around the neighborhood.

"Nice dog breath, Phin!" Madison said, pulling her head away from his nonstop kisses. They headed upstairs, where Madison could towel him off (he'd been out in the cold for so long!). Together they curled up on her comforter for a reunion snooze.

Phin just wheezed and wheezed, happy to be warm—and happier than happy to be home.

That night, Mom made soup and sandwiches for dinner. Madison wasn't all that hungry from the day's excitement, but she joined Mom at the table, anyway.

"While you and the runaway dog were napping, your father called," Mom said with a smile.

"What did Dad want?" Madison asked.

"He's trying to get a flight home Monday or Tuesday. The airport in Denver is still messed up. The storms are in Colorado and out west now. It's a travel nightmare, Dad said."

Madison missed Dad. He'd been gone for almost a week now.

"So he's coming over when he gets back?" Madison asked.

"Yes, honey bear. He'll be here. He promised."

Madison yawned. "I'm so tired, Mom," she said. "I think I'm going to go upstairs and go to bed for real."

"Well, it's been some day, Maddie. I don't blame you. And I'm sure Phinnie is tired, too."

They kissed good night, and Madison headed back up to her room.

She went to crawl into bed but stopped herself on the way. Her laptop was sitting open on her desk but she hadn't checked her e-mail since the power outage the night before.

In the half darkness of her bedroom, she logged on to bigfishbowl.com.

Phin curled up at her feet.

From: MadFinn
To: Bigwheels
Subject: Hello
Date: Thurs 18 Jan 7:23 PM

How are you???? I just checked the
site to see if I could IM you, but
you aren't online. Today was without
a doubt the strangest EVER. I went
skating, but that wasn't everything.
So much happened! Phin ran away,
Ivy got hit with a snowball, and
way more than that. I'll tell you
all about it the next time we
Insta-Message. I'm too tired to
repeat it all right now. I'm going
to bed and it isn't even eight
o'clock at night!

Please write back sooner than soon.
I miss you, Bigwheels!

Yours till the snow drifts,

MadFinn

p.s. I'm putting another picture of
Phinnie on here. Mom took this
during the blizzard. Yikes! Snow
dog!
Attachment: PHINSTORM.jpg

Madison yawned again. Her eyes felt droopy. But she could see that she had some e-mail, and she was too curious not to look.

From: Wetwins
To: The Skates
Subject: Cocoa Party SUNDAY
Date: Thurs 18 Jan 7:01 PM

Hello everybody, the party is ON!!!!!!!!!! This is where Chet and Fiona live: 23 Ridge Road (near intersection of Walker Avenue). Be there at one o'clock. We are making food and hot chocolate, and we'll be doing something fun like playing videos or games. SO be there or be a loser!!!! LOL L8R 4 U!

Madison scanned the e-mail to see if she could figure out the list of people who had been invited. She remembered that Ivy hadn't been standing around when Chet told everyone else about the party. Maybe that meant Ivy wouldn't be asked? Maybe she wouldn't show up?

Madison hoped as hard as she possibly could that Ivy was left off the list. She hoped so hard, she crossed her fingers, toes, *and* eyes.

But then she saw a second e-mail in her box with the same subject line. Unfortunately it was from Ivy, who'd hit REPLY ALL when she got Chet's message. This meant she *had* been invited.

```
From: Flowr99
To: Wetwins
Cc: The Skates
Subject: Re: Cocoa Party SUNDAY
Date: Thurs 18 Jan 7:31 PM
```

Fab! I will TOTALLY see you there, Chet. Thank you again for inviting me. TTFN.
:>) Ivy

Why was Madison so haunted this week by letters from Ivy? Some she could open . . . and some she couldn't open, but the letters followed her *everywhere*.

Madison wanted to screech.

She opened up a new file instead.

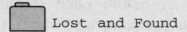 Lost and Found

I thought the real snow that falls from the sky was bad enough, but boy, was I ever WRONG! There are worse storms in my life like I-V-Y. How come she acts so superior to everyone else? And how come she keeps showing up wherever I am? I really doubt if

Fiona would have invited the enemy over! Chet is a chucklehead.

Skating was a disaster. I felt invisible. And Hart pretended to be all nice, but I think he sees me more like a friend and nothing else. At least I hope he sees me like a friend! Aimee whispered to me today that he is always looking at me and asked if I liked him. I could have swallowed my gum! No way, I said. NO ONE LIKES HART except for Poison Ivy. I hate lying to Aimee, but she can't know. I would die of embarrassment if everyone knew that I liked the same person as Poison Ivy.

Just when I think I'm done finding out everything I can about Ivy, she somehow makes my life miserable AGAIN. Like now I STILL have this sealed letter that I found. I keep trying to blow it off—and it keeps coming back to bug me!!! The new plan is that I will show it to her at the party and that will be the end of it. She thinks she knows everything, but I will show her a few things. HA!

Rude Awakening: No one likes a snow-it-all.

Ivy's the real blizzard around here. Just when I think she's gone, she slams me harder than before.

But she better watch out.

This weekend, I'm ready to slam back.

Chapter 11

"You look soooooo good!" Aimee squealed as she and Madison walked into the Waterses' house together.

It was a half hour before Sunday's party's official "start time." They wanted to arrive early and hang out with Fiona alone for a while.

"I missed you guys so much!" Fiona cooed. She coughed a little. "You shouldn't get too close, though. Just in case I'm still contagious or something."

"I missed you, too, Fiona!" Madison leaned in for a squeeze. "And I don't care if I catch your flu. Being sick would be better than everything that's been happening to me."

"I heard that Phin ran away," Fiona said. "But he's okay now, right?"

"Yeah," Madison said. "He had me so scared."

They walked into the kitchen, where Mr. and Mrs. Waters were both putting food out on trays. They had prepared a fondue pot with melted chocolate, marshmallow crispy treats, and other fun munchies.

"Have some!" Mrs. Waters handed Aimee a brownie, but she refused.

"I'm on a diet," she said.

Madison rolled her eyes and took the brownie. "I'll try it," she said, smiling.

"You know there are like a thousand calories in just one brownie," Aimee said. Madison ate it, anyway.

In the living room, a VCR was set up with movies so kids could watch TV if they wanted. In the downstairs family room, another area was set up so everyone could hang out and listen to music.

"This is a real party," Aimee said, impressed. "I thought we'd just be hanging out talking and eating and drinking cocoa. This is serious, Fiona."

"Well, my parents like to overdo everything," Fiona admitted. "They always want us to have a good time."

Madison and Aimee giggled.

Madison loved being at Fiona's house before the party started . . . before Ivy Daly came.

She felt around inside her jacket just to make sure the letter was still there. As soon as she got rid of the letter, she'd lose all memories of her enemy.

Dingdong.

Egg and Drew arrived and went into the living room with Chet. They hooked up the PlayStation and started to play without saying hello to Mr. and Mrs. Waters or the girls.

Fiona grabbed a potato chip and took a seat in the dining room. She wanted to be filled in on all the gossip from ice skating.

Who skated with whom? What happened on the ice?

Most important, she wanted to know . . . what was *Egg* doing the whole time? Her major crush on Egg didn't go away even when she hadn't seen him in days.

Dingdong. Dingdong.

Ivy and Hart, by coincidence, arrived at the exact same time.

Madison hated coincidences. It was the superstitious side of her acting up. She figured that this coincidence meant Ivy would be sitting next to Hart the whole time they were at Fiona's (when not surrounded by her drones, of course).

Madison kept a hawk's eye on her enemy during the start of the party. She had to find the right time to bring out the letter.

But when?

She almost followed Ivy into the bathroom once, until Ivy shot her a look.

"I think I was here first," Ivy said, shutting the door. "You'll have to wait."

There was another moment in the middle of eating when Madison found herself in the kitchen alone with Ivy. But all she could do was stare. She had a total speech block.

"Do you have a problem?" Ivy asked.

Madison took a mouthful of chips. "No," she said, chewing. "I was just zoning out. Sorry."

"Whatever," Ivy grunted.

As Ivy walked away, Madison fingered the letter inside her pocket. Why couldn't she let go? Why couldn't she just tell her the truth? The longer Madison waited to share the sealed letter . . . the bigger deal it became.

After everyone had eaten plates of food from the kitchen, Chet gathered the group in the family room with Twister. But no one really felt like playing a game where you had to bend and crouch.

"We just ate," Dan said. "My stomach is way too full."

He burped for emphasis.

"How gross," Aimee said.

He burped again.

"I know! Let's play truth or dare instead," Ivy suggested.

Fiona started to say, "I don't really want to—"

But Egg interrupted. "Totally!" he said. "Excellent idea. Truth or dare."

The group sat on the floor in a circle. Ivy sat next

119

to Hart, just as Madison had predicted. Everyone else sat mostly boy-girl, boy-girl.

"We should actually play spin the bottle truth or dare," Ivy said, amending her original suggestion.

"What's *that*?" Madison asked.

Ivy demonstrated.

"You spin the bottle and it lands on someone like this." She grabbed a soda bottle from the table and spun it around on the floor. "So in this case it landed on Rose. Now, I ask Rose, 'Truth or dare?' "

"Dare!" Rose blurted.

"Okay." Ivy laughed. "So now I think up a really, really good dare. Like, spin the bottle again and you have to kiss the person it lands on."

"Kiss?" Aimee exclaimed.

"I don't want to play this game, Ivy," Fiona said.

"Oh, don't be a baby," Chet said to his sister. "It'll be really fun."

Aimee leaned over to Fiona. "Maybe it won't be terrible. Let's try."

"Okay, so who's going to start?" Ivy asked. She handed the bottle to her left to Drew. He smiled as he took it.

Drew spun. It pointed back to himself, and everyone in the room laughed.

He spun again, and it landed on Hart's friend Susie.

"So what do I do?" Drew asked.

"Truth or dare?" Ivy reminded him.

He asked Susie which she wanted.

"Truth," Susie said, without missing a beat. "Absolutely."

"Okay." Drew thought for a minute. "Have you ever been to a foreign country?"

"Wait, wait!" Ivy blurted. "What kind of a question is *that*?"

"You didn't say there was a special kind of question I was supposed to ask," Drew said.

"Well, everyone knows that you're supposed to ask better ones than that," Ivy said. "No one cares if she went to a foreign country."

"I do," Madison said.

"I have a better question!" Egg said. He whispered it to Drew.

"Okay." Drew changed his question. "What's the most embarrassing thing that has ever happened to you?"

Susie smiled. She thought for a moment.

Hart cracked up. "I know that one, Susie. Don't lie!"

"Hart, be quiet!" Susie said. "Let me see. . . ."

Ivy made a face. "What are you talking about, Hart?"

"Let Susie answer," Madison said to Ivy. Of course she was curiouser than curious about what Susie and Hart had meant by that comment, too.

"Well, I guess you're right, Hart," Susie said, looking over at Hart again. "That *was* the most embarrassing thing ever. Well, this summer . . . Hart saw me naked."

"WHAT?" Ivy and Madison screamed at the same time.

Ivy covered her mouth. "Get out!"

Fiona giggled.

"You're joking!" Rose blurted.

And the rest of the boys started to laugh, especially Drew. He even started to snort.

"I only saw for a second," Hart corrected her. "And I didn't even know what had happened. But Susie was so embarrassed. She kept apologizing every time she saw me. It was embarrassing for both of us."

Madison couldn't understand how something like that could have happened between Hart and Susie. How could they even look at each other?

Ivy obviously couldn't believe it, either. She had a look on her face like she'd bitten into a lemon.

"Who's next?" Drew said, passing the bottle over to Susie.

Susie spun, and it landed on Chet, which made her laugh. Madison remembered that she'd admitted during skating that she thought Chet was cute.

"DARE!" Chet said. "I am not revealing any truth to you guys. No way."

"Okay, Chet," Susie said. "Then spin the bottle and whoever it points to . . . you have to carry them around the room."

"What?" Egg shouted. "That is so stupid."

"As long as you don't have to carry me," Dan said. Except for a series of gross-out burps, he hadn't spoken much until now. Everyone laughed at the comment, though, since he was the heaviest kid in the room.

Chet spun the bottle. It landed on his sister.

"NO problem, man," Chet said. He lifted Fiona into a piggyback position and circled the family room, throwing her on the sofa at the end of it.

"Thanks a LOT," Fiona said as she crawled back down to the floor.

"Hey," Susie said, smiling. "I was going to tell him he had to lick someone's arm. Be glad I picked the piggyback thing instead."

Chet spun the bottle again and asked Ivy if she wanted truth or dare.

She thought for a moment and then said, "Truth."

Everyone wanted to tell Chet what question to ask, but he didn't want to hear anyone else. He already had a question in mind.

Madison couldn't believe Ivy had chosen truth. But Madison also suspected that Ivy would probably lie about whatever she was asked.

"Which teacher do you have the biggest crush on and why?" Chet asked.

Everyone groaned.

"Why didn't he ask her which person in the room

she had a crush on?" Fiona whispered. "My brother is a dork."

"SHHHHHH!" Chet said. "So what's your answer, Ivy?"

"Well, I would have to say . . . Mr. Danehy," Ivy said. "Because science is my favorite subject."

"What a lie," Madison said out loud.

"Excuse me?" Ivy said. "That is not a lie. Are you calling me a liar?"

"I'm your science partner, and it is SO a lie. And a big, fat, slimy one at that."

"Well, I answered the question, so I get to spin," Ivy said, ignoring Madison and twisting the bottle around on the floor.

Madison's heart sank when she saw where the bottle landed. On her.

"Well, Madison!" Ivy said with glee. "Okay, so do you want truth or dare?"

Madison looked over at Aimee for some kind of life preserver, but Aimee was distracted. Fiona was gazing off into space somewhere, too.

"I'll pick truth," she said at last. "Truth."

"Okay, then," Ivy said. She rubbed her hands together like some mad scientist. "Tell the group what person at school you have the biggest crush on and why."

The whole room tilted. Madison felt her hands get sweaty, too.

She had to lie.

"Um . . . well, no one, really . . ." Madison stammered.

"That is SO not true, Madison," Ivy said. "And you know it."

Madison blinked. "How would you know?" she asked.

Ivy smirked. "Because I do. You have to tell the truth, Madison. Spill it."

The whole circle of friends got silent. Everyone's eyes were on Madison. Even Hart was staring at her.

"We're waiting . . ." Ivy said.

Madison grabbed her knees and rocked back and forth a little.

"Okay, Ivy." Madison took a deep breath. "You got me. I will admit my crush to everyone in this room. I have a crush on Egg Diaz."

"WHAT?" Egg said. "You are the world's worst liar!"

"No lie, Egg," Madison said. "So there. Can I spin the bottle now?"

Ivy sat backward on her hands. "I guess." She looked confused.

Egg was shaking his head. "No way, man!"

Drew started snorting again.

Fiona nudged Madison before she spun the bottle. "Did you mean that, Maddie, about having a crush on Egg?"

Madison shook her head. "No way."

Fiona breathed a sigh of relief. "I thought so, but . . . you were so convincing.".

"Are you going to spin the bottle or what?" Rose asked.

The bottle whirred around so fast that it moved halfway across the floor inside their circle.

"Hart!" Drew shouted.

"Truth or dare, Hart?" Aimee asked.

Madison looked him squarely in the eye. "Well?"

He looked right back at Madison and said, "Truth. Let me have it."

Madison grinned. "Okay."

Right then and there, she decided to ask him a real question. She knew Hart wouldn't lie no matter what. So she took a chance.

"Have you ever liked anyone in this room?" Madison asked. "And I mean 'like' like, not 'good friend' like. You know?"

"I know what you mean," Hart said.

He sat back and looked around the room.

Everyone waited for his answer.

Chapter 12

"The truth is, I do like someone in this room," Hart said. He didn't look at anyone in particular.

Fiona giggled.

"You do?" Madison asked again. "So the answer is 'yes'?"

"Yeah," he said.

"Oh, man!" Egg said. "Who is it? Who is it? Come on!"

"That wasn't part of the question," Hart said. "I don't have to answer with a name unless it's part of the question, right?"

Madison nodded. And of course, she'd purposefully left the name part out. She felt her heart beating, like she'd swallowed something huge.

He liked her?

Maybe.

"Your turn to spin, Hart!" Ivy said. He smiled at her and picked up the bottle. This time it landed on Egg.

He picked dare.

"Okay, then," Hart said, daring him. "I like Ivy's suggestion. Spin the bottle and then you have to kiss the person it lands on."

"Get out of here!" Egg shrieked. "What if it lands on YOU, bozo?"

"Pucker up!" Drew said.

Egg looked nervous. He spun the bottle.

"Aaaaaaaaaaaaah!" Fiona screamed. It landed on her.

"No way, man, I am NOT kissing her. She's sick," Egg said. "I'll catch some nasty germs."

"I'm all better, actually," Fiona said. "You won't get sick."

"Yeah, well, I won't risk it."

"You can't blow this off, Egg. It's the game. Everyone else played fair," Dan said. "Kiss her."

"Kiss her! Kiss her! Kiss her!" everyone started to chant.

Aimee stood up. "Hold it!" she said. "Everyone needs to stop. Chet and Fiona's mom and dad will hear us."

"You didn't say where I have to kiss her," Egg said.

Fiona blushed.

Egg leaned across the circle and kissed Fiona's bent knee.

"There!" he said, proud of himself.

"We need to get more specific about the questions in this game," Ivy said. "Like if we ask people who they like, we ask for names. And real kisses are required."

"That *was* a real kiss, Ivy," Egg argued. "Why do you have to see everyone get embarrassed?"

Ivy just shrugged. "I don't," she said. "I just—I don't."

She cut herself off. The room was silent.

"*Fiona!*" a voice called from outside the family room. It was Mrs. Waters. "Do you or your friends want any more snacks?" she yelled through the doorway.

The boys all jumped up for more food, but the girls stayed put.

"I think this game is history," Aimee said.

"Sure looks that way," said Susie. "I think I'm going home. I have to head back to boarding school tomorrow."

"No! Don't leave!" Fiona said. "Please?"

But everyone started to gather their stuff.

"Plus you have a math test tomorrow," Aimee reminded Madison.

"Oh, wow! The snowstorm made me forget that completely," Madison said.

"And I have ballet practice in the morning," Aimee added.

Everyone got Susie's phone number, e-mail, and

address at school so they could keep in touch. In one day she'd become a good friend.

"Let me know what happens with Hart," she whispered to Madison on her way out. No one else heard.

"Huh?" Madison said. "What are you talking about?"

"He totally likes you," Susie said. "Does anyone know you like him?"

Madison stood there like a mannequin.

"Keep in touch," she said. "I'll call if I'm home from school. And we'll have to hang over the summer."

She leaned in and gave Madison a small hug. But Madison was still too stunned by Susie's comments to move.

"Bye," Madison said, managing a one-word response.

"Bye!" Susie chirped back.

Everyone helped Chet and Fiona's parents clean up the mess around the house. Most of the food had been eaten, but no one had watched any videos. Everyone said their good-byes and bundled up to face the cold outside.

"Wanna walk home?" Madison asked Aimee. She needed some fresh air.

Aimee nodded and called her brothers to tell them she didn't need a ride home. It took them a little longer than usual to make it over to Blueberry

Street with all the black slush and puddles around the neighborhood, but the pair of BFFs made it.

"When Fiona got picked by Egg, I thought I would DIE," Aimee said. "And by the way, what was all that stuff you said about having a crush on him? Are you nuts?"

"He knows it's not true," Madison said.

"Maybe, maybe not," Aimee said. "I heard him ask Drew if you were serious."

Madison smiled. "Now, that's funny. Aimee, he knows the truth. He's one of my oldest friends."

"Yeah, but sometimes friends can change," Aimee said.

Madison stopped. They were standing in front of Aimee's place. They embraced, and Madison walked on.

"See you at school tomorrow!" Aimee called after her.

Madison nodded. She thought about Aimee's last words.

Sometimes friends can change.

Inside her pocket, the Ivy letter was now permanently warped, torn, and smudged. Madison took it out.

She ripped open the seal and read it.

Finally.

Do Not Open Till 7th Grade
Top Secret FOEO (For Our Eyes Only)

131

We Madison Francesca Finn and Ivy Elizabeth Daly do swear that we will be bestest friends until seventh grade and after that, too.

1. We will go to Far Hills Junior High like Janet, and we will be the coolest friends in the whole school.
2. We will always share everything and borrow each other's clothes.
3. We will get discovered by a famous TV agent and become TV stars in seventh grade. But no matter how famous we get, we will always be friends.
4. We will get married someday and have kids at the same time so they can grow up and go to school together like us.
5. We will have a farm out in the country with all kinds of animals.
6. We will travel around the world on our own plane and go swimming in all the oceans.
7. We will never be mad at each other.

After reading the letter, Madison raced home. Even though they'd been enemies now for a few years, Madison suddenly felt a blank space inside where her friendship with Ivy had been. They had all those plans together, and the only thing that had come true was their being at the same junior high school together. She knew they'd had a falling-out, but how did it get so ugly? What had *really* happened?

When Madison came inside, Mom was in her office, working on the Brazil documentary.

"Hey, Maddie!" Mom called out. "Remember those tree frogs we saw in Brazil? You have to come see the footage. It's amazing!"

Madison slunk into Mom's work space and collapsed on the floor.

"How was your party?" she asked. "You look glum."

"Huh?" Madison grunted.

"How was the party at Chet and Fiona's?"

Madison rubbed her eyes. "Okay, I guess."

Mom turned off the frog video and turned on the overhead light.

"Are you crying?" Mom asked Madison gently.

"No." Madison sniffled, wiping her nose with a tissue. "Why do you say that? I am not crying."

"What happened, honey bear?" Mom asked.

"Nothing. Everything. Oh, it's just that I think I've lost my mind, Mom. If you find it, will you let me know?"

Mom laughed. "Sure thing. You want to talk?"

"Not really," she said.

Mom nodded. "Well, I'm here when you need me."

Madison decided she would go online to surf the Internet for a pre-algebra homework helper program instead of obsessing anymore about Ivy. Thoughts of a now imminent math test were giving Madison huge tummy flip-flops. She had to get studying—fast. There were no more snowstorms to save her from the test.

The bigfishbowl.com search engine gave Madison a few different sites where she could practice her equations, multiplication of fractions, and exponents. They had a helpful hints section with special ways to remember rules and the order of things. Madison was looking for fast and easy tricks since she had so much to learn and so little time to learn it!

She learned an acronym to help her solve algebraic equations: PEMDAS (Please Eat My Delicious Apples Soon).

Instantly the whole process seemed to make sense. The letter *P* was for "parentheses," *E* was for "exponents," *M* was for "multiplication," *D* was for "division," *A* was for "addition," and *S* was for "subtraction." When she followed this order to finish her simple-variable equations, Madison felt more confident about the order of operations. Not only could she take this test, but she could ace it! Madison wondered why this part of math hadn't seemed clear before now.

What was different *now*?

After studying for a half hour, Madison opened up her files.

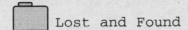 Lost and Found

Rude Awakening: I know why math is hard for me. Sometimes things just don't add up.

Why can't people stay the same? Ivy used to be so sweet. Hart used to be annoying. Life was easier a couple of years ago, before they switched places. Now Hart's the nice one, and Ivy is evil. Seventh grade has been one gigantic algebra problem, and my head is spinning.

When school at Far Hills started, they talked about how this year would be like a transition year and we'd all feel out of place and out of sorts but that would end. It would END. Well, guess what? Endings are a joke. Nothing ever **really** ends.

Like this letter thing. Now that I've read the pact I made with Ivy, I can't just throw it out. It's like a part of me. I can even remember that we signed our names with fruit-scented markers.

She closed the file and went into her e-mailbox.

FROM	SUBJECT
✉ JeffFinn	Fw: This is SNOW funny
✉ TRAVELUSA	Special Onetime-Only Offer
✉ Flowr99	Science

The note from Dad turned out to be blank.

TRAVELUSA was spam.

And Flowr99 seemed familiar at first, but Madison couldn't place the address. She scanned the e-mail.

```
From: Flowr99
To: MadFinn
Subject: Science Lab Notes
Date: Sun 21 Jan 5:11 PM
```

```
I got your e-mail from Egg hope you
don't mind. It's Sunday and I can't
find any of my notes since before
vacation and I need your science
notes tomorrow. Bring your notebooks
to class. C U L8R
```

Ivy hadn't signed it, but Madison knew the person who had written this.

Or at least she *used* to.

Chapter 13

Mrs. Wing was all smiles in Monday morning's computer class.

"This is a fabulous shot, Drew!" she said, looking at the computer screen in his station. Drew was downloading his digital photos from the snowstorm onto the school Web site.

"Oh no, you didn't put that one up there," Madison said when she saw the photo of her and Ivy struggling just before Madison had been "ice tagged" out. "I look so weird. Ick."

"No, you don't look weird at all, Maddie," Mrs. Wing said. "You look like you're having fun with your friends."

"Isn't that Ivy Daly?" another kid asked. "Since when are you friends with her?"

Madison dropped her head. "Since never, okay?

We were on opposite teams. Look, Drew, please take that photo off."

"But you look nice," Egg said, in his best trying-to-impress-the-teacher voice. Egg had an itsy-bitsy crush on Mrs. Wing, and when he was trying for her attention, he would often exaggerate. "Really, really nice."

"Well put, Walter," Mrs. Wing said, taking the bait.

He just grinned and crossed his arms smugly. "I know," he said.

Madison groaned.

After almost a whole week out of school, Madison and all the other students had loads of work to catch up on. It was amazing how much work seventh graders had to do. The snow days had been like frozen time—literally. But that time was long over.

Now Madison was thrust full speed ahead into schoolwork, after-school commitments, the school Web site, interschool social situations, and even gym class (which she was dreading more now than ever before).

"What about this picture?" Drew asked Madison. She looked at it close-up because she couldn't tell at first who was even shown. It was a close-up of two people who were standing on the ice, just milling around.

On the left side was Aimee and their newest

friend, Susie, and then Madison in her rainbow cap, a boy behind Madison, and Egg, hamming it up for the camera. Madison looked a little closer and could see that the unidentified boy was actually *Hart*, and he had his hand on Madison's shoulder.

Wait just a minute! Madison thought. I don't remember Hart Jones putting his hand on my shoulder or anywhere else.

She felt giddy inside.

"Skip to the next picture," Egg said, reaching for the computer mouse.

"No, I wanna see this one!" Madison said. "Can I get a copy of this one, Drew?"

Drew nodded and then scrolled through the rest of the pictures.

There was a great shot of Aimee, Rose, and Ivy. (Madison hated it, though.)

Another photo showed Chet doing a glide on only one skate. He looked like a professional. That was selected by Mrs. Wing to appear on the site.

"What did you do during the snowstorm, Mrs. Wing?" Madison asked her.

The teacher shrugged. "Not a lot. I went to help my husband over at the clinic. Have you been around there recently? They've got a bunch of brand-new cages."

"That's nice," Madison said sweetly. She missed all the animals.

Computer class zoomed by. Mrs. Wing helped

everyone in class work on their graphing skills in anticipation of the big math test. Madison was feeling more and more confident about the test—especially when she repeated her newest "simple-variable equations" mantra.

Please Eat My Delicious Apples Soon.

Please Eat My Delicious Apples Soon.

Upon entering math class, Madison sat in the front row and dumped her bag onto the floor. Taking a deep breath, she rolled up her sleeves, poised her sharpened pencil, and prepared for the worst.

But she knew the first answer right away.

And she knew the second answer, too.

In no time, Madison was whizzing onward through equations, graphs, and other algebraic mazes. She finished the dreaded math test ten min-utes *early*, feeling more confident about her math skills than ever before.

On the way to lunch, Madison was in such a good mood that she stopped in to visit with Mr. Montefiore, the music teacher who led the school band. Her snow day discovery of the old flute in the attic inspired her to talk to Mr. Montefiore about taking up the instrument again.

The attic exploration had not only helped Madison to rediscover truths about friends and parents. It also helped her to find out stuff she'd forgotten about herself.

She was a good flute player. And—like it or not—she had a lot in common with her mom.

Mr. Montefiore was surprised by Madison's visit. He hadn't thought she liked to perform. But when she pulled the old flute out of her bag and played a few notes, *he* changed his tune.

"We'll get you up to speed with your band mates in no time," he reassured her. "I am very excited about this."

Madison played a little more and then put her flute back into her bag.

As she shoved it in, she saw the Ivy letter was there in the front pocket. Madison hoped that her resolve wouldn't fail.

Poison Ivy Daly would see that note today.

Everyone was still buzzing about the snow days during lunch period. Once lunch was over, however, the buzz had died down. It almost always seemed true that on the day after a school break, everyone's brains got tired more quickly. By the time science class rolled around, Mr. Danehy was dealing with a bunch of space cases.

"Did you bring the notes?" Ivy asked as soon as Madison walked into the classroom door. Madison pretended like she hadn't heard the question.

"I asked you if you brought the notes, Maddie?" Ivy asked again, a little more firmly.

"Notes?" Madison played dumb.

"I sent you an e-mail. Didn't you get it?"

"Huh?" Madison was making Ivy frustrated, but she enjoyed it.

Ivy wrinkled her eyebrows and glared at Madison. "Maddie, I have asked you the same question like seven times. Do you have the stupid science notes or what?"

"Oh!" Madison said at last. "No, I don't." She smiled.

Ivy frowned. "Aren't we supposed to be partners?" she asked.

"Yeah, so?" Madison replied.

"Well, partners help each other out. So if we have this pop quiz, then I can look on with you because you're my partner, right?"

"Pop quiz?" Madison's voice dropped. "When?"

"Where have you been?" Ivy chided. "Mr. Danehy said last week . . ."

Madison turned to face the blackboard. She hadn't even cracked her textbook open in days. Everything in the classroom slowed down. Madison started noticing that half the kids had their books out to study.

Hart came into the room just as the final bell rang. "Hey, Finnster! Ready for the quiz?"

Ivy crossed her legs with a huff. "Great, now we can both fail."

Mr. Danehy entered a moment later, but he

wasn't carrying any copies of a test. Madison closed her eyes and said a private thank-you.

"Lucky thing." Ivy snorted.

"Now, class." Mr. Danehy grabbed his pointer and directed it skyward. "There are many things in this class I'd like to point out to you." He aimed the pointer at the students. "For example, you."

Chet raised his hand. "Uh, Mr. D., are we having a pop quiz or—"

"Shhhhhhhhhhhhh!" the front row shushed him.

Mr. Danehy shook his head. "Nope. I want to talk to you about an opportunity instead. I have an opportunity for you kids to improve your grades and make an impact on your community."

"Oh no, not another community service pitch." Ivy groaned.

Madison turned to look at Hart.

When she turned, he was looking right back at her. She saw him lean into his notebook and scribble something on a sheet of paper.

Mr. Danehy kept talking. "Now, as you may know, the Far Hills Annual Science Fair is coming up soon. And I'm eager to have all of you kids involved. Please give me a show of hands. Who's interested?"

One kid in the front row raised her hand.

"Tsk! Tsk!" Mr. Danehy moaned.

Madison was listening, only at some point everything Mr. Danehy said turned into gibberish.

Madison just stared at Hart. She blinked a few

times, waiting to see what he was doing. All at once, he raised his hand, stood up, and started to walk toward Mr. Danehy's desk.

On the way there, he dropped a note onto Madison's counter.

Ivy's eyes were on the note like glue the moment it left Hart's hand.

Madison thwacked her palm over the torn piece of paper and pretended like nothing had happened.

"I saw that," Ivy whispered.

"Huh?" Madison played dumber than dumb.

"I saw." Ivy poked her nose over into Madison's airspace. "Hart dropped something right there. What was it?"

"Excuse me?" Madison asked. "I don't think that's any of your business."

"Yeah, well, I do," Ivy said.

Madison kept her palm firmly planted on the note. She wasn't going to risk Ivy seeing this—whatever it was.

Meanwhile Mr. Danehy was oblivious. He was still droning on about the science fair. Hart interrupted him to ask to go to the bathroom.

How can I read the note without Ivy seeing me? Madison thought. She looked around the room and then back over at Ivy.

Ivy hadn't taken *her* eyes off the hidden note.

"You're not supposed to pass notes in class, you know," Ivy whispered. "I can turn you in."

Madison laughed. "Go ahead."

Ivy raised her hand, and Madison panicked. She reached out for Ivy's arm. They ended up in a mini-tussle over the note.

"GIRLS!" Mr. Danehy yelled. "What on earth is going on back there?"

Neither Ivy nor Madison said a word.

"Madison started it," Rose spoke up from the other side of where they were sitting. "I saw her."

Ivy got a big grin on her face.

Stupid drones.

"Excuse me, Mr. Danehy," Madison said. "But I believe that Ivy Daly was passing notes, and I wouldn't pass it along for her, so she got a little—"

"You are such a liar!" Ivy huffed.

Taptaptaptaptap.

Mr. Danehy hit his desk with a ruler. "That is QUITE enough, girls," he said. "I want to see both of you after class."

Madison and Ivy sank onto their lab stools.

And Madison still hadn't seen the note!

As Hart walked back into the classroom, Madison noticed that Ivy got distracted, so she took that opportunity to shove the note into the front pocket on her bag. She hadn't read it yet, but that wouldn't matter. She'd have plenty of time to look at it later in study hall or up in the media center or after school.

Chet gave her a thumbs-up from across the

classroom. Madison couldn't help but smile back at him. He was an advocate of anyone who got into trouble. And that was her right now . . . TROUBLE.

A while later, when class ended, Hart walked out with everyone else. Madison didn't have a chance to ask him about the note. Meanwhile Ivy had already stood up and approached Mr. Danehy's desk, ready to make her own plea bargain. Madison got up, grabbed her bag, too, and sat down in a chair at the front of the room.

"So, Miss Finn and Miss Daly. Which one of you would like to start with an explanation?"

Ivy raised her hand. "Ooh! Me."

Madison rolled her eyes.

"So this is how it happened, Mr. Danehy," Ivy explained, a smile on her face the entire time. "I was just sitting there listening to you tell us all about the science fair—which, by the way, I really want to participate in—when all of a sudden Madison Finn wrote this note and tried to pass it over to Hart Jones. It was totally not me. It was totally all her."

"And Mr. Jones, apparently. Shouldn't we get him in here, too, then?" Mr. Danehy asked the girls.

"No!" Ivy blurted. "Like I was saying, it was all Madison, and he had absolutely nothing to do with what happened."

"I see," Mr. Danehy said. He made a "hmmm" noise and then turned the floor over to Madison.

"Well," Madison tried to explain. "I was also

listening to you talk about the science fair when suddenly Ivy started to accuse me of having been passed a note or passing a note. Something like that. And I didn't have one. So I got flustered."

"What do you have to say to this, Miss Daly?"

"I can show you where the note is, Mr. Danehy. It's in her bag," Ivy said, grabbing at Madison's orange bag. "In that front pocket."

Madison pulled the bag back into her body. "I don't think so, Ivy," she said.

But Ivy wouldn't give up. Not only was she upset that Madison had scooped her troublemaking scheme, but she was way more upset because the boy she liked had passed a note to none other than Madison Francesca Finn.

Ivy lunged for Madison's bag a second time, only now she grabbed onto the side zipper. With one swift movement, she reached into the front pocket and pulled out the note.

Or, at least what she thought *was the note.*

"YOUNG LADIES! ENOUGH!" Mr. Danehy yelled. "Ivy, you can't just go probing into someone's personal property like that. Give that to me!"

He took the note from Ivy and looked it over.

"This looks like it took an awfully long time to write," Mr. Danehy said. "And what do you say to the fact that your name is on this note along with Madison Finn's name?"

"What?" Ivy said.

He held the note out for her to look at.

"I—I—don't know . . ." Ivy stammered. "What *is* this?"

MADISON FINN & IVY DALY
Friends Forever and Ever and Ever
For OUR eyes ONLY!!!

Madison hung her head. After all of her hesitating and procrastinating, *this* was the way Ivy finally got to see the letter.

By mistake.

"What *is* this, Maddie?" Ivy asked.

Mr. Danehy picked up his briefcase and started to exit his classroom. "The second bell will be ringing shortly, young ladies. I suggest you get to where you need to be."

Madison turned to Ivy. "I found it. During the snowstorm. In my attic."

"Do you remember writing this?" Ivy asked.

"Sort of," Madison admitted. "Do you?"

Ivy let out a deep sigh. "Whoa. This is weird. It's like having a flashback. How long have you had it?" Ivy asked.

"A while. Since last week."

"And you never showed it to me?" Ivy whined.

"It's not like we talk a lot," Madison replied.

"I can't believe you would open this without me,

148

when it says right here that we're supposed to open it together," Ivy said.

She grabbed the note, picked up her bag, and stormed out of the science room, leaving Madison all alone.

 The Letter

After Ivy discovered the letter in the
pocket of my bag, she just took it and I
raced after her and we ended up in the
girls' bathroom down by Mrs. Wing's
computer labs. I followed her into the
bathroom because I had to talk to her.
Even though she is the enemy, I felt
bad. I don't wanna feel bad like
that.

Ivy said that it didn't matter if
we were friends or enemies, that a promise
was a promise. And that I shouldn't have
opened this letter alone.

I NEVER, EVER would have thought that
Poison Ivy would care.

After she left, I sneaked out and ducked into Mrs. Wing's lab. She never checks for hall passes, which is a good thing.

Madison closed the file on the letter. "This all started with his note," she said, digging into her bag's front pocket.

Madison pulled out Hart's note. She didn't have to actually read the note because she already memorized it. But it was nice to hold it and read it again.

Finnster
What is ur e-mail?
Hart

This was a real note from Hart. She wanted to tell someone. . . .
Bigwheels!
Madison went into bigfishbowl.com and pressed NEW MESSAGE.

From: MadFinn
To: Bigwheels
Subject: Need Your Help, Pleez
Date: Mon 22 Jan 4:18 PM
———————————————————————————

Remember how I said in my last e-mail that my week has been zanier than zany? Guess what? It got even CRAZIER. Okay, so Ivy has now seen

the letter. You were right about
showing it to her. It was weird b/c
she even seemed sad that I read it
before I showed it to her. Like
even though we're not friends
anymore, I'm supposed to keep old
promises. That's so hard.

But there is another note now that
is even more confusing! (Drumroll,
please.) It's from Hart. COULD YOU
JUST DIE OR WHAT?????

Okay, so I don't know if this note
means he likes me or what. It says,
"Finnster What is ur e-mail? Hart."

What do you think?

Yours till the math tests,

MadFinn

As Madison hit SEND, she heard the phone ring
downstairs. Mom yelled up, "Telephone!" and
Madison logged off and went downstairs to
answer it.

"Hey, Maddie!" Fiona gushed into the receiver.
"Chet told me you and Ivy got into some massive
trouble in science class today. Is it true?"

"Chet has a big mouth," Madison said.

"Well, yeah." Fiona giggled. "So tell me what happened."

Madison wanted to tell. But she had to leave out the whole part about Hart's note because neither Fiona nor Aimee knew about Madison's undying crush on Hart. And she had to leave out the part about the Ivy and Madison note from second grade because they didn't know about that, either. Maybe Madison would tell them later, but not now.

"Well, nothing really happened," Madison said. "I thought I saw her passing notes. But I was wrong."

"That's it?" Fiona said. "But Chet said you guys were so upset. And someone saw Ivy *crying* in the hallway."

"They did?" Madison asked.

"Well, I'm just glad that you didn't get into trouble and that everything is okay now," Fiona said.

"Where is Aimee tonight? I tried calling her," Madison asked.

"Ballet. Where else?" Fiona said.

Aimee had missed several classes because of the snowstorms, so she was eager to get back to practicing. She'd signed up for private lessons twice a week for a month. That meant Madison and Fiona would be seeing less of their other best friend, at least for a while.

Fiona hung up so she could surf the Web

and Madison went into the kitchen at home for a snack. Mom was emptying the dishwasher.

"Oh! Perfect!" Mom said. "I've got you! Let's run up to the attic for just a moment. I want to show you something I found."

Madison grumbled. She didn't feel like doing much of anything right now except eating peanut butter and crackers. She didn't feel like rummaging through Mom's work materials and organizing boxes. They'd been doing that for days!

But she still managed to follow Mom up the stairs.

Phinnie followed close behind, too.

"Take a look," Mom said, grinning as she pushed open the attic door. "What do you think?"

Madison's jaw dropped open. Mom had *completely* rearranged the attic. On one side there were still boxes and piles, but across the room, she'd covered an old sofa that was up there with a new blanket and added a reading lamp.

"So if we're feeling nostalgic or we just want to have a look around," Mom explained, "it won't be such a big production. So, quit standing there. Tell me, what do you think?"

Madison smiled. "Amazing."

"And I ordered some bookshelves so I can make a better filing system up here. And I was even thinking you might want to put your desk under this window at some point. Like a private room for studying. It's up to you."

Madison couldn't stop smiling.

"Oh! I almost forgot to tell you that Dad is on his way home. He should be back in Far Hills tonight. In fact"—Mom reached her arm out to check the time—"he should be pulling into our driveway in an hour or so."

Madison threw her arms around Mom and dashed back down the stairs. If Dad was coming, she wanted to dress up a little, or at least to get out of her school clothes. She put on some strawberry-kiwi lip gloss for the special occasion.

Dad took Madison out for Chinese food in downtown Far Hills, just the two of them. Stephanie had stayed behind in Denver to tend to more business. On the way home, Madison spilled the beans to Dad about everything that had happened with Hart's note. He sounded encouraging, although dads tend to be more cautious about such matters of the heart, and Madison knew that.

When Dad dropped her off after nine o'clock, Madison was exhausted. But she still found time to sneak back online for one last e-mail check.

From: Bigwheels
To: MadFinn
Subject: Re: Need Your Help, Pleez
Date: Mon 22 Jan 7:54 PM

You won't believe this, but it is
SNOWING like mad here right now!
We have a foot and a half in our
yard, and all the weather reports
now say that we're getting another
storm in Washington just like
yours! I don't ever remember seeing
so much snow! Now I know what
you were talking about last week.
What was that silly joke your
dad sent you? I wanted to tell
my mom. Resend it if you can.

So I read your note about Hart's
note. That is so weird he did
that. And I really think maybe
he is just trying to spend more
time with you because he likes
you, but I don't know for sure
if he means anything romantic.
I can't really tell. You haven't
told me what YOU think. Did he
say anything else? Sometimes I
wish I knew what he looks like.
He sounds so cute.

Write back sooner than soon?

Yours till the hockey pucks,

Bigwheels

p.s. I wanted to tell you something else about friends b/c you seem so sad about that old friend Ivy and I don't like hearing you be sad. What if we made up a secret name for us? You always say everyone else is a BFF, but what if I'm your BIFF? Best Internet friend forever? Hope you like it! C U L8R!

As she logged off, Madison felt warm all over, and not just because she had on her woolly monkey slippers. Even though she had to let go of a friend from the past, she had a BIFF to enjoy the future with—through snow, rain, and whatever bad weather came her way.

Mad Chat Words:

(@@)	You're kidding!
:>D	It's grrrrrreat!
:-~(	I'm going to cry
(::)(::)	Band-Aid (for boo-boos)
?4U	Question for you
911	Emergency
DLTM	Don't lie to me
HHOK	Ha ha only kidding
VF	Very funny
VVF	Very very funny
BTDT	Been there, done that
SWDYT	So what do you think?
W-E	What-ever
BIFF	Best Internet friend forever

Madison's Computer Tip

Sometimes it's easy to forget that whatever you write online can be seen by *anyone*. Even when I'm chatting in a private room, someone from bigfishbowl.com could be monitoring what is said. Or another member could be eavesdropping. **Don't write online messages that contain too much private information.** Sometimes when I send long e-mails to Bigwheels, I forget this rule. I write negative stuff about Ivy or her drones. I probably should be careful. What if Ivy were to read what I wrote?

Visit Madison at www.madisonfinn.com

Book #6: *Lost and Found*

Now that you've read the story . . . how much do you *really* know about Madison and her friends?

1. What does Madison's gym uniform look like?
   a. Gray shorts and yellow T-shirt
   b. Blue polyester shorts and white T-shirt
   c. Pink terry-cloth shorts and red T-shirt

2. Who are the drones?
   a. Ivy and Lindsay
   b. Rose and Joan
   c. Ivy and Daisy

3. Who is Madison's gym coach?
    a. Coach Wing
    b. Coach Roach
    c. Coach Hammond

4. What is Egg's secret goal in life?
    a. To play hockey for the New York Rangers
    b. To be a computer programmer
    c. To become a skiing champion

5. Where do kids from Far Hills go to ice-skate?
    a. Lake Getmeouttahere
    b. Lake Fallontheice
    c. Lake Wannalotta

6. Which boys at school are actually cousins?
    a. Drew and Dan
    b. Drew and Hart
    c. Drew and Chet

7. What causes school to be closed?
    a. A foot of snow
    b. Tornado winds
    c. A major flood

8. When were Madison and Ivy best friends?
    a. Never!
    b. Last year
    c. In second grade

9. Who gets very sick during the storm?
   a. Fiona
   b. Aimee
   c. Madison

10. What is the punch line of Madison's dad's joke that goes: What do you get when you cross Dracula with a snowstorm in Far Hills?
    a. A pain in the neck
    b. The cold shoulder
    c. Frostbite

11. Why can't Madison's dad get to Far Hills for dinner?
    a. He's stranded in Denver.
    b. He doesn't want to eat with Madison.
    c. He's too busy working.

12. What is the name of Madison's mom's production company?
    a. Phineas Phin, Inc.
    b. Budge Films
    c. Nudge Films

13. Why does Madison's mom want Madison to go up to the attic?
    a. To help her lift a mannequin
    b. To help her clean
    c. To have a surprise lunch

14. Which old instrument of Mom's does Madison find in the attic?
    a. A cello
    b. A xylophone
    c. A flute

15. Who is Sk8ingboy?
    a. Hart
    b. Drew
    c. Dan

16. What is Madison's Mom's maiden name?
    a. Francine Fresco
    b. Francine Hooper
    c. Francine Maxwell

17. What does Madison find inside her old secrets box?
    a. Jewelry
    b. Letters
    c. Lettuce

18. Which twosome wrote a mysterious letter five years ago?
    a. Madison and Ivy
    b. Madison and Aimee
    c. Madison and Mom

19. What does Madison finally decide to wear to go skating?
    a. A blue jacket, a turtleneck, and corduroys
    b. An orange sweater and jeans
    c. A wool dress with leggings

20. Who does Madison *think* likes Hart?
    a. Ivy Daly
    b. Rose Thorn
    c. Lindsay Frost

21. What does Drew do the whole time everyone else is skating?
    a. He eats s'mores and licorice.
    b. He sits inside his limousine.
    c. He takes photos with his new camera.

22. What does Madison's mom lose in this story?
    a. Phinnie
    b. Her camera
    c. Her car keys

23. Where is the post-skating cocoa party held?
    a. Aimee's house
    b. Ivy's house
    c. Fiona's house

24. What is the most embarrassing thing that ever happened to Susie?
    a. Hart hit her in the head with a snowball.
    b. Hart saw her without any clothes on.
    c. Hart tripped her when she was walking down a flight of stairs.

25. What question does Madison ask Hart while playing spin the bottle?
    a. "What do you like most in a girl?"
    b. "Have you ever kissed a girl?"
    c. "Have you ever liked anyone in this room?"

26. Does Egg really kiss Fiona during the game?
    a. Yes, he kisses her knee.
    b. Yes, he kisses her hand.
    c. No way!

27. Who is Ivy's older sister?
    a. Jessie
    b. Jennifer
    c. Janet

28. What is PEDMAS?
    a. An acronym that helps Madison solve algebra problems
    b. The name of Mom's latest documentary
    c. The name of a common skating injury

29. Who gets caught passing notes in science class?
    a. Madison and Hart
    b. Madison and Ivy
    c. Hart and Ivy

30. What is BIFF?
    a. Best Internet Friends Forever
    b. Believe in Friends Forever
    c. Best Ideal Funnest Friend

Answers:
1b, 2b, 3c, 4a, 5c, 6b, 7a, 8c, 9a, 10c, 11a, 12b, 13b, 14c, 15a, 16b, 17b, 18a, 19b, 20a, 21c, 22a, 23c, 24b, 25c, 26a, 27c, 28a, 29b, 30a

How well do you know Maddie?

26–30 correct: You might as well pack your bags and move to Far Hills, because you are a *Madison Finn* fanatic!

20–25 correct: You could totally be Madison's BFF, because you know her inside out!

17–19 correct: You think Maddie's pretty cool, and you'd have fun hanging out with her.

14–16 correct: You know a few things about Madison, and you're interested in finding out more about her.

13 or fewer correct: You didn't quite catch all those details about Maddie, but don't worry—there's still lots of time to learn.

Mad Chat Match

Match the following Mad Chat words with their correct meanings.

(@@)	What-ever
:>D	Best Internet friend forever
:-~(	Been there, done that
(::)	Emergency
?4U	Very, very funny
911	So what do you think?
DLTM	It's grrrrrrreat!
HHOK	Very funny
VF	Don't lie to me
VVF	You're kidding!
BTDT	I'm going to cry
SWDYT	Band-Aid (for boo-boos)
W-E	Question for you
BIFF	Ha-ha, only kidding

See next page for answers.

Mad Chat Match Answers

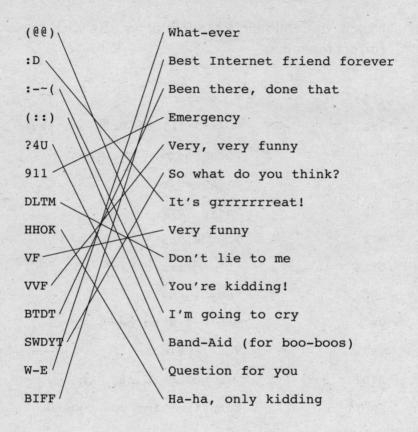

(@@)   What-ever

:D   Best Internet friend forever

:-~(Been there, done that

(::)   Emergency

?4U   Very, very funny

911   So what do you think?

DLTM   It's grrrrrreat!

HHOK   Very funny

VF   Don't lie to me

VVF   You're kidding!

BTDT   I'm going to cry

SWDYT   Band-Aid (for boo-boos)

W-E   Question for you

BIFF   Ha-ha, only kidding